OUTLAW AND LAWMAKER

Rosa Praed was born in Queensland in 1851 and after her marriage in 1872 lived on Port Curtis Island until 1876 when she and her husband settled in England. In a prolific career spanning the late nineteenth and early twentieth centuries, she published some fifty novels and stories. Writing in 1881, in her Preface to *Policy and Passion: A Novel of Australian Life*, she stated that only when Australia had become an independent nation and had 'formulated a social and political system adapted to the conditions of her development and growth' would the country 'possess a literature of her own as powerful and as original as might be prognosticated. But,' she added, 'the time for this is hardly yet ripe.'

Three of Rosa Praed's novels are currently available in Pandora as part of the Australian Women Writers: The Literary Heritage series: *The Bond of Wedlock* (1887), an example of her early work, *Outlaw and Lawmaker* (1893) and *Lady Bridget in the Never-Never Land* (1915) from a later phase in her career.

Dale Spender is an Australian feminist who shares her time between Sydney and London. Her many books include *Man Made Language* (1981; revised edition 1985); *Invisible Women* (1982); *Women of Ideas and What Men Have Done to Them* (1982); *Mothers of the Novel: 100 Good Women Writers Before Jane Austen* (1985); *Reflecting Men* (1987) and *Down Under: Two Centuries of Australian Women Writers*, 1988. She was the founding editor of the journal *Women's Studies International Forum* and she is the General Editor of this series, the Australian Literary Heritage.

PANDORA

AUSTRALIAN WOMEN'S WRITERS:
THE LITERARY HERITAGE

AUSTRALIAN WOMEN WRITERS
The Literary Heritage

General Editor: Dale Spender
Consultant: Elizabeth Webby

Pandora is reprinting a selection of nineteenth- and early twentieth-century novels written by Australian women. To accompany these finds from Australia's literary heritage there will be three brand-new, non-fiction works, surveying Australian women writers past and present, including a handy bibliographical guide designed to fill in the background to the novels and their authors.

The first novels in the series are:

A Marked Man: Some Episodes in His Life (1891) by Ada Cambridge
Introduced by Debra Adelaide

An Australian Girl (1894) by Catherine Martin
Introduced by Elizabeth Webby

The Incredible Journey (1923) by Catherine Martin
Introduced by Margaret Allen

The Bond of Wedlock (1887) by Rosa Praed
Introduced by Lynne Spender

Outlaw and Lawmaker (1893) by Rosa Praed
Introduced by Dale Spender

Lady Bridget in the Never-Never Land (1915) by Rosa Praed
Introduced by Pam Gilbert

Uncle Piper of Piper's Hill (1889) by Tasma
Introduced by Margaret Harris

The companion books to this exciting new series are:

Down Under: Two Centuries of Australian Women Writers
by Dale Spender

A lively, provocative overview of the history of the literary scene and the position of women writers in Australia which shows that any image of the country as a cultural desert was not based on the achievement of Barbara Baynton, Ada Cambridge, Dymphna Cusack, Eleanor Dark, Katharine Susannah Prichard, Christina Stead and the many other Australian women who have enjoyed tremendous international literary success.

Australian Women Writers: The Contemporary Scene
by Pam Gilbert

There are a number of outstanding contemporary Australian women writers about whom relatively little is known. This book fills that gap with a comprehensive discussion of the work of Helen Garner, Kate Grenville, Elizabeth Jolley, Barbara Hanrahan, Robin Klein, Thea Astley, Jessica Anderson, Jean Bedford, Olga Masters and Antigone Kefala.

Australian Women Writers: A Bibliographical Guide
by Debra Adelaide

Covering over 450 Australian women writers, this invaluable sourcebook outlines their lives and works and puts rare manuscript collections throughout Australia on the literary map for the first time. A comprehensive guide to the articles and books written about these women is also included.

OUTLAW AND LAWMAKER

ROSA PRAED

Introduced by Dale Spender

PANDORA

London   Sydney   New York

First published in 1893
This edition first published in 1988 by
Pandora Press
(Routledge & Kegan Paul Ltd)
11 New Fetter Lane, London EC4P 4EE

Published in the USA by Pandora Press
(Routledge & Kegan Paul Inc.)
in association with Methuen Inc.
29 West 35th Street, New York, NY 10001

Set in 10/11½ pt Ehrhardt
by Input Typesetting Ltd, London SW19 8DR
and printed in Great Britain
by
The Guernsey Press Co. Ltd., Guernsey, Channel Islands.

Introduction © Dale Spender 1988

British Library Cataloguing in Publication Data

Praed, Rosa
Outlaw and lawmaker.——(Australian
women writers).
I. Title   II. Series
823[F]   PR9619.2.P7

ISBN 0–86358–223–0

CONTENTS

———•———

INTRODUCTION

———————————•———————————

Friend of Eliza Lynn Linton, acquaintance of Ouida and Ellen Terry, admirer of Oscar Wilde (whom she used as a model for some of her characters), advised by George Meredith, a prolific and popular novelist who was accorded considerable acclaim, Rosa Praed was a remarkable woman. She was born in outback Australia, and had no formal education nor patron to introduce her to the London literary scene. That she wrote as much as she did (more than forty novels, many of them running to three volumes) and as well as she did, is of course part of her claim to fame; that she was able to get her novels published by reputable firms in England, and so gain a measure of acceptance for herself and her writing, is also very much to her credit.

Born Rosa Caroline Murray-Prior on 27 March 1851 on her father's station on the Lower Logan River in Queensland, she was soon aware of some of the hardships – and highlights – of life in the Australian bush. She saw how the isolation, the climate and the lack of support and medical care, all took their toll on her mother; she witnessed natural and unnatural disasters and the price that these exacted in human terms; she saw her neighbours slaughtered by blacks and her father forced to 'sell up'. All these events would later make an appearance in one form or another in her novels.

But if she was influenced by the harshness, she was also moved by the stark and spectacular beauty of the Australian landscape; it is her familiarity with the variable Queensland terrain, and her ability to describe and evoke the most extraordinary settings which characterises much of her fiction. She knew the Australian bush; she knew what it could do to women and to men. Because of her first-hand experience she treated the country with great respect.

The circumstances of her own upbringing could hardly have been more isolated. Her playmates – apart from members of her own family

– were black. With her half-caste friend Ringo she learnt how to dig for witchety grubs; she learnt the aboriginal lore and language, and a great deal more besides. That she would later write authentically about aboriginal culture (for example, in *Fugitive Anne; A Romance of the Unexplored Bush*, 1903) demonstrates her sensitivity and reveals her insights, but that she recognised the humanity of the blacks at a time when it was not orthodox to do so – when they were more frequently attacked as 'savages' – ranks as an even more notable achievement.

Rosa Praed was not formally educated. Her mother, Matilda Harpur, had come from a family more interested in poetry than in profits, and she tried to pass on some of her own love of literature to her daughter. But the opportunities for such indulgence were few; when she was not bowed by the burden of child birth, blinded by the blight (which forced her to live in semi-darkness for long periods of time) there were many other demands made on Matilda Murray-Prior's time and they took priority over Rosa's 'learning'.

Yet, clearly, some of her mother's cultural concerns were transmitted. In June 1866 the *Maroon Magazine* was launched; inspired by Elizabeth Gaskell's biography of Charlotte Brontë, it was a handwritten family magazine to which Rosa, her brother Tom and her mother contributed until 1868, when her mother died. Many of her mother's pieces, including some which give advice to a daughter, are deeply moving and reveal that Matilda Murray-Prior was not without literary ability.

Of her own literary development, Rosa Praed later said that the model of Charlotte Brontë and the reality of the *Maroon Magazine* were responsible for her early scribbling. Like Charlotte Brontë, Rosa Praed found that the family forum allowed her to serve a form of literary apprenticeship; it also provided feedback for her efforts. And in the lonely Australian bush such writing could mean employment, entertainment and emotional stability.

When her mother died, Rosa Praed was not only deeply distressed by her personal loss, she was also determined that she would not embark upon such a hard life and endure such a harsh fate herself. In later autobiographical writings (such as *My Australian Girlhood*, 1902) and in much of her fiction there is an underlying protest against the unjust treatment of women, and it appears that it was when her mother died that Rosa Praed resolved to retain her independence in so far as circumstances would allow.

Ironically, after her mother's death circumstances allowed Rosa Praed much more leeway.

By 1867 Queensland had become a colony and Rosa Praed's father became a member of the new parliament. He was therefore obliged to spend more time in Brisbane and acquired a home on the river at Kangaroo Point. As the daughter of the widowed member of parliament, Rosa enjoyed many privileges (and parties) which stood in marked contrast to much of her earlier, isolated bush life. She attended sittings at the House, witnessed political intrigues, graced political gatherings (many of them organised in the botanical gardens or at Government House) as well as enjoying the more informal pleasures of the time such as waterway pastimes and tennis parties. Many of these experiences are documented in the novel *Miss Jacobsen's Chance; A Story of Australian Life* (1886) in which the daughter of a widowed cabinet minister has but one short season to 'catch a man' and 'make something' of her life.

The natural setting (the verandah overlooking the river) and the social setting of Kangaroo Point, surface repeatedly in Rosa Praed's Australian novels where she has created a fictitious state – Leichardt's Land – which is modelled on colonial Queensland. *Policy and Passion; A Novel of Australian Life* (1881) and *Outlaw and Lawmaker* (1893) are both set in Leichardt's Land and are dramatisations of some of the issues which were familiar to Rosa Praed in her 'official' youth, right down to the heated debates about where the railway should go.

But there were other debates in which she was also involved. In *Miss Jacobsen's Chance*, the author makes it clear that she does not like the way women are pressurised into finding a man, but the degree to which her fiction represents the realities of her life cannot be ascertained. There is no doubt that Rosa Praed's father was intent on seeing her 'settled' and made many attempts to persuade her of the pleasures of marriage; when he met with little success (he was disturbed to find that Rosa rejected all suitors he considered suitable) he resorted to threats. In 1872 Rosa married Campbell Praed.

It was never a happy marriage. It came to be a marriage in name only when Campbell Praed revealed his penchant for extra-marital affairs. It was however a marriage which afforded Rosa Praed much material for her fiction and prompted many questions among her readers; *The Bond of Wedlock; A Tale of London Life* (1887) is an account of a husband who beats his wife and the novel raises the issue of when a wife should be obliged to stay with her husband, and when

she is justified in seeking a divorce. (So successful was this contro-
versial novel that it was dramatised for the London stage in 1887–8
with the title *Ariane*.)

The marriage to Campbell Praed got off to a very bad start. After
a short honeymoon, Rosa took up residence with her husband on Port
Curtis Island, a forsaken and desolate place. Completely isolated, the
house was horrific, the mosquitoes were malevolent and the fleas were
ferocious; the diet was dreadful (damper, salt-beef and goat) and the
life was physically arduous with even the attempts to keep fires alight
proving to be an overwhelming task. When she discovered that she
was pregnant, Rosa Praed came close to despair.

But the setting and the consequences of this episode in her life
also become the fabric of her fiction (with Esther Hagart in her first
novel, *An Australian Heroine*, 1880 enduring many of the ordeals that
Rosa Praed had faced). And another 'event' of this period which
proved to be significant in the author's life was the experience of the
supernatural. It was in desperation, on the island, that Rosa Praed
turned to her dead mother for advice and found an 'answer' in the
form of automatic writing. While Rosa Praed became famous for her
Australian novels she also gained a reputation for her stories of the
spiritual and occult.

She did not have to stay long on the island however. Campbell
Praed was forced to sell up and elected to return 'home' to England.
His wife was overjoyed at the prospect of living a 'civilised life'.

Matilda Elizabeth, Rosa Praed's first child, had been born in
February 1874; the Praeds arrived in England in 1876 and her second
child Humphrey was born in May 1877. And throughout this period
Rosa Praed began to write.

The first move towards the publication of her novels was made by
her brother-in-law who took her manuscript (of what was later to
become *Policy and Passion*) to Fred Chapman of Chapman & Hall;
the manuscript was passed on to the reader for this publishing
company, George Meredith. Recognising the potential of the writer,
Meredith advised the publishers to recommend some revisions and
to keep in touch with this talented woman. And so began a career in
which Rosa Praed was consistently advised to *tone down* her style in
order to meet the requirements of polite fiction and appeal to the
Victorian English reading public.

It was not just at Chapman & Hall where her vital and vigorous
prose was vetted. George Bentley – pillar of the establishment and
publisher to Queen Victoria – was often shocked by the frankness

and freshness of the female writer and did his best to make a lady of her in fact and in fiction. He wrote letter after letter to Rosa Praed, advising her to modify the scope and the style of her fiction, and we can only speculate on what her writing might have been like had she been left to her own devices instead of being compelled to produce prose of propriety.

In 1882, with the publication of her third novel, *Nadine: A Study of a Woman*, Rosa Praed had become an established novelist. Although her novels had been 'toned down' they still exceeded the bounds of pure and polite fiction. She persisted in dealing with ethical issues which placed her in the realm of the risqué.

Both *An Australian Heroine*, her first novel, and *Nadine*, introduce elements of the nature/nurture debate with questions about illegitimacy and heredity, and the extent to which the sins of one generation are visited on the next. *Policy and Passion*, her second novel, continues in the same vein; partly a love story, it also takes up the issue of how far past actions can be put aside. In Australia, where so many people were likely to have a questionable past – where disgraced sons of good family, as well as convicts, could find themselves among the leading citizens and lawmakers – interest in the nature of good and evil, in the permanance of sin and the advisability of pardons, would invariably arise.

Outlaw and Lawmaker continues in the tradition that Rosa Praed established in her earlier novels. Elsie Valliant, like so many of Rosa Praed's heroines must not only learn about love but must come to a decision about the relative attractions of security and passion. Drawing on Rosa Praed's personal experience, with some of the characters clearly modelled on personalities of the day (with *Hansard* as a verifying source), *Outlaw and Lawmaker* is a most realistic romance. With the political intrigues of Leichardt's Land as a background, the spectacular scenery of Queensland as a setting, and the fascination of a new continent and strange customs to lend an air of mystery, some of Rosa Praed's preoccupations with themes of heredity, subordination, convention and morality, are played out in this novel. *Outlaw and Lawmaker* is a thriller with a philosophical framework.

One of Rosa Praed's aims was to 'explain' Australia to a British audience; another was to help develop an identifiable Australian litera-ture; and a third was to explore some of the injustices of the world, particularly as they impinged upon women. With all three aims she achieved a measure of success.

Her novels are a rare combination of a variety of 'genres'; her

Australian novels have elements of the travel story in them: her 'occult' novels encompass considerations usually reserved for historical romances – or for science fiction. And Rosa Praed's willingness to raise political questions – about the subordination of women and of blacks, about the status of a colony and the credentials of its officials – in a genre that was ostensibly refined and reassuring fiction, is not only a testimony to her talents but a revelation about her own nature.

For many years she enjoyed more security in her literary than her personal life. Her husband was a cause for concern, and yet still there was some compensation: it was he who caused her to question men, marriage and conventional morality. Rosa Praed found little consolation in her four children: Matilda, her only daughter, was deaf and mentally disturbed; and all four children died before their mother, meeting violent and untimely deaths.

Rosa Praed sought solace in her friends, some of whom she collaborated with in her writing (she wrote three novels with Justin McCarthy, one of which, *The Right Honourable; A Romance of Society and Politics*, 1886, was a best seller). She went on to find companionship (for 28 years) with Nancy Harward with whose help Rosa Praed wrote twelve novels and four volumes of short stories between 1902 and 1916. Nancy Harward died before Rosa Praed, who had in 1934 added a codicil to her will insisting that she be buried alongside Nancy.

Many questions can be asked about Rosa Praed and there is much about her and her writing that remains to be known but of her there is also much that can be said with certainty: she is an Australian woman writer of distinction who deserves to be reclaimed, read, and respected.

Dale Spender
May 1986

CHAPTER I

•

Elsie

Anyone who has travelled through Australia will identify the Leichardt's Land of these pages, though in the map it is called differently,
with that colony in which the explorer Leichardt met his tragic fate,
and to a part of which he gave his name; and the same person, if he
will examine the map, should have no difficulty in discovering the
Luya district, which lies on the southern border of the colony in a
bend of the great Dividing Range.

The Luya, in its narrowest part, is fenced on almost three sides with
mountains. Here the country is wild and mostly scrubby, intersected by
spurs from the range, and broken by deep ravines and volcanic-
looking gorges. There is scarcely any grazing land, and till Goondi
Diggings were started, the Upper Luya was spoken of as the most
picturesque district in Leichardt's Land, but as offering the least
attractions to a settler of any kind. Even the Goondi 'rush' some few
years back, though it had for a time let loose a horde of prospectors,
did not do much towards populating this particular nook below the
Dividing Range. Goondi became a flourishing township and its output
of gold continued steadily, but though other goldfields sprang up on
the further side of the district, contrary to expectations no gold was
discovered on the Luya waters, and prospectors had now given up
the useless search. Moreover, Goondi was on the very edge of the
district, across the high-road to the next colony, and beyond lay open
country and fine stations for cattle and sheep. Goondi called itself the
township for the Luya district, but as a matter of fact the Luya
had no especial head-centre. It is a secluded corner hemmed in by
mountains, and though at no great distance from the capital of the
colony and within easy reach of civilisation, it is cut off by its
geographical position from the main current of life and action.

The river which waters the district has its rise in Mount Luya, the highest point of the range, then reputed inaccessible to white men. There are strange fastnesses at the foot of Mount Luya – places where, report still declares, foot of European has never trod. The Blacks have a superstitious reverence, amounting to terror, for this region, and in the aboriginal mythology, if there be indeed any such, Mount Luya with its grey desolate crags and mysterious fissures, and, on either side, twin-peaked Burrum and Mount Goondi with its ribbed rampart of rock and black impenetrable scrub, might well represent the lair of Demons or the abode of Gods.

A few stray selectors had settled themselves at the head of the Luya on the small flats and wattle ridges that offered a certain scant subsistence for stock. But these selections had, for the most part, a suspicious reputation, as affording a convenient base of operations for cattle-stealing and such nefarious practices. Certainly, one or two of these petty landowners might be credited with strictly honourable intentions, as, for instance, that unprofitable scion of aristocracy, Lord Horace Gage, who, more romantic than practical, had been seduced by the beauty of the scenery and by a keen artistic instinct, as well as by the fascinating prospect of hunting big game in the shape of wild horses, and of starting an industry in hides and horsehair; or a guileless new chum, such as Morres Blake, of Baròlin Gorge, with a certain ironic humour described himself, taken in by an old hand who was eager to dispose to advantage of a property no seasoned bushman would buy. It may be added that Mr. Blake had accepted his bargain with resignation. He turned the Gorge into a nursery for thoroughbred horses, and seldom visited the Luya, leaving the management of affairs there to his working partner, Dominic Trant. Except, however, for these selectors' homesteads, a great part of the Upper Luya belonged to the Hallett Brothers, and made portion of their station Tunimbah – a troublesome bit of country in mustering time, when the broken gorges and undergrowth formed an almost impregnable refuge for 'scrubbers.'

Tunimbah was one of the principal stations on the Luya, and extended beyond this mountainous region to the open country, where was good grazing land, and where the river was no longer a shallow, uncertain stream brawling over miniature precipices, trickling through quicksands, or dropping into a chain of still, deadly-looking pools – except in flood-time, when it had a way of coming down from its source with amazing volume and rapidity. As the mountains widened out the Luya widened and deepened, and flowed quite sedately through wooded pastures and the paddocks of well-kept head stations. Lower down it washed peaceful German plantations and the settlements of cedar-cutters, who floated their logs on its surface to the township, below which it finally emptied itself into the ocean.

Of the squatters on the Upper Luya, the Hallett Brothers were perhaps the most important, and with the prospect of greater wealth in the future than any others of the settlers in the district. They were young and enterprising, and besides Tunimbah, owned stations out west, which they worked in conjunction with their southern property. Tunimbah was always quoted as the most comfortable and best managed of the Luya stations. Young Mrs. Jem Hallett, the eldest brother's wife, was considered a model housekeeper, and the most dressy woman in the district. She went to Leichardt's Town for the Government House balls, and was a lady not slow to assert her pretensions, social and otherwise. Frank Hallett, the unmarried brother, was popular in the neighbourhood as a capital fellow and a clear-headed man of business. He was particularly popular with ladies, being a good match and a sociable person who got up races and picnic parties in slack times, and liked to amuse himself and other people, and he was vaguely known in the colony as a man of promise. He had been mentioned in the newspapers and publicly congratulated by the Governor on having taken high honours at the Sydney University, and was considered a person likely to distinguish himself in politics. He had gone through one election, and had been beaten with credit. Since then he had been biding his time and hoping that the Luya constituency might fall vacant. Yesterday there had seemed little prospect of this being the case. Now, in a few moments after the first shock of a tragic disclosure, he saw himself member for Luya, and at no very distant date leader of the Opposition in the Leichardt's Land Assembly.

The disclosure was made by a girl.

The girl was standing on a point of rock above the steep bank, at what was called Lord Horace's Crossing. Lord Horace's homestead, Luya Dell, lay behind her. The girl was Lord Horace's wife's sister. The crossing was one of Lord Horace's fads.

He had wasted a great deal of money and labour in making it more beautiful than Nature had already done, and that was quite unnecessary, for Nature had not been niggardly in her provisions.

It was a creek flowing down one of the many gorges of Mount Luya. The creeklet ran between high banks, mostly of grey lichen-covered rock – banks which curved in and out, making caves and hollows where ferns, and parasites, and rock lilies, and aromatic-smelling shrubs grew in profusion – banks that sometimes shelved upward, and sometimes hung sheer, and sometimes broke into bastion-like projections or into boulders lying pell-mell, and it seemed only kept from crashing down by the binding withes of a creeper, or the twisted trunk of a chestnut tree or crooked gum. Then there were mysterious pools with an iridescent film upon their surface, and dank beds of arums, and fallen logs and rugged causeways, and the triumph of Lord Horace's engineering skill – a bridge of unhewn stone that might have been laid in prehistoric ages by some Australian Titan.

The girl stood framed between two great cedars and outlined against a bit of blue sky. Just here there was a gap in the mountains, and a long narrow flat, on the discovery of which Lord Horace prided himself, curved round a projecting bluff and constituted the freehold of Luya Dell. It was Lord Horace who had christened the place. The girl might have postured as a model for some semi-allegoric Australian statue of Liberty. The cairn of rocks, patched with lichen and the red blossoms of the Kennedia creeper, and tufted with fern, made her a suitable pedestal. She was tall, slender, and lithe of limb, with something of the virginal grace and ease of a Diana, and her clinging holland gown was not an altogether un-goddess-like drapery. She had a red merino scarf twisted round her shoulders and waist, and wore a sort of toque of dark crimson upon her trim little head with its tendril fringe in front and knot of brown curling hair behind. Her face was oval in shape, though the features were not exactly classic. At this moment she looked alert and expectant; her dark eyes were dilated and alight, and her red lips were slightly parted in an eager smile. There was a flush on her soft, almost infantine cheek, which was of the warm pale tint of a fruit ripened in the shade. She had one arm lifted, and beckoned excitedly to Frank Hallett, whose pulses tingled at the sight of her.

'Stop,' she cried. 'I want to talk to you.'

As if there were any power on earth except that she herself wielded which just then would have kept him from stopping and talking to her! He raised his hat, and put spurs to his horse. He did not trust himself to Lord Horace's bridge, which was in truth intended more for ornament than for use, but splashed through the shallow stream and scrambled up the steep hill. She watched him leaning forward, raised in the saddle, one hand lightly clutching his horse's mane, his eager face upturned to her. It was an attractive face, bronzed, wholesome, well-featured, with clear eyes frank and straight-looking, a pleasant smile, dark brown whiskers and moustache, and a square-cut, shaven chin. He looked a typical bushman, with a little more polish than one associates with the typical bushman – had the bushman's seat, and the bushman's sinewy, sapling-like figure.

But the girl did not admire the typical bushman. She would have preferred the product of a more complex civilisation. In this she resembled what indeed she was, the typical Australian girl. She had not a very varied experience of the human product of a complex civilisation. Her reading convinced her that she must not generalise by the specimens that drifted to Australia, and of which her own brother-in-law was an example. When she was in a discontented mood she always brought herself into a state of resignation by reflecting that nothing would have induced her to marry Lord Horace Gage.

'Of course I might have married him if I had chosen to cut Ina out,' Elsie Valliant had always said to herself, with the complacent vanity of a spoiled beauty. 'But one must remember that there's honour among thieves, and besides, he is too great a bore for anyone to put up with but Ina, who is a placid angel.'

To be sure, if Lord Horace had been the heir to the marquisate, instead of the youngest of many scantily portioned younger sons, Elsie might have altered her mind, for she had the reputation of being a very worldly and a very heartless young lady. At any rate, this was what her rejected admirers declared.

'He really is good-looking,' she thought now, as she watched Frank Hallett. And she added: 'It is such a pity that he is – only Frank Hallett.'

'Tell me, have you met Braile?' she questioned anxiously, as he pulled up his panting horse and flung himself from the saddle.

'Braile – the postman? No; I've been out on the run. I left Tunimbah early.'

'That's a pity,' said the girl. 'He is brimful of news – dying to communicate it to someone. Mrs. Jem will have a benefit when he gets to Tunimbah.'

'Well, I have no doubt Edith will reward him with an extra glass of grog, and that the mail will be late at Corinda in consequence,' said Hallett. 'What has happened?'

'Braile is never late,' said the girl, not answering the question. 'He is wound up to carry the mails, and nothing short of a creek risen past his saddle flaps will stop him. I have a respect for Braile. The way in which he grasped the dramatic points of the situation was most admirable.'

'What is the situation? You shouldn't tantalise me. I believe it's only some joke. Nothing really exciting now – is there?'

Elsie nodded gravely. 'Enough to excite Braile and Horace, and even Ina – and me. Enough to raise the district and to make you wish you were a bushranger, or the head of police, that you might be in the play-bill too.'

'Then it's Moonlight out again. Have they caught him?'

'It's Moonlight, and if they had caught him should I say that you would like to be in his place?'

'I suppose not. Not,' and the young man reddened and stammered and looked at her in a curious way – 'not if you cared two straws about me.'

He seemed to wait for her reply, but she only stared at the ground, gazing from her lofty position over his head.

'I wish you'd tell me why in any case I should wish to be Captain Moonlight.'

'Because he is a hero,' said the girl.

'Do you think so? Must one wear a mask and rob one's neighbours to be a hero?'

The girl made an impatient gesture. 'You don't understand. You've no romance; you've no ideas beyond the eternal cattle. You are quite satisfied to be a bushman – you are more humdrum even than Ina.'

He did not answer for a moment: 'I am very anxious to know what the news was that old Braile brought. Look here, let me help you down from those rocks. You seem such miles above me. You look as if you had put yourself up for a landmark.'

'So I did. I thought my red shawl would attract attention. I was trying how far I could see down the Gorge – wondering if anyone were in hiding there, and from how far they could see me. I was thinking how easy it would be to hide up in Mount Luya, and wondering – She stopped, and then, taking his proffered hand, stepped from the pointed stone on which she had been balancing herself to a lower one, and so till she was on the level beside him. He finished her sentence –

'Wondering if there was any chance of Moonlight coming along. How should you like to be carried off by him?'

'On his black horse Abatos?'

'How do you know that his black horse is called Abatos?'

'Ah, that's part of Braile's story. Moonlight hardly ever speaks, you know. It is the Shadow who conveys his orders and intentions. But that night Moonlight was heard to say one word as he rode towards the coach, and that was "Abatos."'

'Why his horse's name? Why not a new "swear"?'

'Oh!' she said with a slight accent of contempt. 'Ask Horace to lend you his Lempriere.'

Hallett flushed. 'I am not as ignorant as you think. I had forgotten for the moment. And so you would like to be carried off by the bushrangers?'

'I think I should like it immensely. I should enjoy the opportunity of talking to Moonlight and his masked henchmen. I shouldn't be at all afraid of their not treating me in a gentlemanly and considerate manner. Only, you see, I shouldn't be worth carrying off. Unless Mammie realised on the piano and the sewing-machine – we've not a stick else worth twopence – there would be nothing to ransom me with. And anyhow the piano and the sewing-machine would hardly run to a ransom.'

'Your brother-in-law?' suggested Hallett.

'Poor Horace has telegraphed to *his* brother-in-law. The Bank will come down on the Dell unless Lord Waveryng sends him a thousand pounds at once. Leichardt's Town, and the wedding trip, and the imported bull have cleared him out. No, I should be left to my fate.'

'That seems a melancholy state of things,' said Hallett, with an embarrassed laugh; 'but in the event of such a calamity as your abduction by Moonlight, Miss Valliant, I think there are some of us fellows who wouldn't think twice of selling the last hoof off their runs to buy *you* back.'

The girl laughed too, and blushed. 'Perhaps, after all, I shouldn't want to be bought back. Now I am going to tell you –'

She seated herself on the lowest boulder of the cairn, and he, holding his horse's bridle, leaned against the cedar tree and listened.

She began, 'Goondi coach was stuck up on Thursday night.'

'Ah! So that's it. The brutes!'

'Do you mean the bushrangers? No, they didn't behave like brutes. Two men against a coachful. Think! Peter Duncan, the millionaire, was on the coach, and Moonlight made him sign a cheque for 2,000*l.*, to be cashed at Goondi Bank.'

'By Jove!' exclaimed Hallett. 'That was cheek. Well, I'm glad it was Peter Duncan. The old miser. He deserves it.'

'Moonlight only robs people who deserve to lose their money, and the Government, and the banks, who don't miss it,' went on Elsie imperturbably. 'He protects the widow and the orphan. There was a widow on the coach too. She was an old German woman, and she was hurrying down to Leichardt's Town to say good-bye to her only son. He was to sail in the "Shooting Star," and her only chance of seeing him was by catching the Goondi coach the next morning. She had her savings with her to give him. She offered them all to Moonlight if he would get her into Goondi.'

'And he took them?'

'No,' cried the girl triumphantly. 'He gave them all back to her. Well, Mr. Slaney was in the coach also, and he was in a bad way too. He had got bitten by something, and was blood-poisoned, and he was going to the doctor.'

'Slaney the member?'

'Yes, the member for Luya. Oh, I have been thinking of something. I'll tell you presently. I'm a wretch, but I can't help it. Who could be sorry for Mr. Slaney?'

'You don't mean –'

'Wait, wait. I must first prove to you that Moonlight is a hero. He and his Shadow – you know that's what they call the other man – sacked the mail, got Mr. Duncan's cheque, and then tied up the driver and the passengers each to a separate tree, some way off the road. You see, Moonlight's only chance of cashing his cheque was by being at the Goondi Bank directly it opened, before the coach was missed, or the telegraph wires could be set working.'

'I see. It struck me at first that it would have been safer to have had the cheque drawn on the Leichardt's Town Bank; but of course the other was his wisest plan. Moonlight is a shrewd fellow. Well, Miss Valliant, what is the rest of Braile's story?'

'Ah, now comes the point. Think of the daring! Moonlight meant to leave the coach and the passengers tied up till someone found them in the morning. The old German woman went on her knees to him and cried about her son. Mr. Slaney offered a cheque for 500*l.* if only he would get the coach to Goondi. Mr. Slaney guessed that he was dying.'

'Dying!'

'Wait. Moonlight refused the cheque, but said that he would take Mr. Slaney's word. Moonlight and his Shadow had an argument. The Shadow told him he was a fool. It ended in Moonlight having his way. He gave his horse to the Shadow, mounted the box, and drove the coach to within a mile of Goondi, with Mr. Slaney and the German woman, leaving all the others tied up to their respective gum-trees.'

'And then?'

'Then day was breaking. Moonlight turned the coach off the road, fastened the horses, and remounted his own. Mr. Slaney was groaning with pain. The coach to Leichardt's Town, which the German woman wanted to catch, was to start at eight. The Bank opens at nine. You see what a risk it was. Moonlight explained the situation, and told them he would trust to their honour. He showed the German woman a cross-cut by which she could meet the down coach outside Goondi. Mr. Slaney gave his word that he would not give information to the police, and walked on to Goondi straight to the doctor's house. Moonlight waited –'

Elsie paused dramatically.

'How do you know all these details?' asked Hallett, struck by the vivid way in which the girl told her story.

'Mr. Slaney told the doctor afterwards. Braile had got the particulars at Goondi. And it is easy enough to fill in from one's imagination. I have been thinking of nothing else all day. I have been picturing Moonlight nerving himself to walk into the Bank, not knowing whether a policeman would be there to take him. It seems to me a brave thing to have staked one's liberty on the honour of a poor old German woman and Mr. Slaney.'

'They were true to him?'

'Yes. At nine o'clock, when the Bank opened, a very respectably got-up and quiet-looking bushman went in and presented Mr Duncan's cheque, which he said had been paid him for a mob of store cattle. The Bank cashed it without question. Two hours afterwards it was all over the place that the Goondi coach had been stuck up, and Mr. Duncan bled of 2,000*l*. But Moonlight and his Shadow and the respectably dressed bushman had disappeared.'

'And Mr. Slaney?' asked Frank Hallett.

'Mr. Slaney,' repeated Elsie solemnly. 'Ah, this is what concerns you. The member for Luya died early this morning.'

CHAPTER II

The Legend of Baròlin

'Ah!' Frank Hallett drew a long breath and stood in silent thought for a minute or more. Elsie watching him all the time saying nothing. The interest, half indignant, half admiring, and with a dash of the humorous in it, which Elsie's account of the sticking-up of the Goondi coach and the robbery of the miser-millionaire had excited, faded suddenly, and gave way to a more personal and absorbing excitement. Moonlight's depredations were certainly a mystery and a shame to the district, and to a Government which was supposed to protect the property of peaceable colonists. But the Luya squatters had got into a way of looking upon Moonlight's misdeeds as not calling for very serious vengeance. He did not bail up their stations or steal their valuable cattle and horses, or frighten helpless women or respected inhabitants. There was, indeed, a certain odd chivalry and dare-devilry of the Claude Duval kind in this masked miscreant with the soft voice and courteous manners, who flashed out on moonlight nights to stick up a gold escort and then disappeared into the bowels of the earth, as it seemed, or into the thickets of Baròlin Scrub. It was Moonlight's picturesqueness which appealed to the romantic element in more prosaic natures than that of Elsie Valliant. If truth were told, Frank Hallett was not inclined to judge too harshly a bandit who, granted that he robbed, robbed 'on the square.' No, it was not of Moonlight that he was thinking, but of the fact suddenly borne in upon him that Mr. Slaney's removal threw open the constituency of the Luya, and assured him of the opportunity for which he had been waiting in order to begin his chosen career. In a flash he grasped the personal significance of Elsie Valliant's words. The member for Luya was dead. He himself might now be the member for Luya.

At the same moment a pang of remorse shot through him, remorse that he could so allow himself to speculate on the beneficial results to himself of a fellow-creature's death. But it was not in human nature that he could feel more than a passing pang. Mr. Slaney, though the chosen of the electorate, and the possessor of certain good qualities, as the Moonlight episode showed, was almost as unpopular in the district at large as the miser Duncan, whom everybody hated. Slaney had got into the Legislative Assembly on a reactionary wave, and through the vote of the Irish population on the Diggings. To Frank Hallett he had been privately and publicly obnoxious, and they had had more than one encounter, not wholly of a political nature. Slaney had kept a bush inn, and had made his money, people said, by doctoring the grog. He was a queer, cross-grained person, given to hard drinking, and with his blood in the condition in which a bite from a horsefly might prove a fatal poison. Everyone knew that he would not be returned a second time, and everyone said that Frank Hallett's election, should the seat become vacant, was a certainty. In a quick prophetic glance the young man saw himself in the position which he coveted – the leader of a party – a future premier of Leichardt's Land, a public personage whom the most ambitious girl in Australia might be content to own as her lover.

Then, with a thrill of triumph, he realised that Elsie too must have grasped this point in the situation, and he saw that she had worked her narrative up to it with a distinct appreciation of its dramatic importance. She had waited for him at the Crossing that she might be the first to tell him the news. From this he must infer that she was interested in him – Frank Hallett – and not in the feats of Moonlight, and, as she phrased it, the 'raising of the district.' She was interested in the way in which he would take the information – in the bearing of the incident on his future fortunes, with which, perhaps, she already identified herself. She had divined his secret ambition. Might it not well be that she had divined another ambition dearer and more secret still?

His breath came and went fast in the agitation of his fancied discovery and eager-rushing hope. He had been looking away beyond the Crossing. Now he turned to her, and became aware that she was watching him. In an instant there was the shock of a recoil. The sweet indifference of her gaze, the mere friendly curiosity, the slight touch of feminine coquetry in her smile, checked all his ardour and made him draw back and pull himself together as though he had been hurt. He said, very quietly,

'It is you who have grasped the dramatic points of the situation, Miss Valliant. I think you must have been giving Braile lessons.'

She looked away from him and back again quickly.

'It interested me,' she said. 'I am interested in Moonlight. I should like very much to see him. But,' she added with a little laugh, 'even if he carried me off, as you suggested, I shouldn't get a sight of his face. They say no one has ever seen him without his mask.'

'Perhaps he doesn't wear it in his hiding-place,' said Frank. 'I am sorry for Slaney,' he went on in the same dulled tone. 'And I am glad he kept his promise to Moonlight. I shall always think better of him for that. Yes – I am sorry – though –' He paused.

'Well?' she said, 'though –?'

'Though, of course, his death gives me a chance of standing for the Luya. Not that it matters so much. I should have got in for the northern district.'

'But this will be much nicer,' said she demurely. 'You won't have to go away on electioneering tours, and being our own especial member, we shall have a right to order you about and to be interested in your general career.'

'Shall you really be interested in my career?' he asked, bending a little towards her. She looked at him, letting her big brown eyes rest full on his for a moment or two.

'Why, yes, naturally, and as far as we are concerned, I assure you your duties as member of Parliament will be no sinecure. When Ina, and Horace, and I want anything from the Government – such as a mail twice a week, or a railway to the Luya, or any little trifle of that sort – we shall expect you to make a fuss about it in the House. And then if the Governor does not give balls enough you will be responsible for not voting a sufficient entertaining allowance. And, of course, when you become a Cabinet Minister we shall want you to look after us at the public functions – find us seats in the special saloon Government carriage when there's a show or a railway opening. And we shall want to be asked to all the Government picnics down the bay. Oh, and I must insist on a seat on the daïs – and no one looking askance at me as though I had no right to be there – at the Mayor's ball. And I always did want to be a Minister's wife, so that the usher of the Black Rod might take me to my place at the Opening of Parliament.'

'One might suggest, perhaps, that an opportunity may present itself of securing these advantages,' said Hallett grimly.

'How?'

'Why –' Hallett reddened and stammered, abashed by her clear gaze. 'It would not be so difficult to marry a Minister, would it?'

'Wouldn't it? But there doesn't happen at present to be an unmarried member of the Executive. Still, as you suggest, one may live in hope. There will be new politicians coming on, and I may have a chance yet. I will wait for a change of Ministry. Then your party will be in – and *you* may be in too.'

Her laugh, which was innocent and frank as that of a child, robbed her speech of its audacious coquetry. Elsie said things which no other girl could have said without incurring the charge of being unmaidenly. No one would ever have called Elsie unmaidenly, though they might have called her, and with a good show of reason, an unprincipled flirt, and in spite of her freedom of manner no man would have ventured upon an impertinence towards this young lady, who knew very well upon occasion how to maintain her dignity.

'You are laughing at me,' exclaimed Frank Hallett in a hurt tone. 'You don't think it is in me to become a leader. Well, we shall see. Yes, Miss Valliant, that's my ambition and my intention. I mean to be a political leader, and I think that if a man has pluck and perseverance and a certain amount of brains, as well as a certain amount of money to make him independent of place, he is bound to get to the front and to make a position that he wouldn't be ashamed to offer to a woman he cared for.' The young man's voice shook. 'I think that before very long I shall be on the Ministerial bench, or at any rate in the front rank of the Opposition, and when that day comes I shall ask you for your congratulations.'

'And no one will give them with a more sincere heart than I,' said Elsie gravely. 'And you didn't understand me, Mr. Hallett. I never meant to laugh at you, or to doubt you. Oh, I know well enough that you are considered a coming man. Mamma, and Ina, and Horace, and heaps of other people have told me that of you.'

She stopped and blushed. She knew, though Frank did not, why she in particular had had all Frank's advantageous prospects impressed upon her. Oh, of course, he would be a very good match for a penniless Leichardt's Town belle, and her mother knew it, and Lord Horace, and Ina, and all the rest of their world knew it too.

'Thank you for saying that, Elsie! If you only knew –' the young man began passionately. He came a step nearer her, but Elsie moved and put out her hand in a half laughing, half rebuking manner.

'But I don't know, and perhaps I don't want to know – there, never mind. . . . I want you to tell me something –'

'Tell you – what?'

'Oh, it's nothing – only –'

'Tell me,' she went on with the slightest confidential movement. 'I'm so interested in Moonlight. Do you think it is true – what they say – that he has some secret hiding-place under Mount Luya?'

'How can I know, and why should I care?' exclaimed Hallett exasperated.

'I should have thought you would care, that you might have some idea if there really is such a hiding-place, for you are always about on the run, and they say no one knows the Upper Luya as well as you do.'

'There might be any sort of cave or hiding-place up in the gorges by Baròlin Scrub. Cattle don't go there – except the regular scrubbers that it is no use trying to get at. They used to hunt there for gold. One of these prospecting chaps would have been more likely to come across it, or the Blacks –'

'Oh, but there's a Black's legend,' said Elsie eagerly.

'If you are going to make a legend out of a Black's tale about the Bunyip or Debil-debil –!' he said contemptuously.

'It *is* a legend, and quite a respectable one. Yoolaman Tommy – King Tommy, you know – told me. He says that close to Baròlin Waterfall at the back there is another smaller waterfall, and beside it a huge black rock which is shaped like a man's head, with long grey moss growing upon it, so that it looks as if it were a very old black man with grey hair and a beard. Have you ever seen it?'

'No, Baròlin Waterfall is a *cul-de-sac*. The water is supposed to come from the lake on the top of the mountain, and the precipice cuts the mountain. They say the lake is the crater of an extinct volcano.'

'Let us make a picnic there sometime, and try to find old Baròlin – the Old Man of the Mountain. Do.'

'You couldn't do it. I have never got to the waterfall myself, and I'm a pretty good rider, and Pioneer as safe a horse in rough country as you'd find on the Luya.'

Frank Hallett patted the big powerful bay, who turned from rubbing his cheek against the cedar-tree as if he knew that he was being talked about.

'We might ride as far as we could, and walk the rest of the way,' said Elsie.

'Walk five miles over the Luya rocks and through Baròlin Scrub! There wouldn't be much left of you, Miss Valliant.'

'I am determined that somehow or other I will see Baròlin,' said Elsie, with the wilfulness of a spoilt child. 'Perhaps you don't know why the scrub and the waterfall are called Baròlin?'

'Did King Tommy tell you?'

'King Tommy told me that the white-haired old man was once a great chief who lived in Mount Luya, and was a mighty man of war, against whom none of the other chiefs could stand. He got so powerful that he offended the great spirit Yoolatanah, and Yoolatanah turned him into a rock and shut him up behind the waterfall, which was called after him, Baròlin. The Blacks say that he sleeps, and only wakes when someone goes near the fall. Then he seizes them, and they are never seen or heard of again. So the Blacks will not go near Baròlin or enter the scrub even at bunya time.'

'I thought it was the Bunyip,' said Hallett laughing. 'I know none of the Blacks will go near Baròlin. They always say "Debil-debil sit down there," and as there are any amount of bunyas in the scrub and none to speak of anywhere else, this superstition must be a pretty powerful one.'

At that moment an Alpine call sounded from the other side of the creek. Elsie got up. 'That's Horace. Now we shall hear something more about Moonlight.'

'Why are you so interested in Moonlight?' asked Hallett jealously.

'I have told you. Because he is a hero. Horace – Horace; have they caught Moonlight?'

CHAPTER III

Lord and Lady Horace at Home

Lord Horace was scrambling up the bank, leaning well over his saddle bow and clinging to his horse's mane. His seat was a little uncertain, and it was evident that he was only a spurious sort of bushman, in spite of his rather elaborate bush get-up of Crimean shirt, spotless moleskins, and expensive cabbage-tree hat. He had a stockwhip, too, coiled over his left arm, though he had made no pretence of going after cattle, and had indeed only a few stray beasts to go after. He was a tall, slight, dark young man, with a profile somewhat after the Apollo Belvedere type, fine eyes, and a weak mouth. He was distinctly aristocratic-looking, clipped his g's after the English aristocratic fashion, and had certain little ways of his class, in spite of his efforts to be rough. He had an attractive manner, and apart from his wish to ape bushmen's habits, seemed quite without affectation. He looked, certainly, however, more suited for a London life than for that of an Australian settler, and it was equally certain from his physiognomy that he would never take the world by storm with his talents.

'Moonlight!' he cried out in answer to Elsie's question. 'Been huntin' for him all up the Luya. No chance whatever of their findin' him. I say, Hallett, how do you do, old chap? Let's make a party – get some good black trackers, don't you know? and go out on the trail, eh? – man-catching. It would be rare sport.'

'If you and Mr. Hallett were to do such a thing I'd never speak to you again,' said Elsie indignantly.

'Look here, she has been ravin' about the fellow. I must say I think it was rather a fine thing refusing Slaney's cheque, and trusting to his honour. Slaney's honour! Poor chap, he's dead, so mustn't abuse him. You should have heard the fellows at the "Bean-tree" discussing your chances, Hallett. I suppose you are going to stand for the district?'

'I suppose so,' Hallett answered. 'But,' he added, 'it is too soon to talk about that, with poor Slaney not yet in his grave.'

'Oh, nobody cares about Slaney. The king is dead, long live the king – that's my motto, and Slaney was a confounded Radical, hand and glove with the working-man. I'm a working-man myself, but I ain't a Radical.' Lord Horace talked excitedly and rather thickly. Elsie looked at him, and drew her delicate eyebrows together in a frown.

'I think we had better walk on to the Humpey,' she said; 'Ina will be wondering what has become of us all.'

'Yes, come along, and have a refresher, and talk over things,' said Lord Horace. 'It's a beastly ride from the "Bean-tree." I went over to see if some of those selectors wouldn't get their meat from me – might as well turn an honest penny, you know; and I wanted to hear the news about Moonlight. Macpherson and his men are mad at his having given them the slip, and are scouring the country till they find his hiding-place. They're mad, too, against poor Slaney, for not letting them nab Moonlight at the Bank. By Jove, that was a neat trick, and I like old Slaney, though he *was* a beast. I like him for havin' stood on the square to Moonlight. But come along, and let us talk it over. It's canvassin' I'm thinking of. I canvassed once for my brother-in-law Waveryng – before he was Waveryng, you know – got him in, too, with singing comic songs – I'm first-rate at 'em. By Jove, Waveryng isn't half as grateful as he might be, or he'd do something for me now.'

Lord Horace spurred his horse and cantered on, executing a series of Alpine calls, to which there came a response from the house in the shape of a faint 'Coo – ee.'

Frank Hallett did not mount, but walked beside Elsie, who was silent and looked worried.

'I forgot,' said Frank abruptly, 'I've got a note for you from Mrs. Jem. She wants you to come over next week, and Lady Horace, of course. I believe there's to be a dance or something at Tunimbah.'

'I'm going home next week,' said Elsie.

'But you can wait for that. Nobody wants you in Leichardt's Town.'

'Heaps of people want me, and heaps of things. Mamma wants me; my winter gowns want me, and the fruit wants me. It has to be made into jam, and my dresses have to be made; there's nobody to do them but me. You see Ina used to be the practical person among us – the Prime Minister, the dressmaker, and the cook all in one. And now Ina is gone.'

'Oh, but haven't you –?' Frank began, and stopped awkwardly.

'Haven't we a cook? you were going to say. No, we haven't. Mammie and I do the cooking for each other, and a nice mess we make of it, and the Kanaka boy who does the garden cleans the pots and pans. Now you know all about it. Have you any idea, Mr. Hallett, what Mammie and I have to live upon?'

'No – that is, I didn't imagine, of course, that you were millionaires.'

'We've got exactly one hundred and twenty-five pounds a year, not counting the garden produce – a hundred and twenty-five pounds a year to pay our rent, and to feed and clothe our two selves, and buy all the necessaries of civilisation. I suppose I pass as a civilised young person out in Australia, though I am quite sure I shouldn't if you put me down in London society. Oh, dear, I wonder if I shall ever have a taste of London society?'

'How you always harp on England,' said young Hallett.

'Well, isn't it supposed to be the Paradise of Australian girls, as they used to say Paris was to Americans? I'm certain that one of the reasons Ina married Horace was because she thought he might take her to England. I can't imagine any other.'

Frank laughed. 'Oh, he's a very good fellow, though he *is* a lord, as they say about here. But why do you say that your sister married him because she wanted to go to England? She is not ambitious, she doesn't care about that sort of thing. She is not –'

'Not like me,' Elsie interrupted. 'If I were only half as good as Ina!'

'She married him, I suppose, because she loved him,' Hallett went on uneasily.

'Do you think he is the kind of person a girl would fall in love with?' said Elsie.

'Why not? He is very handsome, and he has nice manners.'

'And he is horribly selfish, and he is shallow – as shallow as the creek at the Crossing. Mr. Hallett, do you know I am worried about Ina. I don't think, somehow, she is very happy. But she is much too proud and much too good to own it.'

Hallett looked uncomfortable. His memory went back to a certain day not many months back – a day when he had confided to Ina Valliant the love he felt for her sister Elsie, and of which he never could think without a painful twinge, a horrible suspicion that she had once cared for him herself. It was true he had no reason for the suspicion – nothing but a stifled exclamation, a quiver of the voice, a sudden paling. The suspicion had been joyfully lulled to sleep, when a month or so afterwards she had accepted Lord Horace, and when she had told him again, and this time firmly and unfalteringly, that she would do everything in her power to further his suit with Elsie. And she had done everything she could. She had asked him over repeatedly, had been sweet, frank, and sister-like, and had seemed absolutely satisfied. And yet when Elsie said that Ina was not happy, he knew that she was only echoing his own miserable thought.

'Tell me,' he said, 'why do you fancy that? Isn't he good to her?'

'Oh, yes. He is always making love to her, if you call that being good. It is really quite embarrassing sometimes, and if I were Ina I wouldn't have it. And then he flies out because the dinner isn't quite right, or because some little stupidity is wrong, and sulks like a spoiled child. It's because Ina doesn't sulk too – because she puts up with his pettishness so angelically, and takes such pains that everything shall be right next time – that I am sure she isn't happy. It's unnatural.'

'Surely it's very natural if she cares for him.'

'Poor Ina,' said Elsie softly. 'Well, she is happy enough, apparently, when she is fidgeting after the chickens and furbishing up her doll's house.'

'It does look a little like a bush doll's house,' said Frank.

They were close to the Humpey now. It was a queer little slab place, roofed with bark, standing against a background of white gum-trees, which, with their tall, ghost-like trunks and sad grey foliage, gave a suggestion of dreariness and desolation to the otherwise cosy homestead. Lord Horace had made the best of the Humpey. It had been a stockman's hut, two slab rooms and a lean-to; and now another hut had been joined to it; which was Lord Horace's kitchen, and there were sundry other lean-to's and straggling shanties which served for guest-rooms and meat-stores. The verandah of the Humpey had an earthen floor, and the posts were of barked saplings. But there were creepers growing around the posts and festooning the bark roof, and there were stands of ferns against the slab walls, and squatters' chairs with crimson cushions which made splashes of colour. Lord Horace's chair had a glass of some spirituous concoction on its arm-table, which his attentive wife had just brought to him, and he was filling his pipe, while Ina, who was only a few degrees less lovely than Elsie, leaned against the post, and waited submissively to be told the day's news. Lord Horace took a great deal of credit to himself for having left the Humpey in its original state of roughness. 'Some fellows, you know, would have gone to no end of expense in cartin' cedar, and shinglin', and paintin', and spoilin' a really good Australian effect,' he was wont to say. 'That's the worst of you Australians, you've got no sense of dramatic fitness. And that's what I say to Ina and

Elsie, when they want me to fill up the chinks between the slabs, and
put in plate-glass windows. A bush hut *is* a bush hut, and there's
something barbarous in the idea of turning it into a villa. Wait till
I've finished my stone house. Then you shall see something really
comfortable and harmonious too. In the meantime, if we can't be
comfortable, let us at least be artistic.'

Those were Lord Horace's sentiments.

The new house had come to a standstill for want of funds after the
foundations had been laid, and it was not likely to get beyond the
foundations, unless Lord Waveryng sent out further supplies; but
Lord Horace talked of it with as proud a certainty as if an army of
master builders were already at work.

Lady Horace came slowly down the log steps, and held out her
hand to Hallett.

'How do you do,' she said, in her gentle little Australian drawl. 'I'm
very glad you have come. Elsie was saying yesterday that we were so
dull.'

'That's because we're on our honeymoon yet,' put in Lord Horace.
'Elsie says it's quite disgusting the way we spoon.'

Frank Hallett noticed that Lady Horace flushed a brilliant red, and
interpreted the blush as a favourable sign. Oh yes, she was happy.
She must be happy. If she had not been happy she could not have
answered so composedly.

'We were planning to take Elsie over to Tunimbah to see Mrs. Jem
Hallett, before she goes down to Leichardt's Town. But we're a little
frightened of Mrs. Jem, because she is so dreadfully grand, and she
might be vexed if we went without a formal invitation.'

'Here is the formal invitation, anyhow,' said Hallett, and he produced his sister-in-law's note, and gave it to Lady Horace, who duly
handed it to her husband, and it was there and then settled that they
would go.

Frank Hallett had brought something else for Ina – some of the
famous Tunimbah figs, which were now going off, and he had brought
a book for Elsie, and while these offerings were being unpacked and
commented on, he studied Lady Horace's face. Ina was not so pretty
as her sister. She was not so tall, her colouring was less brilliant, she
was much quieter. It was a wonder, people thought, that Lord Horace,
who was a fastidious person, had fallen in love with her instead of
with the all-conquering Elsie. But Elsie had snubbed him, and Ina
was besides very pretty and very much more docile than her sister.
She had a sweet little serious face, with a peculiarly delicate

complexion, and a tender resolute mouth. The fault of her face lay in the light eyelashes and eyebrows, which gave her a certain insipidity. She had a very gentle manner, and she did not talk much, not nearly as much as Elsie.

She had been only four months married. Hallett asked her how she liked the Dell, and she told him in her child-like way all about her chickens, and her pigs, and the new garden, and the pump Lord Horace was making, and other domestic details. And she asked him various questions about the working of Tunimbah and Mrs. Jem Hallett's management, which showed that she had thrown herself entirely into her bush life.

He said something to this effect.

'Yes,' she answered. 'I want to make the Dell as much a model of a place in its small way as Tunimbah is in its big way. And then, you know, Horace isn't like a regular bushman, he must have his little English comforts –'

'Which he insists on combining with his Australian dramatic effects,' put in Hallett, 'and that must make management a little difficult for you, Lady Horace.'

Ina laughed. 'Oh, I don't mind,' she said. 'Now I want to show you the last improvement,' and she took him into the sitting-room, which was a very cosy and picturesque place, though the walls were only of canvas stretched over the slabs, and the ceiling, of canvas too, was stained with rain droppings from the bark roof. Lord Horace had been amusing himself by drawing in sepia a boldly designed flight of swallows along one end of the room.

'Not strictly appropriate to Australia, my dear fellow, but I couldn't stand the papers they showed me. I have sent home for something a little more artistic. It should be parrots, of course, or satin-birds – and by the way, those beggars of satin-birds have gobbled up all our loquats – but my imagination wouldn't soar, and Ina is not inventive. I'm trainin' her faculties, but by slow degrees.'

Ina flushed again. Between the flushes she was – so Hallett noticed – alarmingly pale. And surely she had got thinner. But she had taken ever so much pains over the arrangement of the drawing-room, which was in truth exceedingly pretty and full of English odds and ends, from a portrait of Lady Waveryng in full court-dress to an antlered stag's head over the doorway. Ina was proud of her charming room, though she gave Elsie all the credit of the arrangement. 'It was always Elsie who did the prettinesses,' she said, 'Whether it was in our ball dresses or our parlour. Elsie has only to put her hand to a thing and it gets somehow the stamp of herself. I was never good for anything but the useful things.'

Lord Horace sat down to the piano, which was a fine instrument and was littered with music, and struck a few chords. 'You must hear my newest thing. It's one of those spirited bush ballads of William Sharp's, and I've set it to music. Ina and I sat up till all hours last night practisin' it.'

'Yes,' interjected Elsie, 'and you made poor Ina faint by keeping her standing so long.'

'I wanted her to have some port wine,' answered Lord Horace, 'and she wouldn't. It was her fault, wasn't it, Ina, dear?'

'Yes, it was my fault,' said Ina. 'I didn't take the port wine in time.'

'Well, never mind,' said Lord Horace, 'she shall have some port wine now to make up.' He rushed off and brought the wine, which he made her swallow in spite of her protests. That was Lord Horace's way. A glass of port wine for a woman, and a brandy and soda for a man, were his notions of a panacea for ills of body and mind. When Ina had drunk her wine he began his accompaniment again and burst into the song. He had a fair baritone, and sang with a certain manner as of one who knew what he was about. He put a good deal of dramatic go into the rattling words –

'O'er the range and down the gully, across the river bed,
We are riding on the tracks of the cattle that have fled:
The mopokes all are laughing, and the cockatoos are screaming,
And bright amidst the stringy barks the parrakeets are gleaming;
The wattle blooms are fragrant, and the great magnolias fair
Make a heavy sleepy sweetness in the hazy morning air;
But the rattle and the crashing of our horses' hoofs ring out,
And the cheery sound we answer with our long-repeated shout.'

And then came the chorus, which the four took up:

'Coo-ee – Coo-ee – Coo-ee – Coo-ee!'

'My dear Horace,' said Hallett, 'why didn't you try for fortune in the light operatic line? You are much better suited for that than for roughing it in Australia.'

'I did think of it,' replied Lord Horace seriously; 'but the light operatic line is played out in England, there's no chance for anybody now. And then one's people would have thought it *infra dig*. They're old-fashioned, you know – don't go in for modern innovations – the stage cult and that sort of thing. It's not a bad notion of yours, though – an opera of bush life – openin' chorus of stockmen and bushrangers, and Moonlight for a hero. It might pay better than free-selecting on the Luya.'

'It might well do that,' said Elsie, who was rather fond of a passage-at-arms with her brother-in-law.

Lord Horace caught her round the waist and gave her a twirl or two into the verandah. 'A waltz – a waltz, Ina!' he cried. Ina played. There were some blacks outside who clapped their hands and cried out 'Budgery!' and the pair stopped to have what Lord Horace called a 'yabber.' Hallett and Ina were left alone. She let her hands fall from the piano, and her sweet serious eyes met his. 'Mr. Hallett,' she said, 'I think you ought to make haste.'

'Tell me what I ought to do, Lady Horace.'

'I think you ought to make Elsie understand how much you care for her.'

'I have tried to do that. You were wrong. She doesn't care for me.'

'I thought she did,' said Ina faltering. The break in her voice reminded him of the break in it *that* day. Perhaps she was thinking of this too. She went on in a different tone: 'You must not judge Elsie as you would another girl. She is horribly proud, and she is horribly reserved, and she is horribly perverse. Oh, I know all my Elsie's faults.'

'Tell me, Lady Horace, what made you think that she cared for me?'

Ina hesitated, and her soft colour came again. 'I don't think I can do that quite, Mr. Hallett.'

'Tell me,' he urged.

She looked at him and turned away her head. 'Yes, I'll tell you,' she said, in a forced sort of voice. 'It was – do you remember that day at Tunimbah – before I was engaged? – when you told me that you were so fond of Elsie.'

'Yes,' he answered, and his voice, too, was strained.

'It was just after that, that Horace – that I began to think I might marry Horace. One day, when Elsie teased me about it – she never cared very much for Horace, you know, though Mammie liked him so much – we spoke of you – and Elsie told me that you were the only man she had ever known whom she could fancy herself marrying. She told me that she had once fancied – before Horace came on the scene, you know' – Ina laughed a little unsteadily – 'that you had a –

a regard for me. It was absurd, wasn't it? – and that the idea ha
made her unhappy and snappish to me, and that she had hated hersel
for minding. But she had minded. That meant a great deal fror
Elsie.'

At that moment Lord Horace and Elsie came in.

'Mr. Hallett,' she exclaimed, 'I have been telling Horace that w
are to have a picnic from Tunimbah to the Baròlin Waterfall.'

'Elsie is determined to find Moonlight's lair,' said Lord Horace
'Well, I'm on for any fun of that sort. Talking of Baròlin, do yo
know the people there, Trant & Co.?'

'Blake & Trant,' said Hallett. 'It's Blake who is the boss, they say
But how anyone who wasn't quite a fool could have bought Baròli
Gorge!'

'They say Trant is doing a good thing with his horses, though,
said Lord Horace. 'Do you know the chap? He was at the "Bean
tree" to-day. I didn't fancy him. Looked to me like one of those low
bred half-Fenian fellows. I saw 'em when I went salmon fishin' wit
Waveryng to Ireland. I was wondering whether Blake could be on
of the Blakes of Coola.'

'Coola?' repeated Hallett.

'Blake of Coola is about as old a name as there is in Ireland. Castl
Coola was close by our river. Lord Coola was a friend of Waveryng's
I never met him. The Castle was shut up the only time I went ove
It is a common enough name though.'

'I believe my sister-in-law has asked Mr. Trant over to Tunimbah,
said Hallett.

The bell rang for dressing. Lord Horace took his guest over t
what was by courtesy called the Bachelors' Quarters. There was onl
one spare room in the Humpey, and that was occupied by Elsi
Valliant.

CHAPTER IV

●

Elsie's Lover

They were sitting down to dinner when the barking of the dogs announced an arrival. Presently the woman in the kitchen came in with a slip of paper, on which was written: 'Dominic Trant, of Baròlin.'

'By Jove!' exclaimed Lord Horace, 'he has taken me at my word! Saw him at the "Bean-tree" to-day, and asked him to look us up if he was passing. He said he was going straight on to-night.'

Elsie looked excited. 'Dominic Trant! Dominic – what an odd name!'

Lord Horace brought his guest in. Mr. Trant was rather a good-looking man of from thirty to thirty-five. Elsie decided, first, that he was distinctly Irish; secondly, that he was not quite a gentleman. If he had been a gentleman he might have sat for one of Velasquez's pictures, but there was a certain commonness about him which destroyed the effect of his otherwise artistic appearance. He had an accent, too, and Elsie detested a brogue. But he had fine black eyes and a well-featured sallow face. His manner was rather second-rate. He called Lady Horace 'Your Ladyship,' but after the first time or two dropped into familiarity, and was almost free and easy. He scarcely took his eyes off Elsie.

He explained his arrival. He had stopped late at the 'Bean-tree,' later than he had intended. The fact was, he had waited for a telegram from his partner Blake, who was thinking of coming up to Baròlin.

'Your partner doesn't pay many visits to Baròlin,' said Frank Hallett.

'Well, no,' replied Mr. Trant. 'Blake was rather taken in over Baròlin, that's the truth. He was disgusted, and turned the whole shop over to me. It's a fiddling little place is Baròlin, and dull as ditchwater.'

'I expect it will be livelier now that the police are turning out on the Upper Luya to hunt for Moonlight,' said Lord Horace.

'Oh, Moonlight!' said Mr. Trant with a laugh. 'Do ye think they'll catch him?'

'They won't, unless the squatters lend a hand,' said Hallett; 'and it's a queer thing, but the squatters don't seem so down on Moonlight as you'd suppose. He hasn't bailed up any of them yet.'

'They'll not catch him,' said Mr. Trant. 'Anyhow, I'll lend 'em a hand at it.'

Elsie looked at him with an expression of dislike. Trant, whose eyes met hers, noticed it, and coloured. 'You don't want him to be caught, Miss?' he said.

'No,' said Elsie decidedly. 'He is a picturesque figure. We haven't much that is picturesque in the bush.'

'Surely,' said Lady Horace, 'we can be picturesque without bushrangers.'

The talk went on about Moonlight. Lord Horace got excited. 'A man hunt.' That was what he wanted. Big game! You needed sportsmen to take the thing up properly. The police were duffers. And now that there was going to be an election no one would bother about Moonlight. Frank Hallett would be responsible if any of the Luya stations were bailed up.

Mr. Trant looked interested. He turned the conversation on to the election, and they discussed the probability of the Irish vote carrying it in favour of the Radical member. He asked a good many questions as to the strength of the Irish vote, the predominance of Radicalism among the Goondi diggers, and the political leanings of the Luya selectors. Hallett fancied that the man meant to draw him, and showed Mr. Trant that he did not intend to be drawn.

Elsie also scenting Trant's motive, though she could not account for it – surely he could not be thinking of opposing Hallett – plunged into the talk. She had hitherto been very silent.

'Do you ever go to Leichardt's Town, Mr. Trant? – to the balls, I mean?'

Trant looked at her admiringly from under his heavy brows. 'I leave that kind of thing to my partner, Miss Valliant. He is more of a ladies' man than I am. Perhaps,' he added, 'I've never had any great inducement till now to stay in Leichardt's Town.'

'I have never met Mr. Blake,' said Elsie, ignoring the implied compliment.

'Blake goes across the border when he wants a spree,' answered Mr. Trant. 'He runs down to Sydney, and he is rather a card there,

I can tell you. I shouldn't wonder, though, if he were in Leichardt's Town a good deal this winter.'

'It is going to be a very gay winter, isn't it?' put in Lady Horace. 'The Prince is really coming, and there will be the new Governor, and we shall have a lot of balls. Elsie and I are going to have a good time – just like the old times, before I married.'

She got up as she spoke and went into the parlour. The night was warm, as March nights are, and there floated in the fragrance of the stephanotis, which twined one of the verandah posts. Elsie sauntered into the verandah. Lady Horace was going to follow her, but when she saw that Hallett had come out of the dining-room, evidently with that intention, leaving Lord Horace and Mr. Trant, she drew back and let Hallett pass her.

Elsie had gathered a spray of the stephanotis, and was stroking her lip with one of the waxen flowers.

'How do you like Mr. Trant?' asked Hallett abruptly.

'I don't like him at all,' she answered. 'I hate a man who calls me "Miss" and looks at me in that fashion.'

'I am sorry that Edith asked him to Tunimbah.'

'Why did she do that?'

'She said we had been unneighbourly, and that she had heard Mr. Blake was a very charming man, and that for his sake we were bound to be civil to his partner. You know Edith rather likes to play the part of great lady of the district.'

'She does it very nicely. She is so amiable and proper, and well dressed, and well read, and all the rest. She always says the right thing when she is in society. Do you know, I think Mrs. Jem Hallett is rather wasted as the wife of a Luya squatter.'

'I see you don't like Edith. But, never mind. You will come over, won't you, and leave the jam to take care of itself for another week?'

'I will come on one condition.'

'What is that?'

'That you take me to Baròlin Waterfall.'

'I am afraid that you will find it a rougher expedition than you bargain for. It will mean a night's camping out.'

'So much the better. I have never camped out in my life. Promise.'

'I promise, if not now, at some future time.'

'Why not now?'

'The river is up, you know, and then it's very difficult to get a black boy who will go near the Falls. But I will do my best. Do you think there is anything in the world I wouldn't try to do if you asked me?'

Elsie's eyes were like stars as she turned them upon him. It was a way of hers to answer a question with her eyes. But presently she said thoughtfully, 'I don't know.'

'What is it that you don't know?' he asked. 'Don't you know that I would do anything in the world for you?'

'Without any reward?' she said coquettishly.

'There would always be the hope of a reward – the hope –'

'Ah!' she exclaimed, cutting him short. 'You are not disinterested. No one is. There is always the hope of a reward. I am tired of it all.'

She moved away from the verandah post as she spoke, and tossed the sprig of stephanotis from her. It fell on the edge of the steps, and he stooped and picked it up. She sat down on a squatter's chair at the end of the verandah furthest from the drawing-room. The other men had come out of the dining-room. Mr. Trant was talking to Lady Horace. Lord Horace came to the door and called out 'Elsie!'

'Well?'

'Come along in. Let us do Sharp's chorus. Trant says he has got a voice.'

'Trant! I wish Horace wouldn't let him be so familiar,' murmured Elsie *sotto voce*.

'Please ask Mr. Trant to try a solo. I can't sing choruses so soon after dinner.'

'Oh, don't go in,' pleaded Hallett.

'It's too hot inside,' Elsie went on, speaking to her brother-in-law. 'Let us stop here and be comfortable.'

'Well, you are' – Lord Horace began to protest, but was called off by his wife.

'What are you tired of?' asked Hallett abruptly, as he seated himself on the edge of the verandah, almost at Elsie's feet.

'Oh, I don't know. Tired of people – people who – who do everything from personal motives, tired of stupid speeches, and compliments, and all that.'

'Tired of being made love to, he said bitterly – 'that's what you mean – of being made love to by men you don't care for.'

'Well,' said Elsie, quietly stroking her dress, 'a good many men do make love to me, you know, and I can't say that they are profoundly interesting as a body.'

'And there are no exceptions – not even one?' he exclaimed. Does no one interest you?'

Elsie looked up swiftly, and went on stroking her dress again. 'I should like to be made love to by some man who didn't care in the least what I thought of him – a man who would go on his own way straight as a die – not turning, as you all do, to right or left, at a woman's beck – a man with a purpose and a destiny. I don't think I should mind whether it was a good purpose or a bad one – a magnificent destiny or a terrible one – only it must not be small or mean! Oh, a man who would follow his star at all costs. That is the man I should like to know.'

'Go on,' said Hallett. 'Tell me more of what you would like in the man who made love to you.'

'He must never pay me a compliment,' said Elsie. 'He must not want to do what *I* wish. He must make me do what *he* wishes. He must be my master.'

'Oh!' exclaimed Hallett impatiently, 'that is a Jane Eyre-ish idea. No man who truly loves a woman can be her master. To love is to be a slave.'

'How do you know that?'

'Because I love you, and because I am your slave. Elsie, how long is it to go on? I can't stand much more.'

'It shall end to-night if you wish it,' she answered.

'But how? But how?' he cried.

'In this way.' She bent a little towards him and spoke very distinctly.

'I shall say to you, "Mr. Hallett, I am very grateful to you for caring for me, and I am honoured by your affection!" That is how the nice girls talk in novels.'

'Bah!' He gave his shoulders an impatient shake.

Elsie went on: 'I am not worthy of your affection. I am a spoilt, heartless young woman, who has never loved anybody in her life – except Mammie and Ina – after a fashion. I don't think it is in me to love any man – unless he was the kind of man I have described – the kind of man who isn't at all likely to come my way. I am very selfish and very frivolous and very mercenary and very ambitious –'

'No,' he said doggedly; 'I am not going to believe that.'

'It is true though, all the same. The only thing that I care about is excitement. I should die of dulness in the bush. I am nearly dead of dulness now. If I were a man I should fight battles; I should intrigue; I should do reckless things. As I am a woman, all I can do to amuse myself is to make men fall in love with me, and so gratify my sense of power, till –' She paused.

'Go on – till when?'

'Till they want what I don't want to give – till they want to come close to me – and paw me – and all the rest.'

'Elsie, you are horrid.'

'Yes, I know that I am,' she replied composedly. 'But you know that you are all alike. You all want to paw me. Then I hate you. And, what is worse, I hate myself.'

'At any rate, you are frank enough.'

'It is almost my only virtue, and, as you say, I make the most of it.'

'Go on with the rest that you were going to say to me.'

'I would say: "And so, Mr. Hallett, being this sort of person, and being so wholly despicable and so utterly unworthy of you, who are so highly estimable – and respecting you so truly –"'

'Oh, Elsie, don't laugh at me.'

'I'm not laughing at you. I mean every word. You can't imagine how truly I respect you. And so – that's how I would wind up – I'm not worth dangling after any longer, and you had better find some other girl who will be less frank, perhaps, but who will, at any rate, give you something better worth having than what I can give you.'

'Will you tell me first exactly what that is?'

'Honest friendship, and a dash of – how shall I call it? – affection.'

'That's something gained anyhow,' he exclaimed. 'I'm not a bit discouraged; I feel that I have made headway. You said that you were quite frank with me three months ago, and you told me then that there was no affection.'

'I didn't know you so well three months ago. I hadn't had an opportunity of learning how estimable you are. Since then I have seen ever so much of you. I have seen you at home. I have heard your praises sung by everybody. You have done all sorts of nice things for me. I should be unnaturally ungrateful – a monster – if I hadn't some affection for you. But affection expresses everything. There's nothing more. There never will be anything more, and there ought to be a great deal more.'

'Well, I am contented.'

'You are very easily satisfied. My ideal lover, my prince among men, would never be contented with – affection. He would want all that there was more, and if I hadn't got it to give him, he would make me a polite bow and go and look for it elsewhere.'

'That would be because he didn't love you as much as I do. If he loved you he would be satisfied to wait, on the chance of getting the rest.'

'And if he never could get the rest?'

'He would be quite satisfied as long as no one else got it.'

'Ah! but if the prince came?'

'Then he would accept his fate. That's the risk. You know I told you three months ago that I would run the risk. It was part of our compact.'

'Oh, our compact! I had forgotten that we had a compact – a real serious compact. Did we fix any limit for it?'

'You told me,' said Hallett, 'that I might go on caring for you – being your friend – your lover on probation –'

'No, no,' she cried; 'that means too much. You were to ask for nothing.'

'I have never asked for anything – I have never even kissed your hand. I will never do so till you yourself tell me that I may.' Hallett's voice trembled with emotion. 'I will worship you as one might worship a star. And you can do nothing to prevent that. In this sense you can't help my being your lover.'

'In that sense – no. You are very chivalrous. Now that is what I like. I admire you when you are like that. But at the same time I am going to say something horrid.'

'Oh, say it.'

'I think, do you know, that I despise you a little for – for – caring so much. That is like a woman, isn't it?'

'Yes; it's like a woman – at least so the cynics who write novels tell us. Well, about our compact? I am sure it had a limit – tell me.'

'You were to give me a definite answer whenever I asked for one.'

'And you asked me for one just now – and I gave it. You said you could not stand things any longer. So the compact is ended.'

'No. You said I might end it if I pleased; and I don't choose to end it after what you said –'

'What? About affection?'

'Yes. I'll never end while you say that you care for me the least bit.'

'Affection isn't caring. It's what one feels for one's pet horse, or one's dog – or one's friend.'

'Well,' said he stolidly, 'it's enough for me. Since it is that or nothing. I am your friend – till you tell me I am something more.'

'But it is ended. I have no more responsibility. I have told you to go. You know you ought to marry. You are going into Parliament. You will be a Minister. You'll have to have a house and to give parties. Political people ought to be married. They shouldn't go dangling after girls –'

'Not after girls; after *a* girl.'

'Well, they shouldn't dangle after *a* girl. It's undignified – especially after such a girl as I am – no money, no connections – except Horace,

I suppose, being a lord, though an impoverished one, counts for
something – a girl who only keeps a Kanaka boy in the kitchen, and
has to make the jam and clean her own boots – oh yes, I assure you,
Ina and I have often cleaned our own boots. It's – well, it's *cheap*, as
Horace says.'

They both laughed. Just then someone struck a few chords on the
piano. It was Lord Horace. And presently someone began to sing.
This was not Lord Horace, who had a nice little baritone, but not a
voice like this. And Lord Horace's French – though he only aired it
occasionally in quotations, was shaky; while even Elsie, who had only
had a few dozen lessons from a French Sister in the convent at
Leichardt's Town, could tell that Mr. Dominic Trant had lived in
France.

Thanks to the Sister, she could understand every word.

'Ninon, Ninon, que fais-tu de la vie?'

It seemed an appeal to herself. How could such a person sing like
that? She asked herself the question as she got up from her chair and
went into the parlour. Mr. Dominic Trant looked at her while he
sang. His eyes had something mesmeric in them. Irish eyes occasionally have. The man was certainly good-looking, and he did give one
a sense of power. The effect that he had, however, was not quite
pleasant. It was the power of a certain sort of passion – not of the
highest kind. The power also of unflinching purpose – also not of the
highest kind. This seemed to show itself when the man was singing.
He began to interest her. He had only struck her before as being
rather ill-bred.

'Where did you learn to sing French?' she asked when he had
finished.

She had gone to the piano.

'I learned French among French people,' said Trant. 'I thought
you would like that song. It was sent out to me the other day. Do you
understand it. Do you speak French?'

'No,' said she perversely. 'How do you expect an Australian girl to
speak French? So you have travelled a great deal, Mr. Trant?'

'I wish you'd let me translate it to you,' he said, not answering her
question. 'But I am quite sure that you understand it. I could tell that
you did by your face.'

'Sing something else,' she replied; 'something English, please.'

This time he sang a rollicking drinking song. Lord Horace was delighted. 'You must come over,' he said. 'We must practise some glees, and we'll let you have 'em at Tunimbah next week, Hallett.'

Frank had to come forward to explain that his sister-in-law had written or was about to write to Mr. Trant, to invite him to join the party.

'I think it is not unlikely that my partner Blake will be at Baròlin then,' said Mr. Trant. 'I had a telegram from him, as I told you, at the "Bean-tree" to-day.'

'Tell me about Mr. Blake,' said Elsie, subsiding into a chair, and motioning Trant to her side in a way that irritated Hallett. She had put on her coquettish air, which meant that she scented a victim. 'Why doesn't he ever come to the Luya?'

'He does come sometimes,' answered Trant.

'But nobody has ever seen him. I feel a curiosity about Mr. Blake.'

'What do you want to know about Blake?'

'Is he young?'

'No, not exactly. I suppose he is close upon forty.'

'Is he married?'

'No.' Mr. Trant laughed. 'He is fair game – and difficult game.'

Elsie drew herself up a little. She was quite sure now that Trant was very ill-bred.

'What do you mean? Does he not like ladies? You said he was a ladies' man.'

'Oh yes, he likes ladies. He is not a marrying man though, Blake. He doesn't care about anything except –'

'Except –?'

'Except adventure, amusement, making money.'

'But people say that Baròlin isn't exactly a money-making place.'

'Oh! They say that, do they? Well, perhaps they are right. But then Blake makes money in other ways. He has got means. He is a luckier sort of devil than I am – obliged to stick at Baròlin all the year round.'

'I say,' put in Lord Horace, 'is your partner any relation of the Blakes of Castle Coola? Because you know my people know the Coola people; I've been fishin' close there.'

'I don't know,' said Mr. Trant. 'I should think it isn't unlikely. Blake doesn't like being questioned about his people – says he cut the whole lot when he came out here.'

'Got into a row perhaps,' said Lord Horace. 'That would be a Blake all over. They're a wild Irish lot – got a dash of Fenianism in the blood. There was a Blake who got drowned. He tumbled off a cliff or something. Waveryng knew him. He was a chap in a crack regiment, too. Well, it came out afterwards that he had been preaching to the chaps in the regiment, inciting to mutiny – like the Boyle O'Reilly business, you know.'

'Yes, I know,' said Trant stolidly.

'They said there would have been a court-martial if the fellow hadn't died; so it's lucky, perhaps, for him that he was drowned.'

'Well, as he was drowned, he can't have anything to do with Blake of Baròlin,' said Trant, with a laugh.

CHAPTER V

A Gauntlet to Fate

Mr. Trant went away the next morning. Elsie did not go into the parlour to bid him good-bye, but remained in the verandah where she was sewing, and listened to his parting words to Lady Horace, who invited him to repeat his visit. 'Ina has no tact,' murmured Elsie to herself. 'She might have seen that I didn't like him.'

'Where's your sister?' asked Mr. Trant, and Ina's want of tact again displayed itself when she promptly replied, 'Oh! Elsie is in the verandah.'

Mr. Trant came out. 'I have come to say good-bye, and to tell you that I shall be over at Tunimbah when you are there.'

'I don't know that I am going to be there,' said Elsie perversely.

Mr. Trant's face fell. 'If you are not there, I shall come away the next day. ... Do you live up here, Miss Valliant?' he asked, after having waited in vain for Elsie to reply.

'No,' she said. 'I am only staying with my sister, and I am going back to Leichardt's Town almost immediately.'

'Lord Horace wants me to come and sing. It isn't much of a ride over from Baròlin – only about fifteen miles.'

'Oh!' said Elsie.

'Miss Valliant, why don't you like me?'

'Really, Mr. Trant, you ask rather embarrassing questions.'

'But you don't. I see it in your face. You liked me a little after I sang last night. I knew I was having some effect upon you, and I should have liked to sing on for ever. I wish you'd let me come and sing to you.'

'But I'm going away. And besides, I mightn't like you to have an effect upon me.'

'That means that you are a little afraid of me. I know that; I can make people afraid of me.'

'Can you really? How?'

'I don't quite know. By looking at them. I can always make a woman like me, if I want to. I don't often want to. I don't care about them.'

'Perhaps that is why you make them like you. People can often influence others just from the very reason that they don't care about them.'

'I don't think that reasoning ought to apply to you and me. Please don't be offended. I only meant that it would be impossible to look at you often and remain indifferent.'

'In that case,' said Elsie, 'it would be better not to look at me.'

'Much better,' said Trant seriously. 'I quite agree with you. It would not suit my way of life to care too much for a woman.'

'What is your way of life?' asked Elsie, interested in spite of herself.

Trant laughed in a sort of *sotto voce* way that he had. 'You wouldn't understand it if I were to tell you.'

'From the outside it wouldn't seem to be so mysterious,' said Elsie, piqued – 'living at Baròlin and looking after horses and cattle. I understand something about that.'

The black boy came round with Mr. Trant's horse. 'Well, good-bye,' he said in a lingering manner. 'I am very glad to have met you.' Elsie gave him her hand. The black boy grinned as Trant went down the log steps.

'I say,' he said, 'Ba'al you got him Mary belonging to you?'

'Ba'al,'* answered Trant.

'That budgery† Mary,' said the black boy, making a gesture towards Elsie, who pretended not to see or hear. 'Mine think it that fellow Hallett, plenty look after Elsie. Elsie – I say,' shouted the imp – an Australian black is no respecter of persons – 'Mine got him dilly-bag for you.'

The dilly-bag, which had been plaited by the gins, smelled atrociously of the camp, but it was a good pretext for escaping Trant's farewell gaze, and for running round to the store for a fig of tobacco, the purchase-money agreed upon for the dilly-bag.

Trant rode off. Close by the door Hallett was saddling his horse, and Lord Horace was in conversation with a travelling digger, to whom he had been giving out rations.

---

*Ba'al – No.   †Budgery – Good.

'Lord, what infernal cheek!' Lord Horace was saying. 'You'll have to look sharp, Hallett, to beat that.'

'What is it that you are to look sharp about?' asked Elsie, coming towards him.

'It seems,' said Hallett, drawing his lips together, and relaxing them with a determined expression, 'that though poor Slaney was only buried yesterday, the Opposition candidate has already declared himself.'

'What!' said Elsie.

'Posters up on the gum-trees all round Goondi. This fellow has come from the "Bean-tree" this morning, and they had telegraphed it on there. I wonder if Trant knew anything about it.'

'Why, of course,' put in the digger. 'Trant is his partner, and Trant was at the "Bean-tree" yesterday, telegraphing all over the country. Good-day, miss.' He touched his felt wide-awake as Elsie turned to him impulsively.

'You don't mean that Mr. Trant is the Opposition candidate?' she asked.

'It's his partner, miss,' said the digger. 'Blake of Baròlin. He thinks he'll get in on the Irish vote – a flash sort of chap is Blake, they say. You take my advice, Mr. Hallett. Cut in at once, and take the wind out of his sails. You're safe enough on the Luya, but those Goondi chaps are all agin the squatters, and they like blather.'

The man had taken some dirty shillings out of his pouch, and was handing them to Lord Horace in payment for his rations. Lord Horace counted them carefully and thrust them into his pocket.

'Have a nip,' he said, and took the digger to the kitchen, where Lady Horace acted as Hebe, and where his health was drunk, and that of her ladyship, with due formalities. Lord and Lady Horace were popular in the district, and a good many loafers found their way to the Dell. They could always fetch Lord Horace by admiring his amateur bush ways, and he always wound up business by offering them a grog.

'Where are you going?' asked Elsie of Hallett.

'To the "Bean-tree," and perhaps to Goondi, to look after my political interests.'

'Isn't it rather odd that Mr. Blake should have got into the field so quickly. He must have heard of Mr. Slaney's death almost as soon as it happened,' said Elsie.

'I suppose he has been working up the district for some time on the sly,' answered Hallett. 'Trant must have set the wires going. That fellow brought me a telegram from the "Bean-tree," which had been forwarded by Mrs. Jem, on the chance of its picking me up here. My supporters want to see me.'

Elsie noticed that he had pinned into his coat the sprig of stephanotis she had thrown away the night before. 'Why do you keep that withered thing?' she said. 'If you come round to the verandah, I'll give you a better one.'

'Give me the bit you have in your belt,' he said. 'It will bring me luck.'

She took it out with a little hesitation. 'You'd much better have a fresh piece,' and she moved to the house. He followed her. It was only an excuse for getting out of eye-range. As soon as they were in the front verandah he stopped her as she was going to the stephanotis creeper.

'No, give me that.'

'No, I want it for myself.'

She held it back, but he took it from her, and put it to his lips.

'I have spoilt it for you now,' he said.

She still held out her hand. 'How?'

'Because I kissed the flowers. There!' He tossed them away.

She gathered another spray. 'That is a very nice one: and please don't throw it away directly you are out of sight of the house.'

He laughed. 'I'll show you the ghost of it next time we meet.'

'That means that we shan't meet for a long time.'

'Long enough for these to wither. I don't know when I shall be able to get over again. I must canvass the district. We shall meet at Tunimbah.'

'Write and tell me how things are going,' she said.

'Do you really care to hear? Oh! Elsie, it makes me glad.'

'Of course I care to hear. I am immensely excited. I wish I could go to Goondi and canvass for you. I'd make love to the Luya selectors. I'd abuse Mr. Blake to your very heart's content. Blake of Baròlin! Has it struck you that the name sounds rather poetic?'

'Much more so than Hallett of Tunimbah.'

'Well, yes! I love a poetic name. I couldn't marry a man who was called Smith. Two Smiths proposed to me by the way, and they were good matches, and Mammie and Ina scolded me for sending them about their business. To be sure, I couldn't have married them both. Oh, what a bore it is that one must marry – somebody!'

'I can't bear to hear you talk like that. Why must you marry – anybody?'

'Because I've got no other way of gaining my living. Because my prettiness is going – oh yes! Girls in Australia go off very soon. And do you think I haven't heard it said that Elsie Valliant is going off? Because I should hate to be an old maid. Mr. Hallett –'

'Yes?'

'You know we settled last night that our compact was at an end.'

'Did we? I think not.'

'Yes. I told you to go. I gave you a definite answer. There's nothing more to wait for.'

'I think there is a great deal to wait for.'

'I was most splendidly unselfish. I sacrificed myself. You don't even thank me for my disinterestedness. You are to expect nothing from me, and I am to give up the gratification of having the member for Luya – a prospective minister – among my admirers.'

'Let us make a new compact,' he said gravely. 'I don't ask anything from you – except absolute frankness.'

'Oh! that I have always given you.'

'Go on giving it. Let us talk out quite openly to each other. Tell me that you don't care a bit for me – if it is true. Tell me if your affection – you said it was affection – deepens or lessens. I shall never reproach you if you hurt me. I am willing to take my chance.'

'Well, what else?'

'Let us go on in this way. You will know – yes, for I shall tell you unless you forbid me – that I love you. That is not to be gainsaid. I don't care how long I have to wait. You told me that you liked me better than anyone else who has ever cared for you.'

'Yes, but that isn't saying much. I have never cared for anyone.'

'Well, that is all I want – now. I think I like you to be like that. It fits in with my star fancy. I can worship you without a tinge of jealousy. And when you flirt, I know that it only means that you are dull and want amusement.'

'That is a charitable construction to put on my evil doings.'

'I don't mind. It's like the naughtiness of a child that doesn't know what it's doing. One can't think hardly of it when it's so unconscious. That's what you are. You don't realise that you can hurt people. And all that fancy about the hero – the Prince –'

'Yes, the hero – the Prince. Is that like a child, too? But the child's fancies sometimes become the realities of the woman.'

'This is what I meant by absolute frankness. If the Prince comes, tell me, you will be able to trust me. I shall stand aside. I will worry you no more. Wait, and I will wait, too.'

'For my Prince? And how long do you give me to wait?'

'You shall fix your own time. Throw a gauntlet to fate.'

The phrase struck her. '"A gauntlet to fate." I like that. I did not know that you could say such poetic things. Well, I will throw a gauntlet to fate. Well, here's my challenge.' She flung a glove she carried into the air. As it came down she tried to catch it, but it fell almost into his hand.

'That is an omen,' he exclaimed. 'And the time?'

'I challenge fate to bring my Prince along within the year – a year from this day – what is the date?'

'The twenty-ninth of March!'

'The twenty-ninth of next March then. It shall be yes or no, once and for all.'

CHAPTER VI

———•———

The Coming of the Prince

Elsie seemed a little depressed for a week after Frank Hallett's visit. She felt that she had committed herself. To be sure, she consoled herself with the reflection that she had the fullest right to throw him over if her Prince came. But suppose that no Prince came, and that she had reached no further pitch of romantic ardour than she had at present attained?

'I liked him better six months ago,' she said to herself. 'I was almost in love with him. I think I was quite in love with him. I think I was quite in love with him one day when he seemed to like Ina better than he liked me. How horribly selfish, and mean, and small to be jealous! And jealous of one's own sister!'

Lady Horace was a little depressed too, if indeed anyone so equable could be depressed. Elsie accounted for it by the fact that Lord Horace had been aggravating. Lord Horace had occasionally fits of spleen and regret that he had ever left England – fits which were generally brought about by a perusal of his bank-book, and which usually ended in a grumble over dinner, and a reactionary burst of effusion to his wife.

He was away just now, helping Frank Hallett in his electioneering business, and the sisters were alone. They were sitting out in the verandah together one evening. Ina was in a squatter's chair, and Elsie sat on the edge of the verandah, and leaned her head against Ina's knees.

'Ina,' she said suddenly, 'I wish I wasn't such a wretch.'

'What makes you say that, El?'

'I don't know. Frank Hallett, I suppose. It's perfectly horrid of me to want to keep him dangling in a string. Why don't I marry him straight away?'

'Oh, why not?'

'I don't know. That's just it. I like him. He is the only man I have ever been able to imagine kissing me without a shudder.'

'Elsie!'

'Well, it always comes to that in time. There was a moment when I was almost in love with him.'

'Almost!'

'How tragically you say that. There was a moment when it came over me that I had snubbed him too severely, and that he had deserted me for you; and I believe I threw myself on the bed and cried out of grief and mortification.'

'I saw you,' said Ina, 'and I knew from that moment that you cared for Frank Hallett, and that you ought to marry him.'

'Did you really see me, Ina? And you never said a word. That was awfully like you. You'd never let me suspect that you knew how abominably petty I had been. It was all vanity.'

'No, no, Elsie, don't say that.'

'It's true. I've been like that all my life, and I'm ashamed of it. I hate myself sometimes. I can't bear a man who has admired me to take up with anyone else – even my own sister. I'm a mean creature.'

'You know you are not. I've seen you take the greatest pains to dress up girls in your own finery, so that they might have as good a chance of getting partners as you. You have dressed me up in the same way. You have exulted in my little conquests. You know you have, Elsie. And if you were jealous for a moment it was because you cared. Do you think I'm not certain of that?'

'Ina, you are trembling. What's the matter?'

'I can't bear to hear you cry yourself down.'

'I shouldn't have been so horrid, Ina, if you had cared. It's a mercy you didn't, for I might have had a little trouble in getting up to such a height of heroic abnegation. Frank Hallett wouldn't suit you, Ina. He is too solid and steady, and for two angels to marry is a waste of regenerating material. No, Ina dear, you are clearly intended for a sinner.'

The girls laughed, both a little sadly. Elsie went on, 'Do you know, Ina, I think it's a pity we weren't taught to earn our own living. I think it's a pity in a kind of way that we are pretty. If we had been ugly there wouldn't have been so much bother about this marrying business. As it is there's been nothing else for us to do. You are married, and it is all right, or at any rate I hope it is all right for you, but here I am, twenty-two, poor – and in three or four years' time I shall be losing my good looks and there'll be nothing for me to fall back upon. Now if we had been governesses, or even plain needlewomen, there would not have been any necessity for falling in love.'

'Elsie!'

'Oh yes! it is a very disagreeable necessity. The only thing more disagreeable would be to marry without it. It is so difficult to fall in love. I have been trying for all these years, and I haven't succeeded yet.'

'Not even with Frank Hallett?'

'Not even with Frank Hallett, and yet he has everything for one to fall in love with – good looks, though I don't care for those in a man, nice manners, brains – of a sort – money – you couldn't wish for anything more satisfactory. And I think I could be happy with him.'

'Elsie,' said Ina, with an inflexion almost of passion in her voice, 'don't be a spoiled child; caring only for a thing when you can't get it – not valuing what is yours. Don't let it all have been of no use: his love for you; my – my prayers for your happiness with him.'

'You are right, I have been a spoilt child. Mammie has spoiled me, you have spoiled me, though I'm older than you, my poor Ina; and it is I who ought to have spoiled you. It's that which makes me the heartless, freakish thing that I am. And yet – and yet there's always the feeling that the Prince might come.'

'The Prince? Do you mean the Prince that is coming this winter? And what use will that be to you? You don't think you can marry him?' Ina alluded to the visit of a certain sprig of royalty, which was expected to take place that year. 'You don't think you are like Beatrix Esmond, do you?'

'Yes, I do think I am very like Beatrix Esmond. As for my Prince – well, I should be pleased if he wore a periwig and Court ruffles and carried a sword like Colonel Henry Esmond; but that is out of the question, I suppose, in this nineteenth-century Australia, and there are not many Colonel Esmonds in history – or out of it.'

'I think Frank Hallett would do quite as fine things as Colonel Henry Esmond.'

'Perhaps. But do you know, between ourselves, I always thought Colonel Esmond was ever such a little bit of a prig. Ina, I have told Frank Hallett that if the Prince does not come along within a year's time I will marry him.'

'And you are going to flirt with everybody that comes along, with the idea that he may turn out to be your Prince?'

'I think I should know my Prince without trying experiments. As for flirting, I suppose a poor girl may be allowed to make the most of the last opportunity she will ever have. I shan't be able to flirt after I am married, you know.'

'I think you would flirt in your grave. You were flirting the other night with that horrid Mr. Trant.'

'I am not sure that he is horrid. I think that under some circumstances he might be rather interesting.'

'At any rate he is horrid for having sneaked so about the election.'

'They say all is fair in love and war. The two must be hard at it now. I wonder that Frank Hallett hasn't written.'

'I wonder that Horace hasn't written,' said Ina uneasily. 'I don't see how you can expect Mr. Hallett to write when you never answered his letter.'

'Look here,' said Elsie, 'I don't think Horace is quite fit to be trusted by himself. He'll go flirting with the barmaids – you know Horace is a horrid flirt.'

'Let us go over to Goondi to see about getting some things,' said Lady Horace, 'but I don't think that would be a good time. We must have a new colonial oven before the Waveryngs come. Oh! Elsie, what shall I do with them?'

Lady Horace took life placidly as a rule, but she was just now seriously discomposed by the news which had arrived by the last mail, that Lord and Lady Waveryng were about to make the tour of the world, and proposed to include the Australian Colonies in their programme.

Elsie laughed. 'Never mind. Take them camping out. Let Horace look after them.'

'If only the new house were built.'

'Well, I expect you'll find that Horace has anticipated Lord Waveryng's remittance, in shouting champagne to the diggers, and there'll be nothing left to pay for the imported bull, let alone the new house. You'd better make up your mind to go to Goondi.'

It was nearly a fortnight after Mr. Slaney's death and the sticking up of the coach by Moonlight. The excitement over Moonlight's escapade had paled before that of the election. The police patrolled the district, and had explored as far as they were able the fastnesses of the Upper Luya. But the Upper Luya was not easily explored. Every trace of Moonlight seemed to have disappeared, and the police returned to head-quarters to await the next full moon and be on the look out for another outrage.

The Tunimbah festivities had been postponed in view of the election. They had now been fixed for a date after the polling day, and would, it was supposed, inaugurate the entrance of Frank Hallett into public life. In the meantime young Hallett, accompanied by his supporters, harangued the district and started a reputation for making telling speeches. Lord Horace also made speeches of a somewhat humorous description, and exposed his friend to the risk of being unseated on a charge of bribery, from the lavish manner in which he regaled the electors and distributed champagne. If, however, Hallett and his friends were energetic, Blake of Baròlin and his partner, Dominic Trant, were more energetic still. Elsie read the accounts of Mr. Blake's meetings in the papers, and she read his speeches, and contrasted them with those of her lover, not altogether to Frank Hallett's advantage. She began to think that it was perhaps as well she had not been brought into personal relations with the opposing candidate, since she might have found it more difficult to canvass with enthusiasm for Hallett among the Luya selectors. And yet she longed to see Blake. Everything she read about him appealed to her imagination. He was almost a stranger on the Luya, but this was perhaps better for him, since he had come daringly into the country, bold, picturesque, as it seemed irresistible; and had taken it by storm. It was said that he would run Frank Hallett hard, though no one among the squatters doubted that Frank Hallett would win. Blake appealed to the masses. He had the Irish gift of eloquence. He had that terrible Irish passion, and he had the pluck of the typical Irishman and a certain dash of poetry and pathos and romance that is typical also of Ireland. There was about him, too, a dash of mystery. No one knew quite what he did, where he came from, and where he got the money which he scattered so freely. The women adored him, and women have a powerful voice at election times. He was something of the *preux chevalier*, though he represented the Radical interest. All this Elsie gleaned from the glowing descriptions in the 'Goondi Chronicle,' which was on his side, and the sneering remarks of the 'Luya Times,' which was on theirs. It was very easy to read between the lines. Frank Hallett was safe, steady, eminently estimable, but he was not picturesque. The other was picturesque, and that was enough to make Elsie wildly anxious to see him. But probably he was not safe, steady, nor eminently estimable. She had her wish on that very day when she had suggested to Ina that they should go to Goondi. She had gone down to the Crossing – her own favourite Crossing – the place where she had met Hallett. Perhaps she had a lingering fancy that Hallett might ride that way and she would hear some news – something to enliven the deadly dulness of the life at the Humpey. Elsie was getting very tired of life at the Humpey, and was beginning to sigh for her Leichardt's Town parties, and the bank clerks and young gentlemen in the Government offices, who out of the Parliamentary season made up the roll of her admirers. She had taken her book with her, for, unlike Ina, Elsie was fond of reading. It was a book which Hallett had brought her – a book she had often heard of and had never yet read. The book was a translation – Goethe's 'Elective Affinities.'

There was a nook of the creek, set back from Lord Horace's bridge, and out of sight of any passer-by who might cross the bridge. A gnarled ti-tree jutted into the stream – a little tree peninsula. It had great twisted roots covered with ferns, with pale tufts of the scentless mauve violet. The branches of the ti-tree bent down and dipped their red bottle-brush blossoms into the stream, which just here was dark and rather deep, and swirled in tiny eddies round the twigs and bowed roots. There was just room for one person to sit on the islet. The back of the tree and the twisted roots made a famous arm-chair. A log spanned the stream above the islet, and was used by foot passengers. Elsie had crossed upon it. Lower down, the creek ran shallower over a bed of stones and rock crystals, and made a pleasant brawling. There was an intense dreaminess in the air, and there was no other sound but the chirping of grasshoppers, the occasional caw of a cockatoo, or cry of a bird in the scrub close by, and the footsteps of cattle or horses coming down to drink. Elsie was reading the scene in which Edward and Ottilie first discover their love. She put the book down and leaned back against the tree, her cheeks flushed, and a tender smile was upon her lips. She had often read about love, but none that she read of seemed to her so real as this! Should she ever know such love? Was it so rare? Was it possible that in this manner Frank Hallett loved her? Why, then, was it that she felt no returning throb? Elsie wondered vaguely with some dim faint realisation of the greatest of life's mysteries. But it was quite true that she had never loved. People had loved her, but she had never taken much account of what they felt and suffered. It occurred to her now that, perhaps, they had suffered a good deal, and that, perhaps, she might have been kinder.

'I have never taken life seriously enough,' Elsie said to herself. 'I have never taken love seriously either.' And then she laughed softly, as the thought flashed across her how impossible it would be to take some of those bank clerks from the serious standpoint. Life and love had only been a game to Elsie. And yet in the background of her consciousness there had always been a tremendous ideal – so Elsie herself would have phrased it – an image which was sacred, an image of a prince. Only *a* prince. *The* Prince had not ridden through the enchanted forest where the princess slept.

There was a sound of horse's feet now, a more definite tramp than that of the stray animal making for water. A traveller. Could it be Hallett? Elsie would not move. From where she sat she could not see him as he crossed the bridge; but she would see him when he mounted the bank, and if it were Hallett, she would give him a 'Coo-ee' and surprise him. The tramp came nearer. Another odd fancy came into Elsie's mind. She remembered Hallett's rather contemptuous remark when she had described the ideal lover . . . 'A Jane Eyre-ish ideal.' The tramp on the hard ground made her think of the metallic clatter of Rochester's horse rising above the murmuring of rills and whisperings of the wintry afternoon. There was no similitude between this dreamy southern afternoon and the grim frost-bound landscape of the book, but the fancy was in her mind. And there was a dog – another Gytrash – a human-looking shaggy creature with intelligent eyes and a huge masklike head. She could see the dog as it bounded up the bank and turned back to bark. She knew the dog quite well. It was the big collie that belonged to one of the Tunimbah stockmen. Of course the rider was Frank. She coo-eed. The horse was pulled back and turned on the threshold of the bridge. A mettlesome animal. She could hear it snort and quiver. Pioneer was like that. This was Pioneer's colour. She had caught a glimpse of a black hind quarter. Elsie bent forward and coo-eed again; at the same time she plucked an overhanging bottle-brush blossom of the ti-tree and flung it at the rider.

The missile did not hit its mark, but she was wholly unprepared for the effect of her heedless action. There was a plunge, a kick, a rear forward, and the horse and rider darted past, the creature swerving blindly up the bank, cannoning against a she-oak, and then dashing under the low branch of a white cedar. The rider stooped to save himself, but too late. A projecting boss of the tree caught his shoulder and almost dragged him from his seat. He was a good horseman and a man of nerve, and gripping the bridle checked the horse and dismounted. He staggered a little and put his hand to his shoulder. The coat had been torn, and he was evidently severely bruised. The pain of the blow made him turn for a moment quite white. What struck Elsie in the midst of her consternation was that he never uttered a sound.

She herself had given a cry of alarm and self-reproach. She had seen as the horse rushed past that it was not Pioneer, and that its rider was not Frank Hallett. This was a much more spirited and highly-bred animal. The thing was all quivering now, its nostrils distended, and the whites of the eyes gleaming. The stranger patted it with his left hand – it was the right arm that had been hurt. 'Wo, old man! Quiet, old boy!' he said, and turned and saw Elsie.

She had left her islet and was standing – an image of dismay. 'Oh, I am so sorry! I hope you are not hurt.'

The stranger took off his hat. He raised his right arm to do so, and winced with pain.

'Oh, you are hurt. Please let me see. I can't tell you how sorry I am.' He came down to the little plateau where she stood, leading the horse, which though still restive followed him.

Elsie saw the torn coat. She went close to him and touched his shoulder.

'It's nothing,' said the stranger; 'only a knock. It doesn't hurt at all – at least nothing to speak of.'

'It hurts horribly: I can see that, and it is my fault. I hadn't the faintest notion – I thought you were Frank Hallett.'

The stranger laughed. 'No, I am certainly not Mr. Frank Hallett; I am Blake of Baròlin.'

Elsie did not laugh. It seemed to her that she had known from the first moment that this was Blake of Baròlin.

He was picturesque. Oh yes, there was no doubt of that. She could imagine him swaying a crowd. There was something kingly about him. He was tall, and straight, and powerful. He had eyes like the eyes of an eagle, they were so piercing and so steadfast. And there was a Napoleonic suggestion about his firm mouth and chin – a certain combined sweetness and dignity and resolution – a fire and force in the expression of his features and the carriage of his head. Very handsome. But a great deal more than handsome.

'I can feel that it is swelling,' she said in deep distress, taking away her hand. 'It ought to be bathed and seen to at once, or you will be horribly bruised. I don't know what to do. Shall I run up to the house and send the black boy for your horse? You can't lead it like that. It hurts you every time it tugs. Give me the bridle. What's its name?'

'His name – oh' – he paused and laughed rather oddly though – 'he's called Osman. No, you couldn't hold him. He's a young horse, and there's something up with him to-day. I was off-guard or he wouldn't have shied at you like that. I can't think what startled him.'

'It was I. I threw some of these things at him.' She twitched off a ti-flower. 'I threw it at you – at you – at least I threw it' – she laughed nervously – 'at Mr. Frank Hallett.'

'I am sorry, for your sake, that I am not Mr. Frank Hallett.'

'You needn't be sorry. Will he stand?' Blake had strapped his horse round a sapling.

'Yes, I'll just wait a minute or two, if you don't mind, till the twinge has gone off. Then I'll get on to Baròlin.'

'Oh, won't you come up to the house and have it seen to? My sister will be pleased.'

'Your sister?'

'Lady Horace Gage. I am Miss Valliant; I am staying with her.'

'Yes, I heard that.' Mr. Blake made her a bow. 'I beg your pardon for having frightened you.'

'Oh, it isn't – I mean it was all my fault. Please come up to the Humpey!'

'I don't think I ought to do that. You see, Lord Horace and I have been doing nothing but hurl abuse at each other for the last week or so, and I'm on a canvassing expedition to the Upper Luya.'

'Do you think you are going to beat Frank Hallett?' asked Elsie.

'I hope so. Yes, I think I shall beat him. If I do, I suppose you will hate me?'

'I don't know why you should say that. Mr. Hallett is not my brother or – or any other relation.'

'But you wish him to get in?'

'Yes – I wish him to get in.'

'Because he is a friend, or because you are in sympathy with his politics?'

'Oh, his politics! I don't know anything about politics. I don't care in the least whether the squatters get their Land Bill, or whether the agriculturists get things their way, It doesn't matter.'

'Don't you think it matters that the squatters monopolise a great deal of land to which they have no right, and of which poor people ought to have a share?'

'There is plenty of room in Australia,' said Elsie.

'Yes, there is plenty of room, and all the more reason for legislators to see that justice is done. I mean to go against your Squatters Land Bill, Miss Valliant. I mean to fight Mr. Hallett on all his points tooth and nail. I am fighting him now. We are enemies in open field, and you and yours are on his side of the battle.'

'Oh, we are sisters of mercy – Ina and I,' said Elsie laughing. 'In common charity one may bind up one's enemy's wounds.'

'I think my wounds will keep till I get to Baròlin,' he said, laughing too. 'They are not very serious: I will not put your and Lady Horace's loyalty to so severe a test. I am glad you call yourself a sister of mercy, and that you take up so disinterested a position – perhaps I ought rather to say so womanlike a position.'

'Why womanlike?'

'You confess that it is for the sake of friendship, not from political conviction, that you are on Mr. Hallett's side.'

Elsie laughed. He went on: 'Well, at any rate, though naturally Mr. Hallett has your best wishes, I may hope that you will not owe me any serious grudge if I am returned.' He looked down at Elsie with a half smile. Where was all her self-confidence gone?

To anyone else she would have made a jesting reply into which she would certainly have infused a spice of coquetry. Their eyes met. Hers dropped and she flushed slightly. He thought her wonderingly pretty.

'No,' she said weakly.

'Thank you. I am very glad of that. I'm afraid we shall not have the chance of seeing much of you in the Luya, but if I do get in, we shall meet at the Leichardt's Town balls, perhaps.'

'Don't you mean ever to come to the Luya? Do you always leave everything to Mr. Trant?'

'Oh no. I do come to the Luya occasionally. I have been up here several times.'

'We haven't heard of you coming.'

'No, I suppose you haven't heard of my coming. But then you have such big excitements on the Luya that it is not surprising.'

'You mean Moonlight?'

'Ah! He seems to be an excitement. What do you think of Moonlight, Miss Valliant?'

'I admire him. I would give anything to have been in the coach when he stuck it up.'

'Shouldn't you have been afraid?'

'No. Why? I have no money to be robbed of – not even a watch. And Moonlight only robs misers and the gold escort. I suppose he thinks he has a right to the spoils of the earth. And,' she added, 'that's your principle, Mr. Blake.'

'It's the principle of the oppressed. And so you sympathise with Moonlight?'

'I should like to see him,' said Elsie dreamily. 'Do you know that I told Mr. Hallett, the day after the robbery, that I wished Moonlight would carry me off to his lair?'

'You wished to be carried to Moonlight's lair! Well, more unlikely things have happened. I can quite imagine that if Moonlight, as they call him, heard you say that, he might be inclined to act upon your suggestion. What did Mr. Hallett say?'

'I should have to be ransomed, you know – some of the squatters here would try and buy me back.'

'I haven't the least doubt of that. The district would rise in search of you, and they would probably be more successful than Captain Macpherson and his men seem to have been. And – well so much the worse for Moonlight. Good-bye, Miss Valliant.'

'You are going?'

'Yes.' He unbuckled his horse's bridle. 'It will be late before I get to Baròlin, especially if I stop at the cedar-cutters' on the way.'

'Ah, we have been beforehand with you. They have promised us their vote.'

'So you have been canvassing for Mr. Hallett? He is very fortunate. I wish I had been the lucky candidate who secured your partisanship.' He raised his hat again. Elsie held out her hand.

'Is your shoulder very painful?'

'A little; but it is not worth thinking about. I am glad of the accident since it has given me the opportunity of making your acquaintance. I have wished for a long time to meet you.'

'Why?'

'I will tell you some time, when I know you better. It is rather a long story, and it might be disagreeable to you to hear it.'

'I don't understand.' She looked at him wonderingly.

'No? Never mind. It will keep. You are leaving your book behind you.' He picked the volume up and handed it to her, glancing at the title as he did so.

'The "Elective Affinities!" Do you believe in that theory?'

'No. I can't tell. I have had so little experience –'

'I should have thought that you had had a considerable experience.'

'You mean –' she stopped and blushed.

'Well,' he said, 'I mean that you must have tested some of the laws of human chemistry, and are at least in a position to judge what kind of qualities you yourself are most likely to attract.'

'Oh no,' she exclaimed with childlike candour which amused him; 'I can't judge in the least. They are all so unlike.'

'They must at any rate have one common quality.'

'That of being commonplace,' she said.

He laughed and slipped the bridle over his left arm. 'Come, Osman. Good-bye, Miss Valliant.'

CHAPTER VII

———————•———————

'I Follow My Star'

When Elsie Valliant set her heart upon doing any particular thing, she usually had her way. She had set her heart upon going to Goondi during the election week, and so she persuaded Lady Horace to take her. They rode to the Bean-tree Crossing, as the Telegraph Station and German Settlement near them was called, and there picked up the coach to Goondi. It was only a one day's expedition, after all. Two coaches passed in the day, one in the morning and one at night.

Lady Horace was not very hard to persuade. Perhaps she was more excited about the chances of Hallett's return than she chose to show. Perhaps she was a little anxious about her husband, of whom they heard vaguely as 'shouting drinks' to the electors, driving four-in-hand about the country, playing practical jokes upon his opponents, certainly flirting with electors' pretty daughters, and otherwise having what he described as 'a good time.'

Ina was so quiet that no one ever quite knew what she felt or thought; but Elsie had a shrewd suspicion that she was not perfectly satisfied with her handsome and excitable young husband, and Elsie had heard Lord Horace speak more crossly to Ina than befitted the short time they had been married. To be sure he had apologised very penitently afterwards, and had declared to Elsie that Ina was an angel, which she told him had always been perfectly well known in the family. Lord Horace had added that perhaps it might be better for him if she were not quite such an angel, as she would keep him in stricter order, and there Elsie had agreed. Anyhow, Ina seemed to think that he needed a little keeping in order now, and so she said that as she wanted to do some shopping, and as Goondi was the nearest place where she could buy a yard of silk or a reel of cotton, she and Elsie would go.

It was a queer straggling bush town, with a large and floating population, mostly of miners. The claims, with their heaps of stone and scaffolding of machinery, gave it a different appearance from the ordinary township. All day and night the machinery was at work, and all day and all night one could hear the dull thud of the blasting. There was only one street in the township, but it went up- and down-hill for nearly two miles. Goondi was all hills and little wooden houses and heaps of stone and mullock, which is the refuse from the crushing. There was only one hotel – a big two-storeyed wooden house, with verandah and balcony all round, commonly known as 'Ruffey's. Here the rival candidates were staying. Hallett harangued his mob from the north balcony, and Blake addressed his from the one on the south. Lord Horace was waiting outside the hotel to receive them when the coach drove up. His refined, Greek-featured face looked paler than usual from fatigue and late hours. He was very much excited, and could talk of nothing but the election. He began at once to tell Ina of how he had been making himself agreeable to the wives of the diggers and settlers, and of the bush balls at which he had been assisting; of how the men had openly derided him for being a Lord, and of how he had entertained and impressed the ladies by his answers to their questions concerning aristocratic life in England. 'Lord! I have crammed them,' he said confidentially; 'but I think we are doin' it, though it'll be a close shave. Puts me in mind of Waveryng's election. I fetched 'em last night, I can tell you, by describin' all that, and singing 'em the war-cry – I composed it myself – a sort of hash of the "Marseillaise," the "Star-spangled Banner," and "Tommy Dodd." The worst of it is that fellow Trant has got a voice that takes the wind out of our sails, and then he appeals to their feelin's. Blest if he didn't give 'em "The Wearing of the Green" last night – struck up when Blake began about the Irish wrongs – he's a Fenian is that fellow Blake, but he is not a bad sort for all that; and I really felt inclined to blubber, it was so pathetic.'

Hallett came towards them. They were in the entrance-hall, and he was coming down the stairs. From the other side of the hotel floated sounds of the mob he had been addressing. He, too, looked excited, and a little nervous. He went straight to Elsie, just shaking hands with Lady Horace as he passed.

'You see I said I would come,' she said.

'I'm afraid you've come to see me beaten,' he answered in a low voice. 'I mustn't confess to defeat now, but I feel pretty sure of it.'

'But he is a stranger,' said Elsie. 'What has he done? How has he got over the district?'

'The man has power,' said Hallett bluntly, 'and I haven't.'

'Yes, he has power,' said Elsie dreamily; 'I can see that.'

'You've seen him, then?' said Hallett, surprised. He had not heard of that meeting by the creek. Elsie had not even told her sister. 'Take care,' he added in a low voice, 'there he is.' Aloud he said, 'I think we had better go up to your sitting-room, Lady Horace. This isn't exactly the place for ladies.'

A number of men had come in from the outside entrance. They were talking noisily. Trant's voice could be heard above the others. He stopped short at the sight of the ladies, and lifted his hat to Lady Horace, who gave him rather a cool nod. All the men seemed to cluster naturally round the central figure – Blake himself – taller than the others, more erect, and altogether better-bred looking. He, too, raised his hat at the sight of Elsie, but with his left hand. She made a slight movement in his direction. It was more a gesture than a movement, but he interpreted it as she had intended, and came to speak to her.

'I hope your arm is all right now,' she said. 'No, I see it isn't. Why do you wear a sling?'

'The shoulder was dislocated,' he said in an eager confused manner, 'and Abatos pulled all the way to Baròlin, and made a nasty business out of what would have been nothing if I had kept quiet.'

'Abatos!' she exclaimed. 'You called him Osman.'

'Abatos,' said Hallett, 'is the name of Moonlight's famous horse.'

'I suppose I was thinking of that. Someone has just been speaking of Moonlight,' replied Mr. Blake quietly. But Elsie had fancied when she spoke that his face had changed, and that he had grown paler. Was it the sight of her which had agitated him? The girl's heart thrilled with an odd momentary sense of triumph.

'The excitement of an election is apt to confuse one's faculties,' Blake went on. 'You have come into the thick of the fight, Miss Valliant. But I think on the whole' – he turned to Hallett – 'that the warfare is conducted with as little rancour as could be expected, considering the sort of mob we have to deal with.'

'Your mob,' said Hallett laughing. 'Mine is decorous, compared with your wild Irishmen –'

'My wild Irishmen? They are the best-natured and the best-behaved fellows in the world,' Blake insisted good-humouredly. 'They can sing, too, I can tell you.'

'Yes – they can sing,' Hallett admitted, 'and they can cheer in their queer shrill sort of way – I can't always make out whether they are delighted or disappointed. It sometimes sounds to me like a death-wail, and then, by Jove! I am told it is a shout of triumph.'

'You'll hear it to-morrow,' Blake said carelessly, 'and then you will know that it isn't a death-wail – and don't you forget it.'

'I am very curious about it – I want to hear it,' Elsie said in an abstracted sort of way, as if she were talking to herself.

'I don't,' Hallett declared with a laugh. 'Well, Blake, we shall know it all to-morrow. "God show the right," as the old proclamations of battle used to say.'

'"God show the right,"' repeated Blake abstractedly. 'That's what they say in Ireland. Come what will, Hallett,' said Blake, 'you are a good fellow, and a gallant opponent.' Then the little group dispersed.

Sounds echoed all through the wooden building, and 'Ruffey's' was by no means a peaceful haven on this election eve. From the bar down below there came noise of revelry, hoarse callings for drink, snatches of song, rough laughter, and occasionally an oath. In the balcony, on which Lady Horace's sitting-room opened, all this could be distinctly heard. It was an odd place for a young lady to choose, but for the greater part of the evening Elsie Valliant sat there and listened to the din and watched the street below. There was a moon getting near its full, and the long straggling roadway, with its wooden houses – its odd-looking groups of passers-by: rough bushmen, diggers, China-men, blacks – presented a rather amusing spectacle. But Elsie did not seem so deeply interested in the street scene as in a low monotonous hubbub, with one voice distinguishable through the babel, which came to her from the other side of the building, and which she guessed to be that of Blake holding a meeting. There were interruptions every now and then. Sometimes his voice rose so clearly that she could almost make out the words. Sometimes another voice interposed; sometimes there were hoots from below; sometimes cheers; but through it all the one voice declaimed with a force and passion that Elsie felt to be real oratory. She would have given the world to hear what he was saying. She did, indeed, crane her head over the balcony, but after a minute drew it back, afraid lest in the moonlight someone should see and recognise her. By-and-by it ended. The street became quieter, but the noise in the hotel increased. Hallett came up and joined her in the balcony.

'Have you been listening to Mr. Blake?' she asked.

'No,' he replied; 'I have been orating on my own account. Why do you stay out here? It isn't fit for you, with all that noise going on in the bar.'

'I will go to bed,' she said listlessly. 'I am tired.'

'Stay a moment. Come round here; it is quieter. I told you I'd show you the ghost of your flower the next time we met. Here it is.'

He opened his pocket-book and showed her the stephanotis spray crushed between its leaves. 'I have worn it,' he said, 'as one of the old knights you are so fond of might have worn his lady's token when he went to battle. It has been with me all through my battle.'

'Give it to me,' she said, in a strained sort of voice. He did so. Before he could guess her intention, she had crumpled it into a shapeless lump, and had thrown it into the street.

'Why did you do that?' he exclaimed, deeply hurt.

'Because it's worth nothing. It has not brought you luck. It never will bring you any good luck.'

'Have you made up your mind, then, that I am to fail?' he said in a pained voice.

'Yes, I feel it, I know it. He has victory in his face. That man will succeed wherever he goes, and in whatever he chooses to do.'

'In whatever he chooses to do!' Hallett repeated. 'Don't say that. I cannot bear you to say it.'

'Why? I only say what I feel. I never knew any man who gave me that impression in the same way.'

'Do you know why I cannot bear you to say it? It is because he may choose to influence you.'

'Well!' said Elsie with an odd smile. 'That might not be an unpleasant sensation. Don't be angry,' she added hurriedly, seeing the look of pain that came into his face. 'I didn't mean to vex you. Nothing in the world is more unlikely to happen.'

'As that he should influence you, or that he should choose to do so?'

'Both, or either – as you please. Good-night, Mr. Hallett. We have had a thirty-mile journey to-day, and Ina has gone to bed.'

They went in. He gave her a candle, and bade her good-night.

'Do you know where your room is?' he asked.

'Yes; it is a good way along the passage – horribly far from Ina's. I shall lock my door.'

'Don't be frightened if you hear noises. They are not likely to shut up the hotel very early. I think it was a mistake your coming here just at this time.'

'I don't think so at all. I wouldn't miss it for the world. But I should like to know who has the room next to mine. Where are you?'

'On the ground floor. I am very sorry. I will find out who is next you if you like.' He went out. After a minute or two he came back.

'Mr. Dominic Trant has the room next yours.'

'I don't think I like Mr. Dominic Trant,' said Elsie. 'He has such odd eyes. I think he believes he can mesmerise people. All the time we were standing in the hall downstairs, he was looking at me. Tell me – is he going to Tunimbah?'

'I suppose so. Edith says it will be the greatest mistake to get up a coolness on account of the election. She has asked Mr. Blake to come too.'

'I suppose she is right.'

'Yes; Edith has a good deal of tact in these matters, but it would be odd if he should come as the member for Luya.'

'Very odd,' said Elsie. She took her candle and left him. He went down the stairs, and she to her room.

It was, as she had said, a long way down the passage. It was in a wing that had been added to the main building, and there was a bend in the corridor that made it seem more isolated still. She was a little dismayed when she saw that Mr. Dominic Trant was fumbling in his keyhole.

'They've locked my door,' he said. 'It's a queer sort of shop, isn't it, Miss Valliant?'

'Yes,' said Elsie shortly. 'Good-night.'

'You are next me. These wooden partitions are confoundedly thin. Don't be frightened if you hear me coming in and going out. Blake and I are going to amuse ourselves.'

'I hope you will do so. Would you let me pass, please?'

Trant drew back. 'I intend to make you like me, Miss Valliant. You don't now, but I intend that you shall. Do you know that I am coming to Tunimbah?'

'Yes, I know that. Please bring some songs with you.'

'Blake is coming, too. He will be the member for Luya, and Mr. Hallett's nose will be out of joint. Look here, Miss Valliant, I've got something to say to you.'

'I don't think I want to hear it now, Mr. Trant.'

'I shall not be a minute telling you. I know you are a flirt. Everyone says so. You'll be wanting to flirt with Blake. Take my advice, and don't. He is a nasty customer, is Blake. There is nothing he enjoys so much as compromising a woman. He has got no more heart than this key.'

'I don't see what that matters to me, Mr. Trant – or to you.'

'It does matter to me. I know Blake's ways. I don't want to see you let in. I think a great deal of you – a great deal more than you know.'

'I am very much obliged to you.' She turned the handle of her door, and went into her room, leaving him outside. Then she tried the door after her, but to her dismay she discovered that there was no key, and that the bolt was frail and unreliable. She tried to reason herself out of her terror of Trant.

'He has probably been drinking,' she said to herself, 'though he looked cool enough.'

She sat down without undressing. It seemed to her that there were all kinds of disquieting sounds about. The roar of the machinery, which she could not at first understand, was uncanny, and so were the occasional detonations from the blasting works. By-and-by the noise in the bar subsided a little. The hotel itself was fairly quiet. It was now about midnight. She heard steps along the corridor, and they set her trembling again. The steps paused at Trant's door. Someone went in.

Yes, the partitions were horribly thin. She could hear the voice distinctly. It was the voice of Blake, and yet she was conscious that he was speaking almost in a whisper.

'Are you ready?'

Trant murmured something. She could not distinguish the words.

Blake went on, still in the same low clear voice, and with an accent of contempt. 'Naturally you don't understand. One must follow one's star.'

Again a murmur from Trant, of which she only distinguished the words 'eight thousand.'

A laugh – an odd mocking laugh. 'The member for Luya. Droll! There's a certain humour in the situation.' And then a sentence in French. She could not make it out. A sound as of someone moving about and opening and shutting things followed. Presently one went out – both she imagined at first, for there was a complete silence. Elsie could bear it no longer. She must go and find Ina, and ask her to stay with her. She did not know what had frightened her. And why should she be frightened either of Trant or of Blake? But she was frightened for all that. Her nerves were like stretched wires. To remain there till morning seemed an impossibility. She took up her candle and opened her door. The passage was all dark. She would go to

Lady Horace's room. A window in the passage was open, and a gust blew out the candle. She gave a faint cry. At that moment the door of Trant's room opened and a man came out – a man in riding dress, with a black sort of poncho covering his coat. He drew back as he saw her and heard her exclamation. He had no candle, but at that moment the moon came out from under a cloud and shone through the uncurtained window. She saw that it was Blake.

He came towards her. 'Miss Valliant, I'm afraid I frightened you. I did not know that you were so near.'

'I am in the next room. I heard you.'

'You heard me!' His eyes were full upon her. How bright they looked. They had an odd intent expression. There was something wild in their gaze. 'Then you must have preternaturally keen ears, for I spoke in a whisper.'

'I heard you say that one must follow one's star. What is your star? Where is it taking you?'

He continued looking at her in that strange rapt manner.

'Where it has always led me – to danger and to misfortune.'

'To misfortune!' she repeated. 'Oh no, no. Why do you say that?'

'Because fate has been against me, and because I'm in a reckless mood to-night. Does the full moon affect you, Miss Valliant? Does it make you feel that you could do any sort of dare-devil thing? I've got the music of Berlioz' "Faust" in my head. Do you know it?'

'No. How should I know it?'

'True. They haven't performed it in Australia, I fancy. Well, if you ever hear it, note the description of Faust's wild ride with Mephistopheles. I think Mephistopheles is always abroad when the moon is at the full. That's how I feel.'

'You are not going to ride to-night?'

'Yes. I am going for a gallop. That's my way of working off my excitement.'

'You don't seem as if you were excited. You are quite pale and cold and resolute. It is only your eyes that have a wild look.'

'They look wild, do they? They ought not to look wild when they are fixed on you.' They were fixed on her now searchingly. 'Go back to bed, Miss Valliant. Nothing will disturb you. You may sleep as soundly and peacefully as a child.'

'I am frightened. I was going to find my sister's room,' she said falteringly. 'I don't like being here alone – so far from everyone.'

'You should not be frightened. No one will hurt you. What frightens you?' he said.

'I don't know. It's very stupid, I suppose. Things seem odd and eerie – it's so odd my standing here talking to you at this hour.'

'There's nothing so odd in that. Go back to bed. Don't wake up your sister. I'm sorry that I told you about my wild mood. The truth is that I come of a hot-headed race. I love adventure, violent exercise, all sorts of things that stir one's blood, and make life worth living. I love solitude, and for weeks I have been living in a crowd and putting a curb on myself –'

'But there is Mr. Trant. You will not be alone.'

'Oh, Trant understands me, and lets me have my fling. To-morrow I shall be as meek as a lamb, and you won't recognise the spurred and booted desperado of to-night.' He laughed as he spoke, and made a movement with his arms which caused his cloak to fall back. In the moonlight Elsie saw the gleam of something at his waist, and realised that it was the shining handle of a pistol.

'You look like a desperado. Why do you carry that pistol?'

'Oh, that – I had forgotten. Moonlight may be about, you know. It is as well to be armed when one scours the country at full moon.'

A clock struck twelve. He held out his hand. 'Do as I tell you. Sleep well, and look upon this midnight meeting as a dream.'

His touch gave her a curious sensation. 'Your hand is quite cold,' she said. 'What is the matter?'

'Nothing is the matter.'

'It is as cold as death,' she repeated.

'Death – what do you know of death? Go to bed; go back and sleep. Dream happy dreams. Good-night.'

He opened her door for her, and waited till she had gone through and had closed it behind her. She heard his steps going softly down the corridor. Then she shot the bolt and quietly undressed. It was very strange, but she had no thought of disobeying him, no thought now of going to Lady Horace. She felt soothed and satisfied, and yet through all there was a certain thrill of excitement. His eyes with their bright intent look seemed to be gazing at her in the darkness. There was something compelling in the look. It haunted her and gave her a strange dreamy feeling. She did not sleep for a long time. She pictured him scouring the plains on his black horse Osman, and working off the fever of his blood, the hilt of his pistol gleaming as his cloak flew back in the wind. In her fancy he seemed like some mediaeval knight. What a contrast to the dull prosaic bushmen round her, with their eternal talk about cattle and horses, their petty interests and low aims. This man spoke of his star. How strange that he should have used

CHAPTER VIII

The Member for Luya

It was early morning before Elsie fell asleep. She slept late. Ina knocked at her door, and found it bolted and went away again. Later, when Elsie was dressed and went into the sitting-room, she found the whole party assembled there. Lord Horace was talking excitedly. 'Eight thousand pounds' worth of gold. By Jove! it's a haul!' he was saying.

Eight thousand pounds! The words brought a thrill to Elsie. 'What are you talking about?' she exclaimed. 'What does it mean?'

'It means the most daring robbery that ever was committed. The gold escort robbed eight miles from Goondi at three o'clock this morning – six armed policemen to five bushrangers,' said Hallett.

'And the devil, as they say, in the shape of a black horse,' put in Lord Horace. 'I should like to have the chance of a shot at Abatos. What fools they were not to aim at the horse. 'Pon my soul, it's the most extraordinary thing. Etheridge, the sergeant, swears the men are all in armour.'

'Copying the Kellys,' said Lady Horace.

'Copying the mediaeval duffers rather. It's a better sort of armour than the Kellys. That must be chain armour of the best manufacture, or they couldn't ride the distances in the time and do the things they do – unless Moonlight has the power of disappearing into the bowels of the earth whenever he sees fit. It beats me, and I can't help having a sneaking regard for such a plucky fellow. I hope Macpherson won't nab him.' Lord Horace went on walking fiercely up and down the inn parlour.

Elsie sat silent. She, too, was intensely excited.

'The worst of it is that no one cares two straws about the polling to-day,' said Hallett. 'All Goondi is mad over the robbery. I am afraid it will affect the votes.'

'No, it won't,' said Lord Horace. 'I shall drag the voters in – your voters, at least.'

Elsie ate her breakfast listlessly. Hallett looked at her with anxious eyes.

'You look as if you hadn't slept. And you don't seem so tremendously interested in Moonlight as I thought you would be.'

'Yes,' she answered, 'I am tremendously interested. Was anybody hurt?'

'Moonlight has never yet shed blood,' said Hallett; 'and as for the bushrangers, Etheridge says that the bullets glanced by them. He let the police fire. They weren't prepared, and before they had time to reload, Moonlight and his men had closed in on them, and the whole thing was up. They were found gagged and tied to gum trees by a selector who started early this morning to vote. The gold had gone, and there wasn't a trace of the bushrangers to be seen.'

Outside the hotel the mob had become uproarious.

'It's Blake holding forth. You'll hear "The Wearing of the Green" presently. Come along, Horace. Let us see what they are up to,' said Hallett. He was very pale. Elsie went out with Ina into the balcony. It was the same voice that she had listened to the evening before.

'Yes – it's Blake haranguing his wild Irishmen,' Hallett said.

Elsie could hear the voice, but she could not see the man. She could tell by the murmurs of the crowd that it was a large crowd and deeply interested. The sensation was curious and intense. The hush was something almost painful during each sentence of the speaker, and then the wild shriek of applause seemed as if it broke irrepressible out of the very heart of the listeners.

'Blake won't let his fellows forget all about the election, even in the excitement about Moonlight and the robbery,' Hallett quietly observed. 'He's a better tactician than we are.' This was the very thought that had been passing through Elsie's somewhat distracted mind.

She could hardly follow the course of the appeal that Blake was making to his admirers. It was something about the future of Ireland, and the future, too, of Australia. But she did not want to follow the political appeal. She was content to hear the voice – melodious, strong, thrilling, sweet – with sudden spontaneous notes of humour in it, which brought out roars of laughter from the delighted listeners.

Hallett's turn came to address his electors, and Elsie was near, and could follow his words, but they thrilled her to no enthusiasm. She could not understand why Ina was white and cold with anxiety. What did it matter? What did anything matter? It was the other voice that rang in Elsie's ears. But how could she, in loyalty, hope that Blake might be victorious? Lady Horace made no attempt to do her shopping that day, and the colonial oven was not bought – on this occasion at any rate. The excitement in Goondi was far too intense for it to be safe for ladies to venture into the business street; the mob too dense and turbulent. Interest was divided between the result of the poll and the bushranging outrage. There was almost a suspension of all other business. Police patrolled the street. The township authorities were waiting for Government orders. Court-house and telegraph station were surrounded by a swaying crowd waiting the arrival of 'progress telegrams.' Captain Macpherson, the superintendent of police, had started out with all the available force. Native trackers were got together, and further bands were being summoned from the neighbouring township. At evening, however, nothing had been heard of Moonlight. He might, as Lord Horace had said, have disappeared into the bowels of the earth, for all the trace he had left.

Mr. Blake and his supporters were very much in evidence that day. Elsie saw him in the distance – cool, calm, apparently self-confident. She saw him riding down the street of the township on a horse which was not Osman, but which was, nevertheless, a very splendid animal – a mettlesome chestnut, which apparently he had ridden all through the election, for she heard Hallett and Lord Horace discussing it and extolling the Baròlin breed. She looked at the horse to see if it showed any traces of a wild ride, but it was as fresh, and spirited, and sleek as though it had not left the stable for days. Elsie wondered whether he had really taken that gallop, and if so whether it had, as he had said, worked off the excitement. He certainly seemed now absolutely collected, but perhaps his composure was a sign of excitement at white heat. She observed that during the early part of the day Trant was not with his partner, and that when he did show himself he seemed by far the most wearied and discomposed of the two.

Elsie watched the fortunes of the day from her balcony. She saw Hallett go into the Court-house up the street, and then Blake came up to the Court-house door and got off his horse and went in too, accompanied by a few friends, and she assumed that the counting of the votes was going on. She went in and out uneasily from and back to the balcony. Some hours after she saw a rush made towards the Court-house by an excited crowd. Presently she heard a wild outcry

– at first she hardly knew whether of grief or joy – and then broke out the song of 'God save Ireland,' mingled with hurrahs for Blake, and a crowd rushed up waving banners and sticks, some with green ribbons tied to them, and she knew that the victory was won. The crowd halted under the hotel outside, and Elsie assumed that Blake was there, and that he would have to make another speech. So he did. His voice rang out with all the proud vigour of victory; and she heard him tell of the regeneration of Ireland, and the magnificent destiny of Australia.

Lord Horace had worked manfully. It certainly was not his fault that Frank Hallett was not elected. But when the poll was declared, just before the crowd returned to the hotel, it was known that Blake had come in the victor by a majority of twenty votes.

Again Elsie and Blake met in the corridor. She was coming from her room; he was going towards his. She went straight to him, and held out her hand.

'I congratulate you,' she said simply.

'Thank you,' he answered, and held her hand for several moments before she withdrew it.

'But,' she added, 'I am very sorry for Mr. Hallett.'

'He has behaved splendidly,' said Blake. 'He is a fine fellow. We shall not bear each other any animosity. He fights fair, and when the fight is over he shakes hands. We have shaken hands, and have agreed to bury personal differences. Political differences, I am afraid, we shall never bury.'

'Tell me,' she said abruptly. 'What did you do last night?'

'It does not matter, Miss Valliant, since I did not disturb you again. I took care not to do that.'

'No, you did not disturb me,' she answered. 'But I did not go to sleep till nearly daybreak, and Mr. Trant must have come in after that.'

'Yes, he came in after that.'

'Your horse did not look as though you had ridden very far last night.'

'I accomplished my purpose,' he said; 'I worked off my excitement.'

'And you did not meet Moonlight?'

He laughed. 'So Moonlight was abroad last night.'

'Strange, wasn't it?'

'Captain Macpherson has not caught him yet?'

'Have you heard?' she asked.

'He has not caught him yet. I don't think he is likely to catch him.'

'Now that you are member for Luya, Mr. Blake,' Elsie went on, 'you will have to do something to preserve the peace of the district.'

'What should you like me to do?' he said. 'Ask a question in the House, and twit the Government with the fact that all the police of the district are held at bay by an undiscoverable outlaw?'

'No; I don't want you to deprive us of our chief excitement; not that it will matter much to me, for I am soon going back to Leichardt's Town, and frankly, I am full of sympathy for Moonlight. Do you know that one of the troopers says that he speaks a strange language.'

Blake laughed. 'I understand that he was heard to give an order to fire in French, and Captain Macpherson has started the theory that he is an escaped convict from New Caledonia.'

Lady Horace came out of her room just then, and advanced to her sister and Blake. Her eyes had a frightened look. 'Elsie,' she said, 'I should like to know Mr. Blake.' She held out her hand with her charming smile. 'I cannot say that I am glad you have got in, but I am glad, at any rate, that the fight is over.'

'And the hatchet is buried, Lady Horace,' said Blake, acknowledging her salutation with a very courtly bow. 'I suppose you know that the rival candidates and their supporters dine together to-night, and that we shall all make pretty speeches about each other and be good friends henceforth.'

They said a few more words, and then Blake left them. The two sisters went back to the sitting-room. 'Elsie,' Ina said on the way thither, 'don't begin to flirt with that man.'

'Why not, dear?' asked Elsie.

'Because he will make you do what he likes,' said Ina; 'I see it in his eyes.' The light of a gas jet fell on her agitated face and blurred lashes.

'Ina, you have been crying,' exclaimed Elsie. 'What is the matter? Has Horace been doing anything to vex you?'

'No – I –' Ina stammered. 'I am very happy, Elsie, I'm only sorry for Mr. Hallett; and you don't care. You are wishing joy to the man who has supplanted him. You have nothing kind to say to Frank, who loves you. He is in there waiting, and hoping to see you. Oh, go to him, Elsie, and say that you are sorry.'

Ina pushed Elsie in and ran back to her room.

Frank Hallett was there alone. He was standing by the mantelpiece, and looked grim and sad. It struck her for the first time almost that he, too, looked a man of power. He lifted his head as she entered and smiled.

'You see you were right. I am beaten – but only for the Luya. I shall have another chance directly.'

'What do you mean? Oh, Frank, I am sorry.'

'Thank you, Elsie.' He took her hand in his and held it. 'Thank you, dear. That makes up for other things. It is an odd chance, isn't it, that on the very day of my being beaten for the Luya, the Wallaroo vacancy should be declared?'

'Wallaroo! I hadn't heard.'

'Lady Horace knew – it is all over the place. Fletcher has resigned.'

'Yes, yes, I remember, but I did not connect the two things,' Elsie stammered. 'There has been so much to think of – Moonlight and this. You will get in there.'

'And I have another electioneering campaign before me. It will not be a long one, however, and I don't start till after the Tunimbah festivities.'

'You see,' he added with a rather bitter little laugh, 'it is as we thought. The trophies of victory have been turned into the symbols of defeat. We shall be celebrating the triumph of my opponent. Blake's first appearance among us will be as the member for Luya.'

'Oh! Frank –'

'Are you sorry, Elsie? Be truthful.'

'Sorry – for your defeat? Of course I am sorry.'

'But for his victory. Are you sorry for that?'

'I don't think you have any right to question me in this way,' she said proudly.

'No, no, I have no right. But I watched your face this morning, and I watched it last evening, when you were listening to him speaking. I saw that you were straining to catch the words. And somehow, Elsie, you don't seem like yourself to-day. You look as though your thoughts were far from Goondi, and from the election, and from everything that concerns us here.'

'No, Frank, but I am tired. I – I –' There was almost a sob in her voice. 'You are quite right. I am not myself. I don't know what is the matter with me. I did not sleep very well last night.'

'You did not sleep! Did anyone – were you frightened at the noises in the hotel?'

'No.' She hesitated.

'But there were noises,' he said. 'I heard the trampling of horse's feet in the yard. I wondered who could have come so late.'

'It was nothing,' she said hurriedly. 'No, I was not disturbed. Don't hink anything more about my looks, Frank, or about things. It doesn't matter, after all, since you are sure to be member for Wallaroo.'

At that moment Lord Horace's voice sounded in the passage. He ushered in the victorious Blake, pausing as he did so to give some directions to the waiter. 'Heidsieck – spurious, of course, Blake, but not half bad. Hallett, old boy, swallow down animosities; drown 'em in the flowing bowl, and Elsie and Ina must join in. The fight was a fair one, and we're beaten. There's Wallaroo ahead, a dead certainty if ever there was one.'

Hallett came forward, and held out his hand to his rival. 'You are right, Horace, and I congratulate you, Mr. Blake.'

Elsie admired him at the moment very much, but she admired Blake still more, as, with winning courtesy, he responded to Hallett's congratulations.

'If there had been twenty fewer Irishmen in Goondi, you, not I, would have been member for Luya,' he said. 'But, as Lord Horace says, there's Wallaroo ahead, and we shall fight in the Legislative Assembly yet, Mr. Hallett, in as friendly a fashion, I hope, as we have fought here.'

CHAPTER IX

•

A Bush House Party

Tunimbah was considered one of the most beautiful stations on th
Luya. It was almost in the shadow of Mount Luya and of the twi
peaks of the Burrum. Baròlin Gorge – a misty cleft – stretche
up between the two into the dividing range, and seemed to Elsie'
imagination the passage to a realm of mystery.

Mrs. Jem Hallett had the reputation of being a most accomplishe
hostess. She was always called Mrs. Jem, because the elder Mrs
Hallett, mother of the two brothers, was still alive, and occupied
pretty cottage about a stone's throw from the big house. But the ol
lady was an invalid, and took no part in the domestic management o
the station, leaving everything to her clever daughter-in-law. Mrs. Jer
was very handsome – a little self-conscious, but that was hardl
surprising. She had big black eyes, and, unlike most Australians,
rich colour. She was tall also, and elegant, and always dressed wit
great care and taste.

Nothing more unlike the Humpey could be imagined. Tunimba
head-station was an imposing stone house with deep verandahs trel
lised with creepers, a beautifully kept garden, a gravelled courtyarc
and beds planted with flowering shrubs and pomegranate trees an
camellias. It had out-buildings after the newest and most improve
pattern, stables, a retinue of smartly got up black-boys and grooms
trim fences and white gates, and last, but greatest of all, a Chines
cook. The head-station stood on a small hill, and the garden slope
down to a lagoon, as is the case in many Australian homestead:
Beyond the lagoon was the racecourse, and on this particular occasio
– the tenth anniversary of Mr. and Mrs. Jem's wedding-day – ther
were to be given some bush races – a sort of friendly competitio
among the horse-owners of the district – which was rather noted fo

its races – and the horses they intended to run at the forthcoming Leichardt's Town Races.

Mrs. Jem received her principal guests on the verandah facing the courtyard, and herself conducted them to the drawing-room. It was her great aim to be considered English, and she always made a great deal of Lord Horace, who was at his best on these occasions, and imported something of the British country-house element into these bush gatherings. She had been accustomed to rather patronise the Valliant girls in the days before Ina's marriage, and it had been at her house that Lord Horace first met Ina. She, therefore, took credit to herself for the match.

'I am so glad you came, dear. Thank you both, love, for your good wishes. Wasn't it a happy idea putting the races on to our wedding-day? Of course we couldn't possibly have had them at the election time. Oh, such a pity, isn't it, about Frank? We had made so sure. But he is quite certain to get in for Wallaroo, and we must just make the best of Mr. Blake, who is quite charming. Such a pity he is on the wrong side, but Jem says, Elsie, that you must convert him.'

Mrs. Jem had quite a number of people already assembled when the Gages and Miss Valliant arrived. Jem Hallett was a handsome, rather heavy squatter, excessively good-natured, but not as clever and enterprising as his brother. He was far too lazy to go into politics, and contented himself with having the best breed of cattle on the Luya.

Mrs. Jem interrupted her husband's heavy jokes, and sent him off to look after the gentlemen and bring them in to tea. Her drawing-room looked extremely English, with its daintily laid tea-table, and pretty silver things, and with its art muslin draperies and upholstered lounges and arm-chairs. Several ladies were sitting there, and others were playing about in the verandah and on the tennis-lawn. Those in the drawing-room were for the most part matrons, and among them were one or two Leichardt's Town magnates – Lady Garfit, the wife of the Minister for Lands, and her daughter; there was pretty Mrs. Allanby, who gave parties in Leichardt's Town, and whose husband was a stock and station agent; two or three of the neighbouring squatteresses, several young ladies, rivals of Elsie as popular belles, who came in from the verandah when the Gage party appeared. Lady Horace's marriage had produced a certain access of cordiality in the manner of the Leichardt's Town dames, especially now that it was known that Lord and Lady Waveryng were coming out, and would be guests at Government House during the time of the Prince's visit. Formerly, Mrs. Valliant and her pretty daughters had only been admitted on sufferance into the more select circle of Leichardt's Town society, and this gave Elsie Valliant's manner a dash of defiance as she acknowledged their greetings. The girl was full of hatred and malice – at least so she told Ina – and it flashed through her mind that there might be some great person in the Prince's suite who would fall in love with her and marry her, and that she might revenge herself on these second-rate people for all their slights. She was an undeveloped creature, this poor Elsie. There was nothing very great in her, or very noble. She was full of meannesses and littlenesses and jealousies, for which she despised herself in her more exalted moments, but there had never come anything into her life to call forth higher sentiments. She sometimes fancied that if such thing did come, she, too, could prove herself heroic. Ina was better than she. No one acknowledged that more readily than Elsie. But then Ina had not been the idol of a foolish mother, and Ina had never been a beauty.

Elsie had never looked more lovely than she did that evening when she went into the drawing-room dressed for dinner. She and Ina had spent some time in the concoction of the costume, and then Elsie had had a fit of penitence, and had insisted on making something lovely for Ina, too. It struck Elsie that Ina seemed shy and agitated, and she wondered if Lord Horace had been cross. Now that the blush of the honeymoon was over, Lord Horace had fits of downright crossness. And Lord Horace was certainly selfish and exacting. He made his wife do things for him that he would not have required from a Lady Clara Vere-de-Vere. This Elsie resented. What right had he to expect that her sister would act as his valet? Ina did everything that he asked her, and was patient and sweet as far-famed Grizel. But she always said that she was happy.

Frank Hallett took Elsie in to dinner. Lord Horace naturally conducted Mrs. Jem, and Mr. Blake was given to Lady Horace. Mrs. Jem had waived the rules of strict etiquette so far as to give Lady Garfit the precedence over sometime Ina Valliant. Blake and Ina were seated opposite Elsie and Frank. Somehow, whenever she glanced across the table, Elsie seemed to meet Blake's eyes. He had such odd eyes – so deep and piercing. She could never forget their wild gleam on that strange night at Goondi. Blake had a stephanotis flower in his buttonhole. So had Frank Hallett. She remembered having said to Blake one day at Goondi – the day after the declaration of the poll, when they had walked down the street of the township while waiting for the coach, and to hear the latest news of Moonlight, or rather to hear the news of Moonlight's vain pursuers – that the stephanotis was her favourite flower. Blake's voice enchained her attention, and made her listen carelessly to what Frank Hallett was saying. She wondered what Blake was talking about to Ina. She felt almost certain from the way they both looked at her that she herself was the subject of conversation.

She was the subject also of Mr. Dominic Trant's regard. He was on her other side, and devoted much more consideration to her than to his legitimate partner. He would insist upon discoursing about Blake in what Elsie felt to be rather a crude fashion.

'You remember what I said to you the other night, Miss Valliant?'

'I am not sure that I do, Mr. Trant.'

'I told you that my partner was rather a dangerous customer. You know there's such a thing as the biter getting bit. Any woman who plays with Blake will find that she is playing with fire.'

'I don't understand you, Mr. Trant; or how what you say can in any way apply to me.'

'They say you are a flirt. So is Blake.'

'Well?'

'He never cared for a woman in his life, Miss Valliant; but it has always been with him as it is with the sportsman after game. The more difficult it is to get, the more fellows there are after it, the more determined he is that it should fall to his gun. Blake would follow a woman he thought worth his trouble through thick and thin till he had got her down at his feet.'

'And then?'

'Why, then, Miss Valliant, he'd tell her that he had no heart to give, and he would leave her to further enjoy the excitement of going after other game. That is all Blake cares for – the excitement of doing what other people have failed to do.'

'And so,' said Elsie, 'Mr. Blake goes about with women's scalps at his belt, and you fancy that he might do me the honour of wishing to adorn himself with mine. It is very kind of you to warn me. Why are you so interested in my welfare?'

'Because I want you for myself,' said Trant brutally.

'That is very kind of you, too,' said Elsie. 'I like your way of playing a game, Mr. Trant. It is honest, at any rate.' She turned to Frank Hallett, and pointedly avoided Trant. He came up to her, however, as soon as dinner was over.

'I have come to beg your pardon. I'm a rough brute. I throw myself on your mercy.'

'Please don't offend again, then,' said Elsie.

'I'll go on my knees to you if you like. I'll promise anything. The
only thing I'm good for is to sing. Mrs Jem Hallett has asked me to
sing. You'll forgive me when you hear me sing. I am going to sing
something to *you*.'

The man was right. His merit lay in his voice. It was impossible
not to be moved by his singing. They were all sitting out in the
verandah or strolling about the starlit garden, which was full of the
scent of stephanotis, verbena, and Cape jasmine. Mrs. Jem had started
music in the drawing-room, while the dining-room, which was a great
room with a polished floor, was being got ready for dancing. Elsie
had already a little crowd of men round her. Several were Leichardt's
Town admirers. The old fever for admiration was upon her. From
one she accepted a flower. To another she gave one. She had smiles
for all. Then Trant began to sing. A vague emotion seized her, a
sudden irresistible longing for the deeper drama of life. There was
so much beyond all this flirting and dancing and dressing, so much
of which she was totally ignorant. Even Trant with the coarse passion
in his voice represented a world of feeling that she had never entered.
She became silent, and would not answer the young men's banal
remarks.

'Hush – go away, I want to listen,' she said, and sat there, her
profile outlined against dark night, the light from the drawing-room
upon her serious face and shining eyes and slender girlish form; she
sat with her hands folded, quite still. Someone came and leaned
against the verandah post by her side. She knew without looking at
him that it was Blake. She knew, too, that he was watching her, and
the feeling gave her an odd thrill and presently drew her eyes to his.
Trant's songs ceased; and his accompanist went on playing desultory
chords.

Mr. Blake said suddenly, 'Do you do anything – I mean in the way
of music?'

'No,' answered Elsie. 'I do nothing – nothing at least that gives
people pleasure.'

'I should say that you did a great deal which gave people pleasure.
You exist – that is something.'

'I wish you wouldn't pay me compliments in that unmeaning way.
I hate it. It is like everybody else.'

'You would like me then to be unlike everybody else. Thank you.
I like you to say that.'

'Why?'

'Because it shows that you think about me.'

'I don't see that that matters.'

'Oh yes, it does – to me. I have been watching you, Miss Valliant, wondering –'

'Wondering what?'

'Wondering what lies underneath the butterfly existence you seem to lead.'

'Ah! you think I am a butterfly.'

'I think that you know how to *papillonner la vie* as one says, but that is a different thing from being a butterfly.'

'I don't understand much French, but I understand enough to know what that means.'

'It is a great art to *papillonner la vie*.'

'Do you practise it?' she asked.

'I try to. But I have moods in which life seems deadly serious.'

'Were you in one of those moods that night?'

'Ah! No, I was in a reckless mood that night. I have quite got over it now.'

'And you are in the butterfly phase,' she said a little bitterly.

'Why do you say that in such a contemptuous way?'

'I was thinking of something Mr. Trant told me about you.'

'What was that?'

'I don't think I ought to tell you.'

'I can guess what it was. Trant reproaches me with liking ladies' society too much. I am sure he told you that I was a flirt.'

'Yes, he said something of that kind, only he put it more strongly.'

'How? You needn't mind telling me what Trant said about me. I am sure that he has often said the same things to my face.'

'So he told me.'

'He warned you against me, didn't he?'

'Yes –'

'And he described me as a conceited cad who tried to be a lady-killer?'

'No, he didn't say that. He described you as a person who liked to make women fall in love with him, and who went about with hearts as trophies in the way that an Indian carries scalps.'

'Oh! That was putting it melodramatically. Miss Valliant, perhaps you think me a conceited cad when I say that the game of love – or flirtation – has given me some amusement in my life, but that when I found it becoming serious for myself, or for the other person, I have always stopped short, unless –'

'Well, unless?'

'Unless it was a fair contest. Hearts not in it. The best fighter to win, and friends when the fight is over; like our election the other day. Isn't that your idea of a flirtation tournament?'

'Yes – perhaps – I haven't any theory about it.'

'You only practise the game. Well, don't you think that two skilled players might get a good deal of fun out of such a game?'

'I don't know.' Elsie was getting a little uncomfortable, and at the same time was deeply interested.

'Oh yes, you do. Because Trant implied that in this instance it is a case of Greek meeting Greek. Well, Miss Valliant, is it a challenge?'

'If you like to take it so,' she answered recklessly. There was a silence.

'Yes, I do,' he answered seriously. 'I think it is very likely that I shall get beaten; but I accept the challenge. Will you dance this with me?' he asked in a matter-of-fact tone. 'That is a waltz, isn't it?'

She got up. At that moment Frank Hallett came up.

'Miss Valliant, you will give me this?'

Elsie hesitated. Blake said nothing, but his eyes were on her. 'I am engaged to Mr. Blake,' she said at last.

Frank Hallett drew back.

'The one after the next, then? I am going to dance the next with your sister.'

Elsie nodded. 'Yes, the one after the next.'

She took Blake's arm and they went into the dancing-room. He danced extremely well. So did she. Elsie had never felt before during a dance as she felt now. She had at once a sense of intoxication and terror. She had begun to be afraid of Blake, and she had never in her life been afraid of any man. What had he meant by asking her if she had given him a challenge? What did he think of her? What had he heard about her? Well, she would show him that she could take care of herself.

The waltz ended, and they strolled into the garden. The moon was rising, and threw fantastic shadows upon the gravelled walk.

'Mr. Blake,' Elsie said suddenly, 'will you please tell me what you meant when you told me that day by the creek – the day I threw the flower at your horse – that you had been wishing to make my acquaintance for a particular reason? Will you tell me what the reason was?'

'If you wish it,' he said; 'but it is rather a long story. I don't think I can get it into the interval between this and the next dance.'

'I am not engaged for the next dance. We will sit it out – unless you want to dance.'

'No. It seems absurd to say that I would much rather sit it out with you.'

'Why absurd?'

'You forbade me to pay you compliments,' he answered.

They turned towards the lagoon, out of the track of promenaders. There was an avenue of bunyas leading to the boathouse, and the dark pyramidal pine trees looked strangely solemn in the moonlight. Elsie gave a little shiver.

'I hate this walk. It puts me in mind of a churchyard. Come down here. There's a seat close to the house, and I shall be able to hear when the waltz begins.'

She took him into a vine trellis to the right, and they sat down on a bench which was placed in a sort of arbour.

CHAPTER X

Jensen's Ghost

'Well!' she said. 'Why?'

'Why!' he repeated. 'Do you know any people at Teebar?'

'No,' she answered, and blushed at one of her most painful recollections which the name evoked. 'At least not now.'

'No; because the person you once knew, and who lived there, is dead. He was a man called Jensen. I knew him very well. He had a station close by the township.'

'Yes,' she said, in a stifled way.

'He took to drinking, as you know, and killed himself.'

'I did not know. Killed himself!'

'As surely as any man who ever blew his brains out. He did not drink, did he, when you knew him?'

'No. Mr. Blake, I know what you mean, and it is cruel, it is wicked to blame me for that.' She half rose in her agitation. 'It wasn't my fault that he —'

'That he loved you. No, that was certainly not your fault. There must be a great many men who love you. But I was sorry for poor Jensen. He looked a stupid fellow when I knew him, but he was clever enough to write very decent verse. And he looked rather a weak creature, but he was strong enough to be faithful to the one woman he ever loved.'

'What did he tell you about me? Don't be afraid of hurting me.'

'He told me all that had ever passed between you – his version of course – but it was so detailed that I think it must have been pretty near the truth. You encouraged him a good deal.'

'Yes – I encouraged him.'

'I think you were engaged to him for two days?'

'I – I said I would marry him – if I could like him well enough.'

'And at the end of two days – you didn't give it a long trial – you told him that you had only engaged yourself for an experiment, to see what it felt like, and you threw him over.'

'Yes, that is true. I couldn't care for him enough.'

There was a silence. At last he said, 'I saw a good deal of Jensen. I did what I could to reclaim him, but he said he had no faith in man nor woman, and no motive for living. From what I could gather, he used to be a healthy-minded man, fond of sport and of work, and not disposed to take a morbid view of life. You will understand that I was naturally anxious to meet the lady who had been able to effect such a change, but besides, all that he told me about you made me feel that you would be interesting.'

Elsie seemed to be strangling emotion. She spoke in a hard voice, cut once or twice with a dry sob, and with her face turned from him.

'I know what you must think of me. You must think that I am fair game for anybody. You must think that I am as bad as a woman can be. I am certainly not going to excuse myself. I only want to say that I was very young, and that I had never felt deeply about anything, and had no idea that anyone else could feel in that way. I want to say, too, that I had been brought up to think that I must marry well –'

'And Jensen was very well off. Yes, I know.'

'It is horrible. It is humiliating. It is utterly undignified. When I think of it my cheeks burn, and I loathe myself. Do you know,' her voice dropped though she spoke with passionate vehemence, 'he is the only man – except my father – who has ever kissed me. I hate him for that.'

Blake uttered an exclamation of mingled surprise and sympathy. He had never dreamed of this odd kind of virginal pride in Elsie. Her curious unconventionality, her impulsive speech, all that he had heard of her had prepared him for a different sort of woman.

Elsie went on still in that hurried vehement way. 'I hated him the day he did that, and I told him so. I suppose he told you that. I felt that I never wanted to see him again – to be taken possession of – that wasn't what I meant. It is quite true that I had had a fancy that it might be amusing to be engaged. I have always had a curiosity about life and about different kinds of experience. I thought that I should have an entirely new set of feelings, and that this was to be the door to them. You can't imagine anything more childish, and stupid, and ignorant. I don't know why I am telling you all this. I hate myself for doing so.'

'Don't do that,' he said in a different manner from his former one. 'I am very glad that you have told me.'

'I have been trying to forget it all. I would never let myself think of it. I heard that he had died, but I did not know how. As I got to know other men, and saw for how little flirtation counted, and how soon they got over disappointments of that kind, I got to think less about it. And then I never felt deeply about anybody, and how could I know –'

'That anybody might come to feel deeply about you? And so you have gone on flirting with men, and liking them, perhaps, until they too have wanted to take possession of you, and then that fierce thing in you has roused up and has made you cruel. You have never yet met your match – quite.'

The 'quite' was an afterthought. He was thinking of Frank Hallett.

'I hope,' he went on, 'that you won't find your match after you are married. That would be the worst misfortune that could happen to you.'

'Why do you say that?' she asked.

'Because all that you have told me makes me certain that you have the capacity for a feeling which when it comes will almost frighten you.'

'Could one be frightened of love?' she said softly. 'I have often wished that I could really love someone.'

'Don't wish it – unless you are quite certain that the man you love is worthy of your love and capable of giving you back all that you give – don't wish it unless you are certain, too, that the man you love can marry you.'

She shrank together a little. 'I think we had better go in,' she said. 'The dance will begin presently.'

He got up and gravely offered her his arm. 'Miss Valliant, you are going back soon to Leichardt's Town. Will you allow me to call upon you and your mother?'

'Yes, certainly,' she answered, and added, 'We live on Emu Point.'

They walked towards the house. Before they reached the verandah, Elsie stopped and faced him. 'I am very sorry for what I said to you this evening,' she said impulsively. 'I hope you will forget it.'

'I am afraid that I can't promise to do that,' he answered.

'Then at least you will not remind me of it.'

'Ah! that of course I can promise. As far as lies in my power I will try not to remind you of it.'

'Thank you. I think that I will sit down here. If you see Mr. Frank Hallett will you tell him where I am?'

He left her. She had not long to wait. Frank Hallett was walking up and down with Lady Horace, and he had seen her come back with Blake. They both came to her.

'Elsie,' Ina said, 'what is the matter?'

'Nothing,' said Elsie. 'Why?'

'You look scared somehow.'

'I think it must be because I have been seeing ghosts,' said Elsie tremulously.

'Ghosts!' repeated Lady Horace.

Elsie did not answer.

'It must have been the effect of the moonlight in the garden,' said Hallett. 'Those pyramids of rhynca-sporum do look rather like white ghosts.'

Elsie burst into a laugh.

'How like you that speech was! You are really a very comforting person. You always find a natural and reasonable explanation for all one's vagaries, for all one's stupid superstitious fancies.'

'I am glad,' he said gravely, 'that you find me a comforting person. But I don't think that is what you like best.'

'What is it that I like best?'

'Something more romantic. I know that I am a very prosaic kind of fellow. But perhaps that wears best in the long run, and most stupid superstitious fancies do admit of a reasonable and natural explanation.'

They began to dance. The waltz with him was not quite like the one with Blake. She was conscious of this, and she was angry with herself for being so. Why should a girl, when two men waltz equally well, feel a subtler intoxication in the contact and joint motion with the one than with the other? They had only taken a few turns when she stopped him.

'I don't want to dance. I'm tired.'

They went out into the verandah again. He was concerned.

'Something is the matter with you.'

'No. Yes – everything is the matter.'

'Tell me, Elsie,' he said.

'Frank, if I ever give you bad pain – if you are misled by your own fancies, and think me better, and truer, and more sincere than I am, and wake up to find that I am a vain, ambitious, mercenary girl, with no real thought for anyone but herself, don't say that I haven't warned you.'

'You have warned me often enough, and I told you that I was quite contented to take the risk. I can't bear you to talk like that, and yet I'm glad too.'

'Tell me why you are glad.'

'Because if you weren't getting to care for me a little, you wouldn't be troubled – at the thought of the suffering you might cause me.'

'I am troubled – horribly troubled. And of course I care a little for you. I care a great deal, but it isn't the sort of caring I mean.'

'The sort of caring you mean is a romantic dream – the glamour that never was on sea or land, but only in the imagination of romance writers. I don't mind entering the lists with your Prince, Elsie dear. I can wait. He won't come along. Princes like that don't ride through the gum trees.'

'Now,' she said seriously, 'it pleases me to hear you talk like that. It makes me feel that you are strong. I wish that you were strong enough to carry me off and put an end to my doubts for ever.'

'Shall I try?'

'No, no. Give me my year. Frank, I do want to care for you. I am grateful to you for loving me. You'll believe that.'

Elsie slept badly that night. They had danced till long past midnight, and she had tried to drown her guilty recollection of poor Jensen. She had danced again with Blake, and they had talked in the verandah afterwards, not of personal topics – with a tact which she appreciated he avoided allusion to their previous conversation – but of travel, of men and women and books, of life on the Luya and of the wider life beyond. And she had danced with Trant, and he had been very personal, and had expressed his admiration with a certain respectful bluntness which had amused her, and had done more than anything else to distract her thoughts from more painful subjects. She told herself that if he was a little rough he meant no harm; and that his roughness was of a more interesting kind than that of the Luya squatters in general. Elsie was not very fond of bushmen. She preferred the Bank clerks and young Civil servants of Leichardt's Town.

She had danced, too, more than once again with Hallett, and she was doing her very best to persuade herself that the regard she felt for Frank Hallett was the nearest approach she should ever get to love. And then she had seen very plainly that Lady Garfit and her daughter were making up to the Halletts, and that Frank was clearly an object of desire in matrimonial circles. It was perfectly evident that Rose Garfit was in love with him. Rose was another type of the

Leichardt's Town belles. She was not soft and slender and complex, like Elsie, but was a great Junoesque creature, with calm blue eyes and quantities of flaxen hair, a downright sort of girl, absolutely goodnatured, a splendid horsewoman, a good tennis-player, always bright and smiling and equable, and in every way a desirable wife for a well-to-do squatter. Elsie did not actually dislike Rose, who did not want to give herself airs, though she had always seemed to hold herself aloof in a calmly superior way from the lesser fry of Leichardt's Town. This was because of her father's position, and because she was always better dressed, and had carriages and riding-horses, which she – poor Elsie – never had unless some obliging admirer gave her a mount. But Elsie hated Lady Garfit with a holy hatred, for Lady Garfit had snubbed her on more than one occasion, and had done all she could to keep Elsie out of the Government House set, promulgating the report that she was fast and bad style, and even that she rouged. Elsie would have done anything to annoy Lady Garfit, and it was very evident that Lady Garfit was extremely annoyed at Frank Hallett's devotion.

There were other ladies, too, before whom Elsie was not displeased to parade her conquests. She could see that Mrs. Allanby was furious because she had sat out with Mr. Blake, and because Frank Hallett had forgotten a dance for which he was engaged to her, while he in his turn was sitting out with Elsie. But Mrs. Allanby revenged herself by flirting with Lord Horace. And then there was Minna Pryde, of Leichardt's Town, who was more on Elsie's social level than Rose Garfit, who never lost an opportunity of, as she put it, 'spiting' Elsie about her 'beaux.' Minna was dark, and pretty and vivacious, and was certainly not good style, and not at all in favour with the more fastidious of the Leichardt's Town matrons. Elsie was also rather pleased to vex Mrs. Jem, who patronised her, and who, she knew, would have preferred Rose Garfit for a sister-in-law. These uncharitable motives had been more or less preponderant all the evening, but in the stillness of her chamber they melted into a rain of tears. She did not dare to cry out aloud, lest she should wake Ina. The two sisters shared a tiny verandah room, Lord Horace having been sent, with almost all the other gentlemen, to the bachelors' quarters, where, judging from the sounds of revelry that floated on the night, he was doubtless enjoying himself.

CHAPTER XI

•

On the Racecourse

The head station at Tunimbah was astir betimes, and long before the big bell clanged for breakfast, preparations on the racecourse had begun, and flags marked the line of running, and waved on the top of an extemporised Grand Stand. Frank Hallett was waiting in the verandah when Lady Horace and Elsie came out. They were in their habits, like most of the other ladies, since nearly everybody was to ride to the course.

'I thought you might like me to show you your places at the breakfast table,' he said. 'Most have gone in. There are a quantity of people here already, and more coming from everywhere.'

Breakfast was not in the dining-room to-day, but in the old wool-shed – a large slab bark building, about a hundred yards beyond the courtyard, which was always utilised on these occasions, and in which they were to dance in the evening. Tunimbah had once been a sheep-station, in the days before the Halletts had bought it, but sheep did not do well on the Luya. On an Australian station an 'old woolshed' is an institution, and the homestead which possesses one is usually the centre for the festivities of the district.

It was a queer picturesque place, with its dark walls, and beamed and raftered ceiling, and it had been decorated with creepers from the scrub, and now looked very gay indeed, filled with a chattering crowd – bushmen in immaculate moleskins and flaring ties, and with a generally brown, healthy, and excited appearance; ladies in habits, some of home manufacture, others the product of Leichardt's Town tailors, so that there were all varieties, from the honest brown and grey wincey to the Park turn-out with high hats and boots. The girls were, many of them, very coquettishly got up, and stephanotis was in favour for a breast-knot.

Outside, a good many men were lounging about discussing the merits of their horses, settling matters with their jockeys, and taking notes of the new competitors. There was a good deal of interest in the Baròlin horses. The breed was getting a name, and Trant, to use a colonialism, was 'blowing' loudly about his chances of taking the Luya Cup, and cutting out Frank Hallett, who had won it the previous year, with his thoroughbred Gipsy Girl.

Mr. Blake came up and shook hands with Lady Horace and her sister.

'I have been waiting for you,' he said to Elsie, as they fell back a little – 'because I want to sit next you, if I may, and also because I want to ask you if you will ride a horse of mine, which is a perfect ladies' hack, on the course to-day. I heard you telling Lord Horace last night that you didn't like the one you rode from the Dell.'

'Thank you,' said Elsie. 'I should like to ride your horse. But Mr. Frank Hallett has offered me one. I am the luckiest young woman in the world. Everybody has offered me horses.'

'Then your only difficulty will be in selecting,' said Blake.

'I like riding new horses,' said Elsie.

'Then,' said Frank Hallett a little stiffly, but feeling that he was magnanimous, and that he could afford to be so, 'you will perhaps be wise to accept Mr. Blake's offer. If it is the horse he rode yesterday you will be much better mounted than on mine.'

He turned again to Lady Horace.

'Mr. Hallett is very generous,' said Blake.

'Is it Osman?' said Elsie, ignoring the remark. 'The horse that nearly knocked you against a tree that day at the Crossing.'

He gave a little start. 'No. I wouldn't put you on that horse.'

'I shouldn't be at all afraid of him. I never saw such a beauty. Perhaps you will be astonished to hear, Mr. Blake, considering I am a town girl, that I don't mind what I sit, short of a regular buck-jumper. I can even manage a little mild pig-jumping.'

He laughed. 'This horse won't even pig-jump. And I am not surprised at hearing of your being able to do anything – that is courageous and interesting.'

'Thank you. But the last clause was such an evident afterthought that I don't know whether to take that speech as a compliment or not. And you know you weren't to pay me compliments. Mr. Blake, can you imagine what is the one passionate desire of my life – at present?'

'Please tell me?'

'To have a gallop on Moonlight's Abatos.'

'It is possible that you may attain even that summit of bliss, if, as you once suggested, Moonlight were to carry you off.'

Elsie laughed. 'Moonlight isn't in the least likely to show himself in the district, while Captain Macpherson and his men are hanging round. Did you know that he was to be here to-day?'

'Who – Moonlight?' asked Mr. Dominic Trant, who had joined them.

'Good-morning, Mr. Trant,' said Elsie, turning. 'No, not Moonlight; but Captain Macpherson. What an odd expression you have got on your face! What are you thinking of?' Trant burst into a laugh.

'I was thinking, Miss Valliant, what a curious dramatic sort of thing it would be if Moonlight and Captain Macpherson were to meet here as fellow-guests. It's not impossible, you know.'

'It strikes me as most improbable,' said Elsie with gravity. She thought Trant's laugh rather familiar, and certainly ill-timed. 'At least I hope so, for Moonlight's sake. I always confess to a strong admiration for Moonlight – and I hope so for Mr. Hallett's sake too. This is not a public racecourse. The people here are his friends.'

Trant laughed again in a sort of *sotto-voce* manner. Blake was evidently thinking of something else. His brows were knit, and his eyes gleamed darkly from beneath them. They went up the wooden slope to the woolshed, and Hallett showed Elsie and Lady Horace their places. He put himself on one side of Elsie. Blake took the seat on the other. He had lingered to say a word or two to Trant.

'Are you going to run Osman for the cup?' Elsie asked.

'I am not sure. He is entered, but I believe Trant has withdrawn him. Tell me who is that opposite – the man with the sprouting beard who looks like a jockey.'

Before Elsie could reply the question was answered by a young Irishman from a station over the border – Mick Mahoney he was named – who called across:

'And is it after the Scriptures that you are taking a pattern, Captain Macpherson, and are ye making a vow not to cut your beard till Moonlight's brought to justice? I'm thinking that at this rate ye'll have it to your waist.'

'Come, I've had enough of chaffing about Moonlight,' answered Captain Macpherson good-humouredly, 'and you might let a chap enjoy his day off once in a way. I've scoured the Luya from top to bottom – not a trace of him have I found.'

'And been in some pretty queer places, I'll be bound,' remarked an elderly squatter. 'It's an awful rough country is the Upper Luya.'

'Captain Macpherson,' put in Elsie Valliant, 'did you go to the Baròlin Fall?'

'As near as we could get, Miss Valliant, and I wish I might catch Moonlight for that blind alley. But he is too cute, and knows the country far too well.'

'It's a *cul-de-sac*, is it?' asked Mr. Blake, bending forward and courteously addressing the police officer. 'I believe you have been at Baròlin Gorge, Captain Macpherson, and know my partner, Dominic Trant?'

'Oh, to be sure. Mr. Blake, is it? Allow me to congratulate you on your victory – saving your presence, Mr. Frank Hallett, but I am not altogether at one with the squatter-archy, as you know. I'm half a Liberal in Australia – was an out-and-out one in England, which comes to the same thing.'

Captain Macpherson laughed in his breezy way. When not in harness he was a rather happy-go-lucky person, though he was grim and daring enough on the trail. 'Your partner, he's down there, isn't he?' and Captain Macpherson nodded cheerily to Trant. 'How d'ye do? Yes, he was most obliging, was Mr. Trant. Showed us all about, and gave my men fresh horses; put us on a wrong scent, too, with the best intentions in the world. That was a most harmless and respectable horse-breaker, Trant, that we followed like grim death across the border.'

'So I heard afterwards,' said Mr. Trant imperturbably. 'But he sounded uncommonly like Moonlight.'

'Tell me about the Baròlin Fall,' said Elsie.

'It is worth seeing, I can tell you, Miss Valliant, but you have to work your way through a bunya scrub to get to it. And there's a funny thing. None of the black trackers will go near the place. You'd have thought a year or two in the Native Police would have cured their superstition, but my theory is that the Australian nigger is only beaten by the West Indian for sheer terror of what he thinks is the supernatural.'

'No one seems to know where the fall comes from,' said Hallett. 'They say that it's the lake on the top of Mount Luya, which was once the crater of an extinct volcano, and has worked underground to the precipice.'

''Tis a big body of water,' said Captain Macpherson. 'You were asking if the place is a *cul-de-sac*. You might have nicked a bit out of the mountain for all the outlet there is. It's a sheer precipice on each side of you, with a waterfall at the end of it.'

'I want to go there,' said Elsie. 'Mr Hallett, remember that you have promised to get up a picnic, and that we are to camp out for a night.'

'You must wait a bit then,' said Captain Macpherson. 'There'd be no use in ladies trying it after the rainy season. We got bogged the other day. I'd put it off till the spring, Miss Valliant.'

'Is it a promise? – in the spring?' asked Elsie, turning with a bewitching smile to Frank. 'Come, I don't often ask you anything.'

'Certainly, it is a promise,' he answered.

'I shall keep you to it. And you, Mr. Blake, you are to be one of the party.'

'I was going to suggest that you should make the expedition from our place,' said Blake. 'It is quite ten miles nearer, and if we are rough, Miss Valliant, we are at least picturesque.'

'When is it spring?' said Elsie, with pretty imperiousness, turning to Hallett. 'Please soon make it spring.'

'I am afraid it can't be managed before the end of August,' said Hallett, 'and even then it would be cold for camping out.'

'The end of August then,' said Elsie. 'That is settled. I look to you to square Mrs. Jem. The end of August!' she repeated. 'Who knows what may have happened before then?'

Mrs. Jem had got up from the table. The men were anxious to be at the course. Outside the woolshed blackboys in clean shirts and with new scarlet handkerchiefs round their waists were leading horses in side-saddles up and down. The gins and piccaninnies had come from the blacks' camp to see the start. They made impish noises and screamed out admiring remarks as the mounting went on.

'My word, Budgery that fellow!' was the exclamation that followed Elsie.

'I say, Elsie,' cried a toothless blear-eyed creature, plentifully tattooed, with a yellow bandana binding her woolly locks and an old pink tea-gown of Mrs. Jem's slung across her shoulder, 'what for you got him new Benjamin? Mine think it Frank cobbon coola* along you.'

'Is that true?' said Blake. 'Is Mr. Frank Hallett very angry with you? Does he mind your riding my horse?'

'No, why should he?' she answered.

---

*Cobbon coola – very angry.

'*I* should mind very much if you rode *his* horse after having promised to ride mine.'

'Is this my horse?' she asked, pointing to a beautiful bay, which was held not by a blackboy, but by a rather flash-looking stockman – a rakish young Australian, with a fair moustache, twisted on each side to a fine point, and odd down-looking eyes. He was a fine upstanding fellow, lean and muscular, and had the gait of a man born or bred on horseback. It was said on the Luya that there had never been foaled the animal that Sam Shehan couldn't ride. He had been well known in the district from a boy, and was supposed to have done a little cattle-duffing, as it is called, in his younger days, but he had reformed entirely since taking a place with Trant & Blake of Baròlin Gorge, and was such a good hand with stock that the neighbouring squatters were always glad to get him over for a day or two at mustering times.

'Yes, this is the Outlaw,' said Blake. 'How is he this morning, Shehan?'

'Quiet as a lamb,' said Shehan, 'and fresh as a daisy, Miss. He's a bit of a speeler. He'd lick the lot of 'em if he was put into training.'

Elsie put her foot into Blake's hand, and he lifted her into the saddle. Hallett was watching him jealously. Lord Horace had given Hallett charge of Ina. He himself was careering about the course, and had made a rather heavy book upon the races.

Behind Sam Shehan were two other Baròlin hands – twin half-caste boys, who had come in Shehan's train to Baròlin, and who had also turned into reformed characters under Trant's tutelage. Pompo and Jack Nutty used to have the reputation of being up to any kind of devilment in the old days, and they, too, were magnificent horsemen, and invaluable at Luya musterings, because they knew every inch of the country.

Blake mounted his own horse, which was a fiery creature, but not the black one he had been riding on the day he first met Elsie. Baròlin was famous for its horses, and Dominic Trant was no less well mounted. He had a scowling expression on his dark face as he passed Elsie and his partner, but he made no attempt to join them. Elsie was the object of attention to a bevy of young men, but it was a tribute to Blake's power that no one thought of interfering with him.

In an Australian March, one may sometimes have a delightful day, with just a fresh faint foretaste of winter in the air. Sometimes, on the other hand, an Australian March is as muggy and disagreeable a month as can well be imagined. To-day it was bright and clear. There had been a heavy rain a few days previously, and the world looked as if it had been well washed. Never was sky bluer. There was a faint breeze stirring the tops of the gum-trees, and throwing a ripple on to the surface of the lagoon. The grass – where it had not been trodden down by the racers exercising – was thick and lush, and brown with its autumn heads. But the yellowing quinces and swelling oranges and the great pumpkins and squashes were the only sign of autumn. As they rode down by the garden fence, the enclosure was spring-like in its bloom. The prickly pears were growing faintly pink, it is true, and the passion-creeper hung out purple eggs, but the roses massed in quantities – golden Maréchal Neils and pale tea-roses, flaunting cabbage-roses, and dark delicate cottage beauties – a most sweet and gorgeous array. And there was a plant of the Taverna Montana in bloom, its dazzling white flowers nearly as large as a camellia. And the honeysuckle and stephanotis scented the air, and the great vermilion pomegranates were like blobs of sealing-wax thrown at haphazard upon the green.

It was a day to intoxicate the senses.

'Who says that the Australian birds have no song?' said Elsie. 'There's a magpie gurgling away as if he meant to sing at a concert to-night.'

Blake smiled at her, and she smiled back in return. She had forgotten Jensen. She had forgotten her half-promise to Frank Hallett. She had forgotten to ask herself whether or not she could ever love him. She only knew that she was happy, and that the air was sweet, and that Blake looked at her in a way in which no one else had ever looked. There was a grassy track – once the path for water-carts in primitive days, before the erection of the grand pump.

The Outlaw bounded forward.

'Oh, let us have one canter along here,' Elsie cried. 'I want to try the Outlaw. One canter by the creek. Come, Mr. Blake.'

She rode on, shaking the reins and patting the animal's sleek neck, as he danced and curvetted. She looked back at Blake, and laughed like a child. How beautiful she was, and how splendidly she rode! They rode on away from the crowd, cantering, almost galloping, always fast, fast, clearing the little logs and gullies in the way, all along the home paddock and never pulling up till they were at least two miles from the station.

'What will they think?' she said, reining the Outlaw. 'Oh, what a glorious spin! Tell me, aren't you happy when you are going fast like that?'

'Do you call that fast?' he said. 'Ah, you should know what it is to ride for one's life.'

'Have you ever ridden for your life?' she asked, suddenly becoming serious.

'Yes,' he answered, 'and I have enjoyed it as I have never enjoyed anything in the world. Oh, to feel that your life – your very life – all the glory and beauty of this glorious and beautiful world – all the past, and the present, and the future – ambition, hope, a Cause perhaps – all depending on the speed of an animal and lying in the mad rush forwards. There's a wild sense of irresponsibility about a moment like that which I can't describe – can't give you the feeblest idea of. Your will seems to have got outside you, and to be in the night, and the trees, and the free birds and beasts. Every nerve is strung to an excitement which is rapture. It's the very essence of the joy of life.'

CHAPTER XII

●

Beelzebub's Colours

The first race was over when Elsie and Blake reached the course. What could they have been talking about during that homeward ride, to make them linger so long? She had a bunch of wild jasmine in her bodice, which he had gathered for her, and she had promised him more dances than she could remember.

Lady Horace looked distressed. 'Oh, Elsie, don't flirt with that man,' she whispered to her sister, repeating the former frightened adjuration. 'I know that it will bring you harm. Don't make poor Frank unhappy.'

'You seem to think a great deal more of Frank's happiness, or unhappiness, than you do of mine, Ina,' said Elsie poutingly. 'It's enough to make Horace jealous.'

Lady Horace flushed deeply. 'Don't say that; don't ever say that,' she exclaimed. 'You have no right to say such a thing.'

'Horace *is* jealous, is he?' exclaimed Elsie. 'Well, that's better at any rate than being sulky over his dinner, or running after that horrid Mrs. Allanby.'

Lord Horace, however, certainly showed no signs of jealousy. He was in very high spirits, for he had won his first bet, and he had tacked himself to pretty Mrs. Allanby, who was delighted to have a chance of revenging herself on Elsie and her belongings. Blake avoided Elsie for the rest of the day.

The girl wondered why, and showed that she did not care, by flirting extravagantly with every man who came near her. She gave Frank Hallett no opportunity for a *tête-à-tête*, and made Dominic Trant radiant by accepting his very pronounced attentions, with every sign of pleasure. It was Dominic Trant who sat next her at luncheon, and who mounted her again when luncheon was over. Dominic Trant was in high feather, for he had won two races, and expected to win several more.

The Luya Cup Race, the great event of the day, came after luncheon. Each horse was ridden by its owner, and most of the near stations and of the larger selections of the Luya were represented in the entrances. It was supposed that Frank Hallett would be the winner, on Gipsy Girl, but a good many backed Trant. Elsie wondered whether Blake intended to run Osman and to ride him. It was not till the last moment that she was certain. Just before the horses came into line he rode out on a beautiful black, which was certainly Osman, only that equally certain Osman had no white star on his forehead. She remembered this distinctly. Blake looked very well in his crimson and black colours. He seemed a part of the horse, and the fiery creature answered to his touch as though there were a complete sympathy between them.

The race was an exciting one. Frank Hallett took the lead with Gipsy Girl, but half-way round Dominic Trant passed him. Blake followed close. The others were in a bunch, Lord Horace keeping up pretty well, but gradually slackening, and one or two very soon giving up altogether. Again Gipsy Girl got the lead. It was evident that Trant's horse was flagging, and that Blake was holding in. But a quarter of a mile from the winning post, the black shot forward. For a little way he and Gipsy Girl were neck and neck. The pace was tremendous. Both men were bowed almost to the horses' necks. Gipsy Girl's sides were streaming, where Hallett had dug in his spurs. The black was scarcely blown. Close to the post he darted ahead, and Blake came in an easy winner.

There was a great deal of talk about the horse, which Elsie saw had been entered as Osman. As soon as the weighing and examination were over, his cloth was thrown on again, and Sam Shehan led him away from the course.

It was said that he had been stabled the night before in an old shepherd's hut across the river, and that Sam Shehan was so frightened of his being tampered with, that he and the half-castes had sat up all night to watch him.

When Blake came to the enclosure, where the Tunimbah ladies had mostly stationed themselves, Elsie congratulated him very sweetly.

'I feel a particular and personal interest in Osman,' she said, 'since it was through him that I first made your acquaintance. But I have been so puzzled. I felt certain that he had no white mark on his forehead. I remember thinking that he looked quite uncanny in his blackness.'

'You must have forgotten,' said Blake quietly, and presently left her to go and talk to Mrs. Jem Hallett.

'I seem fated to receive your condolences on Mr. Blake's victories,' said Frank Hallett. 'He is always the triumphant hero.'

He laughed as he spoke, but there was a shade of bitterness in his tone.

Elsie wore black and crimson that night. Lady Horace declared that people would think she did so on purpose, as a tribute to Blake, the winner, and tried to persuade her to put on an old white gown instead. But Elsie would not. 'I did not know that they were Mr. Blake's colours,' she answered. 'And let people think what they like.'

Dinner to-night was in a tent in the courtyard, for the dance was to be a more important affair than on the previous evening, and the woolshed was being prepared as a ball-room. Frank Hallett was very busy, when the ladies came out into the verandah, superintending the placing of Chinese lanterns, which were hung upon the bunya trees, and marked the way to the woolshed. Frank came up to Elsie. 'Will you do something to please my mother? Will you let her see you in your ball dress? You know she never appears at this sort of thing.'

'Of course I will, and I will come at once, or after dinner – whichever she likes best.'

'Then will you come now? For the dear old lady goes to bed at nine o'clock, and we shall not have got over the speeches by then.'

Elsie and he went out at the garden gate, and walked to old Mrs. Hallett's cottage, which was on the brow of the hill, overlooking the lagoon, not a stone's throw from the house. The old lady was in very feeble health, and lived the most retired life possible. She very rarely came to the big house, but Frank, who was devoted to his mother, spent the greater part of his evenings with her, and always lunched at the cottage when he was not out on the run. People watched them as they went across, and Elsie wondered what Blake would think, for she knew it would be said that this was a visit of an affianced pair. The thought made her cheeks burn, but gave her at the same time a little thrill of triumph, for she knew that Lady Garfit would be annoyed.

Mrs. Hallett was sitting in her verandah, looking at the sunset, which was gorgeous over Mount Luya, and watching the stir and bustle at the head station. She was a handsome old woman, with hard features and snow-white hair. She had a vacant smile, which contrasted oddly with her otherwise severe face. Her brain was weakened a little, and it was for this reason that she did not mix much with the world; moreover, she was not fond of Mrs. Jem.

She stroked Elsie's dress, and looked at her with her blank smile, which was pathetic in its vacuity. 'You're a bonny creature,' she said. 'It's a pity you're so frivolous. I believe your sister is worth two of you.'

'Mother!' exclaimed Frank.

'But you're quite right, Mrs. Hallett,' said Elsie. 'Ina is worth a hundred of me.'

'It's a pity you let her marry that fliberty-gibbet of a lord,' said Mrs. Hallett, 'but you've been badly brought up, and that's what I'm always telling Frank. I remember your mother quite well, when your father was alive, and scab inspector on the Luya. She was a pretty woman too, and you're like her; but she hadn't a great deal of sense, and I think you take after her.'

'Really, Mrs. Hallett, I think it is very unkind of you to bring me here to scold me, and abuse my mother,' said Elsie with a laugh. 'But now, won't you forgive me, and wish me a merry evening? See, I've brought you a rose.'

The girl knelt down, and tendered her little offering with a bewitching humility, that made Frank Hallett adore her. 'The old lady doesn't mean a word of it,' he said, 'and you're an angel, Miss Valliant.'

'There are two kinds of angels,' said Mrs. Hallett, 'and you're in Beelzebub's colours, my dear. But you look lovely all the same, and I don't wonder that all the men are running after you. That's what Lady Garfit tells me.'

'Oh, so the Garfits have been here to see you,' said Elsie piqued. 'Well, Rose Garfit is a practical and a substantial angel, and she ought to be just what you like.'

'So she is. I like her better than you, but then Frank doesn't, my love, and that's the mischief. Lady Garfit says you're a flirt, and that you are getting yourself talked about with those Baròlin men. Now just come here, and stoop down close. I want to see something.'

Elsie did as she told her. The old lady solemnly wiped her spectacles, and took out her handkerchief, and rubbed Elsie's rose-pink cheek.

'Lady Garfit says you're rouged.'

'But you see that I'm not.'

'There's no telling. Rose Garfit – no, it was Minnie Pryde, or Mrs.

Jem said it – some of you Leichardt's Town girls crush up geranium leaves, and rub your cheeks with them, and it doesn't come off on the handkerchief.'

'I'll go,' cried Elsie rising. 'And if I do rouge, and if I flirt, Mrs. Hallett, and if I'm horrid altogether, you're well rid of me. And I'm going back to Leichardt's Town very soon, and you won't see me till the spring, when we are all coming up to picnic at Baròlin Falls, and perhaps by then you'll have forgiven me.'

She kissed her hand and bounded off the verandah, pulling her cloak over her head. Frank followed, but he was detained for a few moments by his mother. Blake was waiting at the entrance of the tent, having the start, and took Elsie into dinner, and Frank was vexed with his mother.

It was a long repast, made longer by the speeches. The health of Mr. and Mrs. Jem was drunk, and an appropriate speech was made by the oldest resident on the Luya, calling attention to the auspicious occasion, and wishing them a silver and a golden wedding. And there were many more toasts, and among them the health of Osman, winner of the Luya Cup; and the cup was filled with champagne, and handed from each to each, Blake himself drinking after Elsie's lips had touched the goblet.

'I drink to our first meeting,' said he in a low tone, audible only to her.

The lanterns were all alight when they left the tent, and the musicians had already struck up in the woolshed. It was a curious and fairy-like scene, the array of coloured lamps, the solemn bunyas in the dimness of night, and in their density of foliage, almost like pyramids of green marble; the leaden lagoon reflecting the pale stars above and the red fires of the camp below, the shadowy expanse of plain, and the darker patches of scrub and bush, with the rugged mountain beyond – Luya – and the two needles of the Burrum, against the deep mysterious sky, dotted with its myriads of stars, and showing all the beautiful southern constellations. The moon had not risen yet, but its appearance could hardly add any greater glory to the night. Blake got Elsie a programme, and wrote his initials against various waltzes. Frank Hallett watched him doing this with envy and jealousy tearing at his heart. He was an outsider, one among the men who waited, as she stood on the steps of the woolshed, to ask her for a dance.

'Please let me pass,' said Lady Garfit sourly, as she convoyed her daughter. 'Mr. Frank Hallett, I am sure you will give your arm to

Rose. Miss Valliant's would-be partners make quite a block in the gangway.'

There was a general clearance.

'I beg your pardon,' said Elsie innocently. 'But you know, I can't help people asking me to dance, can I?'

Lady Garfit did not vouchsafe a reply.

'You must feel like a queen holding a court,' said Trant, who had pushed his way close to her.

'Oh!' she exclaimed, 'Lady Garfit makes me feel like a beggar-maid dressed up. No, Mr. Trant, you mustn't put your name down so many times. Only once, please. I have promised to keep some for Mr. Frank Hallett.'

Trant's eyes flamed. He left her sulkily. When the time came for his dance, he did not appear to claim it, and Elsie danced it with Blake. Nor did he come to make apologies. Elsie would have been offended if she had not noticed that his eyes glowered upon her whenever she turned hers towards him, and his anger, she felt, was a tribute to her power.

Just then, however, when Frank returned, he was made almost happy by the radiant smile with which Elsie showed him the blanks.

Oh yes, it was a triumphant evening for vain Elsie. She was the belle of the room. Rose Garfit was nowhere, and Mrs. Allanby quite out in the cold.

The sense of conquest was intoxicating. All the men present whom she considered worth captivating she had reduced to abject subjection. Never in her life had she so thoroughly enjoyed herself. Perhaps the enjoyment was all the more intense because there mingled with her triumph and elation a strange sense of dread, a certain vague pain and expectancy which gave a keener edge to life, and might have been the thrill of a new sense. And it was true. There were awakening in her sensations she had never known. It was as if she had now taken a plunge into new deep waters, when all her life she had been floating on a shallow sunlit stream.

CHAPTER XIII

—•—

'Hearts Not In It'

The greater number of the guests left on the morrow. The Horace Gages, and Elsie, as well as the Baròlin gentlemen, the Garfits, and one or two of the Leichardt's Town people had been asked to stay a day longer, to join a riding party, which Frank Hallett had organised, to a picturesque gorge up the Luya. Hallett had done this partly to compensate Elsie for her disappointment in the matter of the picnic, and also because she had promised to ride Gipsy Girl, and he thought that he should thus have a chance of riding with her. He was a little disconcerted when Blake suggested to Mrs. Jem that since Point Row, their destination, was not far from his place, Baròlin Gorge, they should ride over in the morning, have luncheon with Trant and himself, in their bachelor domicile, and take Point Row on their way homeward – or go to Point Row first, dine at the Gorge, and ride back the ten miles by moonlight.

It was the first plan which was decided upon. Before twelve o'clock the outsiders had all departed, and the remaining guests were on their way to Baròlin. Trant had started at daybreak, to make preparations for their reception.

Pompo, the half-caste, remained to drive the pack-horse, and, as he expressed it, 'make him road budgery.' Pompo was an elfish creature devoted to his master Blake, and curiously attracted to Elsie, perhaps because he saw that Blake was attracted in a greater and different degree. Pompo did not like Elsie's riding Gipsy Girl, and pointing to The Outlaw, with an air of reproach, asked, 'What for you no like it yarraman, belonging to Blake?'

'But I like your master's horse very much, Pompo,' said Elsie sweetly. 'Only, you see, I rode it instead of Mr. Hallett's the other day, and it wouldn't be fair to ride it again.'

Pompo did not fully enter into this reasoning, and he made Frank Hallett cross by coming perpetually to examine Elsie's girths, or to ask her if she wanted him to 'make him road budgery.' He rode ahead with a tomahawk slung over his shoulders, and would stop every now and then to cut away some overhanging vine, or to remove a piece of driftwood which the February floods had brought down. The impish creature's bead-like eyes continually turned to Elsie in a half-amused inquiring way, while he acted as guide, and did the honours of the road to Baròlin Gorge, which was certainly rough enough for a guide to be necessary.

It ran along the river bank – a track in places barely distinguishable from the cattletracks, which sloped sideways to the water, with here and there stony pinches, and steep gulleys, almost hidden by the rank blady grass.

Now it ran through a patch of scrub or among glossy chestnut trees, with their red and orange blossoms, or between white cedars on which the berry sprays were already yellowing. When the scrub ended there were melancholy she-oaks, and every now and then a shrub of the lemon-scented gum, which Elsie would snatch at as they passed and crush between her fingers, for the sake of the curious aromatic perfume it gave forth. There was something strange and dreamy in this ride along the bank of the Luya – here scarcely to be called a river – a ride so wild that for the most part they had to go in single file. It all harmonised with that phase of mental exaltation which had come over Elsie during the last few days. Anything might happen in this enchanted forest.

In places the creek would make a bend, winding round a little flat, and then there would be a quick canter, with a warning from Pompo to look out for paddy-melon holes. And then they would mount a stony ridge, with weird-looking grass trees, lifting their blackened spears, and gray-green wattles, and lanky gums, and sparse blady grass. And then, perhaps, they would get away from the river for a little way, and the gum trees would close in around them, and the whirring of the locusts would be almost deafening, and the dreaminess more intense. Elsie would almost call out in terror as an iguana scuttled up a gum tree, or a herd of kangaroo made a dash across the track. Once they had an exciting spin after an 'old-man' kangaroo with all the dogs in full cry, but he escaped them, for the river had twisted round again and they were in scrub once more. And here were deep rippleless pools surrounded by beds of poisonous arums, with the wrack of the floodmark clinging to their pulpy stems; and horrid water-snakes showed themselves from under decaying logs and the fallen chestnut pods had rotted, and there was a moist fetid feeling that Elsie said reminded her of Hans Andersen's witch stories.

They seemed to be going right up into the mountains, which began to close in round them, all the seams and fissures in the precipice showing distinctly. Presently at its narrowest part the valley opened out in a chain of flats, and Frank pointed to a gully cutting down into the neck and said, 'That's our show lion – Point Row – what we are coming out for to see. We shall stop there for tea, and then, if you don't mind a climb, we'll get down the rocks on the other side, and the black-boys shall take the horses round to meet us, and we can come home by the Dead Finish Flats, and have a moonlight gallop if you like.'

'It would be heavenly,' said Elsie. 'Look! Isn't that Mr. Trant coming across the flat?'

It was Trant, who, mounted on a fresh horse, had ridden out to meet them.

'You can canter all the way now to the Gorge,' he cried. 'Come Miss Valliant, luncheon is waiting.'

He contrived to get beside Elsie. 'I expected to see you riding with Blake,' he said; 'but it's a bad road, isn't it, for flirtation?'

'Why do you always drag in that horrible word?'

'Is it a horrible word? I thought it was one you were particularly fond of. You won't pretend that you haven't been flirting outrageously this last day or two. I hope you observed that I haven't given you much chance to-day of flirting with me.'

'I wondered why you had gone away so early this morning.'

'In order that you might have something to eat for luncheon. No it wasn't that. Blake said he'd go. Or a message by Sam Shehan would have done as well. The truth is that you're beginning to make me uncomfortable, and I don't like it.'

'I thought it was you who generally made people uncomfortable – at least you told me that you would make them afraid of you.'

'I told you that I could generally make a woman like me if I wanted to.'

'You said that you made them afraid of you as well. I suppose it's the same thing.'

'I shouldn't say it was the same thing at all.'

'Well, I should think it would be very uncomfortable to be made to like a man you were afraid of,' said Elsie.

'I don't intend to let you make me uncomfortable, Miss Valliant.'

'I am very glad to hear that, Mr. Trant.'

'Perhaps you won't like it so much when I tell you that the alternative is that you should be afraid of me.'

'I don't feel in the least bit afraid of you now. I don't know what there is to be afraid of.'

'Don't you? Well, perhaps some day you may find out. If I set my mind on a thing I always carry it through.'

'Really, Mr. Trant, you are quite melodramatic. When you talk like that, and when you sing as you did the other night, you make me sorry –'

'Sorry for what?'

'That you forget your engagements with me in the very rude way in which you forgot them last night.'

'I suppose you mean my not coming to claim my dance?'

'Naturally.'

'I didn't choose to be thrown a dance as you might throw a dog a bone, when you were sitting out half a dozen apiece with Blake and Hallett. I wanted you to sit out with me. And, besides, you wouldn't take my warning.'

'I didn't know that you warned me against Mr. Hallett.'

'No, but I warned you against Blake. It made me mad to hear people talking about you and him – knowing him as I do, and knowing very well that it was only because you were the prettiest woman in the room, and because Frank Hallett is said to be engaged to you, and he didn't choose that anybody should beat him – more especially Frank Hallett.'

'Do you think it is very nice of you to talk about your partner behind his back in that way?'

'It is only what I have said to his face, and you are quite at liberty to repeat every word. Blake knows it is true. But I've put myself in your power in another way.'

'How?'

'By letting you see that I am jealous.'

'Now, Miss Valliant, this is good going ground.' Blake had cantered up and reined in his horse for a moment.

Elsie touched Gipsy Girl with the whip. Blake rode The Outlaw. They were soon striding on in advance of the others. 'So Trant is jealous! Poor Trant! You must be nice to him, Miss Valliant. He is a very good fellow in his way – Trant.'

Elsie was struck by the cool, half-contemptuous tone in which he spoke. 'Is Mr. Trant very much your inferior?' she asked.

'Good gracious! Inferior! In what way?'

'In birth and position, I suppose. You speak as if he were.'

'I am sorry I gave you that impression. Trant is – well, perhaps his ancestors tilled the soil when mine rode over it. I don't know that that makes much difference.'

'You said once that you came of a wild race.'

He laughed. 'Ah, that's true, and I think I've done my best to carry on the family traditions. I've been wild enough, too, at times.'

Elsie was silent for a minute. At last she began impulsively and stopped.

'I wonder –'

'What is it that you wonder?'

He bent down from his saddle, and looked at her with that curiously sweet smile which he had.

'I was wondering, Mr. Blake, that you, who I suppose belong to some great old family, and who have lived in Europe, and care so much for excitement and – and all that you have talked to me about –'

'Well?'

'That you can be content to live in the bush, and in such a quiet place as Baròlin Gorge.'

'But I don't live in Baròlin Gorge. At least I haven't lived there much as yet. And then you forget that I am going in for the maddening excitement of the Australian political arena. What more could I have?'

'I should have thought you could have had much more in Europe, and that at least you would have had the society of people you cared about.'

'I have society that I care about in Australia.'

'How long is it since you left England, Mr. Blake?'

He seemed to be thinking. 'It is about twelve years since I left Ireland.'

'Ireland – yes, I forgot. Do you care very much for your country?'

'I sucked in patriotism with my mother's milk. It was born in me, with many other things that I should be better without.'

'Better?'

'Happier, at any rate.'

'But you – you ought to be happy,' said Elsie falteringly.

He looked at her lingeringly. Her eyes were turned away. She was sitting very erect. Her profile was towards him. There was a lovely glow on her delicate cheeks, a still more beautiful glow in her eyes, and her lips were sweet and tremulous.

'Yes, I ought to be happy,' he repeated, 'and especially at this moment. Well, I *am* happy, Miss Valliant. Or it would be truer to say that the one man in me is happy.'

'I don't understand.'

'Don't you know,' he said, 'that in most of us there are two beings? Sometimes the one is kept so utterly in subjection by the other that you hardly know it is there. But in some people the two natures are both so strong that life is always a battle. It's the Celt in me that gives me no peace.'

'I don't understand,' she said again.

He laughed. 'No, I don't suppose you do. For your own sake I hope not. And yet sometimes I fancy that you've got a little bit of the same nature in you, and that, to a very faint extent, we are companions in misfortune.'

'Misfortune!'

'Isn't it a misfortune to have the rebel taint. *You* couldn't bind yourself down to the sort of life which would content that very estimable young lady, Miss Garfit.'

'No.'

'Nor could I lead the calm decorous existence of – shall I say Mr. Frank Hallett? – an existence made up of going out on the run managing a model station, observing all the social, domestic, and religious obligations, amassing an honourable fortune by strict attention to business and by prudent investment, loving one woman and cleaving to her. No, I do the Celt injustice there. His morals are his strongest point – my grandmother was French. Miss Valliant, have I offended you?'

'Yes.' Elsie turned to him bright dilated eyes. 'I will not have you speak in that sneering way of Frank Hallett.'

'Forgive me, I did not mean to sneer. And I ought to have remembered what I was told last night.'

'What was that?'

'That he is to be your husband.'

Elsie rode on with flaming cheeks, distancing The Outlaw by a few paces. They were a long way in advance of the others. In the distance was to be seen a cluster of buildings standing back against a hill, which was covered with dense scrub. A little to the right rose Mount Luya, a majestic object, with its encircling precipiced battlement of grey rock, making it look like some Titanic fortress. Its strange rents and fissures and the black bunya scrub clothing its lower slopes made it seem still more grim and gloomy.

'I don't wonder that the blacks think that Debil-debil lives on Mount Luya,' said Elsie.

'Do you see that dark ravine with the two spurs of rock going down from the precipice – just as if a thick wedge had been cut out of the mountain?' asked Blake. 'Do you think it will be very easy to reach Baròlin Waterfall?'

'Is that Baròlin Waterfall?'

'Yes, the dread abode of the great Spirit Baròlin. Captain Macpherson may "blow," as you say in Australia, but I am certain that he and his merry men never got beyond the foot of those rocky spurs. There's a pretty little cascade there, but it is not the real Baròlin Fall. That will not be the scene of your spring picnic, Miss Valliant, unless you are prepared to force your way on foot through scrub as impenetrable as an Indian jungle.'

'How do you know all this, Mr. Blake? I thought you were almost a stranger on the Luya.'

'Trant has told me, and he has heard it from Sam Shehan, and Pompo, and Jack Nutty, who, in the days of their nefarious practices, probably "nuggeted" a good many of Mr. Hallett's calves up here on the Luya, and know every inch of country practicable for that purpose. Here we are at the sliprails, Miss Valliant. I am glad we have reached them before the others, and that I am the one to let them down for you.'

He dismounted and waited at the sliprails till she had ridden through. Then before mounting again he came to Gipsy Girl's side and held out his hand. 'Welcome to Baròlin.'

She put her hand in his. Their eyes met. In her look there was a troubled consciousness. In his there was consciousness too, but it was nevertheless a bold and masterful gaze.

'Will you forgive me,' he said, 'and believe that I meant no disrespect to Mr. Frank Hallett? I admire him immensely. He is a good fighter and a gallant foe. I got to like him ever so much during the election, and I hope you will be happy with him.'

Elsie did not answer. He released her hand. There had been something very strange, she thought, in his clasp. It had given her an odd tingling sensation, which no other touch had ever produced. She wondered whether there was any truth in the idea that some people were magnetic. He looked at her all the time. He went on.

'Yes, I admire Frank Hallett. I don't believe he would do a dishonourable thing to save his life. He has all the sterling virtues. But he is – you must own it – he is something of the Philistine, and

I am a Bohemian rebel to the very core of me, and can't be expected
to feel that deep sympathy with his views of life which perhaps you
feel, Miss Valliant.'

'I think,' she said slowly, 'that I have a little of the Bohemian in
me, too.'

He laughed. 'Oh yes, I know that. Didn't I tell you that we were
something akin? Well, I wonder if you will be as generous a foe as
Mr. Frank Hallett.'

'As generous a foe,' she repeated, startled.

'We are fighting, aren't we? Don't you remember that challenge of
the other night? I accepted it. Don't you recollect our talk that evening
– before I told you of my friendship with Jensen? I beg your pardon
for alluding again to what you said was disagreeable.'

'I understand,' she said coldly; 'you want to avenge Mr. Jensen's
wrongs. That is what you were thinking of.'

'I beg your pardon,' he said again. 'It wasn't to be a case of avenging
anyone or anything – nothing so melodramatic. It was to be a trial of
skill, a tournament between a young lady, who frankly owned that she
had played with a man's heart – and who had ruined his life – for an
experiment, and another person who confessed to having played justly
or unjustly for amusement at the game of flirtation. That's all. There
is nothing melodramatic about it. And it was understood that hearts
were not in the business.'

'Mr. Blake, you are cruel – you have no right – it is unfair.'

'If you think a moment,' he said gently, 'you will see that it is all
fair – a challenge given to a tournament – on certain lines – given
and seriously taken up. I suppose the laws of knightly warfare hardly
apply to a lady, and that your word must be my law, but still you will
admit that to draw back would seem –'

'Well?'

'Forgive me, but wouldn't it seem a little like a confession of
cowardice?'

Elsie flushed, and her eyes gleamed; and a spirit of recklessness
took possession of her. 'Very well; whatever I am, I am not a coward,
and I am not in the least afraid of you, Mr. Blake.'

He bowed. 'That I can perfectly understand. It is I who have cause
to be afraid.'

'Why shouldn't we play the game, since it amuses you and it amuses
me – since it is a case of hearts not in it?'

'Why not, indeed?' he answered. 'It seems to me that one of the
objects of living at all is that one may cram as many experiences as

one can into the few years in which experience can be enjoyed. You are fond of drama, Miss Valliant, so am I. You don't get the sort of drama we should enjoy; on the Australian stage it is too crude – too much of the blood and thunder, "Unhand me, villain!" sentiment – not complex enough for people who by right of nature belong to an advanced civilisation. We don't get an advanced civilisation out here, do we? And so we must make our own drama. I am quite certain that one in which you played the principal part would be bound to be exciting.'

'Thank you.'

'And then,' he went on, 'you like making experiments in human chemistry, and so do I. You remember that book you were reading the day we first met. Experiments in a laboratory are sometimes dangerous. Experiments in human chemistry may be much more dangerous. But I never really cared for anything in which there was no danger. I perfectly realise the danger in this case. . . . Here come the rest. I think I may leave the putting up of the sliprails to Trant.' He mounted again, and they rode together up to the house.

CHAPTER XIV

———— • ————

'Are We Enemies?'

Baròlin was only a bachelor's house, and a bachelor's house of the roughest kind, as Trant & Blake impressed upon their guests. But there were things in it which one does not usually find in a bachelor's dwelling in the bush – notably a piano, which Lord Horace insisted on trying, while they were waiting for luncheon, and which he pronounced to be one of the best cottage pianos he had ever played on. Trant sang at Elsie's request one of his passionate love-songs, which produced a sort of reflex emotion in several of the persons present – excepting perhaps Miss Garfit, who remarked that it was sweet; Miss Garfit had a trick of saying that things were 'sweet,' and the epithet was not quite in keeping with her robust personality. Then there were various odds and ends which betokened a more refined taste than one discovers as a rule among lone squatters – some fine bits of Eastern embroidery, a silver perfume sprinkler, two or three jewelled daggers,and so forth, which Lord Horace pounced upon.

'These are Algerian,' he said. 'My sister has got a lot of 'em. Fancy finding Algerian embroideries in an Australian hut!'

'I am sure,' said Miss Garfit, 'this is far too sweet a place to be called a hut. Have you really been in Algiers, Mr. Blake?'

Blake laughed. 'Ask Trant. He was in a regiment of Irregulars. That's how he learned to speak French so well.'

'And you?' said Elsie. 'Was that where you learned to speak French?'

'As I have told you, my grandmother was a Frenchwoman, Miss Valliant. But I have knocked about among the Arabs a good deal, and I learned to speak –'

There was a sudden crash. Trant had jumped up hastily, and had overturned a chair. Blake's sentence remained unfinished.

'By Jove, you've got some nice firearms here,' said Lord Horace, who had been examining a rack of guns and pistols over the chimney-piece. 'These are stunners – all the latest improvements. I see you are prepared for Moonlight.'

Was it Elsie's fancy, that as Frank Hallett and the other men came up to examine the weapons, a sudden glance was interchanged by the partners? anyhow she thought that Blake rather hastily interposed. 'Never mind those, Lord Horace, I am sure luncheon is ready. Come – Trant, will you bring Miss Valliant? Lord Horace, please show Miss Garfit the way.'

He offered his arm to Ina, and Elsie accepted that of Trant. Luncheon was not quite ready, but the delay afforded opportunity for admiring the view from the verandah of the dining-room, which looked out on Mount Luya. Trant was full of apologies for his bachelor housekeeping, which, however, were unnecessary, for the meal was excellently served, and he was much complimented by Mrs. Jem Hallett, who considered herself an authority in such matters, and who made a mental memorandum that she would always in future give her guests coffee after luncheon.

It was mid-afternoon before the coffee had been drunk, they were again mounted, and on their way back to Point Row. Frank Hallett got beside Elsie at the start, and Blake was fain to content himself with Lady Horace. Ina did not care much for Blake, but she made herself as agreeable as she could, because she wanted to keep him from Elsie. Lady Horace was beginning to be a little frightened of Blake's influence over Elsie.

Hallett was not quite himself, or was it that Elsie was disturbed and preoccupied? 'Have you enjoyed your day?' he asked.

'It is not finished yet. Call no man happy till he is dead, you know.'

He laughed, and then said with some embarrassment, 'You and Blake seemed to be talking very earnestly when you were waiting by the sliprails.'

'Were we? I forget.'

'He was holding your hand.'

'You have very keen eyes, Mr. Hallett.'

'But he *was* holding your hand?'

'Yes, then he was.'

'That was odd, wasn't it?'

'It isn't at all odd when a person holds out his hand and asks you to forgive him. You naturally take it.'

'Oh! he asked you to forgive him! Had he offended you?'

'Yes.'

'By something he said?'

'Yes.'

'I wish I knew what he had said.'

'How inquisitive you are. Well, it was about you,' said Elsie.

'About me?'

'He spoke of you in a way I didn't like.'

'Indeed. I don't mind in the least what Mr. Blake says about me.'

'Your tone shows that you do. He spoke very nicely of you. He said you were a generous foe, and that he admired and respected you.'

'That was very kind of him. Did you object to his praising me?'

'I objected to his calling you a Philistine.'

'Oh! now I understand. Thank you, Elsie.' His whole face beamed. 'You are loyal.'

'Am I? I am afraid not. Don't be a Philistine, Frank. I don't like Philistines.'

They were able to canter almost all the way to the turning off to Point Row. At the bend where the Point Row gulley fell into the Luya a great rock bulged out into the stream. It was covered with a wonderful growth of ferns, birds'-nests, and staghorn, with branching antler-like fronds, which so fascinated Elsie that she wanted to get off her horse and clamber up the boulder to gather them. But Pompo stepped gallantly forward. 'Ba'al!' he cried, 'White Mary plenty gammon. Suppose white missus go up that fellow rock she tumble and break her neck. Then mine dig him hole to put her in.'

The creature swung himself up, grinning all the time, and presently came back with an armful, which he slung on his saddle. They went very slowly now. Pompo first, with the packhorse, all the rest following in single file. The hills closed in on either side, and the gulley was in deep shade. There was a little wind, and the she-oaks by the creeklet made a melancholy sighing. The stream ran over a pebbly bed with big boulders here and there, breaking its course and damming it into a deep black pool. In some places the pool was covered with a strange opaline. Now a rocky wall rose ahead. The gulley made a bend, and the creeklet wound between two fantastically-shaped ridges of grey rock. It was impossible to ride further, and they all dismounted. Pompo unsaddling the packhorse and carrying the saddlebags with the tea-things down through the rocky heads, whence he led the way into what seemed the heart of the hills, while Jack Nutty, the other half-caste twin, and two black-boys drove the horses back and round the ridge to meet the picnickers on the other side of the gorge.

The ladies tucked up their habits, and each with her attendant swain picked her way over the rocks, and across the stepping-stones, and through the tangle of fern and creeper, which choked the entrance to the ravine. It was rough walking. The ravine was a rocky trough. On each side rose a wall of grey volcanic stone hollowed in places at the base, and making tiny caves rich in maidenhair fern. It was broken in others and overgrown with the red kennedia and the fleshy wax plant, and had tufts of orchids, creeping jasmine and tiny shrubs, with blue-green leaves that gave out a strong aromatic scent. The creeklet was here a chain of dark clear pools, the last hemmed in all round by rock, black and looking unfathomable. A sort of natural stair led to a higher plateau, and it was here that Pompo had laid the saddlebags and was building up a fire of brushwood for the making of the quart-pot tea.

The quiet place echoed with talk and laughter, and the scared rock wallabies darted out of their holes, and made for the higher level and for the impenetrable scrub. Some of the party climbed above the plateau, and from here the sun could be seen, a golden flame, through the trees. Among these adventurous ones were Blake and Elsie. Frank, in his capacity of host, remained below with Mrs. Jem, and lifted off the quart pot and sugared and cooled the tea. Rose Garfit held one pint pot and he another, and backwards and forwards they poured the smoking beverage. Elsie did not care for quart-pot tea; she said that she liked the spring water better, and that she wanted to see if there were any late mulgams. Blake was of her opinion, and the two did find some untimely berries. They had climbed some fifty feet. Up here the hoya grew luxuriantly, and there were clusters of the waxen flowers sweet as honey, which Elsie gathered, and with which she pelted those below.

'Elsie, Elsie,' Ina cried; 'come down, you'll be losing yourselves up there, and we shall never get to the horses, and Mr. Hallett says the place is full of snakes.'

But Elsie only laughed.

'Why should I climb down to climb up again? We've got to get over the ridge before we find the horses. Mr. Blake will look after the snakes. You are to take care of me and show me the way,' she added demurely, to Blake, 'though we *have* agreed to be enemies.'

'Are we enemies?' he said in an odd dreamy way. 'Let us suspend hostilities then for a little while. No, I don't think we are enemies.'

Elsie turned from the precipice, and moved about among the shrubs and plants, gathering a flower here and there. There were many that she had never seen before, peculiar to these mountain places, and she gathered them and brought them to Blake with all the interest of a child. There were trees with a glossy green leaf and bright orange seed pods, and there was another plant with a cone of brilliant crimson berries. 'I wonder what sort of flower they had,' she said. 'If one only knew in autumn what things were like in spring.'

'Do you know,' he said, 'that there is a great philosophical problem underneath that remark of yours? If one could only know in autumn what had been the promise of the spring. If in the spring one could only know what the autumn would bring forth, one might in that case make a better thing out of life.'

'Oh!' she cried, 'to know in spring what the autumn is going to bring forth! It would be terrible. It would spoil life. I should hate it. I don't want to know anything. I want to live from day to day, never looking forward.'

'So that is your theory! The mere joy of life contents you?'

'No, no,' she cried impetuously. 'I say so, but it is not true. I want much more than the mere joy of life. I am always looking forward – always wondering what is going to happen – always inventing situations – always expecting people who never by any chance come along.'

'What sort of people?' he asked.

'The people who seem to live in romance, and not in real life,' she answered lightly.

There was a 'Coo-ee' from below. Elsie peeped over the ledge.

'They are coming. Now we are going to where the horses are waiting.'

'They will not be waiting yet. Pompo and the black-boys have to lead them a good three miles round the ridge.'

'And we have to climb down this ridge. Do you know the way?' she asked.

'No, but I'm as good a bushman, I think, as most people. I'll engage to strike the horses at the bottom of the gulley.'

'Mr. Frank Hallett knows the way,' said Elsie. 'He is coo-eeing to us to wait for him.'

'I don't want to wait for Mr. Frank Hallett. I would rather show you the way myself. Will you let me be your guide?'

'If you like' she answered.

'Come then.' He held back an over-hanging withe of a creeper, for her to pass through into the denser bush beyond the little plateau. The ground sloped downward. There was a faint track, but it was difficult to tell whether it was a cattle track, or made by the passage of man. On each side, and all down the hill, were cairns of grey volcanic stone, covered with a yellow-white lichen, that gave them a strange and hoary appearance. The white gums had something of the same eldritch look on account of the withes of greenish-grey moss which hung from their branches. Through their straight lanky stems could be seen glimpses of the grey precipice of Mount Luya. A few jagged grass-trees, some melancholy wattles, and stunted cinchona shrubs added to the wildness of the scene. As they got down into the gulley the rocks became more steep and slippery, and the way more difficult. Blake held out his hand to help Elsie over the stones. She slipped and fell into his arms, but quickly recovered herself, and poised with the lightness of a fawn on a jutting rock. 'You don't seem to like taking my hand,' said Blake resentfully.

'I am a very good climber,' she answered. 'And besides, Mr. Blake, did you really mean what you said? Is everything that you or I do or say to be counted as a move in the game?'

'Most certainly, since we have determined to play the game. But you need not be so proud about accepting help over the stones. It will be I who run a risk, not you.'

'I don't understand you.' As she spoke, she put out her hand to balance herself, for she had slipped again. He took it in his, and with his eyes admiringly fixed upon her face guided her down a bad bit. Again that curious thrill of contact of which Elsie was distinctly sensible. So also seemed Blake.

'Can't you understand,' he said, in a voice unlike his usual deliberate utterance, 'that there might be a risk to a man in touching the hand of a woman like you, if –'

'If?' she asked.

'If he were fighting not so much against you as against himself?'

'Ah!' cried Elsie triumphantly, quoting his own words. 'Doesn't it seem a little like a confession of cowardice?'

'No,' he said, looking up to her from his lower level and then taking her bodily in his arms and lifting her down a miniature precipice; 'whatever I may be I am not a coward, and if you make me love you, Elsie – well, then we shall be quits. You shall love me too.'

'And then?' she said almost below her breath, looking at him with fascinated eyes.

'Then,' he said, with a light laugh, 'the game will be a drawn one, the battle lost for the two of us. We shall go our ways both wounded, and perhaps – who knows? – neither of us sorry, though we may have to bear the pain of the hurt till our lives' end.'

She drew herself from him, throwing her body back against the rock. And at that moment there was a rustle in the dry leaves that choked a fissure almost at her elbow, and the gleam of something black and shining, which disappeared in the rank blady grass. Elsie gave a cry, and darted from the place, leaping past him on to a fallen log.

'What is it?' he said.

'Didn't you see a snake? Ina said this place was full of them, and I had forgotten. I am terrified of snakes. When I have a nightmare it is that I am bitten by a snake, and that I am somewhere out of reach of remedies. What should I have done if that thing had bitten me?' She shuddered.

'I should have sucked the poison from the bite, and then I should have given you ammonia – I always carry it with me in the bush' – he touched his coat-pocket, 'and in the long run you would not be very much the worse.'

'And you would have saved my life?'

'Yes, I suppose so, always allowing that it was a deadly snake, and that it had bitten you.'

They did not speak for some time. Elsie was pale. She moved on hurriedly, looking to right and left as she picked her steps. They had nearly got to the bottom of the ridge when Blake gave a 'Coo-ee.' There was no answer. 'They are a long way behind us,' he said coolly. 'We have come down by a short cut.'

'But where are the horses? Perhaps we have come down quite wrong.' Elsie looked uneasy.

'No, we have not. It is they who have gone out of their way. The horses are down there,' and he pointed a little to the right.

'How do you know?'

'Oh, I know the country. You will see.' He called again, this time with a totally different note from the ordinary Australian 'Coo-ee.' It was a strange wild sound, something like the cry of a bird, a most peculiar and wailing sound.

'They won't know that. What an odd coo-ee,' exclaimed Elsie. As she spoke, the cry was repeated, and from the direction which Blake had indicated. 'That is Pompo,' he said. 'Pompo knows my call. Now, Miss Valliant, sit down on this log and rest till the others come. They will coo-ee fast enough. There, listen. Didn't I tell you?'

And from above and a good way off, to the left, there sounded Ina's coo-ee – then another, in a man's voice.

'Sit down,' said Blake. 'You are panting, and you are quite pale. A few minutes ago you had the loveliest flush imaginable.'

Elsie flushed now. She did not sit down, but leaned against a white gum-tree tapping her riding-skirt with her whip in an embarrassed manner.

'Mr. Blake,' she began.

'Well, Miss Valliant.'

'You were wrong – in what you said – in what you thought. I am not engaged to Mr. Frank Hallett.'

'Ah! I wonder whether that is so much the better for him or the worse.'

'The worse. I am not the kind of girl to make a man happy.'

'I think you might make a certain kind of man intensely happy – and under certain conditions.'

'What conditions?'

'First of all, he must be free to love you – free to make you his wife. And yet' – he paused for a moment, then went on – 'I can imagine the desperate sort of joy – a joy in which minutes would count as years, and a week as a lifetime – the joy of loving you, and conquering you, and teaching you the ineffable bliss of love – opening to you a whole world of new emotions and gathering the first-fruits of your heart, with bliss intensified to an ecstasy of pain by the knowledge that it must end in a week. Perhaps that short-lived rapture might be worth more than a long married life of decorous common-place conventional happiness – a Frank Hallett kind of happiness.'

'Don't, don't say things like that. I don't know anything about such feelings.'

'No, but the time will come when you will know, and then you will remember my words. You will remember that it was as I told you, that you had in you the capacity for passion.'

'Yes,' she answered in a low voice; 'I will remember.'

'You understand now what I meant when I told you that I realised the risk I was running.'

'No,' she exclaimed. 'You talk in enigmas. You speak of a certain kind of man – of certain conditions which don't apply to you.'

'But if they did apply to me? – If I was thinking, speaking of myself?'

'How can that be? You are free. Your life is your own.'

'It is true,' he said slowly, 'that my life is my own. But it is true also that my life may be forfeited at any moment, and that I am not free to link the life of a woman like you with a career so wild and precarious as mine.'

'Wild! Precarious!' she repeated, in wonder.

'You don't know what I mean. It is not possible that you should. I am saying to you what I have said to no other woman in the world – to no other person in Australia. My life is wild and precarious – it is not necessary – not advisable that you should understand in what way. Only understand this – I am the last man to ask a woman I love to share it.'

'I understand,' she said – 'no, I shall never understand, but I know what you wish to convey to me. I thank you for your warning. It was not needed. Will you show me now where the horses are?'

—————•—————

CHAPTER XV

A Verandah Reception

It seemed to Elsie that never, in all her life long, should she forget that moonlight ride. The sun was setting when they found the horses. They waited a little while in, as far as Blake and Elsie were concerned, a constrained silence. Elsie talked to Pompo and the black-boys. She was a favourite with the blacks, and had picked up something of the Luya dialect. King Tommy of the Dell had been her instructor, and King Tommy was old and garrulous, and had even been beguiled into discussing the sacred mysteries of the *Bora*. Elsie had a theory that the most sacred initiation grounds of the *Bora* mystery were somewhere at the foot of Mount Luya, and that hence arose the superstitious dislike of the blacks to going anywhere near the Baròlin Fall. But Pompo only grinned when she hazarded this theory, and declared 'that White Missus plenty gammon,' which is the recognised black formula for avoiding a delicate subject. He was more communicative when Elsie asked about the great Woolla-Woolla, the black parliament, and about the marriage laws of the Luya tribes, the Combo, Hippi, and Haggi families. Elsie had arrived at a due understanding of the fact that the child of a Combo-Hippi must marry a Hippi-Haggi, and their child in turn must wed with a Haggi-Combo, when the coo-ees of the rear party sounded nearer and louder, and presently Hallett and Lady Horace, closely followed by Lord Horace and Mrs. Allanby, made their appearance, and proceeded at once to mount.

It was easy going all the way home. They rode across a series of flats made by the bends of the river. There was no excuse for loitering in twos. Lord Horace and Trant started a chorus – Lord Horace's adaptation of Adam Lindsay Gordon's spirited lines.

The moon was getting near its full, and cast ghostly shadows upon the flat and under the gnarled apple gums and the queer rocky knolls that had a way of starting up on the edge of a flat where the hills encroached towards the river. The way was not so picturesque as that which they had taken in the morning, but it was much better adapted to a night ride. Gipsy Girl knew she was going home, and went fleetly along – Hallett close by Elsie's side, for Blake made no attempt at any further talk, but rode by Lady Horace, who afterwards confessed to Elsie that he was certainly very agreeable. As for Elsie, she felt in a dream. She hardly knew what Frank Hallett was talking about, though she answered mechanically even and found herself laughing. He was telling her about his election campaign, and his coming tour on the Wallaroo, on which he was to start on the morrow.

And the Horace Gages and Elsie were going too, and the party was to break up.

They would meet no more till Parliament opened next month and Leichardt's Town gaieties had begun, and Elsie had, as she said, with her little laugh, got through her jam-making. Ina and Lord Horace were coming down to meet the Waveryngs, who were to turn up some time in the winter. All the while, Elsie was thinking of Blake's strange words, seeing in fancy the dark dangerous eyes which already imagination pictured too often for her heart's peace. What had he meant by saying that his life was wild and precarious – he whose life seemed so steady and safe, who had just been elected member for Luya, who was going through the usual Leichardt's Town routine, and would be at Tunimbah for their picnic in the spring? Why was he afraid of loving her? Why should she not love him? Why might he not open to her that world of new emotion, of which in very truth she had even now caught a faint glimpse? Why? – Why?

The night sounds mingled with her thoughts and increased the dreamlike feeling. There was the strange pouring-water sound of the swamp pheasant, the little sweet guggle, like water trickling, and there were uncanny 'gr – rr – s' and swishes of wings and harsh screeches as the horses' tread startled the waterfowl in the creek, and the bandicoots and opossums from their lairs. And then from the scrub came the dingo's howl, weird and melancholy, and the curlews were wailing in the Boomerang Swamp. The horses' hoofs sounded pat-pat on the dry grass, and how curious the shadows were of the riders as they went by, like the dream shadows of the fairy story! A wild sense of irresponsibility came over Elsie. She almost laughed aloud at her fancy. She imagined a masked and armed horseman on a coal-black steed dashing into their midst, and bearing her away – away into the black depths of the scrub; away into an unknown life; away from all that was prosaic and commonplace, to a land of intoxicating surprises, of daring deeds, and love rapture. And somehow the masked horseman had Blake's eyes gleaming through his visor.

'Elsie,' Hallett said suddenly, 'I am sure that you are dreadfully tired. You haven't said a word for a quarter of an hour.'

'Haven't I – not said a word? I thought I was saying – oh, all kinds of clever and brilliant things. Yes, I am tired.'

'We shall soon be at home. There are the lights across the creek from the men's huts. Have you enjoyed your day?'

'Enjoyed my day? Yes, I have had a very happy day. I shall always remember to-day.'

'I'm glad of that, since it was I who suggested the picnic, though, to be sure, Blake has had more to do with the carrying out of it. You have been talking to Blake a great deal to-day, Elsie?'

'Yes.'

'Do you like him?'

'Yes – no. I don't know. I think I hate him.'

'Why, Elsie! You began by saying you liked him.'

'I wasn't thinking.'

'Then it is clear that it is not Blake who has made you enjoy to-day. And you ought to tell Lady Horace, for she was talking about him, and she seemed uneasy, and she made me uneasy too,' said Hallett.

'What about?' asked Elsie.

'She thought he was getting a kind of influence over you, and that it would lead to no good. It will be a relief to her to know that you don't like him.'

'No, I don't like him. I will tell Ina so. Frank, tell me, do you think Ina is happy?'

'Honestly I don't think she is. But Lord Horace is a harum-scarum chap, and makes her anxious perhaps. By-and-by he will tone down.'

'I will tell you what I think. Horace is selfish, and he is fickle. He has fads. He had a fad for Australian picturesqueness. He fell in love with Ina because she is Australian, and he thought she was pictur-esque. He would have fallen in love with me if I had allowed it, it would have been all the same to him. Just now he is a little tired of picturesque barbarism. He begins to see that the bush life isn't a picnic, and he is taken up with Mrs. Allanby because she is English, and because his soul begins to hanker a little after the flesh-pots of Egypt, and Mrs. Allanby represents the older civilisation. I have no patience with Horace. Ina would manage him a great deal better if she were not so submissive.'

Frank laughed. 'You don't mean to make that mistake anyhow,' he said.

And just then they got to the creek, and the lights of the head station came into full view, and there was a chorus of dogs rushing out and barking to greet their masters.

Elsie had only a few words with Blake that night. 'Good-night and good-bye,' he said. 'We start at daylight to-morrow, and I shall be in Leichardt's Town by nightfall. Can I do anything for you there?'

'I shall be there very soon myself,' she answered.

'Then I shall very shortly take advantage of your permission, and I shall present myself at Emu Point.'

'You will begin your new duties very soon,' said Elsie.

'Yes; Parliament meets in a few weeks, and as I suppose you know, there is a talk of the Ministry going out on the Address. Will you come to hear my maiden speech, Miss Valliant?'

'I never go to the Ladies' Gallery,' she answered. 'I have never taken any interest in politics.'

'You must take a little interest in them now, however – now that both Hallett and I have gone into public life. Which of us, I wonder, will be first in the Cabinet?'

'You are going in for that?' she asked, in slight surprise.

'When I play a game I always play it thoroughly,' he replied.

'Good-night,' she said abruptly, 'and good-bye.' She left him. Trant waylaid her as she was passing along the verandah to her room in Ina's wake.

'Miss Valliant, I have two things to ask you.'

'What are they, Mr. Trant?'

'Will you let me come and see you in Leichardt's Town?'

'Why, of course. I have told Mr. Blake that he may come.'

'I am not Blake, and Blake isn't me. I shall come on my own account. The second request is that you will give me the first waltz at the May ball.'

'I am afraid that is promised.'

'Has Blake been beforehand with me?' Trant's face darkened. 'I won't stand that.'

'I am under a standing engagement to dance the first waltz at all the May balls with Mr. Frank Hallett.'

'Oh! Is that engagement going to hold after you are married, Miss Valliant?'

'I don't see why it shouldn't.'

'Your husband might object, that's all. Never mind, I'm not jealous of Mr. Hallett. You'll give me the second?'

'Promised, too.'

'Blake?'

She nodded.

'Then the third?'

'Yes, the third if you like; always supposing that his Royal Highness or his Excellency the Governor doesn't want to dance it with me.'

'I have no doubt that his Royal Highness will want to dance with you, and the Governor, too; unless he is a staid old married man. I'll risk it for that dance, and I shall book the engagement.'

The cottage on Emu Point seemed smaller than ever after the comparative magnificence of Tunimbah. Nobody had made the jam, and Mrs. Valliant was plaintively querulous. She was a delicate, rather would-be fine woman, who had once been as pretty as Elsie, but who had never had a tenth part of Elsie's brains and brightness, or of Ina's common sense. She looked a little draggled now, and had lost her hair and her teeth, and the badly fitting false teeth of the Leichardt's Town dentist gave her an artificial appearance.

'I shouldn't have minded about the jam if you had come back engaged to Frank Hallett,' she said.

'But I haven't, mother, and there's an end of it,' said Elsie; 'and I don't see the remotest prospect of being engaged to anybody for a long time to come.'

'It is your own fault,' moaned Mrs. Valliant. 'You have got the name of being a flirt and of encouraging men who are no use in the way of marrying. These town men never are.'

'They are very good to dance with,' said Elsie. 'Don't worry, mother. If the worst comes to the worst, and nobody will marry me, I can always end up as a barmaid, you know. I've got attractive manners – to men, at any rate. At least, so they say.'

'And the women hate you; I hear that old cat, Lady Garfit, has been setting it about that Frank Hallett has thrown you over because you flirted so abominably with that new man, Blake.'

Elsie flushed. 'Lady Garfit is jealous because Rose was out of it, and Frank Hallett has not thrown me over. Oh, mother, let us forget for one whole evening that my mission in life is to marry, and help me to look over my old ball dresses, and see what I can do with them for this winter.'

They were terribly poor, the Valliants, and it was not surprising that Mrs. Valliant should wish to marry off Elsie. No one but Elsie and Ina knew how they had to pinch and save, and to what straits they were sometimes reduced in order that Mrs. Valliant might have a decent black silk, with a high and a square-cut bodice, in which to take her place among the Leichardt's Town ladies at such functions as called for her attendance. No one but Ina and Elsie knew how the girls used to toil in the mornings to get their house work done to have the afternoons free for their visitors and for their flirtations, and how late they would sit up at nights to make the pretty, simple dresses which Elsie and Ina wore at the balls and garden parties, and which ill-natured mothers of less attractive daughters declared were bought at expensive shops with borrowed money, which Elsie's husband would one day have to pay back. But as a matter of fact it was Mrs. Valliant's boast that they had never owed a penny, and that Ina had gone to her husband with as respectable a trousseau as any other Leichardt's Town girl could have had. Ina's wedding, however, had crippled the widow's resources for some time to come, and there was little enough wherewith to fit Elsie out for her winter campaign. Yet in spite of their poverty they got along happily enough, and Elsie sang over her work, and Mrs. Valliant, in gloves, swept the floors, and made the beds, and did the clear-starching and ironing so beautifully that the Valliant girls' white frocks were the admiration of the town.

It was a pretty cottage in its way, though it was so small – only four rooms and a verandah and lean-to kitchen, but it had a little garden which Peter, the Kanaka boy, looked after – a garden with flaming poinsettia shrubs, and some oleander trees, and a passion-creeper arbour, and a small plantation of bananas, and some lantana shrubs growing on the bank which shelved down to the river. It was a great thing having this tiny bit of frontage on the river, for the girls had had a boat, which Elsie now managed alone, and which saved her a good deal in omnibus fares and ferryage. The Leichardt River winds about like a great S, and beyond Emu Point there lies the North Side, as it is called, where are all the grand shops and the Houses of Parliament, and Government House and the Clubs, and beyond, again, is the South Side, where smaller folk dwell. The big people have mostly houses with large gardens along the north bank of the river, or off Emu Point. The Valliant cottage was not in the fashionable part of Emu Point, but lay in the neck, and was approached through a paddock of gum-trees, once part of a large property, now gradually being cut up and covered with little wooden houses, in which then lived the genteel poor of Leichardt's Town society.

The verandah at Riverside, as the Valliants' cottage was named, had a trellis of Cape jasmine and thunbergia, and in one corner of it Elsie had established herself with her sewing machine and a garden table, on which were her books and workbasket. The soft April wind from the river fanned her cheeks, and had a touch of chill. Winter was close at hand. The poinsettia was beginning to flaunt its red leaves, and the bougainvillea that covered the verandah roof had a tinge of pale mauve. Elsie was working diligently, and she made a pretty picture as she bent over the machine. She was so busy, and the treadle of the machine made such a noise that she did not hear the garden gate click, and it was not till a shadow came between her and the light that she looked up and saw Blake.

'How do you do, Miss Valliant?' he said quietly. 'I should have been here before, but that I did not get to Leichardt's Town quite as soon as I expected; that is, I got here the evening of the day I left Tunimbah, but I had to go away again immediately.'

Elsie got up from the machine and gave him her hand. She was oddly confused. 'I am sorry that my mother is not at home: she has gone over to the North Side. Will you sit here, or would you rather go in?'

'I would much rather sit here, if I may?' He drew forward a canvas chair. 'I don't recognise you in your new character. I never saw you sewing before. What is it – a gown? It looks very pretty.' He touched the delicate fabric which Elsie was hemming and gathering into frills.

'You will see me wearing it,' she said; 'and I wonder if you will like me in it – white muslin. It sounds very innocent and Miss Edgeworthish, doesn't it? but it is to be glorified white muslin – copied from the print of somebody's picture – a Romney, I think.'

'Yes, Romney would have found you a delightful model – almost as good as Lady Hamilton, and he would have given all the soft richness of your colouring.'

At his compliment Elsie recovered her self-possession. 'Never mind my colouring. Tell me what news there is while I work. I am going to sew all these strips together, if you don't mind.'

'No, I don't mind at all. I like to see a woman working, especially if she is worth watching. One can stare at her without seeming rude, and then it makes one feel more at home. I have some news for you, Miss Valliant; news which ought to interest you very much. I don't think you can have heard it, for they had got it at the Club just as I left.'

'What is it? Is the date fixed for the first Government House "At Home"? I don't know of anything else which will interest me particularly.'

'Really, not even Mr. Frank Hallett's election?'

'He has got in, then? Of course I knew he would get in.'

'Yes, he has got in, and by a good majority. I am honestly glad. By all the laws of justice he ought to have beaten me at Goondi.'

'Why, I suppose the best man wins, wherever it is.'

'I am afraid that in this case it wasn't the best man winning. If he had been an Irishman, he would have had a walk over. The patriotic spirit was roused, and I got the benefit of it. Well, you will see now how we shall fight in the Legislative Assembly. Parliament opens, you know, next week.'

There was another click at the gate. Blake cursed the untimely visitor.

It was Captain Macpherson, who, since the races on the Luya, had developed a tenderness for Elsie. He looked a little cross at the sight of Blake, who scarcely stirred from his seat. Captain Macpherson threw himself on the edge of the verandah, with an air of easy familiarity. He had brought an offering, in the shape of banana candy, and Elsie nibbled at it daintily.

'I wonder you aren't ashamed to come to town. Oughtn't you be looking after Moonlight?'

'Moonlight is the devil,' exclaimed Captain Macpherson. 'I beg your pardon, Miss Valliant, but what can you say of a fellow who disappears from mortal ken on the Luya with the whole army of police and trackers on the look out for him, and then all of a sudden turns up, mask, black horse and everything else, close by Wallaroo; and when the moon is new? Nobody expects Moonlight to be on the rampage unless it's full moon.'

'Ah!' said Blake indifferently. 'And the police have no clue?'

'None in the world, and never will have, unless one of the gang turns traitor.'

'That's my belief, though perhaps I am not the person to state it.'

Another visitor appeared, one who had come in a boat to the landing, and now approached through the banana grove, a young man, very neatly got up, and with a town air, and an evident determination to be equal to all circumstances. He was, in fact, a clerk in the Post Office, and was also honorary secretary to a new club. His ostensible reason for coming was, in fact, to give the information that the committee of this same club had fixed the date for their house-warming ball, and that it would take place the night but one after the Government House birthday ball. He had brought his offering, too, in the shape of two first-blown camellias of the year, which, he said, he had got from the curator of the Botanical Gardens. Elsie accepted the flowers graciously, and took them up and looked at them alternately with her nibblings of Captain Macpherson's banana candy. She seemed to take the offerings for granted, and Blake could not help saying, 'I see that it is the custom to lay propitiatory tribute at the feet of the goddess.'

'That is a very horrid way of putting it,' said Elsie, flushing up. 'They call this sort of thing my verandah receptions,' she added. 'A lot of gentlemen always turn up when there is anything going on.'

One or two others turned up later, and Elsie went in and came out presently, followed by the Kanaka boy with a tray and the tea-things. Then Elsie requested Mr. Saunders, the young man in the Post Office, to cut some bread and butter, and there was some joking about the next cake-making day, and it transpired that on one occasion Elsie's admirers had been turned into amateur cooks, and had helped to bake a batch of biscuits. Certainly there was very little formality about Elsie's verandah receptions. The Kanaka boy in his gardening clothes stood gravely waiting to get hot water as required, and Elsie requested her guests to help themselves from the various bunches of bananas hanging from the verandah rafters. 'Riverside is famous for its bananas,' she said to Blake; 'bananas and strawberry guavas, those are our attractions, not counting the chucky-chucky tree by the river. Will you come some time and help me to get chucky-chuckies?'

Mr. Holmes, one of Elsie's army of detrimentals, proposed a pull on the river before the weather got cold, and Elsie gravely made the appointment and accepted an invitation to meet somebody else on the North Side, and get an ice at the Leichardt's Town Gunter's. About sunset Mrs. Valliant appeared. She made Blake think of the descriptions he had read of the American mother. She was a personage equally unimportant in the general scheme of things.

CHAPTER XVI

Trant's Warning

Every one said that this was going to be one of the gayest winters there had ever been in Leichardt's Town. The Birthday Ball was heralded by several smaller entertainments. The Garfits gave an impromptu dance, to which they were compelled to invite Elsie, though before Ina's marriage she had not been asked to the Garfits' less formal entertainments. The Prydes had a picnic, which wound up with a dance, and the arrival of the new Governor was an occasion for social functions of a public character. Lord Horace and Ina came down and established themselves in an hotel boarding-house on Emu Point, and Blake found it convenient also to take up his temporary abode there, though he had to cross the river to get to the Houses of Parliament. A great many gentlemen lodged at Fermoy's, as it was called, its proprietor being a certain widowed Mrs. Fermoy, who took a motherly interest in her lodgers and carefully made it known that she had no matrimonial intentions. Mr. and Mrs. Jem Hallett did not patronise Fermoy's. They took a small furnished house on the North Side, and Mrs. Jem at once made it evident that she intended to belong to the Government House set, she was so ultra-English in all her ways. Frank Hallett naturally stayed with them, but very few days passed on which he did not on some pretext or other find his way across the river to Emu Point. Indeed, at this time Miss Valliant's admirers were a small source of revenue to the proprietors of the Emu Point ferry, there were so many of them, and even if they did not actually call at Riverside they haunted the Point in the hope of meeting Elsie on her way to and from the North Side. They were certainly a great worry to Mrs. Valliant, who thought that the detrimentals kept off desirable suitors, and who was afraid that Frank Hallett's constancy would give way under the strain to which Elsie subjected it. She consoled herself by the reflection, since Elsie gave her the assurance, that the two understood each other. In any case it was useless to try and curb Elsie's humour.

The girl was in a wild mood. She had never before rushed so eagerly into excitement. She seemed to live for amusement, getting through her household duties by dint of rising at an unearthly hour in order that she might rush over to the North Side on pretence of shopping, and stroll about the streets and the gardens with Minnie Pryde, seeking whom she might entrap into her toils. It was not a very dignified or a very womanly manner of proceeding, and, as Elsie sometimes told herself, a nice girl, like Rose Garfit, for instance, would have behaved very differently. 'But I'm not a nice girl,' Elsie said passionately one day to Ina, who had been remonstrating with her upon her conduct. 'A nice girl would never have done the things I've done. And what does it matter, Ina? If I disgust Frank Hallett – well, so much the better. I think that is why I do it.'

But Frank Hallett was always the same, always devoted, always timid of obtruding his devotion, very quiet sometimes, often sad, but ready at any moment to answer at Elsie's beck.

He was a good deal occupied just now with his new duties. There was a great measure coming – a great measure for Leichardt's Land, involving the destinies, so its opponents said, of that promising young colony, and if it were carried – indeed so also its opponents said – involving the immediate ruin and destruction of the colony's best interests. The question was one of a loan to which Sir James Garfit's Ministry had pledged themselves, and it was whispered loudly that Sir James Garfit's Ministry would be defeated.

Elsie was not at the Opening of the Assembly, which was performed in all manner of state by the new Governor, a prosy, rather pompous old man, with a wife who had set herself the difficult task of reforming the morals and manners of the Leichardtstonians. Elsie listened to the salvo of guns which announced the conclusion of the ceremony while she ironed a white frock to wear at a concert the next evening, to which she was going with the Prydes. She felt a little out of things and cross because Minnie Pryde was more favoured than she was – to say nothing of Rose Garfit. The thought flashed across her mind that perhaps next year she might be taking her place as the wife of one of the Ministers in that august pageant, and that Minnie Pryde would be nowhere, and even Rose Garfit obliged to give way to her.

'I wonder if he *will* do anything,' she said to herself. 'He is certain to be asked to join the Ministry, if Sir James Garfit keeps in, and Mr. Leeke really resigns for him.'

Mr. Leeke was the Minister for Mines, and he was in precarious health and anxious to get to England, and it was generally supposed among the squatting politicians that he was keeping his post only till Frank Hallett was ready to step into his shoes.

Elsie put the iron back on the stove, and took up another, testing its heat against her delicate face. Her eyes took a far away look, as she stood for a moment or two with the iron in her hand. 'I wonder if he will remember the violets?' she murmured, but it was not of Frank Hallett she was thinking.

She was to go with Ina to the House that afternoon, when Frank Hallett would move the debate on the Speech. It had been said that Blake would speak also. Ina and her husband had asked her to lunch with them at Fermoy's, and she wondered whether there was any likelihood of Blake being there also. She knew that there was no chance of either Blake or Frank Hallett calling that forenoon, but she expected Minnie Pryde, and perhaps some of her various admirers, who would give her the news of the opening.

Minnie Pryde came early. She came fortified with banana candy, and sat down on the verandah steps prepared for what she called a 'jabber.'

'The Garfits have fastened on to Lady Stukeley,' she announced, 'and so has Mrs. Jem Hallett. I think she must have got her dress from England.'

'Who, Mrs. Jem – yes, I know she did – why?'

'It was the very cut of Lady Stukeley's. Oh, Elsie, why can't we have our things from England? I declare I'd marry anybody who would let me have a box every year from London. . . . There were a lot of new men there,' continued Minnie, 'several new Western members, and then the private secretary and aide-de-camp – only he is married, and his wife *is* a dowdy, I can tell you. Well, I can tell you, too, that I was rather glad you weren't at the Opening,' said Miss Pryde, with an air of fine candour. 'The new men wouldn't have paid so much attention to me. You always cut us poor things out. As it was, I rather enjoyed myself.' Just now there was a truce between Elsie and Minnie Pryde. Minnie thought it more diplomatic, on the whole, to be good friends with her rival.

'Well, I'm glad of that,' said Elsie, a little disdainfully. 'I don't know why you should say that I cut you out.'

'With a certain sort of man,' replied Miss Pryde, weighing her

words as though she were mentally discriminating. 'There are some
men who might like a girl like me best. But the English sort – and
some of the Australian, for of course the Halletts are Australian –
and men of a mysterious kind – heroes of romance – such as Mr.
Blake – go in for you. You are more – more, well, I don't know how
to put it – more like a girl in a book.'

Elsie laughed, not ill-pleased. 'And Mr. Blake? – he was there, of
course?'

'Of course. He came in with the rest when they were sent for, like
a lot of school-boys, and stood at the Bar of the House. How funny
it seems; I don't know why they shouldn't have been there all the
time. And then the Governor read his speech, with the aide-de-camp
in a tight red coat and the private secretary in another on each side
of him, and Captain Briggs, of the surveying schooner, in a blue
uniform – to represent the Naval forces of the colony, I suppose –
and Captain Macpherson for the military! Oh, it was funny, I can tell
you. I felt inclined to call out to Macpherson, "What about Moonlight?" – and Lady Stukeley, who was in green velvet, and *such* a
diamond star fastening her bonnet, nodded when the Governor came
to anything impressive. And afterwards, when all the swells had gone,
we went over the House. And Mr. Blake came and spoke to me, and
asked me where you were.'

'And you told him, I suppose, that since I didn't happen to have a
father or brother or cousin or very great friend in the Cabinet, I was
naturally not invited. Are you going to hear the speeches this evening,
Minnie?'

'Well, I will, if Ina will let me go with her,' said Miss Pryde, 'though
I'm not as a rule keen on speeches. But somebody said that both Mr.
Blake and Frank Hallett are going to speak, and that there's to be
ruction over the Loan Clause. I should like to see Rose Garfit's face
if Sir James is beaten.'

It was settled that Minnie Pryde should walk with Elsie to Fermoy's
and see Lady Horace about five o'clock, and in the meantime Mrs.
Valliant went on with the ironing, and Elsie consulted Minnie about
her dress for the May ball and other festivities. They were in the
middle of their finery when Mr. Dominic Trant appeared, and he was
followed by several other of Elsie's and Miss Pryde's admirers. On
this afternoon, when the Public Offices closed early, there were always
sure to be some young gentlemen at Riverside.

Mr. Trant attached himself at once to Elsie. He had puzzled her
a little by his manner of late. Sometimes he had been sullen, even

morose, sometimes tragic, sometimes he was ardent, and his dark eyes glowed with a sort of fierce excitement which was almost alarming. But Elsie had been a good deal taken up with other thoughts, and had not paid much attention to Mr. Trant. He amused and distracted her, and fed her vanity, and that was all.

To-day he was in a tragic mood.

'When are you going back to Baròlin?' Elsie asked.

'You can answer that question better than I,' he said.

'How?'

'It is you who keep me in Leichardt's Town. Do you suppose I care in the least for this fooling about hotel billiard-rooms and tea-parties, and for philandering up and down Victoria Street? And yet I hang about Grandoni's half the morning, and eat ices and drink sherry cobblers in a way that plays the deuce with my digestion, on the chance of your turning up anywhere about; and I haunt the ferry steps, and I parade up and down the bunya walk in the Botanical Gardens – all for you.'

'That is very foolish of you, Mr. Trant.'

'Is it foolish?' He bent towards her. They were sitting on the boat-house steps in the banana grove, whither Elsie had gone on pretext of finding some still ungathered 'Lady's fingers' which had ripened on the stem. Elsie was now daintily peeling one of the bananas, and Trant watched her with fixed eyes. 'I don't think it is so foolish, though it may seem so to you now, Miss Valliant, because you don't care for me. Do you suppose that I am not aware of that? If you care for any one in the world it is for Blake –'

'Mr. Trant!' Elsie half rose. 'You have no right to say such a thing.'

He put out his hand to detain her. 'No, don't go, don't be indignant. After all, it is only what everybody else is saying, and I know of two chaps who have a bet on as to whether you will marry Blake or Frank Hallett within the year. I'm out of the running altogether, you see, but for all that I'm not afraid to enter the lists, and I think I've as good a chance as either of them; though you won't let me tell you how fond I am of you.'

'Oh, please go on, Mr. Trant. It is very interesting. I don't think anybody ever, ever made love to me quite in this way.'

'I'm not making love to you just now. That will come later, and when I do make love to you I warn you that I shall be a tornado. I shall sweep you off your feet; you'll *have* to listen to me. I'm only stating facts now. Of course I know very well that Blake is much more the kind of fellow for a girl to fall in love with than I am. I don't imagine for a moment that you will ever fall in love with me. I shall make my *coup* in a different way. I shall carry you off.'

Elsie laughed outright. 'Oh! really, Mr. Trant! Like a Border knight, or Moonlight –?'

'Yes,' said he grimly, 'like Moonlight.'

'And how shall you manage it? Will you appear booted and spurred at one of the Leichardt's Town tennis parties and seize me – gallop off with me in front of you? Or will you waylay our jingle when we are going to the Government House ball? Or will you wait till we are on the Luya again, and imprison me in some stronghold in one of the gorges?'

'That would probably be the wisest thing to do,' answered Trant, still grimly. 'We shall see, Miss Valliant. Many a true word is spoken in jest, you know. In the meantime I don't mean to bother you except for a dance or two now and then, and there's no occasion for me to leave Leichardt's Town just yet. I shall wait and watch the game. Only listen to this, I've warned you once, remember, and it's disinterested of me to warn you again. Don't let Blake fool you. He will never marry anyone; he has got other things to think about. He only cares about women for the sake of amusement; but is quite capable of making you believe that he is madly in love with you just to cut out Frank Hallett, or for the excitement of the thing, and then he will throw you over as he has thrown over other women before you.'

Elsie turned quite pale. 'Mr. Trant, you amuse me rather when you talk like that, it is unlike other people. But there are limits even to amusement, and I beg that you will not speak to me of either Mr. Blake or Mr. Frank Hallett in that way again.'

'Very well,' said Trant doggedly, 'I have warned you, remember. As I said, it is against my own interest. My game is to let Blake have his way. After that will come my turn, and then I shall clear the course by sheer strength of will. It will be a *coup d'état*. You know I told you that I always succeeded in what I had set my mind on.'

'I congratulate you.'

'I don't intend to live this sort of life for much longer, Miss Valliant. I don't mean to bury myself at Baròlin. I have done that for a purpose; I wanted to make money. When I marry, my wife will be in a position to enjoy herself, and to see the world.'

'That will be very nice for your wife, Mr. Trant, when you have one.' Elsie got up. 'Do you know I think it is time for me to get ready to walk to Mrs. Fermoy's. I am going to have tea there, and afterwards Ina is to take me to hear the speeches.'

CHAPTER XVII

●

In the Ladies' Gallery

The Ladies' Gallery was crowded. It had been set about that Blake was an orator, that his speech would be a stirring one, and already the picturesque personality of the man had impressed Leichardt's Town society. Besides this, it was known that Frank Hallett would move the Address, and people were interested in Frank Hallett as a coming Minister.

There is no tiresome grating in front of the Ladies' Gallery in Colonial Houses of Parliament, and any member who chose to look up might have easily recognised the stolid features of Lady Garfit and the placid pink and white prettiness of her daughter, and just behind, they might have seen Ina Gage's delicate, rather pensive face, Miss Minnie Pryde's black eyes and brunette complexion, and Elsie Valliant's more distinguished beauty. Both Blake and Frank Hallett did look up, and Elsie noted the different bearing of the two men, each of whom was to make his maiden effort in that assembly. Frank was evidently nervous – grave, absorbed, and hiding embarrassment under a mask of reserve. Blake was indifferent, unconcerned, always giving a sense of latent power, always with a certain kingliness of bearing, and at the same time a certain dare-devilry of which Elsie was keenly conscious. It seemed to her that his eyes sought hers, and that his face changed ever so slightly when their glances met. Her heart was beating strangely. She gave a violent start when Frank Hallett's voice sounded behind her.

'Are you quite comfortable?' he asked.

'Yes, quite, thank you,' she answered.

'I am afraid you find it rather dull up here,' he said, 'and it will be a few minutes yet before we get to my part of the business.'

'You are looking rather pale. Are you nervous?'

'Horribly nervous. I am sick with nervousness.'

'But that won't last.'

'No,' he said, 'once I begin I shall get on well enough. It's the interval of waiting that sets my nerves going. It's like lying in the trenches, you know, before the enemy have come up. Now I must get back to my place.'

He ran downstairs. He had hardly settled into his place when the Speaker began to read the speech which the Governor had delivered that morning. The instant the reading was done Hallett got on his legs and set himself to his task of moving the reply to the Address. Elsie went through a moment of breathless anxiety while he was standing, waiting before he spoke, and then she heard his voice, and felt reassured. After a minute or two of nervousness Hallett went on with his speech composedly and well. Elsie did not care very much about the substance of the speech, but it seemed to her to be well composed, and was delivered with the fluency which only just stopped short of being monotonous. It went over a great variety of topics, to which she paid little attention, but she could hear that it was received with great favour on Hallett's side of the house, and with respectful attention on the other. She was glad to find that there were no ironical cheers or bursts of interruption, not, perhaps, quite realising that a speech which escapes from these tributes of opposition is seldom a speech likely to make a name for the orator.

Hallett sat down amid very cordial applause from the house in general. She could see that everyone was glad to find the young man doing well in his first attempt, and she felt all but delighted at the result. He had certainly not failed. On the contrary, he had evidently succeeded. It was exactly what she had expected of him, and she was content with him. Perhaps she could have wished for something a little more dazzling, something thrilling, like that speech she had heard from the verandah of the hotel at Goondi, of which she had been able to catch only the voice, not the words. But still to wish that Hallett should be dazzling would be to wish that Hallett were not Hallett, only somebody else.

Then a rough and mumbling voice was heard, and she became aware that somebody was seconding Hallett's motion. This was a poor and scrambling performance, and had only the merit of being quickly done. Then the Speaker put the question, and then the Leader of the Opposition spoke.

Mr. Torbolton made a severe attack on the policy of the Government on all its lines. The girl could recognise by the sound and movement of the house that the attack was a heavy one, and told severely. Then there was a reply from the Ministerial side, delivered by Mr. Leeke, the Minister of Mines, into whose shoes it was said Frank Hallett was to step, and she was getting into rather a drowsy condition when suddenly the Ministerial speech came to an end, and in an instant she heard again the voice that had thrilled her at Goondi. She saw that a new speaker had arisen from the Opposition side, and bending eagerly forward she recognised the face and figure of Blake, and in another five minutes the girl had learned for the first time in her life the difference between a born debater and a man who makes a good speech. Blake's voice sometimes fell to such subtle modulations that it seemed to caress the listening ear, and at other times rang out with the vibrating strength of passion, or hissed with the scornful tone of sarcasm. The assembly which had listened with such patient approval to Hallett went wild over Blake. From the Ministerial side there came angry interruptions and contradictions. From the bench of the Opposition came bursts of enthusiastic cheers and shouts of delighted laughter. She hardly knew what it was all about, but she knew well enough that it was a vivid and pitiless attack upon the policy of the Government, and that the Ministers seemed to quail under its effect.

Some member standing in the Ladies' Gallery said to Lady Horace when Blake sat down, 'Well, now, Lady Horace, whether we like it or whether we don't, I think we must call that a great speech.'

Sir James Garfit rose at once, thus paying the quite unusual tribute to Mr. Blake's speech by rising at that period of the evening to reply to a new member. When the Premier began his speech, Elsie's interest in the debate collapsed.

Lord Horace, who was in the men's gallery, separated from that in which his wife and Elsie sat, leaned excitedly over the railing.

'I say, Elsie, Blake's stunnin'. I wish it was our man. In the face of that there's no use in consoling ourselves with the reflection that dear Frank is safe and respectable.'

A little later Elsie knew almost without turning round that Blake had come into the gallery and was behind her. She turned to him in her quick impulsive way, and said, 'Oh, why didn't you tell me you could speak like that?'

'Did I do it well, really?'

'Yes, splendidly,' she said. 'The house felt it. I never heard a real speech before.'

'I am glad of that,' he said, quietly bending over her – 'glad, tha' is, that you were pleased. I wanted to please you.'

There was a short interval, in which the House emptied, and the party in the Ladies' Gallery went out and snatched a sort of dinner at an hotel not far off. After they came back the debate droned dully on. Blake came up again, and lingered in the gallery. Most of the time he talked in whispers to Elsie, and more than once Lady Garfit turned angrily and frowned on him.

It was now nine o'clock.

'I am sorry,' said Blake, 'that there is no terrace here, where I can ask you to come and have coffee.'

'No terrace?' repeated Ina vaguely.

Lord Horace, who had caught the remark, looked annoyed. 'Blake means the terrace of the House of Commons. Don't ask Waveryng what it means, or he will think I have married a –'

'An Australian girl, who doesn't know anything about your fashionable London life,' put in Elsie hotly. 'You had better prepare Lord and Lady Waveryng, Horace, for the depth of barbarism they'll be plunged in here, otherwise they mightn't survive the shock of an introduction to Ina and me.'

'When do the Waveryngs arrive?' asked Blake.

'Lady Stukeley told me at the Opening to-day that she had heard from my sister, and that they would very likely be here for the May ball. They are going to stay at Government House,' said Lord Horace a little sulkily. He was annoyed because Lady Stukeley had not taken quite kindly to Ina, and that was Elsie's fault, for Lady Garfit had prejudiced the lady of Government House against these forward Australian belles.

Elsie got up. At that moment Frank Hallett entered the gallery. She turned to him. 'What is going to happen? I am tired, I want to get back; Ina is tired, too. If Horace likes to stay, I dare say somebody will see us across the river.'

'I wish I could,' exclaimed Hallett, 'but Leeke is going to speak; ought not to leave the House.'

'Since I am not so anxious to hear Mr. Leeke, Lady Horace, please let me take you to Fermoy's,' said Blake.

Lord Horace announced his intention of going to the club. It was Frank Hallett who escorted Ina down the stairs. She turned her pale face to his with a sisterly smile. 'Frank, I haven't had an opportunity of saying a word. You did speak splendidly.'

'Thank you, Ina; you don't mind my calling you Ina just once, do you? I feel horribly down to-night. I'm nowhere beside Blake. He is the coming man.'

'Is it Elsie who has vexed you, Frank?'

'Oh no; not Elsie, not, at least, any more than usual. But she has altered somehow lately. Don't you see it?'

'Yes, I see it. But Elsie was always capricious.'

'You know I care for Elsie more than for anyone in this world, Ina.'

'Yes, I know that.'

'I'm not jealous of Blake – not in the ordinary way. I have been keeping myself a little aloof from Elsie lately on purpose. She has given me her promise that if her prince, as she puts it, doesn't come along within a year, she will marry me –'

'Ah! Elsie's prince!' Ina laughed nervously.

'Ina, a horrible fear has struck me these last days. Suppose that Blake should turn out to be Elsie's prince.'

'Oh no, no!' Ina cried. 'I cannot bear that man. There's something about him; I can't describe the feeling he gives me. He is not true.'

'He is good-looking, and he is a gentleman; and I believe, judging from his speech to-night, and the effect it has had, that he will very soon make a mark. I don't know anything against him. Why shouldn't she marry him? If she is in love with him I shall not put myself forward – I shall not stand in the way. I shall wish her happiness with all my heart, and I shall always remain her friend.'

'And yet you said that you had a horrible fear. You can't help feeling as I do about Mr. Blake.'

'Ah! Frank cried, 'I am human, and I love her. It's because of that that I want her to have her chance, and Blake, too. I won't let myself think ill of him, if I can help, but a fellow is a man after all, Ina.'

They went out into the night. Minnie Pryde came beside Lady Horace. 'I know that you two, anyhow, won't be talking sentiment,' she said. 'I saw pretty soon that I had better make myself scarce, as far as the other two are concerned.'

Ina and Frank both laughed discordantly. 'Oh! I forgot,' cried Miss Pryde. 'Don't mind me, Mr. Hallett, and look here, oughtn't you go back and listen to Mr. Leeke? He had got up just as we left.'

Hallett bade good-night to Ina, and paused for a moment to shake hands with Elsie. It seemed to him that she and Blake were lingering a good deal behind.

'Good-night,' Elsie said sweetly, 'and please when you get into the Ministry, see that I have a place at the Opening.'

They had got out of the lighted space round the House of Assembly, and were walking down a dim street bordered with houses and gardens, which led to the ferry. On one side lay the Botanical Gardens. At the end of the road they had left, and beyond the House of Assembly, were the great gates of Government House with their flaring lamps. The heavy fragrance of datura blossoms weighted the air. Ina and Minnie Pryde walked on alone.

'Won't you take my arm?' said Blake.

She put her hand within his arm, and they walked on for a few moments in silence. He put his hand out and touched her cloak. Are you sure that you are warm enough? The nights are beginning to be cold.'

'Yes,' said Elsie. There was an odd restrained tenderness in his manner which set her pulses tingling.

'Did you miss me to-day?' he asked suddenly.

'Yes,' she answered.

'But you had your usual crowd, your verandah reception; you didn't want me?'

Elsie did not reply for a minute. 'It was too early for my verandah reception,' she said coldly. 'No,' she exclaimed presently in a hard tone, 'I didn't want you in the least. It was a day off, you know. I wasn't playing the game. I hadn't got to be thinking all the time of the next move.'

'The next move,' he said seriously, 'what is it to be? We have gathered chuckie-chuckies and sat on the boat-house steps, and danced, and sat out, and ridden, and done all the usual things that belong to the game of flirtation. There remains only one yet of the minor experiences.'

'The minor experiences?'

'The experiences which belong to the initiatory stage of flirtation. I have found you perfectly charming, horribly dangerous. I confess it.'

Elsie turned her soft face towards him, and their eyes met. He could see by the faint light of a growing moon that she blushed.

'Yes, horribly dangerous,' he repeated.

'What is the other experience?' she asked.

'A row by moonlight. I should prefer it with you alone, but I suppose the proprieties forbid. Shall it be Lady Horace or Miss Pryde who chaperons us?'

'I will go for a row with you the next time you come in the evening. I am glad you warned me that it is part of the game.'

They had reached the ferry steps. Miss Minnie Pryde called a fairy musical 'O-o-ver.' The plash of the oars sounded nearer and nearer as the boat approached. Blake stepped on to the bow, and held out his hand to each of the ladies. One or two others were crossing as well. The stern was filled, and he took his seat in the bows. Several of the passengers were from Fermoy's, and knew Lady Horace and her sister. The talk fell on the evening's debate. Mr. Anderson, one of the young men, praised Hallett's speech.

'I tell you what it is though, Lady Horace,' exclaimed another, 'that chap Blake beat him into fits. I say, can you tell me who he is? They call him Monte Cristo. He chucks half-sovereigns to the railway porters, and rides thoroughbreds fit for a king.'

'Oh, hush!' murmured Ina faintly, and turned the conversation with some rapid question. Blake had probably not heard the remark – at least so Elsie imagined. He sat still in the bow, looking like a Monte Cristo indeed, only his eyes were tenderer, surely, than those of Dumas' hero. Elsie's young bosom fluttered. At last she was in the land of romance. And yet there was a dim terror in the background of her maidenly satisfaction – a terror of unknown forces which might at any moment break from their chain.

When they had got out of the boat and mounted the ferry hill there was a halt. Fermoy's lay in one direction, Riverside in another. It was only a little walk to Riverside, and the sisters had often gone across the paddock alone. To-night Ina seemed particularly anxious that Elsie should wait at Fermoy's for Lord Horace to escort her.

'Then I might wait all night,' said Miss Valliant. 'No, thank you, Ina, I shall go straight home, and you get to your bed.'

'You will let me see you to your gate,' said Blake, in a low tone. Mr. Anderson stepped forward, entreating that he might be the favoured escort. Minnie Pryde, who lived quite at the end of the Point, had secured her own particular swain, who was also a lodger at Fermoy's.

'No,' said Elsie firmly. 'Mr. Blake is going to take me, and you, please, look after my sister. Good-night, Ina. Good-night, Minnie. Ina, I shall come down to-morrow and see how we are going to the Garfit's.'

The Garfit dance was to take place on the morrow.

Elsie and Blake were alone in the soft scented night. Many of the eucalyptus in the paddock had been left standing. Elsie said that they made her think of the Bush and of the Luya.

'And, perhaps, of your future home,' said Blake.

'Perhaps,' said Elsie coldly. 'If it is going to be my fate to marry a bushman.'

'Do you know what your fate ought to be?' said Blake. 'You should marry a rich man, who would take you to Europe and place you in a position to which your beauty entitles you. You should have everything that the world can give to a beautiful woman. You should be caressed, flattered, fêted, adorned, surrounded by every luxury, and set in a fitting frame.'

'Thank you,' said Elsie; 'you draw a pleasant picture.'

'But that will not be your fate,' Blake went on. 'You will marry Frank Hallett, or another. You will never rise above the level of prosperous Australian Philistinism. You will never taste the finest aroma of romance and of enjoyment. You will never know the fascination of danger. You will never experience the subtle emotions which make one day better worth living than a lifetime.'

'Have you gone through all this?'

'In part. Life has always been for me a drama. I started with the intention of getting all I could out of it. I think I have succeeded pretty well, though it has been as much bad as good. I don't care in the least about life as life. But, as I told you one day, there is something in me fierce and untamable, and I confess also morbid, which craves for some other outlet than that of the decorous Philistine routine.'

'And so you contrive to get that outlet?'

'Yes.'

'I can't imagine how! Surely not in the life I see you lead?'

'There are excitements even in the life which you see me lead,' he answered evasively.

'Such as this evening, for instance. But that can mean nothing. It must be easy for you to excel among such men as are in the Assembly here.'

'You should not disparage them. The Governor was telling me that he has been deeply impressed by the ability and statesmanlike foresight of Sir James Garfit. Look, Miss Valliant. Did you ever see the river so beautiful? What would you not give to have a row to-night?'

He pointed to the shining flood, flecked by the moon's rays, and with the mysterious shadows of the bamboos on the opposite shore mirrored on its surface.

'If it had been the days when Ina and I were alone here, we should probably unmoor the boat and go.'

'May I not be Lady Horace for to-night?'

'Ah! Ina would not do it now. She has grown so staid since her marriage. Horace would tell her that it was not the sort of thing an English lady would do.'

'Come!' He held open the wicket which led into the garden. The banana trees looked weird in the moonlight. The cottage was all dark. There was a light only in Mrs. Valliant's room. At the click of the gate, the casement was opened, and Mrs. Valliant said 'Elsie.'

'Yes, mother, I am coming presently. Mr. Blake has brought me home, and I have an irresistible longing just to go down to the boathouse and see the moonlight on the water.'

'Can't you see it from the verandah?' said Mrs. Valliant weakly.

Elsie laughed. 'Poor mother! I shall come presently, dear. You can't think how hot and stuffy it was in the gallery. I couldn't sleep if I went to bed now.'

'Oh, well!' said Mrs. Valliant resignedly, and she closed the window.

The whole proceeding struck Blake as amazing. The mother was more amazing than the daughter. He was still more astonished when, as they walked along the little path, Elsie turned to him, and said abruptly 'Good-night.'

'But you are not going in?'

'No, but I don't want you. Good-night.'

'But the river, and the row?'

'Good gracious! What do you think of me?' she cried fiercely. 'I understand you very well. You are playing your game; I am playing mine. Good-night.'

She walked on, and disappeared among the bananas, without again turning her head. He heard her go down the steps. He heard the sound of the boat pushing off. He saw her a few minutes later seated with the oars, rowing to the opposite side. It was quite bright enough for him to observe the grace of her movement, and the poise of her figure, and of her flower-like head upturned to the night.

She was on the water about a quarter of an hour, long enough to row across and back again. She gave a start when she saw him standing just where she had left him.

'Why didn't you go home?'

'Because I wanted to see that you got in without any harm coming to you. I couldn't insist upon going with you, but I could at least give myself the satisfaction of watching for you.'

'Thank you.' She held out her hand. And then he saw that her eyes were wet, and that there was a great tear-drop on her cheek.

'Elsie!' he exclaimed. 'You have been crying?'

'Yes,' she cried recklessly, 'and do you know why? Because I, too, have something in me that is fierce and untamable, and because I am not like you – I can find no outlet in my life.'

She darted from him and ran into the house. He walked slowly back to Fermoy's through the paddock.

CHAPTER XVIII

---•---

'Ninon, Ninon, Que Fais-tu De La Vie?'

Elsie wore at the Garfit's the white dress that Blake had seen her stitching. She had copied it from an old print. It hung in soft folds to her feet, and she had a little frilled fichu of muslin knotted at her breast, and where it was knotted there was a big bunch of Parma violets, and she carried a large bouquet of violets in her hand. The violets had been sent to the cottage that morning. Elsie knew who had sent them, and perhaps the sending of the violets had something to do with her radiance. Everyone said that Elsie had never looked so beautiful.

The Garfits had a large verandahed house some little way out of town on the north side. They always gave pleasant parties. Sir James was a jovial, red-faced person, who on these occasions dropped the cares of State as though they had been a garment. Rose was always amiable and ladylike, and Lady Garfit was at her best in her own house.

Sir James was, however, on this evening more pre-occupied than was usual with him. There had been another stormy debate that day. Mr. Torbolton, leader of the opposition, had been seen in the refreshment room in close conclave with Blake. The talk ran that Blake's speech had done more than anything to shake the Ministry. Sir James had given particular instructions to his womenkind that they should 'cotton up' to Blake. Blake was an enemy whom it might be well to conciliate.

Lady Garfit, therefore, had arranged that Rose should dance the first dance with Blake. Rose was not an exhilarating companion. Her conversation consisted mostly of remarks to the effect that Lady Stukeley was too sweet, and that the Prince was almost certain to be in Leichardt's Town for the Birthnight Ball; which – had Mr. Blake heard? – was put off till the 12th of June on account of the uncertainty about the Prince. Lady Stukeley had told Lady Garfit that they were expecting a telegram every moment to fix the date. This was not deeply interesting to Blake. He fired a little when Miss Garfit asked him if he did not think Miss Valliant looked lovely. It was such a pity that she was such a dreadful flirt, and got herself so talked about.

Miss Garfit was getting up riding parties – they were to be Parliamentary riding parties – it was only on Wednesdays and Saturdays that the members were free. Would Mr. Blake join them, and had he that lovely horse which Miss Valliant rode at the Tunimbah races, in Leichardt's Town?'

'Yes;' but Blake made a bold shot. It had been promised to Miss Valliant, and he (Blake) was bound to escort her.

Oh! but Rose Garfit would be greatly pleased if Miss Valliant and Lord and Lady Horace would join their riding parties. Lord Horace was always amusing. Didn't Mr. Blake think so?

No, Blake could not quite agree with her. He thought Lord Horace was a bit of a cub, and that his wife was much too good for him. The only decent member of that family was Lady Waveryng.

Miss Garfit looked a little horrified at this familiar criticism. Had Mr. Blake known them in England?

No, not in England; at least, only by hearsay; and he changed the conversation with a compliment on Miss Garfit's dress.

He got his opportunity at last with Elsie. There were certainly no traces of tears on her radiant face this evening. She lifted her bouquet.

'Thank you ever so much. It goes so beautifully with my dress.'

'I have something to confess. I have committed perjury for your sake.'

'For my sake?'

'I swore just now that The Outlaw was devoted to your service this winter, and that I was in duty bound to escort you. I think Miss Garfit wanted to borrow The Outlaw. She is getting up Parliamentary riding parties, and I believe that she intends asking you and Lady Horace to join them.'

'Do you really mean that I am to ride The Outlaw?'

'If you will honour me so far. He is here, at your service, as I said. You have only to say when you want him sent over.'

'Horace has horses. I am sure Ina would like to ride. Mr. Blake.'

'Yes, Miss Valliant.'

'Please forget what I said last night.'

'Once before, when you asked me to forget something that you said, I told you that I could not promise to do that. But I'll promise that I won't remind you of it. Besides, you said nothing that was not altogether charming and womanly.'

They were just going to join the dancers. Trant passed them with Minnie Pryde, and it seemed to Elsie that there was a meaning expression in his eyes. But she forgot all about Trant while she was dancing with Blake. Later on she had a waltz with him, and he complimented her on her dress and upon her violets.

'I know that Blake sent you that bouquet.'

'Yes, he did.'

'If I sent you a bouquet one night, will you wear it?'

'Certainly, with pleasure, if it matches my dress, and it won't be a matter of great difficulty to arrange that, for my dresses are not so various or so numerous.'

'You couldn't have anything prettier than the one you are wearing to-night. Everyone is saying that you look lovely.'

Trant's conversation was this evening carried on in the strain of somewhat extravagant compliment. Perhaps Elsie was wanting in fine discrimination, anyhow she preferred it to his more tragic mood. She was having her fill of admiration just now. Frank Hallett was the only drawback to her enjoyment. He looked sad, she fancied, reproachful, and he did not very often ask her to dance, but devoted himself to Ina. 'Oh, why hadn't he fallen in love with Ina?' Elsie said to herself. 'That would have settled everything, and she would have suited him far better than I ever shall.'

One of the riding parties came off. Before the second could take place the Ministry had gone out, and Mr. Torbolton had formed a new cabinet.

It was no surprise to anyone that Blake was offered an important place in it. Certainly, to secure a seat in the Government after having been in the House only a few weeks was an achievement, but Mr. Torbolton was only too glad to gain such an acquisition to his ranks.

The re-elections occasioned a temporary absence from town on the part of the new Ministers. Blake was, however, returned without a contest.

And meanwhile the little whirligig went round. Elsie was very gay. She had several new admirers, and the verandah receptions became a feature of the day. Lord Horace started a four-in-hand, and was in boisterous spirits. Mrs. Allanby was usually on the box seat. Poor Ina looked paler than ever and more anxious; but she was a loyal little creature and said nothing of her domestic trials even to Elsie. During Blake's absence at Goondi, Frank Hallett came a little more to the fore, and was a frequent visitor at Riverside, but he still kept to his line of not obtruding his love. One day Elsie asked him why he had so changed.

'I have not changed, and I shall never change,' he answered. 'I am always here – always ready to do anything that you want me to do. But you are quite free, Elsie, and I wish you to feel so. It is not I who have changed.'

'Do you mean that I have changed?'

'Yes, you have greatly changed, and I can only guess at the meaning of the change.'

'Tell me how I have changed,' she said.

'You are restless, and your moods vary. Sometimes you look perfectly wretched; at others wildly happy. You are a barometer, Elsie, and the influence which affects your moods is Blake. You are expecting him now?'

'Frank, you insult me.'

'I don't want to. I think you are under the spell of some evil enchantment. It is not wholesome, honest love. That is why I am patient, and why I feel certain that it will pass away.'

'And then?'

'Oh then – then it may be my turn.'

'Frank, I deny everything. Mr. Blake and I are playing a game – that is the whole truth. We agreed to see which could hurt the other most.'

'It seems to me a dangerous game, Elsie – and, as you play it, not a very womanly one.'

'Dangerous! Perhaps; but for whom? Do you think that I am going to let myself be beaten? He has hurt other women, he shall not hurt me. You think I am unwomanly because I flirt with him openly; because I sit out dances with him, and allow myself to be talked about; because my manner gives people some reason for saying that I am in love with him. Well, we shall see. When he asks me to marry him I shall refuse him, and all the world shall know it.'

'Elsie! You are undignified. I say again, you are unwomanly.'

'So Ina tells me. Well, you can give me up. Frank, I sometimes think that there is an evil spirit in me, and that you are right – that I am under a spell. It's true that I am eaten up by a demon of vanity, and selfishness, and reckless pride. I want to be first. I cannot bear that any man should get the better of me. It is horrid, I know it. Very well, but I am myself. I want to do something wild; I want to feel, I want to know. Ah!'

She gave a sudden start, and then drew back and kept very still, for at that moment Blake entered.

They were spending the evening in Lady Horace's sitting-room at Fermoy's. Lord Horace and some choice pals were in the verandah smoking. There was whisky on the table. Ina was sewing, and Trant had just gone to the piano.

He began his song as Blake came in, 'Ninon, Ninon, que fais-tu de la vie?' and only nodded at the sight of his partner, and went on singing. It was a song that always affected Elsie curiously. Blake shook hands silently with Lady Horace, and seated himself beside Elsie. Hallett moved away.

When the song was over, Blake said, 'I came to tell Lord Horace that the Ullagong is signalled.'

Ina, who had moved towards them, gave a little start. 'Then the Waveryngs will be here to-night.'

'Not to-night, Lady Horace,' said Blake, pitying her evident alarm - 'at least not till the small hours of the morning.'

'Oh! do you think,' said Ina tremulously, 'that I need go with Horace to meet them?'

'No,' he said; 'why should you? It will be far too early.'

'I am so nervous about them,' said poor Ina, 'and it may make a great difference to Horace their liking or disliking me. That is what Horace says.'

Ina was off her balance, or she never would have so betrayed herself.

'They are quite sure to like you,' said Blake; 'and you will like them. Lady Waveryng is a charming woman – kind and unaffected, and he is a good fellow.'

'Do you know them?' said Elsie, in surprise.

'I know all about them,' he answered. 'They will not know *me*, but some of my people lived in Ireland near the 'Waveryngs.''

'Oh! I know,' said Ina. 'Then you are one of the Blakes of Castle Coola. Horace was wondering.'

'I have relations in Ireland, and they live at Castle Coola,' answered Blake. 'That is how I come to know about the Waveryngs. But I would rather you didn't talk about it, Lady Horace, if you don't mind, though there is no particular secret. The fact is I wasn't a credit to my family, and I left Ireland in disgrace, and have never had a word of communication with my people since. I am as dead to them as if I were dead in reality.'

Elsie looked at him in a startled, pained way. It was the first time she had ever heard him speak of his people in Ireland, or in any definite manner of his past. Ina looked surprised, too, and a little pitiful. She was beginning to like Blake better than she had done at first.

'You need not be afraid of my talking about what you have said, Mr. Blake,' she answered; 'I shall not even tell Horace if you would rather not.'

'Thank you, Lady Horace; certainly I would rather not. You are very good, and I am sure you are very loyal to your friends.'

Ina flushed. 'I must let Horace know about the Ullagong,' she said. 'I hope he won't go over to the north side to-night.'

She went out to the verandah. Lord Horace was greatly excited at the prospect of his sister's arrival, and declared he must start off to the north side at once, and find out when the Ullagong would really be in. He said that he would stay at the club and beguile the time at billiards, and proposed that Hallett and Trant should accompany him. Trant accepted the invitation, and Ina cast an imploring glance at Hallett, who had not intended to go over yet. He changed his mind, however, when he saw that Elsie seconded Ina's beseeching look, and the three left together. The other men followed shortly. Blake remained chatting with Lady Horace and Elsie. He told them about his second Goondi election. They discussed his new post, and the responsibilities attaching to it.

'One very serious responsibility you will have, at least,' Ina said laughing. 'We shall blame you now, Mr. Blake, if Moonlight bails up any more coaches, or robs any gold escorts. Horace says that the police are in your department, and that you are now Captain Macpherson's chief.'

Blake laughed too, a little strangely, Ina and Elsie thought.

'Yes, that is so. Odd, isn't it? Odd that I should have to sign the warrant against Moonlight, if it ever comes to that.'

'I hope it will never come to that,' said Elsie. 'I have a curious feeling about Moonlight; I don't know why. I want him to escape. I want him to go away and take his money with him and begin a new life.'

'Perhaps,' said Blake, 'that is what he means to do. Perhaps it is some grim fate which has pushed him into his evil ways; some terrible necessity of his nature which makes the excitement of robbery and adventure an outlet for all his fiercer passions, and his better self may – for all you know, Miss Valliant – be struggling with the baser self, and urging him to flee temptation.'

Something in his tone made Elsie look at him wonderingly. He seemed uneasy under her gaze, and got up restlessly, and with a forced laugh added, 'It would hardly do to advance these theories, would it, in defence of Moonlight at a meeting of the Executive? Miss Valliant, I see you making a move; may I be permitted to take you home?'

'Thank you,' Elsie said simply. 'I ought to go now, Ina dear; you should get to bed. Don't bother about the Waveryngs. Leave them to Horace.'

She kissed her sister, and presently she and Blake were walking along the dim, straggling street on their way to the Riverside paddock.

They hardly spoke at first. At last he said abruptly, after some banal remark about Leichardt's Town gaieties, 'Have you missed me?'

'Yes,' she answered fearlessly. 'And now tell me, have you missed me?'

'Oh, no – not in the least. I have only thought of you in almost every hour of daylight, and in some few hours during the night. I have only counted the days till I should get back to Leichardt's Town and to you. Does that satisfy you?'

She did not answer for a moment. Her heart was beating wildly. Presently she said, 'Is this another move in the game?'

'If you take it so. I am going to ask you something, a great favour: will you pull me across to the other side and back again?'

'Yes. Come.'

She ran on a little in advance of him and reached the Riverside fence first. Instead of taking the path which led to the cottage, she went down another, through the banana plantation and to the river bank. The boat was lying at the steps. The tide was at full, and lapped the drooping branches of the chuckie-chuckie tree with a caressing sound.

Elsie threw off her cloak and stepped into the boat, which she untied. She looked, he thought, like some nymph of Greek days in her white dress and with her slim, erect form and well-poised head bare to the night. The stars shone brightly, and the sky was intensely clear. She motioned him to sit in the stern, and shook her head when he asked if he should take an oar, then pushed off into mid-stream.

Her strokes were long and vigorous. He watched with fascinated eyes the movements of her lithe young body as she bent backwards and forwards to the oar. She never spoke a word, but rowed straight across and then turned and rowed him back again.

'Now,' she said, 'don't ever say that I made any fuss about doing what you asked me. Give me credit for being courageous at any rate, when you think of the way in which Lady Garfit would tear my character to shreds if she could see me now.'

'Elsie,' he exclaimed, 'I believe that for a man you loved you would brave any danger. I believe that you have it in you, and that you neither know yourself nor does your world know you.'

She stooped to fasten the rope on the boat – they were on shore again now. When she answered it was in a serious and altered tone.

'No, I don't think I have ever known myself. I am quite sure my world doesn't know me. And I think you are right. I do think it is in me to brave danger for the sake of a man I loved. But then I never believed it was in me to love a man like that.'

'Ah!' he cried, 'you know it now, and it is I who have taught you. You love me.'

They were walking up the little hill to the cottage. Both paused. She turned on him her big, troubled, star-like eyes.

'Elsie,' he repeated triumphantly. 'I have won the game; you love me!'

He put out his arms and caught her to him in a wild embrace. There was something almost brutal in his impetuosity. He kissed her cheeks, her hair, and then her lips. Elsie had never dreamed of kisses so passionate and unrestrained. For a moment or two she yielded to his ardour, and then a swift and agonising sense of humiliation overcame her. 'How dare you! What right have you?' she cried – 'Oh, you are cruel, you are base!'

She tore herself from him and he saw her no more.

CHAPTER XIX

---•---

The Club Ball

Elsie sobbed all night the sobs of outraged maidenhood. He had conquered. She knew it too well. His kisses burned on her lips, and the burning was sweet agony. She loved him; but – and here came the hideous doubt – did he love her? Had he only been amusing himself? Had he only been revenging dead Jensen? Oh! what concerns of his were this dead man's wrongs? Had he only been playing out the game at which he had challenged her skill?

If he loved her, she told herself, he would come on the morrow. He would come in proud humility, and ask her to forgive him, certain of her pardon.

She heard the steamer bells as the Ullagong, with the Waveryngs on board, steamed up the river. She got up and looked out through the blur of her tears. It was grey dawn – the dawn, she thought, of her day of destiny. Would he come? She determined that she would torture herself no more with speculations. She got up and dressed, and set herself savagely to her household tasks.

It was perhaps fortunate that Mrs. Valliant was too pre-occupied with the thought of the Waveryngs' visit, and the effect it would have upon Ina, to notice the pale face and wild eyes of her eldest daughter. She could talk of nothing but Lady Waveryng. Would Ina meet her sister-in-law at the wharf? Would she call at Government House that afternoon? Lady Stukeley would now be obliged to take some notice of Ina's family. It was she who suggested that Elsie should walk down to Fermoy's and learn something of Ina's arrangements.

Lord Horace was in the verandah, talking excitedly to a plain, rather heavy, good-natured-looking man, in a light tweed suit, and with something of the tourist air. The man's eyes rested admiringly on Elsie as she stepped along the side path, not daring to look at any of the other windows which opened on to the verandah, lest, perchance, she might encounter Blake. But Blake was at his office, as befitted a new minister anxious to learn his duties; and there was no need for that startled flush which caught Lord Waveryng's attention.

'By Jove!' she heard him say, 'do they breed 'em like this out here?'

'My wife's sister, Miss Valliant,' said Horace, as she opened the gate of the verandah. 'Elsie, this is Waveryng. Brought 'em straight along to see Ina, in spite of the Stukeleys.'

'Lady Stukeley will understand perfectly,' said Lord Waveryng. 'Em made it straight. Of course Em wanted to see the new sister-in-law.' And thus Elsie gleaned that the Waveryngs meant to be nice.

'They're bricks, ain't they?' said Horace aside.

Ina was in the sitting-room, where a very trim, very handsome, very decided, and rather voluble lady had taken possession of her. Lady Waveryng was a beauty. She was very like her brother, Lord Horace, and had charming manners; though her once lovely complexion had got a little spoiled in the hunting-field. Hunting and yachting were the two things she liked best in the world. Elsie heard her say she only wished their yacht had been big enough to go round the world in, but on the whole she wasn't sure that she did not prefer ocean steamers; and the passengers made it more amusing. They had had a perfectly lovely time in Ceylon. Singapore was so interesting, and the whole Torres Strait route delightful.

'And this is Elsie, I am sure,' and she got up as Elsie entered.

'Horace sent us your photograph with Ina's, to show us how easy it was to fall in love with Australian girls.'

Lady Waveryng shook Elsie's hand warmly, and then she kissed Ina.

They must fly. She did not know what the Stukeleys would say to her. And there was so much to be done. And she understood there was to be a ball that evening somewhere; and her maid had been so upset with sea-sickness that she would have to go and do her own unpacking.

They started off, Horace with them. Lady Waveryng kissed her hand as she turned the Ferry Hill, and walked along leaning on her silver mounted stick, looking, in her neat tailor-made dress and dainty hat, Elsie thought, unapproachably simple and thoroughbred.

'You see, Ina, you needn't have been frightened of them,' said Elsie.

'They're coming to the Dell,' said Ina. 'They say that they're longing to do some Bush travelling. Lady Waveryng wants to hunt kangaroos.

She says I must call her "Em." We are to dine at Government House this evening – a family party; and, oh! Elsie, I am so sorry, but you'll arrange to go with the Prydes or Mrs. Jem Hallett, won't you, to the Club Ball, and wait for me in the cloakroom?'

'The Club Ball?' said Elsie. 'Oh! I had forgotten.' And in truth her heart and mind had been too full for the thought even of a ball to find a place there. 'It doesn't matter,' she said. 'Yes, I'll arrange somehow.'

'And your bouquet, Elsie,' said Ina. 'Do you think Mr. Blake will send you one this time?'

'No,' exclaimed Elsie almost fiercely; 'he will not send me one. 'Why should he? Let us go over to the gardens, Ina, and beg some azaleas and camellias from the curator.'

She did not get back to Riverside till her verandah reception hour. She had a wild fancy that Blake might be there waiting for her. Ministers were not tied to their offices like the humble fry of civil servants and bank clerks. The bank clerks were there – and Dominic Trant was there, but no Blake.

It was Trant who brought her a bouquet; and a very beautiful one of tea roses and maidenhair fern and crimson double geranium. He had been at some pains to find out from Lady Horace what Elsie's colours were to be.

No other bouquet had come, and she said she would wear this one, and thanked him very prettily. He wondered what had happened to her, and why her manner was so strained and conscious. Man-like he attributed it to his own influence. Was it possible that he was beginning to affect her? He had an immense faith in his power of influencing women. His dark eyes glowed passionately upon her face. To flirt with him at that moment was a distraction, and an anodyne to the fierce pain which tormented her. She felt a wicked pleasure in playing with him as a cat might have played with a mouse. Yes, she would give him some dances. She would not say how many. They would wait until they were in the ballroom. What was it that he wanted to say to her? If it was going to be anything very interesting and exciting, she would listen with the greatest pleasure. She wanted to be amused, taken out of herself. Did he think he could do that for her?

'Yes,' Trant answered deliberately. He thought he could at least interest her. He would not promise not to offend her. Perhaps a little at first she might be jarred; women were always jarred by what was real in a man. He meant to be his real self.

Mr. Anderson and Minnie Pryde came in. Minnie was dying to hear all about Lady Waveryng.

They sat in the verandah till it was nearly dressing time; and no one else came. Blake never appeared.

In the evening the Prydes called for her in the jingle – Minnie and her father, who was in one of the Government offices – there was no Mrs. Pryde – and they drove round by the bridge, and along the river embankment, till they got into the string of carriages waiting to pass towards the awning stretched out from the entrance to the Club House. The club was a pretty, low building, with wide verandahs and a big garden, gay with coloured lanterns. The covered way from the street was hung with flags; the ballroom looked very brilliant with its decorations of flaming poinsettia against a background of palms. Where had all the crimson flowers come from? There was nothing else – garlands of red geraniums and euphorbia and vivid pomegranate, deepening into the darker tones of the red camellias and azaleas and the great flags of poinsettia. Minnie Pryde bewailed her pink dress which was quite out of harmony with the prevailing colouring.

'Oh, Elsie, how clever of you to find out what they were going to decorate with,' she cried, looking admiringly at Elsie's cloudy white gauze with its splashes of crimson at waist and bosom. Elsie's cheeks were almost as bright as the crimson flowers, but the colour came and went, and there was a frightened look in her eyes.

Frank Hallett, who was one of the stewards, was waiting near the doorway.

'Your sister asked me to tell you not to wait in the cloak-room,' he said, 'She may be late. We've been dining at Government House, you know, and Mr. Blake and I managed to get away before the rest, because of being stewards. Mrs. Jem will chaperon you till Ina comes.'

Mrs. Jem was gorgeous in maize and black lace, which suited her brunette colouring and her affectation of matronhood. She had taken her place among the higher magnates, and did not smile quite as sweet a welcome to poor pariah Elsie as Frank Hallett would have wished. But Mrs. Jem was wise in her generation, and she had a shrewd notion that Lord Waveryng would take to Elsie, and it was quite evident that Elsie's position in Leichardt's Town society would be somewhat changed by the Waveryngs' stay at Government House, and the admission of Lady Horace into that inner circle from which she had been in her girlhood so rigorously excluded.

'Yes, lovely,' said Mrs. Jem, in answer to a remark of Lady Garfit's.

'But you know I always said that Ina was so much better style, and the rouge is quite evident to-night. It is such a pity.'

But even as she spoke Elsie's cheeks belied the accusation. The girl went deadly white for an instant, and then the crimson tide welled up again. Blake was coming towards them. There was not a shadow of consciousness in his manner. He stopped to salute Mrs. Jem and engage her for a set of Lancers. Yes, he had been dining at Government House. He had thought that Miss Valliant might be with Lady Horace. He bowed ceremoniously to Elsie. 'How charming Lady Waveryng was, and how nice to see her so devoted already to Lady Horace; though, of course, she was certain to be that.'

Was it Blake who was uttering these banalities? Elsie waited. He had not yet asked her to dance. Trant was hovering near, watching her with jealous eyes, and now he pushed himself forward. 'Miss Valliant, this is my dance.'

Elsie looked at her card. It had got pretty well filled already. Frank Hallett's name was down several times, and the bank clerks had been given a sop apiece, and the more important dancing men – the unmarried members of the Assembly – and some strangers from a neighbouring colony, had each set down their initials. But Elsie had kept some blanks, on which she had placed a hieroglyph of her own. 'No, you have made a mistake. It is the next one. This is a gallop. They are not keeping to the programme.'

'Oh, they won't do that until the great people come,' said Blake. 'And here they are, and we stewards must go and receive them.'

The band struck up 'God save the Queen.' There was a little confusion at the entrance, and presently the Governor's fine head appeared, above the blue collar of his uniform, and Lady Waveryng's tiara of diamonds at his shoulder. 'How handsome she is, and how like Lord Horace!' murmured Mrs. Jem. The Leichardtstonians wondered that they had not thought more of Lord Horace, and a pang shot through Lady Garfit. Oh! why hadn't she managed to marry him to Rose? Lady Waveryng's diamonds and aristocratic head seemed the visible symbol of poor little Ina Gage's unmerited social advancement. Lady Waveryng had an air and an aplomb that could only belong to an aristocrat. And she was so simple and so unaffected, and looked about with such evident interest, pointing to the poinsettia leaves, and saying something to Blake as she passed him that produced a bow of evident acknowledgment of a compliment on the taste of the stewards. Lady Waveryng's eyes went back to Blake in a puzzled sort of way. 'Do you know who he is, and if he belongs to the Castle

Coola people?' she said to the Governor. 'I can't get rid of the impression that I know his face. But I don't know which of the Coola people he could be. All the brothers are dead.'

Sir Theophilus Stukeley did not know. He had never met any of the Castle Coola people; always avoided Ireland, and thanked Providence that he had not been born an Irish landlord.

Lady Waveryng laughed. 'Oh, but the Coolas are of the landlord type – thorough Tories; at least, Lord Coola is at any rate. Waveryng has some fishing near them, and that's how I came to know them. But he has all the traditions. It's so sad that all the sons are dead, and the property must go to some dreadful English lawyer, whom one of the daughters married. It seems quite out of keeping that the Castle, Banshee and all, should go into Sassenach hands. Oh! Mr. Blake, I beg your pardon.' She became suddenly conscious that Blake was close to her, and that he was devouring what she said. 'I am sure you are one of the Coola people, aren't you? Please tell me, are you related to Lord Coola?'

'In a hundredth degree,' he answered. 'All the Blakes, I suppose, came originally from the Coola stock.' He withdrew reflecting that he had involved himself in complications.

The Governor and Lady Waveryng went to the upper end of the room. Lord Waveryng had Lady Stukeley on his arm. Ina came in with the aide-de-camp, and Lord Horace with the private secretary's wife.

'By Jove, that sister-in-law of Horace's beats them all to fits!' said Lord Waveryng. 'I am going to ask her if she will dance with me.' He led Elsie out for the first waltz after the state quadrille, in which imposing ceremonial she had naturally no place. He found her very charming, so he confided to his wife, and with a delightful sense of humour. She had asked him how he and Lady Waveryng bore the shock of the introduction to Horace's barbarians. She had also informed him that lords and lesser members of the aristocracy were at a discount on the diggings, and they had never been able to get up a sufficient sense of the honour to which Ina had been raised. She thought, however, that acquaintance with Lord Waveryng might now enable them to realise their advantages. She said all this with grave simplicity, looking into Lord Waveryng's face with her beautiful, shy eyes, always keeping that expression of vague pain and alarm.

All this time Blake had never asked her to dance. He had danced with Lady Waveryng, with Ina, with Rose Garfit. He had smiled at her in an absolutely conventional manner when their eyes met, but he had never shown the least desire for any private conversation. What did it all mean? Had he been mad last night? Had she been mad or dreaming? Or was it merely that the game was played, and that he wished her to understand this, and that her claims upon his attention were at an end?

Well, he should see that she did not care. She smiled upon Trant with reckless witchery, and let him take her into the square of garden behind the Club House – a dim patch of fairyland – palms outlined against the pale moonlit sky, coloured lamps hanging on the fantastic branches of the monkey trees and gleaming in thickets of bamboos. The bamboos made a soft rustling in the night wind; the datura flowers scented the air with their heavy fragrance. There were little tents here and there, and cane lounges, with bright red cushions, set in secluded corners.

To one of these Trant led her. Her shoulders were bare, and she shivered slightly as he came close to her. 'It is too cold to be out in the garden,' she said.

'Cold, no not in the least! But see how thoughtful I have been.'

He liften his arm and showed her a white wrap which he had been carrying half concealed by her bouquet. He had asked permission to hold that for her while she had finished her dance with Mr. Anderson.

'It is Ina's,' said Elsie. 'Thank you.'

He put it on her shoulders. She took her bouquet from him. 'Thank you,' she said again. 'I don't think there's anything you can do for me except amuse me.'

'I shall not amuse you,' he answered, 'I am too deadly serious for that.'

'Deadly seriousness may be amusing sometimes. Go on, Mr. Trant. Talk – talk –'

'What shall I talk about – you or myself?'

'Or both. Do you like my dress? Do you think I look nice?'

'You look beautiful,' he said deliberately. 'Every time I look at you, I – I want to kiss you.'

She shrank. 'Don't please talk like that.'

'I said I should jar upon you if I allowed myself to be real, didn't I? That's what I really feel though. I want all the time to take you in my arms, and cover you with kisses. I would do it too – if –'

She got up. 'Please take me in. I don't like you when you say wild things.'

'Don't be afraid. I have too much respect for you to offend. Besides,

my time isn't yet. When I kiss you it shall be with your permission –
unless –'

'Unless what?'

'Unless I see that you will never freely give me permission. Then
I shall take it. But I do things in a big way, Miss Valliant – not in a
hole-and-corner fashion. It wouldn't suit me to snatch a kiss in a
garden, and see you go off in a fit of indignation, thinking me an
odious cad. You wouldn't think me a cad if I seized a kiss in some
wild lonely place, with not a soul in earshot; a place like Baròlin
Waterfall, let us say, where you would be utterly helpless, and at my
mercy. There'd be something big about that; you'd be too frightened
to tell yourself I was a cad. You'd be frightened enough almost to
imagine me a hero. And then, perhaps, I shouldn't take the kiss.
Perhaps I should act a chivalrous part, and in the end, maybe, you
would give it to me of your own accord.'

Elsie laughed. There was something in his wooing that, rough as
it was, appealed to her. Instead of moving away, she sat down again,
and leaned a little towards him, huddled in her cloak.

'Well,' he said, 'I am beginning to interest you, am I not? I know
exactly what sort of woman you are. I think a man might have a chance
with you, if he carried you off by force. Elsie listen –'

She shook her head, and made a gesture of rebuke.

'Yes, I shall call you Elsie, this once. Elsie, Elsie. It is a beautiful
name. I delight in the name. Elsie. I say it to myself when I am alone.
I kiss you in imagination when I am alone. Elsie, I love you.'

'Mr. Trant –'

'You can't prevent me from loving you; I have the right to do so,
just as much as Blake; only he doesn't love any woman, he is not
capable of loving anybody but himself –'

Elsie gave a little inarticulate cry of pain.

'Something happened last night between you and Blake. Oh, I know
it as well as if you or he had told me. I haven't been with Blake all
these years for nothing. I know the signs of his face. I know what it
means when he puts on that sort of mask he is wearing to-night. It
means that the devil is in him, and that he will go his way, come what
will. Don't be his victim, Miss Valliant. It's for your own good I say
it; don't believe in Blake.'

Elsie turned on him, her face quivering with passionate anger.

'Be silent on this subject! Say what you choose about yourself –
that doesn't matter, it's only amusing, it interests me in a way – but

don't insult me by mentioning Mrs. Blake's name in connection with mine. I will not have it!'

'Very well. But I have warned you. And I have as good a right to make love to you as Mr. Frank Hallett, and that, according to Leichardt's Town gossip, means a good deal, if, as they say, you were engaged to him before Blake came on the scene. There, I am offending again. We'll leave Blake out of the question.'

'I was never engaged to Mr. Frank Hallett. Now you have said what you wanted to say, and there is an end. You are quite right, no one could prevent you. But when I have given you my answer, the incident will be closed, as they say.'

'I haven't asked you for an answer,' he said imperturbably. 'I don't want to close the incident. I intend to open it again. I love you and I mean to marry you.'

Elsie laughed nervously. 'Really, Mr. Trant, am I not to have a voice in the matter?'

'Oh yes, later on; but you must get accustomed to the idea. I'm not a poor man, Miss Valliant – it may be as well that I should mention this – and I intend very shortly to cut this life – for good and all. I have had enough of it. I propose in a few months to leave Australia, and to take my money out of the place. I shall not have done such a bad thing out of Australia' – Trant laughed his odd laugh – 'and then I shall go to Europe, and I shall enjoy life.'

'I am glad to hear it.'

'I shall be in a position to give my wife most of the things that a woman likes – travel, amusement, society, dress, luxuries, and what ought to count a little, unbounded devotion. That does count for something with a woman, doesn't it?'

'It depends on who offers it.'

'I'm not such an odiously unattractive fellow – at least, I've managed to make some women care for me. I know I could make you care for me, if I set to work in the right way. Anyhow I mean to try.'

'It will be no use at all, Mr. Trant. It will be only a waste of time.'

'We shall see. I think you will have to admit later that I am a man of determination.'

'Miss Valliant, I have been looking for you everywhere! This is our dance.'

The speaker was Lord Waveryng. Elsie got up and took his arm, and they went into the ball-room.

CHAPTER XX

Lord Astar's Attentions

As they went in from the dim garden and through the verandah, which was like a conservatory, with its decorations of palms, Elsie's dazzled eyes seemed to see in the glare of the ball-room beyond only one face and form, and those belonged to Blake.

He was standing close to the doorway. Elsie wondered whether he would move away when he saw her; but he turned straight to them. But Elsie noticed that he kept his eyes on Lord Waveryng, and she noticed, too, an odd, watchful expression in the eyes that she had never seen there before. Lord Waveryng spoke a word to him. He, too, kept his eyes with a hard, puzzled stare on Blake. He said, 'You see we weren't so long behind you in getting here after all. But old Stukeley is hard to move when it's a case of Mouton Rothschild '68 – capital wine that! – not damaged in the least by the voyage.'

'Not damaged at all,' replied Blake in a mechanical tone.

'I say,' said Lord Waveryng abruptly, 'do you happen to remember what Lafitte Coola used to give us at the Castle on high days?'

Blake returned the look which Lord Waveryng gave him quite unflinchingly.

'No, I don't remember,' he said, and turned to Elsie. 'Miss Valliant, I am afraid I am rather late in my application, but I must plead my steward's duties as a claim on your mercy. May I hope for the honour of a dance?'

Elsie's heart throbbed so violently that she instinctively put the hand which her bouquet shielded against her side. She dared not look at him. The thought of the wild scene of the night before maddened her almost into fury. What right had he? How dared he think that he could trifle with her so?

'I am sorry,' she said, and her words fell like drops of steel, 'but I am engaged for every dance.'

Blake said nothing. He only bowed, and Lord Waveryng put his arm round Elsie, and steered her into the dance.

'I can see,' he said, when they paused presently, 'that Mr. Blake is not quite in your good books. I wonder how he has offended you.'

'Oh no,' said Elsie, trying to speak calmly, 'he has not offended me, but of course at this time in the evening I have no dances left.'

'I would give a good deal,' said Lord Waveryng, 'for the cheek to ask that man whether he is Morres Blake come to life again. I think I shall do it by-and-by.'

'Who is Morres Blake?' asked Elsie.

'Lord Coola's brother, a fellow that fell over a cliff, and was carried out to sea and drowned; at least, so they said. But you see somebody might have picked him up, and he might not have been drowned; and what gives the theory a spark of probability is that Blake would have been had up to a certainty on a charge of inciting his regiment to Fenianism, if he had not got killed at the nick of time for his family and for his own reputation, we won't say his life, since if he *was* drowned, he lost that anyhow.'

'Ah!' Elsie drew a deep breath. Things seemed to suddenly become clear to her.

'It must be ten or twelve years ago,' Lord Waveryng went on. 'I met Blake – the Morres Blake, you know – twice at Castle Coola, and I don't often forget a face. In fact, I've got an astonishing memory for faces, Miss Valliant. I ought to have been a Royalty.'

They went on again. In the next pause Lord Waveryng talked of Lord Horace. 'I'm going up to see the Dell,' he said. 'I hear Horace's works have come to a dead stop for want of funds. Well, if he is likely to keep out of mischief – and he ought to with such a charming wife – I might see if I couldn't do something. He is my wife's favourite brother, though I can't say I ever had a great opinion myself of Horace's capabilities; but he is a good-hearted chap, and I had a lucky haul with the Two Thousand – I suppose you know that I go in for racing a bit, Miss Valliant – and I might give Horace a helping hand. He'll not get another penny from his father.'

For Ina's sake Elsie rejoiced at Lord Waveryng's benevolent intentions, and thought how pleased her mother would be to hear of the excellent impression Ina had made. That was very evident. Lady Waveryng was sitting now beside her sister-in-law, and they were on the most affectionate terms.

Frank Hallett came next on the list of Elsie's partners. 'Why are you not dancing with Blake this evening?' he asked abruptly.

'I don't know,' said Elsie simply; and it hurt him to hear the note of pain in her voice. 'Frank,' she said hurriedly, 'please don't talk to me about Mr. Blake. Let us talk of other things – of how I am enjoying myself, for instance.'

'Are you enjoying yourself, Elsie?'

'Of course I am. I have had a success. Every one has been telling me that I look very well. Lord Waveryng has been charming. I have been honoured by an offer of marriage.' She laughed hysterically.

'An offer of marriage?' he said anxiously.

'I did not accept it' – she still laughed – 'but it was – exciting. Come, Frank, don't let us lose any of this lovely waltz. I am in wild spirits to-night.'

Poor Elsie! And yet when she went into the cloak-room in the early dawn it seemed to her as though her heart must break, so agonising was the pain of it. All the pretty colour had gone from her face. As she stood in the corridor waiting for the jingle which was to take them over the bridge to Fermoy's, she looked like a ghost, with wild eyes.

'Are you very tired, Miss Valliant?' said Blake suddenly, beside her.

She gave a great start. He was still impassive. 'Yes, very tired,' she answered.

'Have you had a pleasant evening?' he asked, in the same tone.

'Yes, thank you,' she answered. She lifted her eyes, which had not dared to meet his. They met them now, and something in the expression of his eased her pain. For there was pain, too, in his eyes, and a great yearning.

'Mr. Blake,' she exclaimed involuntarily, and made a faint movement of her hand towards him. He put out his hand, and took hers. 'Good-night, Miss Valliant,' he said; 'do you see that faint red streak in the sky, and do you know that in another hour it will be sunrise? Sleep well, and when you wake, don't –' he hesitated, and pressed her hand as he relinquished it. 'Try not to think too hardly of me.'

The girl said not a word. She moved proudly past him. 'Ina, I am sure the carriage is there,' she said, and at that moment Lord Horace came crossly to them. Lord Horace had taken a little more champagne than was good for him. 'What an infernal time you have been with your cloaks,' he said. 'Come along, I can't see the thing, and we may wait here till Doomsday for it to fetch us. Come and get into the first jingle we can find that will take us to the ferry. We can walk the rest of the way.'

A few minutes later Blake stood on the steps of the club house lighting his cigar. He was going to walk to the ferry. Lord Waveryng joined him.

'You are going to walk, I see. So am I, and our ways lie together as far as the turning to Government House.'

The two men stepped out into the fresh, scented air of the early morning. There were faint sounds of awakening birds and insects, and the greyness was so clear that the colour of the begonias, which festooned some of the verandahs along the roadway, showed curiously brilliant. They exchanged a few commonplace remarks about the scenery, the vegetation, and the beauty of the river. Then Lord Waveryng halted suddenly, and turned on his companion deliberately, taking his cigar from his mouth.

'I think I ought to tell you,' he said, 'that I never forget a face, and that I recognised you almost as soon as I heard your name this evening. I presume you have good reasons for not wishing to be identified as Captain Morres Blake of the –?'

'I have the best reasons that man can have,' said Blake. 'Lord Waveryng, I'll be as frank with you as you are with me, and you know my reasons almost as well as I do.'

'It's twelve years ago,' said Lord Waveryng, 'and things have changed a good deal since then. This Parliamentary movement has made a difference. I don't suppose the authorities would want to rake up that business. The reason why I tackled you at once is that I don't know whether you know that Lord Coola's two boys died of diphtheria last year, and that you stand next in succession to Coola.'

'No,' said Blake startled; 'I did not know it, and I am truly sorry.'

'It is worth your thinking about,' said Lord Waveryng. 'I thought I had better tell you.'

Blake was silent for a few moments. At last he spoke. 'There were four lives between me and Coola when – when I left Ireland, and there seemed a probability of several more. It was not to be supposed that my brother would not marry again after Lady Coola's death; and who could have dreamed that my brother William would have been carried off so young – and now these boys! Poor chaps! It is like fatality.'

'Yes,' assented Lord Waveryng, 'seems like a fatality, don't it? Anyhow, you may be the next Lord Coola.'

'Coola will marry again now,' said Blake decidedly. 'He is bound to do it.'

'I don't think he will,' said Lord Waveryng. 'He believes in his first wife's ghost. It's a kind of mania. You Blakes are all a little queer, you know.'

'Yes, I know very well,' answered Morres Blake bitterly. 'It's in the blood. That queerness is responsible for a good deal.'

Lord Waveryng looked at him keenly. 'You are sane enough,' he said.

'Am I?' cried Blake passionately. 'I'm mad, I tell you – mad – mad!'

'You were mad when you threw your chances away and went in for that Fenian business: but it was the aberration of youth. They tell me that you make a good colonial politician. Curious, isn't it, when one comes to think of it, that you should be Colonial Secretary of Leichardt's Land?'

Blake laughed strangely. Again there was silence.

The men walked on, puffing their cigars. They had reached the place where the street divided into two, one leading to the ferry, the other past the Houses of Parliament to the great gates of Government House. Here they paused.

'Lord Waveryng,' Blake said impulsively, 'I trust you.'

'I never betrayed confidence in my life,' said the other, 'at least, I hope not willingly. If you wish to be thought dead, why, as far as I am concerned, you are dead. But I think you make a mistake in not facing the music.'

They shook hands and parted; but Blake did not go straight to Fermoy's.

Careless of what might be thought of him, he walked on through the paddock in which Riverside Cottage stood. He looked wistfully at the little closed-up house and at the verandah in which was Elsie's chair, and where her work-basket still lay on the rough table. He was only driven away by the sight of Peter the Kanaka, up betimes to gather rosellas for the shop on the Point, which bought such garden stuff as the widow had to dispose of. He slipped down among the lantana shrubs that grew close to the garden fence, and made his way back by a circuitous, but less public track, along the river bank to Fermoy's.

During the days that followed the Club Ball, Elsie Valliant's mental and moral condition might have been expressed in the plaint of Mariana, though, to be sure, the outward circumstances of her life were very different from those of the lady of the Moated Grange. Life at Leichardt's Town was at high pressure; life at Riverside Cottage was at high pressure too. The verandah receptions were more brilliant and more sought after than ever, and gained *éclat* from the presence of the Waveryngs and an admixture of the Government House set; not, certainly, in the persons of Sir Theophilus and Lady Stukeley, but in the shape of the aide-de-camp and private secretary, and of the more or less distinguished strangers who frequented Government House at this time. There was always some bustle of coming and going, of flirtation, or of making ready for flirtation. But still Blake came not.

They met often, and yet not so often as would have been the case a month before. It seemed to Elsie that Blake avoided all the informal parties which once, for the sake of a waltz or talk with her, he had welcomed so eagerly. And at the more ceremonious functions, there was an excuse for the formal nature of their intercourse. Naturally, at the public balls and at the Government House At Homes it was not to be supposed that the Colonial Secretary could devote himself exclusively to one pretty girl. Blake paid attention to a few of the Leichardt's Town young ladies, and to Elsie there was in this fact a faint consolation. At any rate she could not feel jealous of Mrs. Torbolton, or of the wife of the Minister for Works, or even of Lady Waveryng, who declared herself charmed with Blake, and made him into a sort of cicerone. But in truth the girl's own being was torn in tatters. Wounded pride, love, the sense of humiliation, and insult, made her days an anguish and her nights a terror. And yet she laughed all the time, and she flirted with everybody and made herself into a very scorn of Leichardt's Town matrons by reason of her unblushing levity.

Just at this time, one of the minor Royal Princes, who was making a tour of the colonies, paid a long-expected week's visit to Leichardt's Town, and the occasion was one of wild excitement and of enthusiastic demonstration of Antipodean loyalty. Elsie had the satisfaction of seeing Blake in official capacity, taking part in the various pageants, as one of the committee of reception; and in spite of her misery, and her anger against him, she felt a savage pride in the manner in which he acquitted himself. She was at the great ceremony of the landing, and at the Mayor's Ball, at the School of Arts, in the evening. She was also at the races, at which one or two of the horses which had exploited at Tunimbah ran, with less credit to themselves and their owners; she was at the picnic in the Government steamer, in which the Prince was shown the bay and the islands; and at all the functions for which Frank Hallett's efforts and the reflected glory of the Waveryngs secured her a place. It was all very brilliant, and she had her fill of admiration. The Prince was greatly taken by her beauty, and danced with her so often as to fill his guardians with a half-amused alarm. Perhaps this was why Lord Astar, one of the Prince's suite, made violent love to Elsie, and short of absolutely proposing marriage, did everything which could be expected from a suitor for her hand. Lord Astar found the verandah receptions very much to his taste, and on the days when he was off duty during the latter part of the Prince's visit, might usually be seen seated at Elsie's feet, with his legs dangling over the edge of the riverside verandah in the most approved colonial fashion, or else lounging on the steps that led to the boat-house, another favourite scene for Elsie's flirtations. The Prince would have liked to take part also in Elsie's verandah receptions, but on this point the Stukeleys and the noble Admiral who had him in charge were inexorable.

Lord Astar was amusing, and clever, and fascinating, and he was very much a man of the world. Elsie had never met any one of his type, though since the arrival of the Waveryngs her experience of the English aristocracy had extended somewhat beyond her brother-in-law. It struck her that Lord Astar's type was most nearly approached by Morres Blake in his lighter moods. Certainly nothing more widely removed from the type could be conceived than Frank Hallett.

It may have been with some wild idea of making Blake jealous that Elsie flirted so desperately with Lord Astar. All Leichardt's Town – that is, the portion of it which constituted society – remarked her behaviour on the day of the races. They were in the Grand Stand – Ina and her husband in that portion which was railed off for the Government House party and the higher officials, but Elsie, with the Prydes, in a less exalted position. She was looking lovely in a grey dress with soft lace at the neck and a bewitching bonnet made out of the breast of an Australian bird. Lord Astar admired her dress, and Elsie told him that she had sat up all the night before to finish it. She also informed him that the bonnet, or at least the bird which composed it, had been a present from King Tommy, of Yoolaman.

'And so the Prince is not your only royal admirer,' said Lord Astar. 'Are lower mortals privileged to lay tributes of loyalty at your feet?'

As he spoke, Elsie became suddenly aware that Blake was passing along the gangway behind her chair. She felt that he stopped, knew instinctively that he had heard Lord Astar's speech and was waiting for her reply. A demon of recklessness seized her; she looked coquettishly up at Lord Astar and answered very distinctly, 'Certainly. Tributes are always welcome.'

'Miss Valliant,' Blake's incisive tones seemed to cut the air, 'Lady Horace has gone down to the saddling paddock, and she asked me to bring you to her.'

Elsie started. Blake moved a chair beside her.

'You will come?' His eyes were full upon her.

She rose obediently; it would have been impossible for her to disobey the mandate of those eyes. Lord Astar bowed and made way for her.

'I shall not forget,' he said very low.

Blake piloted her down the stairs of the Grand Stand. When they stood on the lawn he turned and said deliberately, 'Lady Horace is not in the saddling paddock. I don't know in the least where she is, and she did not send me for you. I brought you here to tell you that you must not accept presents from Lord Astar.'

'Surely,' said Elsie bitterly, 'that can be of very little consequence to you.'

'No, it is not of consequence to me,' he answered, 'but it is of consequence to yourself. I know Lord Astar. I know the sort of reputation he has in regard to women. You compromise your reputation by allowing him to pay you the attentions which have been making you so conspicuous these last few days. Please take my word for this. He is a more dangerous opponent in the game which we have been playing than I have been. Don't play that game with him; the consequences may be disagreeable.'

'In what way?'

'In this – Astar is quite capable of insulting a woman who places herself in a false position.'

'And you,' she cried passionately, 'have you not shown yourself capable of insulting a woman who was fool enough to place herself at your mercy?'

He turned very pale. An impetuous answer rose to his lips. He uttered one vehement word and checked himself.

'I beg your pardon,' he said. 'I have nothing else to say. I have no justification for the impulse that made me take you in my arms that night. I can only ask you to believe that there has never been in my mind a disrespectful thought of you. And then –' he paused and went on in a different tone, 'the situation was understood between us. It had been a challenge. There had been an open fight, and I had suffered severely enough to make me feel a savage wish to show you that you were beaten.'

They had walked on, not in the direction of the saddling paddock, but among the gum trees at the back of the Grand Stand, where, the view of the course being obstructed by the building, there was little or no crowd; indeed, except for a few stragglers in care of luncheon carts, the spot was almost deserted. Elsie turned fiercely upon Blake. Her eyes were flashing; her bosom heaving.

'What right have you to say that I was beaten? You said that I – that I cared for you. What reason did I give you for thinking so? Wasn't I playing the game too? Do you think I have fallen so low as to give my heart to a man who – who has shown me that he despises me? I despise you, Mr. Blake; I *hate* you!'

Blake stood perfectly immovable. 'I am glad of that,' he said quietly. 'I wish you to hate me. But you are quite wrong in the other thing. I do not despise you.'

'Why – why?' stammered Elsie. 'Why should you wish me to hate you?'

'Because it would not be for your happiness that you should love me.'

'And why?' she repeated with the persistency of a child.

'Because,' he answered, 'I cannot –' He stopped, and added more calmly, 'Because in my scheme of life, marriage has no place.'

Elsie turned, and they walked a few steps back without speaking.

'You have not given me credit for much cleverness, Mr. Blake,' she said. 'You evidently don't seem to think that I am able to take a hint. I fancy that you warned me before we – before we challenged each other – against cherishing any false hopes.'

The bitterness of her tone hurt Blake keenly.

'Thank you,' he said. 'It is a wholesome lesson for me to be made to feel that I am a conceited ass.'

Again they walked on in silence. They were near the Grand Stand.

'Please don't go up for a minute or two yet,' he said. 'We have wandered from the question.'

'And the question is –'

'Lord Astar's obvious intention of making you a present, which will probably take the form of an article of jewellery. Miss Valliant, I beseech you, for your own sake –'

'Hush!' she exclaimed passionately. 'I don't want you to say anything more. I am old enough to take care of myself; and if not, I have others who have a better right to protect me.'

'Very well. Forgive me for my presumption. I will not offend you again.' He turned deliberately. 'We had better go back now,' he said, and conducted her to the stand, leaving her in her place beside Minnie Pryde with a ceremonious bow.

Elsie did not speak to him again that day. Lord Astar came back presently, and hardly quitted Elsie's side the rest of the day. When they got home, Minnie Pryde insisted on telling Mrs. Valliant of Elsie's conquest.

The silly woman was beside herself with delight. Elsie married to Lord Astar! Ina's marriage was as nothing in comparison. Why not? If the Prince admired Elsie, why should not Lord Astar marry her? She had been quite right in giving Frank Hallett an undecided answer – quite right in keeping that pushing, handsome Mr. Blake, and his less handsome and more pushing partner, at a distance. Ah, Elsie was her pride and her joy! Elsie would yet be the glory of her old age.

The girl burst into a passionate fit of tears. 'Oh, mother, mother!' she cried. 'For pity's sake leave me alone, and expect nothing of me.'

CHAPTER XXI

---•---

'At Government House'

It was the last night but one of the Prince's stay, and the Birthnight Ball, long after date, had been fixed for that evening. The occasion was to be one of unusual splendour.

Mrs. Valliant, in her rather shiny black moiré and a feathered cap, had been persuaded to emerge from her retirement and to chaperon Elsie. Not that there had been any difficulty in persuading her. She had always made it a point of duty to attend the 'Queen's Birthday' Ball. At the other balls she had allowed Ina and Elsie to be chaperoned by any obliging neighbour, but upon this occasion she felt that loyalty demanded an effort, and moreover it was her only opportunity of witnessing her pretty daughter's triumph. She was a good deal assisted in the effort by Lord Horace's present of a lace shawl, which, as she said, made her look fit to stand even beside Lady Waveryng in all her diamonds. To-night she was in a state of feverish excitement, almost as great as that of Elsie herself, and her delicate face, which had the remains of Elsie's beauty, was flushed like a girl's, as she put the last touches to Elsie's hair and dress. Elsie's dress had been a present, too, from Lord Horace. It was white, and floated about her in fleecy clouds, the little satin bodice moulded to her pretty, slight figure, and great bunches of Cloth of Gold and La France roses at her breast and on her shoulders. There was a bouquet of roses, too, on the table, which she had made herself. Oddly enough, Frank Hallett had sent her no bouquet this time. Perhaps he thought she would wear Blake's or Trant's; perhaps he remembered that she had once before discarded his for one that Blake had sent her. But Blake had sent her none now, and Trant had been called suddenly to Baròlin, and was hardly expected to be down in time for the ball, and so Elsie had been obliged to go herself to the curator of the Public Gardens and beg for the roses, which were not as perfect as she would have liked. There were so many more important persons to be provided with flowers.

But while she was dressing, a special messenger arrived with a box. Peter, the Kanaka, brought it to Elsie's room. The messenger had said that he must take back an assurance that Miss Valliant had received it, and so Mrs. Valliant went to the door. The messenger was a suave, gentlemanly person – Lord Astar's servant, and he had come from Government House.

The box contained another bouquet, wired as if it were straight from Covent Garden, and tied with pale pink streamers. It was composed entirely of the most exquisite La France and Maréchal Niel roses, and was in a silver holder. At the bottom of the box lay a little packet and a note. When Elsie opened the packet she gave a cry of surprise and delight. The light flashed from a star of pearls and diamonds. It was the temptation of Marguerite; and Elsie, notwithstanding her many Leichardt's Town seasons, her numerous flirtations, and her daring unconventionality, was in truth as innocently ignorant of evil intent to herself in the mind of man as was Marguerite when she opened Mephistopheles' casket. Elsie's lovers had always been chivalrous. The note was only a few lines:

'If you will honour me by wearing the accompanying little trinket this evening, I shall interpret it as a sign that you accept my love, and that I may hope for the fulfilment of my most ardent wish.

'Devotedly yours,
'ASTAR.'

Elsie drew a deep, long breath. It was almost like a sigh of pain, but it was not pain or dismay or indignation which brought it forth. To her the note had but one meaning. It had never entered her mind that a man could approach a woman with words of love meaning anything but the one thing – marriage. Of course, he wished to marry her. It was very strange, very sudden. That was all. To-night she must make up her mind whether or not she would accept this brilliant destiny, nay, she must decide now, this very moment, since her destiny depended upon the clasping round her neck of the jewel Lord Astar had sent her. Well, there was no great difficulty in deciding. Here was some balm for her poor torn heart and wounded pride. Now, at least, she could prove to Blake that she had never loved him. She could show him that if he despised her there were others more highly placed than he who thought her worthy of being lifted to a rank far beyond any that he could offer her. And yet – the stab was agony – she loved him. She had never realised it so keenly as now.

Mrs. Valliant watched her in breathless interest. She, too, had seen the flash of the diamonds, and she had no doubt of what the note contained. She, too, was in her way as innocent as her daughter. She knew nothing of the wickedness of the world or the ways of men like Lord Astar.

'Elsie!' she cried. 'Oh, tell me, what is it?'

'It is from Lord Astar,' replied Elsie dreamily.

'Yes, yes, I know. But show me – how beautiful!' She held the ornament to the light and then away from her, and gazed at it in an ecstasy of pleasure. 'It is magnificent – a present for a queen! Oh, Elsie, and it is settled! And you let Minnie Pryde go on with her chatter, and you never told me – me, your mother, and I have been so anxious. He proposed to you to-day. I knew it was coming – I saw that it was coming! No one could have watched him yesterday without seeing – he couldn't tear himself away, he couldn't keep his eyes from you. Was it to-day, Elsie, that he proposed?'

'No, he hasn't proposed to me.'

'But the letter?' said Mrs. Valliant bewildered. 'What does he say? It can only mean that'

'Yes,' said Elsie slowly, 'I suppose it means that.' She gave the note to her mother, who read it eagerly, and then looked at Elsie with an expression of bewildered joy, mixed with a certain vague terror. Then she read the note again aloud, and her expression became one of confident triumph.

'Yes, of course it means that. "His dearest wish – that you will accept my love." I think it is beautiful, so delicate, such a romantic way of putting things; and to send this! It's like what one reads in books – oh, Elsie, and he is so rich – Horace was telling me. Of course, it's quite natural. Ina married to Horace, and the Waveryngs so taken with her, the difference in position wouldn't strike him. Oh! what will the Garfits say now, and Mrs. Jem Hallett, who didn't think you good enough to be her sister-in-law? And now – Lady Astar! Oh, Elsie, it is so wonderful! I can't believe it!'

The poor woman ran on in her delight, never for a moment doubting her daughter's good fortune. Elsie said not a word.

At last Mrs. Valliant exclaimed, 'Elsie, how strange you are! Aren't you happy? Tell your mother who is so proud of you.'

'Yes, I am happy,' Elsie said. 'And so, mother, you wish me to wear Lord Astar's star?'

'Why, of course. He will understand, as he says, that you accept his love.'

'Accept his love,' repeated Elsie. 'And I have none to give him in return. But that doesn't matter, mother.'

'It will come,' said Mrs. Valliant. 'How can you *love* him, when you have only seen him about five times? Though it seems to me that it would be hard to help loving any one so good-looking and fascinating as Lord Astar. I am not afraid of that.'

She fastened the star round Elsie's throat, where it gleamed, as Mrs. Valliant said, like an electric light. They tried it in several positions – in her hair and in front of her dress, but decided that it looked best upon her neck.

Elsie was strangely silent. All the way to Government House she was silent too. It was a long drive, round by the south side and across the bridge. Minnie Pryde and her father were with them, an arrangement by which Mrs. Valliant was spared half the price of the cab. They did not have a jingle this time. That was well enough for a club dance, or a private party, but for the Queen's Birthnight Ball – and the Prince there – and Lord Astar! – No! At the last moment Mrs. Valliant had done violence to her economic soul, and had countermanded the jingle, and had asked the Prydes if they would go halves in a closed landau.

'Oh, Elsie, look!' cried Miss Pryde, as they drove in at the great gates.

The grounds had been turned into fairyland. The avenue of young bunyas was like an avenue of overgrown Christmas trees – pyramids of coloured lamps. And all the paths were outlined in coloured lamps, and Japanese lanterns were dotted about the trees and festooned the colonnades, and over all the full moon shed a ghostly radiance. Within, it was even more like fairyland still. Canvas rooms had been thrown out – bowers of palm leaves, poinsettia, flowering yucca, and rich calladiums, and all the rarest tropical plants. In one place a miniature fern-tree gulley, with stuffed birds perched on the huge fronds as if about to take flight. Murmuring cascades, mossy grottoes, and banks of maidenhair and rock lilies. And further on, a mass of azaleas, and then a camellia tree, and here and there moss-bordered pools with fountains playing and waterlilies floating about. Of course Ina and Lord Horace were with the Waveryngs and the inmost circle of the Government House party – Lady Stukeley, in the magnificence of

172 Outlaw and Lawmaker

crimson velvet, rose point, and diamonds that paled somewhat in glory beside Lady Waveryng's tiara, that was celebrated, but which were, nevertheless, finer than anything of the kind which the Leichardtstonians had ever seen. It was really an imposing sight, and Elsie wondered whether a drawing-room could be much grander – the great ladies in their jewels, the Prince and his suite with their decorations, and the uniforms and gold lace, and cocked hats and swords, that made up a background to the central figures. Everybody who had any sort of right to wear a uniform had put it on to-night, even to Minnie Pryde's father, who had once had some kind of appointment in a volunteer corps, and Mr. Torbolton, the Premier, who looked very uncomfortable, and nearly tumbled over his sword.

When Elsie had got over her entrance greeting, and the little bob to Royalty, to which a course of six days' state pageantry had already accustomed her, she found some amusement in watching the Leichardtstonians as they filed past and performed their obeisances. Frank Hallett came presently, and put his name down for some dances, and found Mrs. Valliant a seat, from which she could see the dancing when it began. He gave a startled look at Elsie's glittering decoration; the girl flushed crimson in contrast to his sudden paleness. It seemed to her that every eye in the room must be fixed on that star. Certainly the eyes of Blake were arrested by it, and he, too, turned a shade paler, and his own eyes gave out a flash as he noticed the ornament and guessed its history.

'I congratulate you, Miss Valliant,' he said, very low, in a voice of concentrated fury and bitterness. 'Lord Astar has excellent taste in jewellery.'

'Lord Astar!' Frank Hallett caught the name, and turned to Elsie with a sudden passionate jealousy. 'Come out with me,' he said hoarsely, forgetting Blake's presence – forgetting everything but a sudden awful fear that seized him. 'I want to say something to you.'

'Not now,' answered Elsie calmly. 'Please forgive me, Mr. Hallett. I forgot when I let you put your name down for the first waltz that I cannot dance it with you.'

'You are engaged to me for that waltz,' said Blake.

She looked at him. His eyes never flinched from her face, but held hers with a compelling power. Elsie realised what a subject of hypnotism must feel in the presence of a master of that gift. She would have given worlds at that moment to have been able to assert her will and contradict Blake. It was impossible. She was spellbound. She began to speak, and the words died on her lips.

'You are engaged to me,' Blake repeated. 'In the meantime may I offer you my arm, till,' he added as they turned away, 'Lord Astar is at liberty to claim his property?'

Still Elsie was spellbound. They walked on a few steps. At that moment the music began, and the formal reception ended. The first quadrille – a state business – was being formed. The knot of men behind the Prince broke up; the Prince was leading off Lady Stukeley. Lord Astar came hurrying to them. He was flushed, and looked excited. There was the light of an evil triumph in his eyes.

'I have been watching you, and watching for you,' he said to Elsie. 'That abominable bowing and scraping seemed never ending, and of course I was tied. Miss Valliant, I'm tied still, you understand, for this quadrille, and I believe it's Mrs. Torbolton – one of the wives of an official dignitary – sounds Mormonish, that speech, doesn't it? I'm on duty, you understand. Once this dance is over I'm free till supper time. I claim the first waltz – the dance after the quadrille.'

Elsie looked at Blake. She stammered – 'I think – I believe – I am engaged.'

'No!' exclaimed Blake, making a profound, and it seemed to Elsie an ironic, bow. 'I resign my claim. Lord Astar has an evident right.'

'You are very good,' said Lord Astar coolly and somewhat superciliously, glancing at Blake. 'But you needn't take the merit of the sacrifice, though I am much obliged all the same. Miss Valliant *was* engaged to me.'

'The next waltz, and' – he whispered to Elsie – 'don't let too many fellows put their names down. It's to be mine – this evening; oh, if you knew how beautiful you look –'

He hurried off to where Mrs. Torbolton was sitting; poor lady, she would much rather have danced with one of her husband's colleagues. Blake gave his arm again to Elsie; he had turned aside while Lord Astar had been speaking.

'Shall we dance? I will find a place among the lesser fry.'

He placed her opposite Minnie Pryde and Mr. Anderson. Minnie's eyebrows went up in astonishment at the sight of Elsie's star. 'My goodness!' she exclaimed, 'to think of my not noticing it when you took off your cloak in the dressing-room! *Who* is it? Not –' and she gave a significant flash in Blake's direction.

Elsie held herself haughtily erect and vouchsafed no sign. Miss Pryde was not to be rebuked. 'It's not His Respectability of Tunimbah, that I'll swear! I always said he had no chance. Oh, Elsie,' and Miss

Pryde's voice sank to an awestruck whisper, 'it's not, it *can't be*, the Prince?'

'How do you know it isn't paste?' whispered Elsie back, as they parted hands. It was in the contact of the ladies' chain that Miss Pryde had jerked out her interrogatories.

'Tell your grandmother!' replied Miss Pryde, with more pertinency than elegance.

Lord Astar claimed Elsie directly the dance was over. He had found no difficulty in depositing Mrs. Torbolton on a chair, for the good lady was scant of breath, and glad to secure a permanent position till supper time. His dance had not been unprofitable. He had taken advantage of the pauses in the quadrille to lead the conversation to the subject of Elsie. Miss Valliant, he soon discovered, was not a favourite in Leichardt's Town. Mrs. Torbolton thought it was really her duty to warn the young man – he was quite young, and no doubt he had a mother who would be sorry to see him fall a victim to the most designing flirt in Leichardt's Town. Elsie, it may at once be said, had refused Mrs. Torbolton's son, and the young man had gone to the diggings, and had lost his money and taken to evil ways, a second instance of the fatal effect of Elsie's charms. Mrs. Torbolton hated Elsie, and perhaps it was not unnatural that she should. 'Yes, she was certainly very pretty,' Mrs. Torbolton grudgingly admitted. But then everybody knew that Elsie painted, and made herself up in a way that was not respectable. And she took presents from gentlemen, and went to lengths that really would astonish Lord Astar if he knew. In proof of it there was the fact that in spite of her undoubted beauty she was not yet married. Mr. Frank Hallett was supposed to be in love with her, but Mrs. Jem herself had declared quite lately that Mr. Hallett was evidently doubtful about tying himself to a girl so talked of – now that he was likely to take a prominent position in politics, and when it is so important that the wife of a public man should be above suspicion – 'Caesar's wife, you know,' addded Mrs. Torbolton – and she had gone on to a highly-coloured relation of some of poor Elsie's escapades, the Jensen episode among them. Lord Astar was not at all ill-pleased at Mrs. Torbolton's confidences. He had often been just a little uneasy on the score of the Horace Gages and the Waveryng connectionship, but clearly it counted for very little. Lady Horace was a harmless little creature, utterly ignorant of the world, and not likely to assert claims of any sort. Lord Horace, as every one knew, was the scapegrace of the family – the half-witted scapegrace, which was a far less dangerous person than the clever black sheep –

and but for Lady Waveryng's infatuation for him, and consequently the help that Lord Waveryng gave him, no one would ever trouble their heads about Lord Horace's personal or family dignity; no, that would not matter at all when the Waveryngs left Australia, which would be very shortly. It was unlucky that they should be on the scene just now, but with a little management things could be kept dark. And as for Elsie, the penniless daughter of a defunct scab inspector, and a pretty dressmaker – Lord Astar had informed himself on the subject of Elsie's parentage, and he smiled in amused appreciation of the hereditary instinct which aided her in the concoction of those very tasteful costumes to which she so frankly owned – the girl who 'made up' and who accepted presents from her admirers; the girl of whom the Leichardt's Town matrons fought shy, and of whom the Leichardt's Town young ladies were jealous; the girl who was a sort of Pariah among her kind, and who loved dress, and luxury, and jewels, and who was devoured with a curiosity about life, about the world, who wanted to travel, who wanted 'experience; she did not mind what kind of experience' – so poor Elsie had stated – 'as long as it was experience;' ah, well, was not this the natural and fitting conclusion? And he would give her experience, and of a not very unpleasant kind. The battle would be even; the bargain would be a fair one; after all she deserved her fate. For Lord Astar was quick enough to see that the girl was not in love with him, and that it was only the glamour of rank, wealth, and perhaps a glamour of the senses which had intoxicated her.

There was in his manner a certain familiarity, a certain freedom, when he came to claim her, which jarred on Elsie, and roused in her the first faint feeling of alarm. But this had vanished when he piloted her into the dance, and guided her swiftly, surely, and with a perfection of finish of style and movement which was very delightful to Elsie. She herself was one of Nature's dancers. She loved the exercise, and she danced as few women can who have not made it a profession. When the dance was over, he took her out into one of the canvas conservatories. 'I have been all around,' he said, 'I know the quiet nooks. Here is one you'd never suspect.' He pulled back a corner of the canvas, which was flapping loosely under an overhanging branch of palm leaves, and drew her through. They were in a little vine trellis, naked now, and with the moon shining through the interlacing boughs of an old Isabella grape vine, and at the end of the trellis was a small summer-house, unlighted, except by one Japanese lantern. He led the girl, half shrinking, half wretched, half glad, to a bench in the summer-house. Then he took her two hands, and drew her to him, leaning a little back himself while he looked at her with bold admiring eyes.

'My own darling. You are so beautiful; and I love you so. If you knew how I watched the door this evening, and how my heart jumped when I saw the flash of those.' He placed a sacrilegious hand upon the girl's warm soft neck.

She shrank from his touch.

'You were glad that I wore them.'

'Glad! I told you what it meant – my dearest wish! Darling, you didn't hesitate. You knew what it meant?'

'I asked my mother if I should wear them,' said Elsie simply.

'You asked your mother. By Jove!' Lord Astar stroked his moustache. And then he laughed, and put his arm round Elsie's waist, and would have kissed her, but she eluded the caress.

'What a shy little thing we are! Not one kiss?'

'Not – not yet,' she said, still shrinking.

He bent down and kissed her neck, and then her arms, and then her gloved hands, and back again to her dimpled shoulder. She put up her bouquet to shield herself from the rain of kisses. She had kept her lips – but these scorched and hurt her.

'No; let us talk.'

'Kissing is better than talking, when one has such a delicious soft thing as you to kiss. Haven't plenty of other men found that out and told you so?'

'I don't know whether they have found it out. They have not told me so.'

'Not, really! Am I the first?' he asked jestingly, incredulously.

'Almost the first. Yes, the first.' She made a mental reservation – the first man whom she had freely allowed to kiss her, and whom she intended to marry. Blake had kissed her, but that had been a theft, an outrage.

'You all say that,' he said laughing. 'But the ladies of Leichardt's Town tell a different tale.'

'Ah!' She gave a little wounded exclamation. 'Please don't tell me what they said. I know it was something cruel. Tell me –'

'Tell you what?'

'Anything that is not too hard for me. Tell me what made you first think of this?'

'If I had a looking-glass I'd put it in front of you and ask you to read the answer to that question in your own face. I love my love with an E, because she is – hang it, there's not an adjective for Elsie, except elegant, and that does not express you. I love my love because she is the loveliest woman I've ever seen. Will that do?'

'And you will give up everything for me – only because I am pretty?'

'Give up everything!' he repeated. 'Gain everything, you mean.'

'It is giving up – when you don't know a girl, and when it's a girl like me, with no connections – or – or anything to speak of, only a little Australian savage, and when even –'

'When – what?'

'When she doesn't even love you as much as she ought.'

He turned himself to her and looked into her face with a curious surprise. She was looking out into the night, and her expression puzzled and her indifference piqued him into still wilder admiration. He laughed in a strange way. 'I think I could make you love me – quite as much as you ought, if you will trust yourself to me.'

Now she turned to him seriously. 'Very well,' she said. 'I will trust myself to you. If I had not thought that you would make me love you, and if I hadn't wanted to try, I would not have worn this.' She touched the diamonds at her neck.

He threw his arm round her. She knew that he wanted to kiss her, and something in his eyes made her shrink. She got up hastily. 'Not now,' she said. 'I think I should like to go back to the dancing.'

'No, no,' he pleaded. But she was firm. Nor would she let him kiss even her hand. He thought this was coquetry, and told her he bided his time.

CHAPTER XXII

───────── • ─────────

'We are Engaged to be Married'

The dance that should have been Frank Hallett's was claimed by the Prince. Of course the royal request was a command, and Elsie danced with the distinguished guest of Leichardt's Land, to the envy and admiration of the Leichardtstonians. Lord Astar had written his name down for the dance following, and he came almost immediately and took her away. They went round the room once, and then he said hoarsely in her ear, 'You are fooling me and playing with me. You won't listen to what I have to say, and yet you have as good as promised to be mine.'

Elsie's hour had come. She let him lead her into the garden. They went to the little summer-house to which he had taken her before. All the way he poured out words of ardent devotion.

Frank Hallett watched her go out with Astar. He watched for her return. It seemed to him as though some horrible fate were keeping him from her. He could hardly prevent himself from going up to her when she was dancing with the Prince, and when she was on Lord Astar's arm. There was something about Elsie to-night which filled him with uneasiness. He was certain that she was very unhappy. He had watched her face while she was talking to Blake, and told himself that it was Blake she loved. Why was she flirting with Lord Astar? What was the meaning of that glittering star? He was standing moodily against a background of palms at the entrance to the ball-room, when he heard his own name spoken, and in Elsie's voice, –

'Frank!'

He hardly knew the voice, it was so thin and so frightened. He turned. She was standing there alone; he could not see Lord Astar. She was deadly pale except for a bright red spot on each cheek, and her eyes were like flames. 'Frank,' she said, still with that strange quietude, 'will you take me away somewhere – somewhere where nobody can see me?'

'Elsie,' he exclaimed, 'what is the matter? Come with me, my dear. I will take care of you.'

He gave her his arm. As she clung to it he felt a tremor all through her body.

'Not there,' she cried, fancying he was going to turn into the ballroom. 'Take me home. Oh, Frank, take me home.'

'Your mother is there,' he said. 'She was asking for you a moment ago. I told her you were with Lord Astar. Won't you go to her?'

'No, no' She shuddered. 'I can't go in there – I can't, I can't.'

Her composure was deserting her. He threw a hasty glance round. Another dance had begun. To the right was a refreshment room, now empty. He took her in there and put her on a chair. By this time she was trembling violently. He went to the table and poured out a glass of champagne cup, all that he could find in the way of stimulant, and made her drink it. 'I am sorry it is not something stronger,' he said. 'Elsie, tell me: are you ill? Has anything happened?'

'Yes – yes – I am ill. Take me home, Frank; now, at once. If I stay here I shall faint, or go mad. Take me home.'

'Tell me where your cloak is,' he said quietly, 'and if you will wait here for a few moments I will fetch it, and will send for a carriage.'

She felt in the bodice of her dress for a cardboard number. He noticed then for the first time that there was a great scratch upon the white skin, and that the diamond ornament was gone from her neck.

He asked no questions, but went silently to the cloak-room. After a few minutes he came back with her cloak, and wrapped it round her. She was cowering in a corner of the room, having moved from the chair in which he had put her, and she had her face turned from the door, as if she were afraid of being seen.

'Come,' he said. 'I was lucky. My flyman was just outside the entrance, and I got the cab at once.'

He led her out into the colonnade. She had a lace scarf over her head, and she pulled it round her face, still in the same dread of being recognised and spoken to. 'Do you want me to tell your mother, or to send any message? Would you like her to go with you? If you would I will take you a little way down the drive, and you will be able to wait in the cab while I bring her to you.'

'No,' she said. 'I would rather go with you alone. Mamma will think I am with Lord Astar; she will not mind.' Elsie gave a wild little laugh, which broke into a sob. 'Stay,' she said, and taking her programme she wrote upon it, 'I have gone home with Mr. Hallett. Please don't mind about me, but stay with Ina. I am tired. – ELSIE.' She folded the programme and wrote her mother's name upon it, all with the same feverish haste, and put it into his hands, while he helped her into the cab. 'Give it to some one to give to her,' she said, 'and then come back to me and take me away. I can't bear it any longer. Oh, Frank, make haste and take me away.'

He went back for a moment to the entrance to the ball-room, bidding the cabman to drive on and wait a little lower down the drive. He looked round for a trustworthy bearer of Elsie's message. By good fortune Lady Horace was coming out of one of the tea rooms on the arm of Morres Blake. He went up to her. 'Lady Horace, may I speak to you for a moment?'

Blake withdrew a few paces. Ina looked at him anxiously. 'Where is Elsie?' she asked; 'I cannot find her.'

'Elsie is with me. Ina, something has happened to upset her – I don't know what, unless that cad, Lord Astar – –'

'Lord Astar!' Ina repeated. 'Oh, Frank, mamma said something – nothing is settled. I will not let Elsie be carried away into doing what she will all her life regret. Trust me, Frank. I have been looking for Elsie ever since. You mustn't judge poor mamma hardly. You mustn't be hard on Elsie.'

Ina spoke in great agitation. She laid her little hand on his arm beseechingly. He looked at her puzzled.

'I don't quite know what you mean,' he said. 'I judge Elsie hardly! You know how I love her. Lady Horace, you may trust her with me. She wants to go home. She doesn't want Mrs. Valliant – I asked her. She wants to go home with me. Perhaps she will let me help her. She asked me to send this to Mrs. Valliant. Will you explain?'

Ina took the folded programme and read what Elsie had written.

'Yes, I will explain; I think I understand why Elsie doesn't want mamma. She thinks mamma might be angry. Poor Elsie! Take her home, Frank, and be kind to her.'

Ina's voice was trembling. Frank wondered why she showed so much emotion, but he did not wait to ask any questions. Ina turned toward Blake, who was standing apart watching them, with a curious expression on his face.

'I beg your pardon,' Ina said with quiet dignity, 'Mr. Hallett wanted to tell me that my sister wasn't very well, and that she does not want to frighten my mother and to take her away. She is only tired, and there's nothing wrong; and so he is going to take her back to Riverside, and I will explain to my mother. It would be such a pity to interrupt mamma's pleasure, for she is enjoying the sight, and she so seldom goes anywhere, and there is nothing really wrong with Elsie,' Ina added conscientiously. 'She is only tired.'

Blake bowed, and she took his arm again, while Hallett made his way out to where the cab was standing. He gave the order to the driver – 'Riverside Cottage, Emu Point, round by the bridge,' and got in beside Elsie. He saw that in those few minutes her composure had been broken down completely. She was crouching in a corner of the cab, and was sobbing hysterically. He took her hand in his, and soothed her as if she had been a child. 'Elsie, dear, try not to be unhappy, Elsie! Nothing can happen to you now. I am here to take care of you. If I can't be anything else I can be your brother, dear; and I can take care of you.'

'You don't know; you don't know,' she sobbed.

'I think I can guess,' he answered grimly. 'Lord Astar dared to send you that diamond thing that you wore – and he took advantage of your – your ignorance and thoughtlessness in accepting a present of which you probably didn't know the value. You took it as you might have taken a flower from me, and he inferred from it that you cared for him.'

'No,' she said; 'don't think better of me than I deserve. He did send it to me. He asked me to wear it as a sign that I would accept his love. I thought he wanted to marry me; and I would have married him for his rank and his money, though I didn't love him. I was bad enough for that, Frank. And then –' She fell again to shuddering sobs.

'Go on, Elsie.' Frank's voice was deep with passion. 'Tell me everything.'

'I can't, I can't. How can I tell you of my disgrace? How can I expect that you will ever speak to me or look at me again? If you knew how low I have fallen – what men think of me.'

Frank gave a low, grim exclamation. 'Well, Elsie, tell me as if I were your brother. Try for to-night to think of me as your brother.'

'It was mamma who said I must wear that, and the bouquet; it came while I was dressing. I had told him at the races that – that he might send me something. I did it; how can I make you understand? Mr. Blake was behind me; he warned me against Lord Astar. He had no right; his speaking made me mad. I wanted to show him that I did not care.'

'Ah!' Frank drew in his breath, as if with pain. 'I understand. It is Blake whom you love.'

'No, no!' she cried with passion; 'I hate him. I never wish to see him again.'

'Is that true, Elsie?'

'Yes, Frank, I will tell you the truth. I did think I cared for him. We were playing at a game that was deadly for me, and I wouldn't own it. I thought I would make him care. It was a fair challenge. I can't blame him for anything. One of us had to be hurt. It is I who was hurt, but I would not let him know. I hate him now. He exulted over me. He dared to tell me that he had won. And I said no, no. I wanted to show him that it didn't matter to me. It was for that, partly. You know I always meant to make a great match if I could. I never hid that from you. It was partly because of Mr. Blake, and to get away from everything, that I wore Lord Astar's diamonds. Mamma thought that he wanted to marry me. We were both of us blind; foolish, oh, how utterly foolish! we didn't think how I must seem to him fair game. And he must have laughed. It makes me laugh now.'

She burst into hysterical merriment that was terrible to hear.

'Don't, Elsie; don't – don't laugh like that, my dear. There is no shame to you, because he was a villain. The unutterable cad. He has dared –'

'At first I thought he meant that we should run away, to be married. He said if I would meet him the next day, and he would get off going with the Prince, and take me to Sydney; and afterwards to England. And then – when I understood –'

'What did you do? My God! If I had heard him –'

'I don't know what I did. I tore the thing off, I think I threw it at him. And he tried to keep me. And then I came to you; I thought at once of you, Frank. I knew that you would take care of me.'

He took her hand in his, and put his arm round the little trembling form.

'I will take care of you, with my life. Only give me the right.'

'The right,' she repeated, as if she did not realise what it meant. 'Oh, I knew that I could trust you, Frank, there is no one like you.' She clung to him, and her shivering ceased. 'Frank,' she went on, in a broken childlike way – 'he didn't kiss me; I didn't let him kiss me. That's all the comfort I have. No one ever kissed my lips except –' and she fell to shivering again.

For answer, Frank Hallett bent down very quietly and kissed her forehead. He laid her head against his shoulder, and she seemed to find comfort in the caress. 'Elsie,' he said, 'I want you to listen to me. You know how I love you – no, you never can know quite how I love you. I would have given you up to Blake, if he had wanted to marry you, and you had loved him so that to marry him would have been for your happiness. I have kept away from you these weeks because I didn't want you to feel bound in any way, or to have any remorseful thoughts. I said from the beginning that I would take my chance, and wait your time. But I think that the time has come now for me to speak.'

'It is generous of you,' she said, very low; 'now, when no one can respect me; when I have given the two – when Lord Astar and Mr. Blake have a right to despise me.'

'They have no right,' cried Frank. 'You are yourself, pure, sweet, womanly as you have been always. I don't know what has passed between you and Blake. I don't want to know. No man can be so unutterable a scoundrel as to despise a woman for loving him – and you love Blake, my poor Elsie. It breaks my heart to see it, and yet I know it quite well.'

'And in spite of that, you – you want –' she said breathlessly.

'And in spite of that, I want you to marry me – that's what I want, Elsie. I want to have the right to protect you. I want Lord Astar – I want all the world to know to-morrow that you are my affianced wife. I am not a great match, Elsie dear, but I am great enough to protect you now. And you mightn't do better,' he added, with an odd little laugh.

'Oh, Frank, you hurt me.'

'I don't want to do that. And I don't want to take any advantage of you – and of your weakness to-night. If you don't want to bind yourself, let it be understood between us that our engagement is only before the world, and that in reality you are as free as you were yesterday. I shall not vex or worry you, Elsie. I shall not even ask you to kiss me. Everything shall be as you wish. I understand you and how you feel.'

'No, Frank, you can't do that. And I couldn't sacrifice you, just to my pride, for that's what it comes to. If I were to accept you now, to-night, it would be for always, and because I meant to try and make you as good a wife as it is possible for me to be.'

'Will you have me, then, Elsie?'

'Frank, you don't want to marry a girl who has just told you that she cares for a man who – who would not marry her and has let her see that he despises her.'

'Yes, I do want to marry that girl. It is nothing to me what any other man feels about her.'

'But it should be something to you – what she feels about some other man.'

There was a short silence. At last Frank spoke. 'I am willing to take my chance of your being cured of that. I have been watching you. Perhaps you thought I was too dense to see or to understand. But love makes people quick at forming conclusions. I formed mine about you and Blake. I thought he didn't care for you in the way that a man cares when he means to marry a girl in spite of every obstacle – I can't help feeling about Blake that there is some obstacle – some mystery in his past.'

'Ah! You feel that too?'

'Yes. It may be nothing disgraceful; I don't know. Why should I think so? The man is a gentleman. I like him in a kind of way, though he is my rival. But when a man loves a woman beyond all things, he goes away, or else he does his honest best to win her. He doesn't play at a game of flirtation to amuse himself and gratify his sense of power, and let her run the risk of being hurt in it, as you have been hurt, my poor Elsie.'

'Don't speak of that. I *will* cure myself. I will not let myself be beaten.'

'It's because you say that that I am safe in taking the risk. I know you, Elsie; how true and good and pure you are in the very depths of your nature. You have only been playing at life, and at love. You haven't known anything of evil, or of the realities of the world. It may be that only in marriage you will learn what love means – and oh, if it might be for me to teach you! You have never cared for anyone in the real sense of the word. Of course I know that you don't care and never have cared for me in that way, though I believe that you have a more solid affection for me than you ever had for any one.'

'That is true, Frank.'

'I don't believe that you have ever loved Blake in the real sense either. You were dazzled by him at the beginning. There was a glamour of romance about him, and he has a way of compelling interest and admiration. Oh, I saw it all at Goondi, at the election time. And Ina saw it too. Ina always said that you were only fascinated, and that it would pass away. Ina has been my best friend all through. If it hadn't been for her I should have given up hope.'

'Frank, it is Ina you ought to have cared for, not me.'

Frank winced. He did not answer. There was a little silence.

Presently he said, 'Elsie, I am right. You will get over this girlish fancy; I am not afraid. I will wait.'

They had crossed the bridge, and had passed out of the long straggling street of the South Side, as it was called, and now they were in a quiet road, bordered with gum trees, which gave out an aromatic fragrance into the night. Elsie had grown calm. Frank still kept his arm about her, but he had attempted no closer caress. They drove for some little way in silence. The lights of Emu Point and of the houses in Riverside Paddock began to show in front of them.

'Elsie,' Frank said, 'will you tell me what you are thinking?'

'I will tell you when we reach home,' she said quietly. 'I will give you your answer then. Don't speak to me till we reach home.'

He obeyed her, and they did not speak another word till the cab drew up in front of the little garden gate of the cottage. There was a light in the drawing-room, and Peter, the Kanaka, was acting as watch-dog in the verandah. Frank helped Elsie to get out, and told the cabman to wait. 'I will see you in,' he said in a matter-of-fact way, 'and then I shall go back to Government House, and bring Mrs. Valliant home.

Peter, the Kanaka, had got up from his blanket, in which he had been sleeping in the verandah, after the fashion of an Australian Black. He rubbed his eyes at sight of Elsie. She bade him wait and watch still for Mrs. Valliant, speaking quite composedly, and then turned to Frank. 'Will you come in for a minute and hear what I have to say?'

He followed her into the little drawing-room, which was lighted by one lamp, turned low. She raised the wick and stood by the table, a little tremulous again now, but never, he thought, had he seen her look more beautiful. She had let her cloak drop, and the lace from her head. Her pretty ball-dress was scarcely crushed, and the roses on her bodice were fresh and overpoweringly sweet. She had thrown away the bouquet. On her face were still traces of tears and humiliation, and her eyes shone very brightly. On her neck was the deep angry scratch which the point of the diamond star had made. She put out her two hands to him, and he held them in his and stood looking at her.

'Well, Elsie; what is it to be?'

'It is to be as you wish,' she said. 'Only – only Frank, don't expect too much from me yet. I will try – I will try hard to forget.'

'Thank you, dear,' he said gently. 'That is all I ask. God bless you, Elsie, you have made me very happy.'

'Tell them, tell them to-night,' she said feverishly. 'I want everybody to know – tell them at the ball. Tell mamma. But don't tell her anything else, Frank. Let that be between you and me. Let it never be spoken of again from this night. Only see that Lord Astar knows.'

'He shall know,' said Frank grimly. 'And I will tell your mother. She wouldn't have been sorry six months ago. Perhaps she will be disappointed now. But,' he added, 'Ina will be glad.'

'Yes, Ina will be glad,' Elsie said thoughtfully.

They were standing, he with her hands in his, both with trouble in their eyes. 'I must go,' he said, rousing himself from the contemplation of her face. 'Good-night, my dear,' he added wistfully. 'Try to sleep happily.'

Still he did not relinquish her hands. 'Frank,' she said falteringly, 'it seems a strange way to be engaged.'

'Yes, we are engaged,' he answered, with an effort at brightness. 'We are engaged to be married; and you have made me very happy. If it seems strange – but the strangeness will wear off in time, Elsie.'

He let her hands go. 'Good-night, dear.'

'Frank,' she said, appealingly, 'Frank, I didn't mean – won't you kiss me, Frank?'

CHAPTER XXIII

•

Mrs. Valliant's Blessing

Ina Gage was waiting anxiously for the reappearance of Frank Hallett. Mrs. Valliant's uneasiness about Elsie had been quickly allayed. She had soon got into the fretful mood. Mrs. Valliant was one of those women in whom sweetness is apt to turn to a pettish sense of ill-usage. 'There's never any calculating on Elsie's moods,' she said to Ina. 'She was quite well and happy when she got here. Something has gone wrong. Ina, you don't think it's possible that she has refused Lord Astar?'

'I think it is very possible,' said Ina; 'and if she has refused him, and feels that you will be vexed, it is quite easy to understand why she went home.'

'But why couldn't she have come to me – why go off in that extraordinary fashion with Frank Hallett? I am glad it was Frank Hallett, and not that Mr. Blake. Look here, Ina; if anything has gone wrong about Lord Astar, take my word for it that the fault is Mr. Blake's.'

In other respects Mrs. Valliant was enjoying the ball. She liked the fine sight. Lady Waveryng had been particularly nice to her, and so had Lady Stukeley. Mrs. Valliant exulted in the discomfiture of Lady Garfit, to whom it was quite evident that the Waveryngs had not taken a fancy, and though her enjoyment was considerably marred by Elsie's departure, and though she suffered some qualms of doubt and disappointment thereat, especially as Lord Astar had taken no notice of her beyond the first greeting, she was of a hopeful nature and accustomed to vagaries on the part of Elsie, and trusted that all would come right in the end.

She was at supper when Frank returned. Ina, who had been one of the privileged guests at the royal table, had got out before the general company, and he met her as he was looking for her mother.

'Mamma is in the supper-room,' said she. 'Tell me about Elsie.'

She saw at once signs of emotion and elation on Frank's face.

'Ina,' he said, 'you must congratulate me. She wished every one to know. She said she wanted them to know to-night.'

A strange look came into Ina's face, an odd far-away look. He thought at first that she had not quite taken in his meaning.

'She has said that she will marry me,' he said simply.

Ina drew a deep breath, and a faint colour came into her cheek, which had been very pale.

'Oh, Frank! Then it is settled?'

'Yes, it is settled; as far as anything can be settled. I told her that she should be free to break it off at any time, if she felt that she did not care for me enough. She is still free, of course. But she says she does not wish that, and that her promise is a binding one. Will you tell Horace, and anyone else that you please?'

'And Lord Astar?'

'Lord Astar!' Frank exclaimed passionately. 'I have to thank Lord Astar,' he added with some bitterness, 'for having brought this about. Don't talk to Elsie about Lord Astar. She does not wish it. The day after tomorrow – no, to-morrow, for it's morning now – he will have gone out of our lives – for ever, I hope.'

There was a rush of people returning from the supper-room. Ina turned. 'There is mamma,' she said. Mrs. Valliant was on Blake's arm. It struck Frank as odd that Blake should devote himself to Elsie's mother. He went towards her, and Mrs. Valliant turned with faded coquetry to Blake.

'Here is Mr. Hallett come to give me news of my naughty daughter.' She made a step towards Hallett. 'Did you leave Elsie? and will you help me to find our fly? though I don't know what to do. It is so awkward. You see we came with the Prydes, and they won't want to go yet. Minnie is living on in hopes that the Prince will ask her to dance, but he has danced with none of the girls except my Elsie; he has been devoting himself to Lady Waveryng, which is quite natural, of course.'

'My trap is at your service,' said Blake, 'if you would like to go back to your daughter. I am very sorry Miss Valliant was not well. I hope she is better.'

'Thank you,' said Hallett stiffly; 'Miss Valliant was only tired. I have got a fly here and I will take you home,' he said to Mrs. Valliant.

'Shall we go and find Miss Pryde, and explain that we are going? I believe that I was engaged to her for the dance before supper. I must make my apologies.'

Mrs. Valliant took his arm, and Blake went up to Lady Horace. As they walked through the ball-room, Hallett said –

'Mrs. Valliant, I have got some news for you. Elsie has promised to be my wife.'

Mrs. Valliant turned on him a bewildered face. 'Lord Astar!' she gasped. 'Lord Astar had asked her to marry him. I expected to hear that everything was settled.'

'Lord Astar did not ask Elsie to marry him,' Frank said sternly. 'He meant nothing more than idle flirtation, Mrs. Valliant; please don't speak to Elsie about Lord Astar. I have to beg this of you. She never cared for him. She wants to forget – to forget that she ever thought it possible for a moment that she could care –'

'I don't understand,' said Mrs. Valliant in a perplexed manner.

'Elsie and I understand each other,' answered Frank. 'We understood each other this summer on the Luya. I was only waiting – waiting till Elsie had made up her mind; and now she has made it up, she says, for good and all. There's nothing now but for you to say that you will give her to me. I am not afraid that you will say no. We talked of this before.'

'Yes, we talked of this before,' repeated Mrs. Valliant, still bewildered. 'Of course I'm very glad, Mr. Hallett – Frank, I suppose I ought to say now. I am very glad that you care for Elsie, and that she cares for you. She did not tell me there was any understanding between you – she rather let me think – but there, it's no use going back on what Elsie says – she will always go her own way, and she doesn't take me into her confidence. It's a little hard, considering that I'm her mother, and that I think of nothing but of her good. Ina was quite different, Ina always talked to me and told me things. I'm sure this evening when we started – if any one had told me that Elsie would go back from the Government House ball engaged to *you* I should have laughed in their face. If it had been Mr. Blake I should have been less surprised. But it only shows –'

Mrs. Valliant stopped short, struck by the expression of Hallett's face. 'I beg your pardon,' she said humbly; 'but you know Mr. Blake did pay Elsie a great deal of attention when he first came.'

'And that is past,' said Frank decidedly; 'and I know that the subject is almost as distasteful to Elsie as the subject of Lord Astar's attentions. Elsie has promised to be my wife, Mrs. Valliant. I mean to take care of her. I don't mean that she shall be vexed or worried by anything that it is in my power to shield her from. But never mind that. Won't you give me your blessing and accept me as your son, and tell Elsie when you see her to-night that you are glad?'

'Yes, I will,' said Mrs. Valliant. 'It's the best thing that could have happened. I won't talk about Mr. Blake or about Lord Astar to Elsie or anybody, but this I must say, that I am glad it's you, and not Mr. Blake. I never liked that man somehow, and I'm certain – as certain as I'm standing here – that he is fond of Elsie. I could see it this evening in the way he looked, and the way he talked.'

Frank said nothing. This should have been poor comfort, and yet there was an odd pleasure in the hearing of it. He was better pleased that Blake should love Elsie, and should be disappointed, than that he should have been flirting with her merely for the gratification of his own vanity and the humiliation of hers.

They found the Prydes. Mrs. Valliant's excited manner told that something had happened. She was not proof against Minnie's eager whispered questioning.

'Is she engaged?' Minnie asked. 'Oh, do, only just tell me that.'

'Yes, she is engaged,' answered Mrs. Valliant. 'It's all quite sudden and unexpected though; I am sure I might have known it was coming months ago, but Elsie is so odd and so reserved. She might just as well have told me it was Frank Hallett, instead of letting me beat about the bush and getting herself so talked about with other people.'

'Frank Hallett!' exclaimed Minnie, in genuine astonishment. 'Well, I never thought it would come about like this. I thought there was something up with Lord Astar, though Daddy said it was nonsense, and that he'd never be allowed to marry a girl like Elsie. I beg your pardon, Mrs. Valliant, I don't mean of course that Elsie wasn't as good as any of them, but you know what I mean.'

'No, I do not,' said Mrs. Valliant with dignity. 'Lord Astar had serious intentions, I know for a fact. Why Elsie has refused him I cannot think. But, of course, Elsie knows her own heart best, and if she has cared for Frank Hallett all this time –'

'Rubbish,' said Miss Pryde. 'I know Elsie is not in love with Frank Hallett. Anyone could see that. If she is in love with anybody I should say it was with Mr. Blake – I am sure it seemed so in the beginning of the winter. But I think she is very wise, and I am sure I hope she will be happy.'

Minnie Pryde was not slow in imparting her news to her partners, and amongst them to Blake.

'Yes, it is really true,' she said. 'Mrs. Valliant told me, and Mrs. Valliant as good as told me that Elsie had refused Lord Astar for Frank's sake. I don't believe it, do you?

'I think Miss Valliant is quite capable of even that,' said Blake. 'When did the engagement take place? I am curious to know.'

'This evening. He must have proposed in the cab on the way home. What can have made Elsie go away? There is something behind, I am certain; and I shall find it out to-morrow.'

The news spread through the ball-room. 'So your sister is engaged to that typical young Australian, Frank Hallett,' said Lady Waveryng to Ina. 'I'm glad of it, my dear, for I think she is a young lady who will be the better for settling down, and I meant to give you a little hint that it was not quite wise of her to flirt so desperately with Lord Astar.'

'I'm sorry for Morres Blake,' said Lord Waveryng later, 'for I've a very shrewd suspicion that he was a good deal more gone than he cared to own on the beautiful Elsie. Well, she has done very well for herself. Old Stukeley tells me that young Hallett is a rising man, and very well off.'

'My dear, you look dead,' said Lady Waveryng kindly, struck by her sister-in-law's paleness. 'You ought to go home. Let Waveryng go and find Horace.'

'Horace is in the supper-room,' said Lord Waveryng, rather grimly. 'Yes, I'll fetch him, with pleasure.'

'Ina,' said Lady Waveryng, 'I want to talk to you. I want you to let us come up with you to the Dell as soon as the Prince has gone. You are too wildly dissipated, you Leichardtstonians, even for me. I don't think this life is healthy for Horace – too much larking round, driving four-in-hand, billiards at the club, and nipping and champagne suppers. Horry is so stupidly social and good-natured; it has always been his fault. I think he is a little disheartened about the Dell, isn't he? It hasn't paid as well as he thought. He was telling Waveryng that he wanted to take up more land and make a larger place of it; and that would give him more occupation, wouldn't it?'

'Yes,' said Ina faintly, 'he wants more occupation.'

'You don't keep him in order, my dear,' Lady Waveryng went on. 'That's what Horry always wanted. He ought to have married a martinet, not a sweet, docile, submissive little creature like you; you let him sit upon you too much. Did he tell you that I gave him a lecture the other night for leaving you so much alone?'

'No. But you mustn't, indeed, Lady Waveryng – Emily, I mean.

Horace is very kind, and if I am sometimes alone, it is what I like. You mustn't ever scold Horace because of me. He is the best husband in the world.'

'Well, I'm glad to hear it,' said Lady Waveryng, putting up her eyeglass. 'He has certainly got the best wife in the world. And what I want to tell you is that you must get him to go up to the Dell, and take us very soon. We haven't much longer to be here; and Waveryng is quite ready to do something, if he sees that the money is not going to be thrown away – Waveryng likes the idea of taking up land and founding a sort of estate; and we might come out again, you know, and see how you are getting on.'

Ina expressed her gratitude. Presently Lord Waveryng came with Lord Horace, who was excited and full of Elsie's engagement. 'I've been telling 'em in the supper-room,' he said. 'A capital fellow, Frank Hallett; the best fellow in the world. By Jove, Astar was hit, I can tell you. You should have seen his face. I shall chaff Elsie about it to-morrow. Look here, Ina, you can get over to Fermoy's all right,' he said, as they went out after having said good-night to the Waveryngs. 'I'll put you in the fly, and then I'll go to the club. I've promised some fellows to look in.'

Ina made no protest. Lord Horace was surprised at her quietness.

'What has come to you?' he said. 'You are like a death's head. I wish you would brighten up a bit. You make people think I ill-use you. Em gave me a talking to the other night for neglecting you. If you want to make yourself out a martyr, for heaven's sake don't try it on with my people. You won't get any good of that. Em is devoted to me. She always was.'

'I am very glad,' said Ina faintly. 'I never complained, Horace. I want you to be happy in your own way. I am a little tired to-night, that's all. Em wants us to go back to the Dell, dear, and to take them with us, and I think we had better go.'

'Waveryng means to fork up, I suppose,' said Lord Horace sulkily. 'It's a little hard to drag a fellow up just when there's a chance of amusing one's self. But I suppose we had better go, and you can ask Elsie to come with us if you like. We'll get up a kangaroo hunt, or bush races, or something to amuse Waveryng.'

So it was settled, and Ina rejoiced in the thought that for her the Leichardt's Town season would shortly come to an end. She was a brave little person, this poor Ina, and no one guessed that the fox was gnawing her under the cloak that she wore so decorously.

Mrs. Valliant had a few words with Elsie that night. What she had were not altogether satisfactory. The house was dark and Elsie had gone to bed when Mrs. Valliant and Frank stepped on to the verandah. It was Peter, the Kanaka, who told them that Miss Elsie was in her room. Frank went away, and Mrs. Valliant sought her daughter.

Elsie was lying awake, her tangled hair all about her pillow, and Mrs. Valliant fancied that she had been crying, her eyes looked so red and so bright. But she was now, at any rate, perfectly composed.

'I suppose Frank has told you,' she said, as soon as her mother entered. 'You were quite wrong, mamma,' she went on in a hard tone; 'it would have been much better if you had not advised me to wear Lord Astar's star. It only gave him the right to insult me.'

'Elsie,' cried Mrs. Valliant, 'how was I wrong? What do you mean?'

'You were wrong in thinking that Lord Astar could possibly wish to marry me. He only wanted me to run away with him. He made me understand quite clearly – I didn't at first – that marrying and running away with a girl were two different things.'

'And you can tell me this – quietly like that?' cried Mrs. Valliant. 'I'd have wanted to kill him.'

'I think I did want to kill him,' said Elsie, in a low voice.

Mrs. Valliant raged hysterically after the manner of a wild woman.

'Does he think that because you have no father or brother there is no one to call him to account? There is Horace. Horace shall know. Horace is as good as he is; and Ina has married into a great family. No one shall insult my daughter. I will go to-morrow to Government House. I will insist upon an explanation and an apology.'

'No, mamma, you won't do anything. You will put the whole thing out of your mind, as I am going to do from this night. We brought it on ourselves, and I have deserved everything.'

'And Frank Hallett knows?'

'Frank is a hero, and a gentleman,' cried Elsie. 'There is no one like him in the world. I shall marry him, mamma, and I shall make him as good a wife as it is in my nature to be. I don't think I'm really bad. I think I can make him happy. That's all that matters.'

'I think a great deal matters besides that,' said Mrs. Valliant. She was in a tearful mood, and kissed Elsie, and talked about the trousseau, and about the difficulty of finding money for it, and the disadvantage to a girl of having no male relatives, all in the same breath. Then seeing that Elsie was moody and unresponsive, she stopped, picked up the finery which the girl had taken off, smoothed the ribbons, put the roses in water and folded the gloves, and then came back to the bed. 'Well, good-night,' she said timidly. 'I shall not call you to-

CHAPTER XXIV

———•———

'Good-bye, Elsie Valliant'

Lord Horace's evening at the club and Minnie Pryde's confidences to her after-supper partners had spread the news of Elsie's engagement far and wide. At the meeting of the Assembly the next afternoon, Frank Hallett was congratulated both by his own side and by several members of Mr. Torbolton's ministry.

'I thought it was going to be one of my colleagues,' said the Premier, with a significant look at Blake; 'but this is much better, and I congratulate you heartily.'

Frank did not ask Mr. Torbolton why this was much better, since presumably Mr. Torbolton should have wished his colleague to be preferred in any suit on which he had set his heart, but accepted the congratulations in a grave reserved manner which was not much like that of a triumphant lover. He took his seat, and went about his business, and even made a speech, and all the time there was present with him the wonder whether it was really himself – Frank Hallett – who was seated in that house on the front Opposition bench, which was next best to being in the Ministry, Elsie's affianced husband, having gained his dearest wishes both of the head and of the heart, and altogether the most fortunate of men, and if so, why he did not feel more elated at his success? Perhaps the reason lay in the fact that Morres Blake was sitting opposite to him. Morres Blake made a speech, too. All his speeches were brilliant, but this was more than usually so. As he listened, Frank Hallett had a dull sense of defeat and disappointment. He did not grudge his rival the glory, but was glad that Elsie was not there to listen to his eloquence. Perhaps it was remorse for his pettiness that made him congratulate Blake when, later on, he passed him in the lobby.

'I hear that I have to congratulate you on a different and far more important matter,' said Blake, after he had thanked him. 'I think you have won a prize, and I do congratulate you in sincerity.'

He did not wait for Hallett's answer, but turned away with an abruptness that was out of keeping with his ordinary courteous self-command.

Another of Elsie's admirers received the news that day. This was Trant. He heard it at Fermoy's on his arrival there early in the afternoon. Some business had detained him at Baròlin, and he had not arrived in time for the Government House ball. It was Lord Horace who gave him the intelligence. Lord Horace was loafing about the verandah, looking rather the worse for his late evening. He observed with a mischievous amusement the red flush that mounted to Trant's cheek, and took a delight in aggravating his discomfiture. Lord Horace was quite aware that Trant was one of the number of Elsie's hopeless admirers.

'Yes, it is quite settled. I think very likely the marriage will be soon. We are all delighted. She couldn't have done better, you know – not even if you had been the favoured individual, you know, Trant. You ought to go and offer your congratulations.'

'Yes, I will,' said Trant sulkily.

'We've had a stunnin' time, almost as good as the Goondi election,' continued Lord Horace. 'The Prince's visit has wakened up Leichardt's Town a bit. Now we've all got to go back to the nursery, like the good children that have come in to dessert. I say, you must help me to get up something for Waveryng. They're coming up to the Dell, you know; a kangaroo battue, or a bushranging lark, something typical and Australian – not that Waveryng has much notion of the value of local colour.'

Trant gave an odd sort of laugh. 'I dare say Moonlight would oblige you if he knew what you wanted.'

'Moonlight has laid low this full moon,' said Lord Horace. 'Well, think it out, Trant, and in the meantime you go and wish Miss Valliant joy, and if you see my wife there, tell her, will you, that I want her.'

Trant went off. It was a little before the hour of Elsie's verandah reception, but he thought he should have more chance of finding her alone. Lady Horace was there, and the two sisters were sitting in the verandah in earnest conclave when he arrived. It struck him that Lady Horace looked very pale and ill, and that she had been crying. Elsie was flushed and excited. She laughed gaily when she saw Trant, and came forward with outstretched hand. Perhaps she was pleased to be relieved from the *tête-à-tête* with Ina.

'Why didn't you come down for the ball?' she asked.

'I was kept on business,' said Trant. 'You don't suppose I didn't ant to be at the ball, did you, Miss Valliant?'

'I don't know,' said Elsie. 'It was a very good ball – at least, so they aid.'

'Why do you say "they said"?' asked Trant. 'Weren't you there?'

'Oh, yes; I was there, and I fulfilled my mission of making the eichardt's Town ladies jealous. The Prince danced with me, and he id not dance with any other of the girls. Ina was honoured; but then he is not a Leichardt's Town girl now. He didn't dance with any of ie others, did he, Ina?'

'No,' said Ina, 'he danced with no one else – of the girls.'

'There. Think of that, Mr. Trant. It may be written on my tomb-tone! "She danced with a Prince." There was nothing possible for ie after that. I came away. That's why I don't know much about the all.'

Trant looked mystified. 'Is it true?' he said.

'Is what true?'

'You know well enough; what they are saying everywhere. At ermoy's they can talk of nothing else.'

'Yes, it is true. Ina, you are not going?'

'By the way, Lord Horace told me to tell you that he wanted you,' aid Trant; 'it seems rather a blunt way of putting it, Lady Horace. I ive the message as it was given.'

Ina took up her gloves and parasol. 'It is to settle about going up) the Dell. Elsie, you will come?'

'Oh, yes,' said Elsie. 'Anything for a change. Good-bye, Ina dear. shall see you in the evening.'

Trant stood looking at Elsie.

'Why don't you sit down? You make me nervous.'

'Come down to the boathouse,' he said; 'I want to ask you omething.'

'Well, there is a horrid glare here,' replied Elsie coolly. 'If you like, e'll go to the steps.'

When they were seated, she said, 'What is it? Please be melodram-tic. Please be interesting. Please do something that will make me for ie moment think of you and nobody else.'

'Does that mean that you are thinking of somebody else in a way iat is disagreeable?'

'Yes.'

'That's a strange confession for a young lady who has just gone and got herself engaged. It can't be of Mr. Frank Hallett that you are thinking?'

'What does that matter to you?' said Elsie. 'I suppose I may pity Mr. Hallett, if I like?'

'Upon my soul,' said Trant, 'I think he is even more to be pitied than I am.'

'I don't think you are to be pitied at all. What is it that you wanted to ask me?'

'What has Blake got to do with this?' he said.

Elsie flushed more deeply than before. 'I would rather, if you please, that Mr. Blake should be left out of the question. I think I have said that before.'

'Yes, you have. I warned you, remember. Now look here, you said I might be melodramatic. You remember what I said to you here, not very long ago? I told you that I always succeeded in what I had set my mind on.'

'I remember that you threatened to carry me off, and that it wasn't quite settled whether you were to perform that feat – you'll have to have a good horse, Mr. Trant, for I am very heavy – at one of the Leichardt's Town tennis parties, or at the Government House ball, or if I am to be imprisoned in one of the Luya gorges – do you recollect that?'

'Yes, I recollect, and I meant it. I warn you. I am not a man to stand tamely by and let another man carry off the girl he loves, especially when she doesn't love that other man. You in love with Frank Hallett, that solid lump of respectability! You are meant for life, for adventure, for emotion. You were meant to be a poet's inspiring angel, or the brave companion of a hero's reckless deeds.'

'I – I have heard something like that before,' said Elsie faintly. 'But it was not you who said it.'

'It was Blake. And he has said it to me. Blake has got blood in his veins: he understands you. Blake and I are alike in more ways than one. We are alike anyhow in understanding you. But you weren't meant for Blake, Miss Valliant. He wouldn't marry you, if he could. He has told me to "go in and win," and I mean to win. Before the year is out, you will be my wife.'

'Indeed, Mr. Trant, that is a bold prophecy; and now I think you have been melodramatic enough. Let us talk of something else.'

'No,' said Trant, bending close to her, 'not till I have told you again that I love you. I worship the ground you tread on. I worship the

flowers you touch. Give me that rose; it can't hurt you to do that –
the one you have in your belt. Give it to me,' he repeated imperiously.

It seemed to Elsie that his black eyes had something of the compelling power that was in Blake's eyes. They were fixed full on hers, and
his hand was outstretched. 'Give it to me,' he said again.

Almost against her will she took out the flower and gave it to him.
He kissed it, and put it away in his breast. 'Do you believe that I love
you?' he said.

'I suppose that you do in a kind of fashion. I wish you wouldn't. It
is of no use, and all this is rather amusing in its way, but what's the
use of it? I never gave you any reason to think –'

'No, you never gave me any reason to think you could care for me,
and perhaps that is why I am so madly in love with you, why I would
risk heaven to win you; not that I believe much in heaven, except the
heaven which you could make for me.'

'Mr. Trant,' said Elsie, with some little dignity, rising as she spoke,
'let us be friends, and forget all this. I am sorry for having let you
talk to me in the way you have done. I have been a vain, foolish,
heartless girl. I have only cared to amuse myself. I am afraid that I
have sometimes done it at the expense of others. I want to change. I
am going to marry a man whom I respect, and for whom I have the
deepest affection. I should like to think that from now I may do
nothing that will make me unworthy of him. Let us start afresh, and
be friends, and don't say any more stupid things.'

'I don't want to start afresh,' said Trant doggedly. 'I mean to go
on as I have begun. I love you, and mean to have you – by fair means,
or by foul, if fair won't answer. I warn you. Don't ever say that I
didn't. Only one thing I want you to know. You are the thing in the
world that I have set my heart on, and I've never failed yet.'

Elsie made no answer. She walked slowly back to the cottage, and
Trant followed. Mrs. Valliant was in the verandah, and was talking to
Minnie Pryde, who, as soon as she saw Elsie, rushed to her with a
torrent of congratulations. And, oh, had it been Mr. Hallett who had
given her the beautiful star, and would Elsie let her see it again?

No. Elsie was sorry, but she couldn't let Minnie see the star. Elsie
had become suddenly grave, and she seemed shy, and altogether,
Minnie said afterwards, more like an ordinary engaged girl than one
would have imagined possible in Elsie.

Elsie had a great reception that afternoon. Mrs. Jem Hallett
appeared, which was a wonderful condescension, but she had learned
by some occult means that Lady Waveryng was going to call also. The

Waveryng advent had considerably altered Mrs. Jem Hallett's views in regard to this alliance. She was very gracious to Elsie. Of course she, Elsie, would come and stay at Tunimbah. Mrs. Valliant was included in the invitation. And how amusing it would be to have the wedding on the Luya – from the Dell, a real bush wedding – Lord Horace would manage it so beautifully. Lord Horace was always talking about local colour, and they might have a procession of blacks, and King Tommy, of Yoolaman, at its head. What did Lady Waveryng think of that? And perhaps it might be worth Lord Waveryng's while to put off the New Zealand trip.

Everybody had gone when Frank came. Elsie was grateful to him for the tact which had kept him away. She was grateful, too, for his calm, matter-of-fact way of taking the situation. There were no lover's raptures. He made no claims. It was with bashful humility that he asked to be allowed to put a ring on her finger.

'Every one will wonder why you haven't an engagement ring,' he said, and took it from its case. 'I thought you'd like diamonds best,' he added awkwardly. The ring was magnificent. Elsie could hardly have believed that Leichardt's Town could furnish forth anything so perfect. She told him so, and again she held up her face baby fashion for a kiss.

He kissed her with more lingering tenderness than he had done the night before. 'Elsie,' he said, 'there's one thing I want you to understand. Your happiness is first of all things to me; far, far beyond my own. You have given yourself generously, my darling, and you say you won't make any reservations. Well, this is what I want you really to take in and think over. If ever you have any doubts or regrets; if ever you get to feel that you'd be happier with another man, you are as free as though this had never been put on your finger. You've only got to tell me. I'll never reproach you, or make it hard for you. I'll help you all I can and in whatever way I can – if not as your lover and husband, then as your brother.'

The tears were in Elsie's eyes. 'Frank,' she said, 'we will never speak again of what I told you the other night. We turn over the leaf, and begin a new page from to-day.' Then as if determined that there should not be any more sentiment, she rattled on about her afternoon's visitors, and Mrs. Jem's cordiality, and the coming visit to the Luya, and the picnic which Frank had promised her.

There was one ordeal which Elsie had to face, and which she dreaded more than anything connected with her engagement. This was the meeting with Blake. The Prince went away the next day, and

Blake, in his capacity of minister, went with the Government House party and the officials, and the great people of Leichardt's Town, to see him on board the man-of-war in the bay. Elsie did not go, though upon this occasion she had been invited, and the Prince expressed deep regret at her absence. Ina went with the Waveryngs, as in duty bound, and had the pleasure of discussing her sister's engagement with Lord Astar and receiving his congratulations. She would gladly have avoided him, but it was hardly possible, and Ina did not know what had taken place at the Government House ball. She had only a vague feeling, founded upon something which Lord Horace had indignantly reported of the club gossip, that Elsie had placed herself in a false position by her too open flirtation.

Frank Hallett did not go down to the bay with the other great people of Leichardt's Town. He stayed and spent part of the day with his fiancée. Ina was a good deal left to herself that day, for Lord Horace, to Lady Waveryng's annoyance, was making himself rather unpleasantly conspicuous with Mrs. Allanby. Lord Horace had, as Lord Waveryng put it, a little too much champagne on board. Lady Waveryng had come to the conclusion that the sooner her brother went to the Dell the better. Everybody was a little glad that the royal festivities had come to an end. It was Blake who paid attention to Ina, and saw that she had everything she wanted, and was taken care of. Ina had always disliked Blake. To-day she felt almost tenderly to him. She was certain from the way in which he had alluded to Elsie's coming marriage that he had a tenderness for her, and would, if he could, have married her himself. Ina never stopped to inquire why he could not marry Elsie. It seemed a received fact that Blake was not a marrying man.

It is rather the fashion in Leichardt's Town during the Session for members to pay calls in the morning. Blake walked across the paddock from Fermoy's the next day, and found Elsie alone and in the verandah sewing.

He came so softly that she did not even hear the gate click. When she saw that it was Blake she got up in some confusion, and then sat down again very pale.

'I beg your pardon for coming so early,' he said. 'I have got to be at the House – that is one of the penalties of being a minister now.'

'Yes,' she said faintly.

'I want to ask you,' he went on, 'to forget an episode which I bitterly regret, and to let me be your friend. I asked you the other night not to think too hardly of me. I ask it again now.'

'I don't think hardly of you,' Elsie answered, in a low voice, not lifting her eyes. 'I think hardly of myself. I have had a bitter lesson.'

'Poor child!' he exclaimed, in a moved voice; and he turned his face away as if to hide the pain he felt. 'You humiliate me,' he cried; 'you are a noble woman and a true woman. And I – but if you knew everything you would not blame me so much.'

'I don't blame you,' Elsie said, her voice, too, quavering. 'I have told you so. I – I ought to thank you, Mr. Blake,' she cried impulsively. 'I feel somehow that you didn't want to hurt me, and that you don't quite despise me.'

'God knows that is true enough,' he said.

'Then,' she went on, still with impulsive eagerness, 'let us agree to forget all this winter in Leichardt's Town. Let us begin afresh from to-day and be friends – good friends.' She held out her hand. He took it in his, and looked at her wistfully.

'You see,' she said, embarrassed by his gaze, and trying hard to be calm, 'I have made a new beginning for myself. I want to be different and to be more worthy – of – she hesitated – 'of the man I am going to marry.'

'Elsie,' he cried, 'tell me, are you happy?'

'Yes, I am happy,' she answered, after a moment's pause and struggling with all in her that was rebellious. 'I am happy. Frank Hallett's future wife ought to be happy.'

'You are right,' he answered. 'To me henceforth you will be Frank Hallett's wife; the wife of one of the best fellows that ever lived. You will be no longer Elsie Valliant after to-day. Good-bye, Elsie Valliant.'

He raised her hand to his lips, kissed it passionately, and left her without another word.

CHAPTER XXV

—————•—————

'The Colonial Secretary on the Luya'

Luya Dell was in a state of excitement. Workmen were busy at the new house, and curious looking 'lean-to's' had been extemporised under the white gum trees at the back of the homestead. Lord Horace was in his element. He was determined to impress his sister and her husband with a true idea of Australian picturesqueness. He had been for some time beating up the blacks for a corroboree. He would have beaten the kangaroo coverts if that had been necessary. He had beaten up the youths of the neighbourhood, distinguished by their 'local colour,' which was Lord Horace's way of characterising Australian-isms. He was organising a wild-horse hunt, and would have cheerfully consented to being 'bailed up' by Moonlight and his gang as an exemplification of his theory of Bush romance. His one regret was that neither 'Em Waveryng' nor his brother-in-law had any notion of the artistic values as applied to a pioneering life.

The Waveryngs had put in a trip to some great sheep-station, between the Leichardt's Town season and the visit to the Dell, and this interval and the assistance of Lord Waveryng's provisionary cheque had enabled Lord Horace to prepare for festivities. Lord Waveryng had since drawn another cheque, and Lord Horace had rushed into the Tunimbah drawing-room one day, radiant with glee, to announce that the Dell was now out of the hands of the bank, and that the creek was dammed, water laid on, and the tiled bath-room of the new house near completion.

Mrs. Jem Hallett raised her eyebrows slightly. She was a good woman of business.

'Waveryng has gone into partnership with me,' said Lord Horace. 'We are going to breed stud cattle.'

'You had better breed kangaroos and sell their hides for saddles,' said Jem Hallett, with his fat laugh.

Lord Horace was offended.

'I don't know why Waveryng and I shouldn't do as well with our stud cattle as Blake and Trant at Baròlin Gorge have done with their stud horses.'

'By the way,' said Mrs. Jem Hallett, 'have you heard anything about Mr. Blake? I have written to ask him to come and stay. Frank and Elsie are bent on the picnic to Baròlin Waterfall, and he made me promise to let him know when it was coming off.'

'Blake has taken ministerial leave, and has disappeared,' said Jem Hallett. 'I heard somebody say that he was hipped at Elsie's engagement.'

Jem Hallett's 'chaff' was truly Australian in its directness. Elsie, who was paying her first visit to Tunimbah as Frank Hallett's affianced wife, coloured; and Frank looked annoyed.

'He is inspecting the northern police department,' he said quietly, 'and he will be down in Leichardt's Town directly.'

'He had better inspect the southern police department,' said a squatter of the neighbourhood, who was staying at Tunimbah. 'It's a disgrace to the colony that they haven't caught Moonlight.'

'Oh, Moonlight has been keeping quiet since that Wallaroo business,' said Jem. 'Perhaps he has left the district.' And then Lord Horace declared his ardent desire to have the Dell bailed up during the Waveryng's visit. 'Em says she is going to write a book of her doings and impressions in the Antipodes,' he said, 'and I'd give anything for her to have a real live bushranger adventure.'

'It might be managed, perhaps,' said Blake himself, who entered that very moment, accompanied by his partner, Dominic Trant.

There was a general confusion, and a volley of exclamations. Blake shook hands with Mrs. Jem, and apologised for having taken her unawares. He was on his way to Baròlin. He intended, he said, to take advantage of her invitation later. He then went straight to Elsie, who gave him her hand without speaking. She had turned a little paler, and before he had been in the room five minutes she made an excuse to leave it, and strolled out into the garden with Frank.

Blake watched them uneasily through the French windows which opened on to the verandah. So did Trant. Mrs. Jem, who was an observant person, noticed that Blake looked pale and worn. Trant she thought, had more than ever the desperado air. Jem Hallett clumsily chaffed the Colonial Secretary on the failure of the police to bring Moonlight to justice.

'There's a chance for him,' said Lord Horace, 'if he only knew it. My sister, Lady Waveryng, has done the maddest thing, all through some stupid mistake of her maid and Waveryng's man – so much for being dependent on old servants!'

'What have they done?' asked Mrs. Hallett.

'Don't give notice to the bushrangers,' said Lord Horace. 'They have brought her diamonds with her to the Dell; part of them are the historic Waveryng diamonds. Of course they ought to have been sent to the Bank, and Waveryng insists on their being taken over to Goondi, and Captain Macpherson has promised him a police escort.'

'Why can't they be kept at the Dell?' asked Mrs. Jem.

'I suggested to Waveryng that we should lock 'em up in the flour bin in the store. It struck me as the safest place. No one would ever dream of looking for family diamonds at the bottom of a flour-bin, would they now? He doesn't think our padlocks are safe though – tried one yesterday – we don't lock up much as a rule, at the Dell, and he prefers the Goondi Bank.'

'And what do you suppose the Waveryng diamonds would be worth, roughly speaking, now?' asked Trant.

'A good many thousands,' replied Lord Horace. 'I wish I had the value of 'em, that's all. Have you any objection to the police escort being employed on private business, Blake? You needn't be afraid of Hallett asking a question about it in the House. He is the only member of the Opposition here just now.'

'I have no objection,' said Blake dreamily. 'Good gracious!' and he pulled himself together. 'Why should I object? Of course the safety of Lady Waveryng's diamonds is a matter of concern to the State.'

'Why, Mr. Blake,' said pretty Mrs. Allanby, from the depths of a squatter's chair in the verandah, where she had been ensconced listening to all that was going on, 'that's against your principles as a Radical, isn't it? I've heard you say that there ought to be no heirlooms, and no tying up of capital in family jewels. We have none of us got any family jewels, and so you needn't be afraid of hurting our feelings by saying so. Now, Lord Horace, please don't hurt my hand. I have got some rings, and I wear them on my right hand, remember.'

This was Mrs. Allanby's way of covering a devotion that was serious to her as well as to Lord Horace.

Mrs. Allanby had a way of rippling on, not waiting for an answer, emphasising her remarks by upliftings of her large dark eyes in a fashion that was effective. Lord Horace, at the sound of her voice, had darted across through the French window.

'I didn't know you were out here. I came over to see you,' he murmured.

'What have you done with your sister and brother-in-law?' she asked.

'They are looking round among the cedar-cutters. Waveryng wanted to inspect the local industries; I thought Ina could manage that business. They only came up yesterday, and it was my only chance of coming over and seeing when you would all come along to the Dell.'

'You must settle that with Mrs. Hallett,' said Mrs. Allanby. She got up, uncoiling herself, as it were, with a certain serpentine grace. Mrs. Allanby was of the type of woman, slender, lithe, secretive, self-contained, and fascinating, which has something of the snake in it. She was always gentle and low-voiced, and plaintive; her movements were soft, her eyes were dangerous, she had a sleek small head and irregular features, and a complexion sallow by day, but which at night, and when she was inwardly excited – outwardly she never seemed excited – became brilliant. She and her husband did not get on together. He was a brute, and had not a penny. It was her brother in New Zealand, she said, who found her an allowance for her personal requirements. She stayed about a good deal, and was always beautifully dressed. But then she was like Elsie in this respect, that she had the knack of putting on her clothes, the gift also of millinery. Ill-natured people said of her that she was a terrible flirt, and intensely designing, and that she was looking out for some one to run away with, and so give Mr. Allanby a chance of divorcing her, and herself and him the chance of a new beginning. It was certain, however, that her conduct was irreproachable, or Mrs. Jem Hallett would never have had her at Tunimbah. She made herself very useful to Mrs. Jem, played well, recited dramatically, and was a most agreeable companion and an adroit flatterer.

She and Lord Horace strolled up and down under the vine trellis which was now beautiful in its spring green. They talked low. Lord Horace had more than ever the air of a sun-bronzed Apollo in bush-man's garb. He was without doubt very handsome, and had that English air which to so many Australian women is so irresistible. Mrs. Allanby was not so clever as Elsie, and did not require intellect or even sterling worth in her admirers. She made Lord Horace tell her of the Waveryngs, and particularly of his twin sister. Em would stand by him through thick and thin, he declared; only Em had taken a tremendous fancy to Ina.

'Poor Ina,' softly murmured Mrs. Allanby.

It was about tea-time. Mrs. Jem always had tea English fashion, with delicious scones and shortbread and daintinesses generally. Lord Horace delivered himself of his messages. Ina wanted Elsie to go over at once; of course Frank might come too. Ina was consumed also, it appeared, with a desire for Mrs. Allanby's company, and of course – a half after-thought – for that of Mrs. Jem and her husband, only that Jem had got to be such a luxurious beggar, and Mrs. Jem mightn't like to camp in the new house; he knew Mrs. Allanby didn't mind, because she had told him so. Lord Horace proceeded to explain that they had given up the greater part of the Humpey proper to Lord and Lady Waveryng; though, bless you, 'Em' didn't mind roughing it – she wanted to go and milk the cows that morning – but Waveryng was rheumatic and afraid of new walls. But there was the new tiled bath-room which must surely atone for all deficiencies. Even at Tunimbah they couldn't boast a tiled bathroom.

Mrs. Jem thought it would be delightful to ride over for the day. Of course if Mrs. Allanby liked to stay there was nothing to prevent her, but she (Mrs. Jem) was rather tied by the babies; and Jem had his mustering, and it would be a much better plan, as there was so much more accommodation at Tunimbah, if she might arrange with Ina and Lady Waveryng to spend a few days there and have the picnic to Baròlin on that occasion. And then Mr. Blake was appealed to. Was Pompo superstitious, and how near could they get to the Fall, and did he think there was any truth in the theory Captain Macpherson had started, that Moonlight had a hiding-place in Mount Luya; and did Mr. Blake know that Captain Macpherson had sworn to unearth the bushranger in his lair, and that he counted on the assistance of the Baròlin half-castes for that purpose?

'The Baròlin half-castes were at Captain Macpherson's service,' Blake said gravely, but he did not think that Moonlight's lair – if he had one – was in that direction; and as for the Baròlin Falls, he certainly did not think they would prove worth the trouble of a march through a bunya scrub and the chance of being swallowed up in a quicksand. He was sure that Mrs. Hallett and Miss Valliant, to say nothing of Lady Waveryng, would decide that a gorge a little beyond Point Row, of which he knew, was quite sufficiently picturesque to camp out in.

'It was only the camping out that mattered,' bleated Mrs. Allanby.

'To camp out in the very heart of the mountains and among the Blacks' old Bora grounds sounded so delightfully romantic.'

Then Lord Horace told them of the corroboree he was working, and it was decided that the Hallett party should stay at the Dell for this event.

Blake seemed to avoid Elsie during this short Tunimbah sojourn. He and Trant were going to ride over to Baròlin after dinner, and Lord Horace was persuaded into the moonlight ride also – their ways lying together for a certain distance. Trant, however, took every opportunity of getting to Miss Valliant's side, and devoured her all the time with his bold gaze in a manner that annoyed Hallett extremely.

'I think the fellow must have been drinking,' he said afterwards to his brother. 'He reminded me of that new chum who went on the burst, and those black eyes of his have a queer reckless way of staring at one.'

But Trant had not been drinking; he was only intoxicated with love.

'Miss Valliant, when are you going to be married?' he said abruptly.

'I don't know,' answered Elsie composedly. She was not afraid of Trant; indeed, if it must be owned, there was a kind of excitement in the sight of his passion, which took her mind away from the flatness of a wooing that had esteem only as a responding quality. 'Not for some time yet,' she added.

'Well, remember,' he said, 'I mean to have my chance. I've not had my chance yet.'

'Your chance of what?' she asked.

'Of making you care for me; of doing something that will oblige you to admire me.'

'I can't imagine an opportunity for your being heroic,' said Elsie, 'but I shall be delighted to admire you if you give me an occasion for doing so.'

'We shall see,' said Trant darkly.

Blake asked the same question, but in a very different tone.

'Will you tell me something?' she said humbly. 'I should like to know, if I may, when you are to become Mrs. Frank Hallett.'

'Why do you wish to know?' she asked falteringly.

'Why? Oh, for several foolish reasons. One is that I shhould rather like to see the last of Elsie Valliant, and when she is dead and buried and done for, it will be time for me to "up stick and yan," as the blacks say. I am thinking of shifting my hurdles. Don't I get Australian in my way of putting things?'

'What do you mean?' she asked.

'Only that I am tired of Australia and of Australian life. I have the demon of restlessness on me again. I am not sure that I shall not go back to Ireland, and to quote Lord Waveryng, "face the music."'

'But why Lord Waveryng?'

'Something he told me set me thinking. The Coola curse is on me; the curse which dooms one Blake in a generation. I am the doomed Blake of this generation. And just lately the feeling has haunted me. I have the most curious sense of coming calamity; though I don't know that it is curious,' he added thoughtfully.

'Oh, Mr. Blake, I can't bear to hear you talk so recklessly. And there's no reason for it. It is some strange fancy that you have in your mind. Why should you be doomed? – you who have been so successful, who have everything in the world to make you happy.'

'Have I? Everything in the world to make me happy! There is one thing wanting for that, Miss Valliant, and it was offered me by fate on a certain moonlight night, not very long since, and I took it in my arms, and I let it go again –'

'What do you mean?' she asked again, growing very pale.

'Nothing that there is any use in saying. I must not see too much of you, or I may be doing something for which I should be sorry. A man can be brave and cool enough, and hard enough in a crisis, you know, Miss Valliant. It is when the crisis is over that he gets unnerved.' He gave an odd laugh, that seemed to her intensely sad. 'This is wild talk for a sober, staid Colonial Secretary of Leichardt's Land. What would Mr. Torbolton say if he could hear me? But I have got the Celtic temperament, and I can't help my queer forebodings and superstitions and mad impulses, and generally melodramatic way of looking at things, and you know I said to you once a man must follow his star –'

'I don't want to interrupt you,' put in Lord Horace. 'But if you are going to ride over with me this evening, Elsie, we ought to be seeing about the horses. What sized swag shall you have?'

'I am not coming to-night,' said Elsie, rousing herself as if from a dream. 'Frank will bring me over to-morrow.'

'Oh, Elsie, dear,' cried Mrs. Allanby reproachfully. 'And I had set my heart on that moonlight ride. Thank how beautiful Mount Luya would look from the gorges. It would be so romantic.'

'Has not a moonlight ride through the gorges any attraction for you?' said Blake, in a low voice.

'Yes,' she answered, in as low a voice as his.

'Then why don't you come?'

She did not answer.

'Are you afraid of me?'

'No,' she answered.

'You will have your future husband to take care of you,' he said bitterly. 'I promise not to annoy you with wild talk.'

'It does not annoy me, it only makes me –'

'What – contemptuous of my weakness?'

'No, no – Mr. Blake, you remember, we agreed to let the past be past. We agreed to be friends. Will you let me be your friend, your sister, and tell me, as you would tell your sister, what it is that is troubling you?'

'I will tell you some time,' he said; 'but not now, and not as I would tell my sister. I will tell you –'

He paused. His eyes fixed themselves on her with doubt and tenderness, in a way that thrilled Elsie.

'When will you tell me?' she asked.

'The day before you are married,' he answered.

Mrs. Allanby came purring towards her.

'Do go with them to-night.'

'Very well,' said Elsie abruptly. 'I have changed my mind, Horace. We will go.'

They set out after an early dinner. Was there ever such a September night? – fragrant with aromatic gum and the white-cedar flowers, full of strange sweet noises and mysterious rustlings, and plaintive calls of curlew and swamp pheasant; and as they rode by the creek, the uncanny swishing of the wings of startled wild duck. The mountains stood forth clear against the sky. Lord Horace had exaggerated when he spoke of a moonlight ride, and Mrs. Allanby called him to account for inaccuracy. It was only a horned moon yet, but it was brilliant, and the stars were bright and the station horses knew the track well. But it was only when they crossed the little plains in the river-bends that there was any opportunity for *tête-à-têtes*. For the greater part of the way the road was too narrow to allow of two riding abreast. Trant enlivened the night with his songs. He, too, seemed in a wild mood, but it did not direct itself especially towards Elsie.

Frank Hallett kept close to his fiancée. He had asked her if she would like him to ride with her. There were times when he almost maddened Elsie by his submission to her moods, and by his resigned acceptance of the fact that she loved Blake.

'Forget it, forget it,' she had said wildly that very evening. 'Yes, ride with me – don't leave me for an instant.'

And so he remained near her bridle rein, and had Blake wished it he could not have talked to her. He fell behind with Trant and for some little time the two carried on a low-toned conversation, in which there were dissentient notes borne occasionally to Elsie, who was nearest in advance. Once in a sudden bend of the track, where the trees grew thick, her habit hooked itself to a jagged branch, thus detaining her for a moment or two, and she caught what they were saying. Trant was speaking angrily.

'Look here! I'm not going to let this chance go because of any damned sentimentality on your part. The thing is as simple as A.B.C., and I intend to carry it through.'

'We will discuss the matter later,' said Blake haughtily.

'No, we've got to be on the spot, and you'd better settle to-night about going over to-morrow.'

Blake's horse almost cannoned against Elsie's as he came round the bend, and she lifted a frightened face from the disentangling of her skirt.

'Miss Valliant, can I help you?'

He had dismounted instantly.

'It is only my habit caught; oh, thank you, Frank.' Frank had turned hastily, not having perceived the accident. 'It's all right, I'm clear now.'

She rejoined her lover. A moment ago her breast had been stirred with a strange revolt. She had moodily watched his square determined bushman's back as he jogged along in front of her, and had compared it with Blake's easy, graceful, rather rakish bearing. Why was Frank so stolid, so good, so commonplace? There were moments in which she felt that Trant, in even his second-rateness, was the more inter-esting of the two. Now she had a sudden reaction. The words she had heard had given her a sense of doubt, repulsion, and insecurity. What was the secret in the life of Blake, which made him speak so strangely – which made him different from all the other men she knew? Perhaps it was not a romantic, an heroic secret, a fateful mystery for which he was not responsible, but the secret of unworthy deeds – of a past of which he was ashamed – a past with which Trant was linked – nay, a present, for had not Trant's words implied some sort of immediate action? What did it mean? What could it mean? Elsie shuddered as though something unclean had touched her. There was peace and safety with Frank. She rode close to him, but she said nothing. All the time her mind was tossed with wonder and suspicion and dread. By-and-by they came to the fork of the Luya, and the two roads branched in different directions – that to Baròlin going as it seemed into the mountains – into the heart of Mount Luya, while the way to the Dell led round the mountain and now over comparatively easy ground.

They all reined in their horses, and said good-night.

'Mind, I shall expect you some time tomorrow,' said Lord Horace. 'How long are you spared from your ministerial duties, Blake?'

'Oh, I'm fairly free,' he answered; 'that's the beauty of being a responsible member of the Cabinet.'

'And old Stukeley has gone to his summer retreat on the Ubi, so that you won't be overdone with meetings of the Executive, and Torbolton and Grierson of the "Lands" are deep in the budget and the new Land Bill. The Colonial Secretary ought to have a pretty easy time – only Moonlight on your conscience!' said Lord Horace.

'Yes, only Moonlight on my conscience,' and both Blake and Trant laughed, again Elsie fancied in that odd way they both sometimes had.

'Well, Macpherson, of the Police, is to turn up at the Dell some time, and you had much better meet him there and consult. It's handier to Goondi than the Gorge. And mind, Lady Waveryng is countin' on that escort for her diamonds. Whatever happens, the Waveryng diamonds have got to be looked after.'

'Oh, yes,' cried Trant. 'Whatever happens, the Waveryng diamonds have got to be looked after. You'll see us over at the Dell, Horace. Good-night.'

Lord Horace did not relish being called Horace pure and simple by Dominic Trant. 'Confound the fellow's cheek!' he said to Mrs. Allanby, but his sense of humour got the better of his irritation. 'He makes me think of that chap at the Bean-tree, Frank, when we were canvassing, and I was trying on the aristocratic dodge. "Lord! He a lord! Lords don't live in bark huts. I ain't agoin' to call him lord. He's just as much a lord as I am.'

'And the chap was quite right,' said Lord Horace, 'and he made me feel ashamed of myself. Handles should be dropped in a free country, especially when they're only handles by courtesy.'

CHAPTER XXVI

———————— • ————————

'Copy' for Lady Waveryng

The Waveryngs were a success. Ina was perhaps happier with 'Em Waveryng' than she had been during her short married life. Em was sweet, warm-hearted, and utterly without affectation. She had no nonsense about her, and in spite of her weak devotion to Lord Horace, she was not by any means blind to his faults. She was, however, like a doting mother who pardons everything to her darling, and is prepared in the long run to uphold his vagaries. Lady Waveryng, notwithstanding, found it a little difficult to pardon Lord Horace for Mrs. Allanby.

She was sufficiently ill-advised to speak to Ina on the subject of Lord Horace's flirtation. But Ina would have none of it. She was exaggerated in her defence of her husband. Lady Waveryng reported what she had said to her brother, and Lord Horace went in a shame-faced kind of way to his wife.

'Em says you have been fightin' for me like a bantam hen for her chick,' he said. 'Don't do that, my dear. You may come to find that I don't deserve it.'

Something in his tone struck Ina.

'Why do you say that, Horace?' she said.

'Because it's true. I'm a bad lot – always was. You know I told you before I married you that I couldn't see a pretty woman without wanting to flirt with her.'

'Yes, I know you did. And I don't mind in the least your flirting with Mrs. Allanby.'

'By Jove, I see that plainly enough,' he answered sulkily. 'If you minded and made a row sometimes, life would be a little more amusing.'

Ina's soft face flushed. 'I know that Mrs. Allanby is much cleverer than I am, and altogether more the kind of woman that men admire,' she said, with some dignity. 'I am quite willing that you should amuse yourself; I am quite aware that you have not always found me very entertaining. I – I often think, Horace, that our marriage was a great mistake' – Ina's voice faltered, but she went bravely on – 'still it is a mistake that cannot be mended now. And if I thought you were wronging either Mrs. Allanby, or me, or yourself by your flirtation, I think you would find that I did mind a little, and that I should not hesitate to say so.'

Lord Horace did not answer for a minute or two; then he said, 'Why do you say that our marriage is a mistake?'

'Because you yourself have told me so,' Ina answered.

'That was only when I was in a rage, and the cooking was abominable. A fellow who has been accustomed to a decent style of life in England can't be expected to put up with Australian roughness.'

'I thought you called it picturesque,' said Ina, with unconscious sarcasm.

'So it is – the outside of it. And there's a freedom about it that's splendid. I never could stand all that cut and dried conventionalism of English society, and even English sport. Over there it's all a question of money. Given a certain income and you know exactly what you can afford to have. You can't have a moor and a deer forest on a precarious six hundred a year. Here you can have as good, and no scale of income to measure by. But I suppose I'm like the boy who wanted to have his cake and eat it too. The life is magnificent – out of doors – only I want indoor comfort as well, and I'm getting a little tired of it. I tell you what, Ina –' he stopped rather guiltily.

'What are you going to tell me?' she asked presently.

'Nothing; only if Waveryng is as good as his word, and the investments turn out as they ought, we might put a manager here and take a run home.'

He had been discussing it with Mrs. Allanby the night before. Ina said nothing.

Lord Horace was very full of his corroboree. 'I don't know what you fellows of the Executive will do to me,' he said to Blake, who with the rest of the Dell party was lounging in the verandah of the Humpey. 'I've been doing my best to get up a war among the natives. There's three tribes of them,' he went on to explain, 'the Moongan and the Baròlin and the Durundur, and they are all at loggerheads with each other. It's quite a romantic affair, a sort of Paris and Helen and Siege of Troy business.'

'Oh, do tell us,' murmured Mrs. Allanby.

'Is he cramming me?' observed Lady Waveryng. 'Remember I am going to write a book. Let us hear the Blacks' Iliad, Horace.'

'This is it. Paris – otherwise Luya Tommy – ran away with Helen, commonly called Bean-tree Bessy. Paris is a Moongan. Helen is of the Baròlins. Helen has a husband who is of the Durundur tribe, and he is a chief also, and not by any means of a complaisant turn of mind. He resents the theft of his wife, or else his terms for the transfer are too high to be within Paris Tommy's means. Menelaus Tommy – they are both Tommies – is disposed for battle, and the Durundurs are a mighty tribe, so that the only chance for Paris and Helen, there being no Troy convenient, is in the Baròlins and the Moongans joining forces and fighting the Durundurs, and this is what I have been trying to compass – all for the benefit of your book of travels, Em, so I think it is rather hard of you to throw doubts on my veracity.'

'I have promised you the proceeds of that book anyhow, Horace,' put in Lady Waveryng, 'so that you are an interested party.'

'Oh! then that accounts for Horace's zeal, and now I understand why he was so anxious to soothe the free-selectors and the cedar-cutters, who object to having the Blacks encouraged about the place,' said Lord Waveryng. 'It's all with a view to ultimate profit in providing "copy" for Milady.'

'I've managed it,' Lord Horace went on triumphantly, 'with a considerable expenditure of rum and tobacco – doled out in driblets. If I had given it in a lump, the Tommies, Paris and Menelaus, might have struck a bargain, and the dramatic *motif* of the corroboree would have been done for. Yesterday there was a little throwing of spears, and the end of it is that the Moongans and the Baròlins have agreed at my suggestion to have a big corroboree and a "woolla" – that's what they call their Parliamentary Council, Em – the night after to-morrow, and then to go forth and fight the Durundurs. Get your note-book ready, Em dear. It's to be a real swagger thing in corroborees.'

Lady Waveryng's book was a stock joke. It afforded a pretext for the trotting out of all the oddities available, and gave point to the various expeditions and Bush experiences. She insisted upon learning everything that had to do with station routine, and handled saddles as if she had been born in a stock-man's hut, and she was learning to crack a stock whip, to plait a dilly-bag, and to make a damper. Lord Waveryng took life less enthusiastically, perhaps because he was a little gouty. Racing and stud cattle were his hobbies, and he was interested in the Baròlin and Tunimbah breeds, and rode about a good

deal, admiring the scenery and getting a fair amount of amusement ou
of the free-selectors and the proprietors of the grog-shanties.

A black-boy was despatched to Tunimbah, and Mr. and Mrs. Jen
Hallett turned up the next day in time for breakfast. The party was ;
large one, for Blake and Trant were there also, and naturally Franl
Hallett, and besides the Waveryngs, Mrs. Allanby and Elsie.

Elsie was strangely subdued, indeed almost melancholy. Do wha
she would to distract her thoughts – and surely in the attentions o
her lover and the discussion of future plans there was enough t
distract them – she could not keep them away from Blake, and th
mystery of his life – for she was certain there was a mystery. Apar
from Blake and her immediate matrimonial prospects, Lady Waveryn
as the typical aristocrat, the embodiment of that sphere of life fo
which Elsie had always vainly sighed, afforded fertile subject fo
reflection. Elsie could not help being impressed by Lady Waveryng'
thorough-bred simplicity, her dignity, combined with perfect freedor
of manner, her absolute refinement, and all those delicate niceties, an
all those indefinable characteristics which make up what is technicall
termed among the lower classes a 'real lady,' as distinguished from ;
fine lady. Lady Waveryng was a 'real lady,' but she was not in th
very least a fine lady – except indeed when she was in her full panopl
of diamonds and velvet and Venetian point. Elsie pondered a goo
deal upon these qualities of Lady Waveryng's. She began to realis
how entirely impossible it would have been for Lady Waveryng to d
many of the things which she, Elsie, had done, so ignorantly and s
innocently. She could not imagine Lady Waveryng 'on the rampag
for beaux,' which was Minnie Pryde's inelegant way of expressing ;
fashion peculiar to some of the faster young ladies of Leichardt':
Town, of sauntering about the Botanical Gardens, or up and dow
Victoria Street, ready to meet the salutations of their admirers wit
smiling readiness for flirtation. She could not imagine Lady Waveryn
holding verandah receptions, or receiving tribute from her variou
adorers, or allowing herself to be taken home by a young man afte
a dance, like a servant-maid keeping company. Elsie grew hot an
red as she thought of that walk from Fermoy's, of many other walks
of many other episodes. She was unconsciously learning lessons. Sh
would never again be the Elsie Valliant who had 'got engaged' t
Jensen, for fun, and broken the young man's heart, the Elsie Vallian
who had challenged Blake to a flirtation tournament, and who ha
been the object of Lord Astar's disrespectful attentions.

CHAPTER XXVII

─────── • ───────

'The Corroboree'

Yet never had Elsie seemed sweeter, more womanly than at this time. All who remarked her observed that her engagement had greatly improved Miss Valliant. Blake watched her closely, and made up his mind that she was unhappy. But beyond the ordinary intercourse of a bush house, which necessarily implies a good deal of familiarity, he did not seek her society. And she made no effort to force his confidence, or to talk to him from the inner view of things. She only wondered within herself whether he and Trant had settled their differences as to the matter of that enterprise, whatever it might be, in which Blake's 'damned sentimentality' stood in the way. She speculated much upon the nature of that sentimentality, and even conjectured whether it could possibly have any relation to herself.

There was no lack of interest and amusement at the Dell. Lord Horace was a good host; and Ina in her quietude and gentleness made her guests happy. She was gentle and sweet to Mrs. Allanby, who must have been a serpent indeed could she have overtly prosecuted schemes for the undermining of poor Ina's happiness. As for the men, they had plenty to do. There was duck shooting on the creek, and an attempt at a shooting luncheon, which became a very scrambling picnic, in which no pair could apparently succeed in finding any other pair. The day after Jem Hallett's coming was signalised by the wild-horse chase, from which the ladies were naturally excluded, though Lady Waveryng pleaded hard to be allowed to risk her neck, but in which Lord Waveryng joined with some trepidation, and the promise of a black-boy in attendance to steer him home, should he find the country too rough. He came home, however, safe and sound, swinging a chestnut tail as a trophy, and full of Blake's feats of horsemanship and the magnificent performances of the Baròlin horses as bestridden by the two half-castes, Pompo and Jack, Nutty, and the stockman, Sam Shehan.

'Never came across such fellows for sticking. They're like the what-de-you-callems in the Greek mythology. And to see the places they went up and down, and the astonishing knack they had of disappearing over a precipice, and getting swallowed up in a gulley,' Lord Waveryng said. 'They seemed to know every inch of the country. I tell you what it is, I am not surprised at your failing to catch Moonlight's gang if it's made up of natives and colonials of the pattern of Mr. Sam Shehan and the half-castes.'

He addressed Captain Macpherson, who had appeared almost simultaneously with the wild-horse party, only from an opposite direction. He had come from Goondi, where there had been what he called a 'mining ruction.'

Captain Macpherson had brought with him some police reports and subject matter for conference with his chief. The new Colonial Secretary, he informed Lord Waveryng, showed an extraordinary aptitude for the details of his department, and especially for those connected with the police force. In the matter of Moonlight, indeed, the instructions from headquarters had been unusually precise and frequent. The police had been sent hither and thither on what had turned out to be mistaken information. Anyhow, there had been two more robberies of gold escorts, and Moonlight was not yet captured. As he expatiated at dinner upon the zeal of his chief, Captain Macpherson wondered why Lord Waveryng laughed drily, and why Blake himself seemed to see a sardonic jest where certainly none was intended. Macpherson resented, as an impertinence, Trant's somewhat Mephistophelian laugh.

'A distinct humour in the situation, eh?' said Lord Waveryng later, in the verandah, lighting his cigar, and looking curiously at Blake as he spoke. 'Control of the police force! Seems odd, don't it?'

'Extremely odd,' replied Blake imperturbably. 'I quite agree with you. There is a distinct humour in the situation. Possibly, my dear lord, a deeper humour than even you are aware of.'

'How about my lady's diamonds?' asked Captain Macpherson, strolling out into the verandah.

'Oh, Captain Macpherson,' cried Lady Waveryng, 'do relieve me from the responsibility of these wretched things. How Briggs could have misunderstood me, and how she could have supposed that I should want my jewels in the Bush, I can't imagine. I never wore them except during that week with the Prince. She and Lord

Waveryng's man had distinct orders that they were to be placed in the Bank.'

'I am afraid, my dear, that your orders weren't very clear,' said Lord Waveryng, rather grimly. 'I never knew Prentiss misunderstand any order of mine.'

'Where are the diamonds now?' asked Captain Macpherson.

'In the medicine chest, lying in the trays where lint and diachylon plaster and surgical appliances belong,' said Lord Horace. 'Fortunately, it's a large medicine chest. That is the only receptacle in the house that has a safe key, and they put a Bramah lock on it, on account of the poisons.'

'Horace wanted us to put them in the sugar bin,' said Lady Waveryng.

'No, Em. The flour bin, I said, it's deeper. And sugar is sticky, especially ration sugar, and the after associations might have been unpleasant. However, Waveryng preferred the medicine chest, which during the day is watched in turn by Miss Briggs and Mr. Prentiss, my lady's woman and my lord's man.'

'And indeed,' said Elsie, 'it only needs candles and a pall to make one think that they are watching a corpse.'

'Mr. Prentiss occasionally flourishes a pocket revolver,' observed Lord Horace, 'and Miss Briggs has, I believe, armed herself with a cutting-up knife from the meat-store.'

'I am sure that it would be a brave robber who tackled Briggs,' said Lady Waveryng.

'At night,' continued Lord Horace, 'Waveryng sleeps on the medicine chest, and keeps a carbine on his pillow. I warn any here who may be burglariously inclined that those diamonds are not to be filched without bloodshed.'

'And my waking hours are made hideous by Lord Waveryng's reproaches for my carelessness,' said Lady Waveryng plaintively; 'and my dreams are haunted by troops of past and future Waveryngs bewailing the loss of those historic jewels.'

'Are they really historic: and are they really so valuable, my lady?' put in Trant in that rather obsequious manner which had annoyed Elsie at first, and now jarred on Lady Waveryng.

'They are certainly historic,' she answered curtly; 'though I can't say it is much to the credit of the family, since the finest of them were a present from Charles II. to a fair, but frail, Lady Betty, who was an ancestress of my husband's, and they are supposed to have been part of the Crown jewels. They are considered valuable by connoisseurs.'

'Well,' said Captain Macpherson, 'if it will relieve your mind, my lady, I am expecting a company of four troopers from over the border to meet me here to-night; and they'll take your diamonds in charge and start with them at daybreak to-morrow for Goondi, where they will deposit them safe in the Bank till you go back to Leichardt's Town. What is the matter, Trant?'

Trant had risen, and was peering over the palisading of the high verandah out into the night, palely illuminated by a moon nearing its full.

'Only I thought I heard something in the creepers – a snake, perhaps. They are beginning to come out now. Are you quite wise, by the way, to talk openly about the diamonds and your plans for taking them to the Bank? How do you know, for instance, that Moonlight has not got a scout among the blacks that are hanging round for this corroboree?'

'Oh, nonsense,' exclaimed Captain Macpherson. 'That isn't likely.' But he looked startled by Trant's suggestion, and annoyed at being convicted of an imprudence. 'You are right,' he added with native honesty, 'I ought to have held my tongue. By Jove! there are the troopers now.'

Four men in blue uniform rode up towards the Humpey, and gave a military salute. Captain Macpherson and Lord Horace hurried out to meet them at the back entrance to the Humpey.

'Oh, listen!' cried Elsie; 'and look!'

There was a sudden blaze of camp fires illuminating strange fantastic forms, on the crest of the ridge opposite the Humpey. A barbaric rhythmic chant broke on the still air. It was the night of the corroboree.

Lady Waveryng started up. She did not want to lose any of the sight. Frank Hallett told her that he had made all the arrangements. They were to take up their position at a certain distance – not too near, and he would tell them when they must depart. They must not be shocked. He warned them that the dance might offend the squeamish.

'I don't suppose it can be worse than the Assassouis at Algiers,' said Lady Waveryng; 'I went to see that.'

The ladies went off, and came back presently wrapped in dark ulsters. As they were leaving the house, Captain Macpherson joined them, and went up to Lord and Lady Waveryng, who were together.

'I've been talking to the sergeant,' he said, 'and they want to push on to-night. They want a bit of a rest now, as they were riding last night. If you'll have the diamonds ready and give them to me after the corroboree, say, they'll go off quietly and be at Goondi before morning.'

Lady Waveryng went back to give some orders to the inestimable Briggs, and Trant and Blake waited for her, while the others strolled slowly in the direction of the camp fires, which had only been a signal blaze, and were now dwindled to a circle of red spots against the background of gum trees. Frank Hallett had chosen a place of view, and led them to a fallen log, near which an assemblage of gins had congregated, at some little distance from the scene of the revel. This was a clear space for the fringe of scrub, marked out by the circle of ember-lights with a huge bonfire laid ready for lighting, in the centre, and behind it a gigantic and fantastically designed semblance of a human figure, of which the outlines could now be but dimly discerned. From the dense scrub at the back, shadowy barbaric forms now and then emerged, and strange wild sounds and the clash of weapons proceeded. These were the warriors preparing themselves for the dance. The gins were waiting for the signal, and crowded round the strangers, grotesque uncouth shapes, with naked bosoms and bare arms, and gleaming eyes, jabbering and gesticulating, and clamouring for tobacco and food. It amused Lady Waveryng to distribute figs of tobacco, cut into small pieces, which Blake handed her. Blake was in wild spirits. The excitement of the corroboree seemed to have infected him. He laughed, he chattered with the gins, he flung bits of tobacco for them to scramble after. His eyes shone, a mad gaiety possessed him. Trant, on the other hand, looked heavy and serious, as though his mind were preoccupied. Elsie observed that Sam Shehan and the two half-castes were also present, lounging in the background, the half-castes conspicuous in their white shirts and red handkerchief-belts and neckties, grinning and cutting capers in impish glee, but taking no part in the corroboree itself. Sam Shehan leaned against a tree, dour and unprepossessing, so much so that Elsie said to Trant,

'I can't imagine why you employ that man; he has such a horrid face, and you know people used to say he was a cattle stealer.'

Trant laughed. 'He is a reformed character now, Miss Valliant, and he is devoted to me and Blake. You see we gave him his chance. A fellow can't help being born with a sour expression, can he? His appearance is against him. There isn't a better stockman than Sam Shehan on the Luya.'

'The half-castes look as if they ought to belong to a pantomime,' said Lady Waveryng. 'I never saw such droll creatures. I'd like to take

Pompo back with me. Will you let me have him, Mr. Trant? He shall be well-treated, I promise you.'

'Pompo would pine and die if he were parted from me,' said Trant. 'Do you know, Lady Waveryng, that I've got a sort of mesmeric power over that black-boy. I believe if I told him to cut off his hand he'd do it.'

'Is he as devoted to Mr. Blake?' asked Ina.

'No,' said Blake; 'it's fear keeps him in subjection, as far as I am concerned – fear and devotion to Trant. I haven't got Trant's knack with the blacks.'

The gins pressed closer. The camp odour became objectionable, even in the fresh night air, and Lady Waveryng shuddered. Lord Horace came excitedly towards them. He had been in the scrub dressing-room of the warriors. He confessed to having plied them with rum. 'Now look out, Em. They are going to begin.'

There was a signal shout – a sort of Banshee cry, ending in a war-whoop. The gins scuttled off to gather up their boomerangs, and squatted in a semicircle in two rows along the line of the fires. Then sounded the music – a queer savage chant in long monotonous cadences, with something at once eerie and exciting in its strains. The gins in the front row sang, those behind swung their boomerangs together, keeping clanking time to the music. From the blackness of the scrub a cohort of grotesque forms came stealing. Suddenly the huge bonfire, which had been made of quickly inflammable material, blazed forth, and the circle of the corroboree was a glow of red light. The gigantic figure in the centre looked like some monstrous idol. It had a rough-hewn painted head, gleaming white and dead black, cut out of new peeled bark and with withes of grey-green moss floating down its shoulders. 'Baròlin, Baròlin,' shouted the half-castes. It was a suggestion of the Waterfall rock, the legend of the great chief. The figure was built up in bark. Its solemn arms were extended as if for prey. Brilliant patterned handkerchiefs in crimson and yellow were drawn about its neck, and a red blanket concealed the lower part of the form. The red flames of the bonfire leaped, extinguishing the moon's rays, and throwing darting shadows among the tall gum-trees, black-stemmed and hoary with moss. The gins leaned forward, their bare black bosoms palpitating, their arms swinging, their boomerangs and nullas clashing. White and red-tipped spears quivered in the earth, making a sort of palisade against the scrub.

Then dancing began. Troop after troop of demoniac beings pressed from the scrub and ranged themselves round the centre idol. They were naked save for a belt about the loins. All were painted in white and red and yellow; some to represent skeletons, others had crawling snakes meandering upon their limbs, others fishes, others in a nightmare pattern, meaning nothing; and on their heads were cockatoo feathers, white and pale yellow, and plumes from the parrot's breast. They danced round the idol, making all kinds of graceful silent gestures in time to the music, which changed as the figures of the dances varied.

Elsie sat as if in a dream. She had been seated between Frank Hallett and Blake. Her dress touched Blake. She was conscious almost of something electrical, highly charged in him – a suppressed agitation, though he sat perfectly still. An odd fancy struck her that he would not move lest he should lose the contact of her dress. Was it a dream – the hellish merriment, the savage gestures, the fiendish shouts and yells, in which there seemed a note of such unutterable melancholy? And the brassy glow rising and falling, the solemn idol with its staring painted eyes and outstretched arms, the circle of gins, women like herself – torn perhaps by love and longing, as she was torn now. . . . And the wide silent Bush, and all the vast barbaric world. And here this little group of civilised beings, the old world and the new meeting, Lord and Lady Waveryng, Lord Horace, Ina, Frank, Blake, Trant. She heard Trant speak at the moment. He was bidding good-bye to Lady Horace and Mrs. Jem Hallett, saying that he meant to take advantage of the moonlight and go back to the Gorge to meet a butcher he was expecting the first thing in the morning.

'And fancy keeping a butcher waiting, Mr. Hallett, and for us poor beggars who don't sell a hundred head in the year! I couldn't trust Sam Shehan to soothe his wounded feelings.'

'A butcher, Lady Waveryng, is the aristocrat of the Bush,' explained Jem Hallett. 'We all bow down to him. Good luck to you, Trant. But what do you want with your paltry free-selection sales, and your partner Colonial Secretary of Leichardt's Land? It's incongruous.'

Elsie laughed. Wasn't everything incongruous? She was thinking so while Trant pressed her hand and tried to put some meaning into his good-bye. . . . The interlude was over. She went back upon her own foolish fancies. Yes, there they were, sitting side by side on that dead gum-tree, all different types, all collected from different ends of the earth, and yet all so curiously linked together. Was she not beside the man who was to be her husband? And on her other side, touching her very skirt, was the man she loved. Oh, yes, she loved him, she loved him. If he would but take her in his arms now – before them all – as he had taken her that night, and press upon her lips kisses as hot and passionate, would she resent the kisses? Would they not seem very life of her life? . . . Now there came a move. Ina called softly to Frank. She wanted to ask him a question, and he got up and went round to her, and then involuntarily as it were, and as though each had been tortured and oppressed by that other presence, Blake and Elsie turned to each other.

What was it that made his eyes so strange to-night? What spirit of recklessness and passion and wild yet restrained impulse leaped out of them, and kindled in her a well-nigh overmastering emotion? He seemed to draw a little closer to her, and then to check himself. The shouts grew louder and wilder. The gleaming forms went faster. The red lights became lurid. The acrid barbaric odour intensified. Elsie felt giddy and faint. She half rose, in an unsteady swaying movement. Blake's arm touched her. They were at the very end of the log. He had risen and had noiselessly drawn her away; and before she knew what had happened they were apart from the rest in the night alone. He had supported her to a little clump of wattle, growing close and making a kind of bower, which sheltered them from observation. Neither said a word. The hood of her ulster had fallen back, and her head was upraised and her eyes were meeting his, the gaze of both intense, beseeching, and terribly sad. Still neither said a word. But he drew her quite close to him as they leaned against the wattle tree, and bent his head to hers, and their lips were joined.

CHAPTER XXVIII

————•————

'I Love You, Elsie'

He kept her fast. It seemed an eternity in a moment. No explanations were given; none were needed. She knew that he loved her. He was recalled to himself by a sort of shuddering sob in her.

'Elsie, my darling,' he said very quietly and gravely, and yet always with that thrill of repressed excitement, 'You are not to be angry with me for what I have done. If we had sat together there one moment longer, I must have done this before them all; and that would have been worse for you, my poor child, for though I love you, Elsie, I cannot marry you, my dear. You must marry Frank Hallett, and he will make you happier than I ever could.'

'I must marry Frank Hallett,' she repeated in a dull, nerveless way. The pride and the anger had all gone out of her. It did not occur to her to upbraid him. It seemed to her that they were both bound in a fate for which neither was responsible.

'Elsie,' he said, 'I'm in a mad mood tonight. That dancing has set every nerve going. I can't restrain myself. Oh, darling, it's worth a great deal to have such a moment as this! I shall try to keep away from you after to-night. You'll not see me again now. I shall not be here to-morrow; perhaps you will never see me again. I shall make arrangements for leaving this country as soon as may be. I take my fling to-night.'

'What are you going to do?' she said, still in that dull voice. 'I don't understand. Make me understand.'

'Make you understand!' he repeated, and laughed. 'Yes, I'll make you understand. You know I promised you, the day before you are married. I shall not leave the country till then. Then I shall have the satisfaction of knowing, at least, that you will thank Heaven I had honour enough not to make you my wife.'

Again they were silent for a few moments, and the hellish uproar went on, and seemed to them far away. And now somebody else was speaking on the other side of the wattle-clump. It was a voice Elsie recognised as that of Sam Shehan, the stockman. She knew his surly tones. She had been listening to him just before she had spoken against him to Trant. She only caught the concluding words, 'All right. I'd better slope now. We shall be there with the horses.'

'They're safe planted?' It was a voice she knew too – and yet she could not be sure – it was low, and the whisper was so gruff.

'Down by Holy Joe's waterhole, the old place. What about the Captain? It can't be that he funks this job?'

'Funks! No. It's damned sentiment.'

They passed on. Elsie had drawn herself from Blake's arms. She had been recalled to the world. And yet her brain was bewildered. Was it Trant who had spoken? What had he meant? The phrase had struck her – 'damned sentiment.' Perhaps that was the connection of ideas which made her think of Trant. He had applied it to Blake.

She looked at Blake, and she saw that he, too, had pulled himself together and was standing watchful and alert, and with a set, determined look upon his face. 'What does it mean?' she asked. 'That was your stock-man. He is going to do something wrong – what is it? – is it cattle-stealing? And it sounded like Mr. Trant's voice. It couldn't have been Mr. Trant. It can't be anything you know of. Tell me.' She caught his arm. And yet the idea was absurd. His laugh dispelled her vague fancy.

'Cattle-stealing! Yes, most likely. If Sam Shehan is up to that devilry it must be stopped. Trant? Why what are you thinking of? He went away half an hour ago; and now I think of it that couldn't have been Sam Shehan, for he had to have the horses ready, and they were all going together. No, Elsie, my dear, whatever Trant's sins may be, he is not accessory to cattle-stealing.'

'Oh, I did not mean –' she cried. And of course it hadn't been Sam Shehan, she said to herself. It was one of the loafers about the Dell. All colonial voices had the same drawl. Lord Horace would encourage what are called in Australia 'sundowners' by his free handed hospitality, and it was such a bad plan. And everybody knew that the Upper Luya was infested with small settlers who 'nuggetted' the calves of the large owners, and, when occasion offered, stole their cattle. Had not Frank told her that the Halletts were the principal sufferers? He had prosed on this subject only a few nights back, conscientiously endeavouring to convey to her his sources of income, and wherein the income was precarious. And how bored she had been. As if she cared whether the Hallett Brothers branded so many thousands and sold so many thousands more or less in the year.

With Blake's next words she threw away the whole matter, and he seemed to have thrown it away too.

'Elsie, my love,' he said, 'I want to tell you something to-night, this last night which will never come again, no, nor any other night like it. I want to tell you that you are the only woman in the world whom I have loved, and whom I have wished to marry, whom I would have married if things had been different. I have fought against you, but you have conquered, and I tell you so this night. But if you were to say to me, now this moment, "Morres Blake, I will go with you wherever you please, and I will be your wife, not counting cost," I would put you back – gently, gently, my darling – with anguish at my heart, and I would refuse your proffered love, and I would bid you give yourself to the man whose wife you have promised to be, and who is worthy of you.'

She said not a word, but he felt her frame shaking with a suppressed sob, as he held her two hands which he had taken in his.

He went on. 'The feeling you have for me is only a sort of glamour, and will pass. I was wrong ever to tell you that you would not be happy leading the safe, decorous existence which Frank Hallett offers you. You will be happy, you must be happy. You will have children round you on whom no baleful heritage will be entailed. You will forget me – I shall seem to you, looking back, only like a dream of the night – for I shall not trouble your life after you are married. I shall only wait for that, and then I shall go away.'

'Where?' she murmured.

'God knows! Back to Ireland, I think. And then? Well, never mind. I have promised to tell you before you are married what my life has been and is. And now, my love, good-bye, and God bless you for your sweetness to me this night. I won't kiss you again. I am not worthy to kiss you. That was a wild impulse. Now I cannot. I am not fit to touch you. And yet –' He raised her hands one after the other to his lips.

Some one called 'Elsie, Elsie, where are you?'

'Good-night,' he said, 'good-bye. Before you are awake to-morrow morning I shall be gone. I, too, have business to see to.'

They came out from the wattle grove. The party from the Humpey had left the log. Lady Waveryng and the Jem Halletts were already half-way down the ridge, but Lady Waveryng's voice floated back

during a momentary lull of the Blacks' shouts. She was saying, wit
her English laugh –

'It really was too suggestive, you know. The Assassouis are not i
it.'

Frank Hallett approached her. He knew in his heart, knew by th
look on Elsie's face, that he was in the pitiful position of the supplante
lover. But he bore himself with a certain stolid dignity.

'I am very sorry to have left you,' he said. 'Ina wanted to speak
me. I was afraid you would find that dancing and everything rath
too much for you. I am so glad Blake took you away.'

'Well, I think after a certain stage a corroboree is not quite a scer
for ladies,' said Blake with commendable composure, 'and so Lad
Waveryng seems to fancy. That screeching has tried even my nerves
he added. 'I have got the only ailment I ever suffer from – torturir
neuralgia – and was thankful to escape for a few minutes with Mi
Valliant from that Walpurgis saturnalia. If you'll excuse me I think
shall go and turn in at once. I've got to join Trant to-morrow mornir
at the Gorge as early as may be. It isn't altogether the case of
butcher,' he added, addressing Frank with an air of candour. 'Th
man who is coming from over the border is something else beside
being a butcher, and, as a matter of fact, we are in treaty with hi
for the sale of the Gorge as a breeding paddock. Trant doesn't wa
it to get about yet, but, of course, Hallett, I am safe with you; an
besides, it may come to nothing.'

He turned off to one of the supernumerary huts which served as
bachelor's quarters, where he and Trant were lodged, and Elsie an
Frank were alone.

'Elsie,' Frank said quietly, but with a break in his voice that belie
his composure, 'you love that man still?'

'Oh, Frank,' she cried, 'be kind to me! Don't ask me anything t
night.'

'Kind to you!' Frank repeated. 'Have I ever been anything but kir
to you? If it's to end, Elsie, let it end now.'

'Do you want it to end?' she asked.

'Tell me that he wishes to marry you – and that you wish to marr
him, and you are free from this moment.'

'I can't tell you that. He doesn't want to marry me.'

'And yet he hangs on about you – he looks at you as I saw hi
look to-night, he plays with you, he makes you untrue to yourself
and to me!'

'Don't say that – don't, don't! I don't understand him. I shall nev understand him. There is some mystery – I don't know what. Perhaps he doesn't really love me – no, I am sure he cannot really love me!' poor Elsie cried out of her tortured soul. 'Perhaps he is married already – there has been such a thing even out of books. One thing is certain – he doesn't want to marry me, and he is going away, Frank; he will trouble us no more.'

'Trouble us! Then you wish our engagement to go on?'

'It must be as you like. I'm not worth loving. And yet, oh Frank, if you leave me, I shall be desolate indeed.'

'I shall never leave you unless you send me away. You know what I said to you, Elsie, when you agreed to become my wife. I said that it might be an engagement before the world till such time as you could make up your mind whether you loved me well enough to marry me, and I said that if you decided that could not be, I would never blame you. I meant that then, every word, and I mean it now, and I had no right to say what I did to you a moment ago about ending it at once. But a man may be tried beyond his true self, and that's how it was to-night. I'm not a fellow who has nerves in a general way, but somehow my nerves seem on edge to-night. I shall not ask you another syllable about Blake. I will wait patiently.'

'Oh, Frank, you are very generous!'

'Am I? You said that to me, I remember, that night – after the Government House ball. I thought then only of protecting you against the world, Elsie, and against what people might say, and the need passed. And now it seems to me there's even a greater need; but it's the need to protect you not against others so much as against yourself.'

They had reached the Humpey. It was only ten o'clock. They had scarcely been an hour at the corroboree and so much had happened. The four troopers were drawn up in the back verandah, apparently waiting. They touched their caps to Elsie, and Hallett asked them when they were to start.

'Twelve o'clock sharp, sir. We turn in for an hour's sleep first. We shall be as fresh as larks, and at Goondi by breakfast time, and we're off again to-morrow – a Moonlight trail, I believe,' the sergeant added mysteriously. 'Government orders. That's why we are doing this job to-night.'

Lord Waveryng came out with Captain Macpherson and Lord Horace. He had some sealed packets in his hand. Lord Horace beckoned to the sergeant, and they all went into the verandah room known as 'The Boss's Office,' where Lord Horace transacted the business of his property. 'Where's Mr. Blake?' asked Captain Macpherson, putting out his head.

'He has a bad headache and has gone to bed,' replied Hallett, 'and he is starting the first thing in the morning back to Baròlin Gorge. Do you want to speak to him?'

'Oh no, it doesn't matter. I won't disturb him now. He wishes me to go over and see him to-morrow at the Gorge. I had intended going on to Goondi at once, but I believe there is some official matter about which Mr. Blake wishes to consult me.'

Captain Macpherson's wiry little frame dilated with importance. He liked being consulted on an official matter by the Colonial Secretary. He went back to the office. Elsie walked away to the sitting-room where the other ladies were yawning and waiting till the troopers had been dismissed. After a little while the sergeant came out of the office, his big square frame looking the thicker because of the sealed packets which were securely fastened into his breast pockets, and his inner man made glad, physically and spiritually, by Lord Horace's valedictory 'nobbler' and Lord Waveryng's bank note. The sergeant assured Lady Waveryng that she need have no fear as to the safety of the historic jewels, and seemed even prepared to emulate the Sancy feat in defence of her property. The troopers were also served with a 'nobbler' apiece, and they were all sent to lie down on their blankets in the kitchen till it was time to start, Captain Macpherson taking the responsibility of awakening them.

Elsie went to bed, but not to sleep. Her room in the new house looked out towards the hut where Blake was lodged. She wondered if he were sleeping. She wondered if he was as miserable as she – no, that was impossible, or he could never have thrust her away so determinedly. She wondered what was the bar between them – she wondered, and her wonderings ended in sobs.

She heard the troopers ride away, with the black-boy who was to accompany them to Goondi and bring back the bankers' receipt for the diamonds in order to assure Lord Waveryng of their safe delivery. She heard the tramp of the horses' feet as the men rode towards the Crossing, lost at last in the more distinct sound of the Blacks' war-cries.

Blake did not appear at breakfast and nobody knew what time he had started for the Gorge. His horse had slept in the yard, saddled by his half-castes, and it was supposed he had got it himself, and had ridden off before any one was stirring; the corroboree had lasted late, and all the Dell hands, including the workmen employed on the new house, had been assisting thereat. The staid Mr. Prentiss enlivened his lord's dressing hour by accounts of the doings which would have proved that, as Lady Waveryng had said, the African Assassouis were not in it. Mr. Prentiss had an appreciation of local colour which delighted Lord Horace. Lady Waveryng declared that he also was contemplating a book of travels.

Lady Waveryng spent the morning in elaborating and copying her notes. The Jem Halletts started for Tunimbah immediately after an early luncheon, arrangements having been made whereby the Waveryng party were to transport themselves to Tunimbah in the following week. On this occasion the picnic to Baròlin Waterfall was to take place. Captain Macpherson went with them as far as the turning to the Gorge. There was an air of depression about the Dell. The Blacks even looked played-out after the corroboree, but showed signs of animation in the shifting of their camp and the sharpening of their weapons, preparatory to the forthcoming battle. But, alas! the Iliad of Durundur and Baròlin was not to become history. Lord Horace and Lord Waveryng rushed in laughing, to announce that the two Tommies – Paris and Menelaus – had amicably settled their differences. Menelaus had retired in all the dignity of his chiefdom, consoled for the loss of Helen by a half-bottle of rum, half a ration of flour, tea and sugar, sundry odd fig-ends of tobacco – collected from Lady Waveryng's bounty – and finally a £1 cheque. Lord Horace having accomplished his corroboree, had stepped in to prevent the war. Bessy of the Bean-tree was to be married that afternoon to Luya Tommy, according to all the rites of her tribe, and Luya Tommy had already given orders at the hut that Bessy's dinner was to be put on the same plate with his.

Lady Waveryng wanted to see the wedding. Here was 'copy' not to be lost. She would ransack the store to find a present for the bride, and her wardrobe for a wedding dress. Miss Briggs remonstrated on the score of unsuitability, but to no avail. Bean-tree Bessy was actually married in a crimson moiré skirt, trimmed with black Chantilly lace, which had peeped modestly from under Lady Waveryng's dress in the Royal enclosure at Ascot, and had thus been, so to speak, in very touch with Imperialism personified, to say nothing of the fashion and aristocracy of England – so do extremes of the Empire meet. But Lady Waveryng was not present at the marriage ceremony; for just as they were going up to the camp, there was a confusion and a commotion outside, and Prentiss rushed round to the front verandah, having been the first to hear of the disaster, his face white as death, his knees trembling.

'The diamonds! Oh, my lady, the diamonds! They've been stolen!'

'Stolen?' cried Elsiej Valliant, starting forward, as pale as Prentiss.

'Who has stolen them?' thundered Lord Waveryng.

'Moonlight!' dramatically exclaimed Prentiss.

CHAPTER XXIX

———•———

Lady Waveryng's Diamonds

It was too true. The celebrated Waveryng diamonds were now in the possession of a gang of masked bandits, presumably Moonlight and his followers. The troopers and Benbolt, the black-boy, had come back to tell the tale. Never was man of mettle and responsibility more crestfallen than the sergeant. He handed Lord Waveryng his bank note back again. 'I don't deserve it, my lord, and you'll believe me when I say that I'd rather have had my leg cut off – I'd rather have lost my life than that this should have happened. But I'll get them – we'll have them back, my lady. Two of us went on to Goondi. The Government know of it by this time. All the telegraph wires in the colony are working – he can't escape. I'm off to the Gorge as soon as Lord Horace will put me on a fresh horse, to tell Captain Macpherson and the Colonial Secretary. The country shall be raised; the Luya shall be scoured. No, they shan't escape us this time, unless Moonlight is the devil incarnate, and that he must be to have known what we were carrying last night and to have taken us the way he did.'

The sergeant's story was after all a simple one, though he was incoherent in its telling. He took some pride in recounting the diabolic ingenuity of the trap that had made it impossible for him to offer any resistance. Moonlight had surely known that not even the muzzle of a revolver would have intimidated him. The bushrangers had chosen their spot, it was in Monie's Gorge, half-way to the Bean-tree – a mountain with a slice out of it – boulders of rock lining the track, and only room on the road for horsemen in single file; and who would think of going round the rocks, which looked as if they were part of the precipice behind, and who could have suspected a scooped-out hiding-place, as if it had been made on purpose for midnight robbers and black horses that had the devil in them as much as their masters?

He was jogging along – his hand on his revolver – every sense alert, from description, when, lo! a lasso had been thrown – it might have been a looped stockwhip that had jerked him from his saddle, causing him to scrape the rock – the sergeant showed the traces of the abrasion, but apparently no other hurt. Simultaneously, it appeared, other lassoes had been thrown, and with unerring aim, over two of his mates. The black-boy's head was covered later. For himself, he remembered only the darting onward of his horse, leaving himself grounded, the apparition of a masked man on a coal-black steed – Abatos, of course – a pair of gleaming eyes upon him, a revolver at his forehead, and a sudden, swift throwing over his face of a thick cloth saturated with chloroform. He had felt his hands being pinioned, and then he remembered no more. When he had come to his senses he had found himself in the hollow of a boulder, with a narrow belt of young white gums between him and the precipice, the diamonds gone, the horses gone; and his companions, including the black-boy Benbolt, like himself, securely tied, each to a gum tree. The robbery had happened not ten miles from Luya Dell. Every man of them had been chloroformed. The whole thing had been done almost without a word. Four assailants were declared to; there might have been more; one of the troopers was certain there were five. What had become of the horses no one knew. The men had lain gagged and bound for hours. It was a lonely road, and they might have been there now had not Benbolt managed, with the aid of his toes, to get himself free. He had untied the others, and they had walked to the Bean-tree, as being the nearest point of humanity. They had divided, as the sergeant had related – two going to Goondi to report, the rest, having got the Bean-tree settlers to provide them with horses, coming back to the Dell.

The matter was comical enough for laugher. Elsie did laugh hysterically, and was led away by Frank. Lord and Lady Waveryng were far too upset and indignant to see the ludicrous aspect of the affair. Lord Horace was wildly excited, and all for raising the district on the instant and chasing Moonlight to his lair.

There seemed nothing for him to do, however, at present, but to horse the troopers as speedily as possible, and go with them to Baròlin Gorge, to consult with Blake and Captain Macpherson. He came home late in the evening. It was Elsie who met him. She had wandered down to the Crossing in the moonlight, unable to control her impatience and anxiety. She and Ina were alone with the Waveryngs, for Frank, escorting Mrs. Allanby, had gone back to Tunimbah. All day Elsie had gone about a pale ghost, with frightened eyes, saying little, but starting at every sound and every footstep. She could not have defined in set form the fear that held her. All day the words she had heard at the corroboree the night before kept repeating themselves in her dazed brain. Had it been Sam Shehan who spoke? Was it Trant who had used the phrase 'damned sentiment'? And if it had not been Trant, what extraordinary coincidence that another should have employed it! And in any case, why should Trant have in the first instance said the words in relation to Blake? For that, of course, had been self-evident. Like balm came the thought of Trant's curious admiration for herself and rivalry with Blake, and she remembered what Blake had said about leaving Australia and selling the Gorge. Was it not possible that he and Trant had had a difference on this point, that jealousy had inflamed Trant, and prompted the accusation of weak sentiment? It was a relief to her to dwell on this idea. She persuaded herself that it was fact.

She watched for Lord Horace from the cairn on which she had stood watching for Frank Hallett. Oh, what an immeasurable distance she seemed from that careless girlhood! All along the creek towards Baròlin there was a level tract with the mountains rising on either side, and closing in beyond, and she could see a long way off. She could see that there were two horsemen coming. One was Lord Horace; the other, she knew, was Blake. The girl's heart bounded with delight and dread. She should see him; she should speak to him; he had come on purpose; he had guessed of what she might be thinking. Oh! how could she ever dare to confess it – that he, her hero, could even by the remote association of partnership with Trant be implicated in so sordid and mean a thing as a diamond robbery?

But no. At the bend of the creek the two men pulled up; they said a few words – of which the murmur was only faintly wafted to Elsie – and then they parted, Lord Horace riding towards the Crossing, Blake turning on in the direction of the Bean-tree. And then a curious thing happened. He stopped dead short and whirled round, and in the bright moonlight Elsie, with quickened sight, could see his face turn towards where she stood on the pinnacle of the cairn. He had seen her in the moonlight, in her white dress, outlined against the dark gum-trees; he wished her to know that he had seen her, and that he was true to his resolution and would not come to disturb her again.

Elsie watched him ride away till the two forms of horse and rider were lost in the shadows and the night. She crept down from the cairn and stood on the top of the bank as Lord Horace shambled up.

'Elsie,' he cried, 'what the dickens are you doin' here?'

'I wanted to know – have they done anything? Was that Mr. Blake with you?'

'Yes, he wouldn't come in – said he must get down to Leichardt's Town, to work the official wires, I suppose. He wants to catch the coach from Goondi to-morrow morning. He's a queer fellow, Blake.'

'Queer! Why do you say so?'

'Oh! I don't know. There were we all in the devil of an excitement, Macpherson raging, and wanting to organise a scouring party on the instant – all of us cursing and spluttering and vowing vengeance on Moonlight, and Blake as cool as a cucumber all the time, looking bored with the whole concern, and with a quiet dreamy way, as though his mind was in the clouds, or too full of the sale of the Gorge to bother about Moonlight.'

'The sale of the Gorge. It was true, then?'

'True! Good Lord, why should it not have been true? The man was there – a meat-preserver in a small way – sells to the big establishments, and wants to go in for something in the breeding line. He and Trant were inspecting when we arrived.'

'Mr. Trant was there!'

'Why, my dear Elsie, I think you must be loose of a shingle, as our Australians put it. Didn't you hear Trant say good-bye, and tell us he was going straight over to meet a butcher? Well, he did go straight over, and he did meet the butcher; anyhow the butcher and Trant were there, and had been right enough when Macpherson got over three hours before me. Are you thinking that Trant stole the diamonds? It would be a convenient theory. And do you know that my first suspicions fell on Sam Shehan? But it won't hold water.'

'Sam Shehan!' Elsie said, still in a dazed way. She seemed able only to repeat vaguely Lord Horace's words.

'Sam is a very bad hat, or was, as we all know. It was a fluke, Hallett tells me, that he didn't get seven years for cattle stealing from Tunimbah. It struck me as not at all unlikely that Sam Shehan may have given information to Moonlight. The informer must have been some one on the spot, for it was clear that Moonlight knew exactly how the diamonds were done up and carried, and the right man to tackle; he must have known, too, the exact hour at which they started. And what beats me is how it was done in the time, and how, supposing it was Sam Shehan, he could have got the news to Moonlight and been at the corroboree – for I saw him with my own eyes.'

'Yes,' said Elsie.

'And have started with Trant and the half-castes before ten. Trant swears he never left his side, and that they were on the run the first thing this morning, getting in some fats ready for the butcher. Of course the theory of Trant's implication does away with that alibi. But it's too absurd. Neither of the theories will work. Time's against it, for one thing, and all the facts. The butcher was there; the fats were there – in the paddock; Sam Shehan and the two half-castes were there, and as far as I could see, not another soul about the place.'

'Did you tell Mr. Trant of your suspicions of Sam Shehan?' Elsie asked.

'No, but I hinted 'em to Blake; and, by Jove, it was the only time he flared up; said he'd answer for Shehan with his life, offered to have him put under arrest if we liked; wanted the mere shadow of a suspicion cleared off him. Well, as I said, facts are facts – and Macpherson was the first to declare that we must look elsewhere. The other theory is that Moonlight is in with the Blacks, and was at the corroboree himself and heard us talking about the diamonds – what fools we were! – and got all the information he wanted. It was extraordinary quick work. Anyhow, I think the diamonds are pretty safe. They can't dispose of 'em, and they wouldn't be likely to break them up at once. And there'll be such a hue and cry and raising of the country that Moonlight's hiding-place isn't likely to remain undiscovered for long. One thing we may be fairly sure of, that the lair is somewhere hereabouts; and Trant declares that if it is anywhere in the Luya, Jack Nutty and Pompo, who know every inch of these parts are sure to find it. That's something comforting for Em, at any rate.'

Lady Waveryng, however, was not a woman to fret vainly over the inevitable. Lord Waveryng was far more of a 'grizzle,' as she termed it; and he did 'grizzle' considerably over the diamonds, and worried the police and the Government of Leichardt's Land not a little in his anxiety for their recovery. The Government did their best, and Blake was as eager in his efforts to hunt down the robbers as Lord Waveryng could have wished, though he was heard to say that from such a Radical Government as that of Mr. Torbolton he could expect but little sympathy, and not much respect for, locked-up capital in the shape of diamond heirlooms.

Lord Waveryng went down to Leichardt's Town to interview himself the heads of the police department and to stir up the Government in his cause. He was the guest of Sir Michael Stukeley, who called together a special meeting of the Executive to confer on the question of capturing Moonlight. The aristocratic section of Leichardt's Town society was stirred to its core. The anti-ministerial news-papers were fierce in their denunciations of a supine administration which could allow not only meritorious colonists but illustrious visitors to be the prey of an outlaw, who with a band of not more than four men could hold at defiance the whole police force of the colony.

'When five ruffians can keep at bay battalions of police,' wrote the *Luya Sentinel*, 'what confidence can the inhabitants of Leichardt's Land feel in the present guardians of public order?' There were veiled allusions to Fenian proclivities on the part of the Hon. the Colonial Secretary, and a hint of possible sympathy with rebels, robbers, and insurgents against the law generally. 'Why were not the robbers hunted to their den? Why was not the country scoured forthwith by police, by the military if necessary? Why were not black trackers put on the trail? Was it not fear, abject fear, on the part of the police officers, as well as the indifference of a Socialist Government, which stood in the way of such rigorous measures? So far it certainly appeared that as long as the bush-rangers chose to keep in their hiding-place in the Ranges, there was small probability of the district being rid of its scourge. In no other district would such hiding-place be possible;' and here the *Luya Sentinel* waxed enthusiastic over the mountain fastnesses, which were the barren pride of this unprofitable corner of Leichardt's Land. It would appear that the Luya had the monopoly of not only all that was picturesque in scenery, but all that was romantic in legend and superstition.

Captain Macpherson swore by all his gods that the taunts of the *Luya Sentinel* should be no longer deserved; and during the next three weeks the indignation of the local press became ridicule at the aimless wanderings of the chief of the police and his troopers among the gorges and ravines and scrubs of the Upper Luya, where, upon one occasion, they got hopelessly bushed, returning to Tunimbah in a sorry condition, having staked a valuable horse in a fall over a concealed precipice, and broken the arm of one of the troopers. The Blacks' superstition also stood in the way of a thorough scouring of the heads of the river, for even the half-civilised trackers objected to venture into that mysterious region, haunted by Debil-debil and the spirit of the mighty Chief Baròlin. Besides, the bunya scrub and spinifex thickets were impenetrable alike to man and beast, and must be equally so to the bushrangers, Captain Macpherson argued. On this Baròlin expedition, Captain Macpherson made Baròlin Gorge the centre of operations, and the half-castes and Sam Shehan acted as pioneers. Dominic Trant also was zealous in the service, while the stockman's prodigies of bushmanship and indefatigable pushing through country that might have appalled the bravest rider, lulled all Lord Horace's vague suspicions. Not a trace or sign of Moonlight could be discovered; not a clue to prove that he had made for this direction after the robbery. The search round Baròlin was given up, and then a new theory, founded on private information supplied to Blake, as Colonial Secretary, by an anonymous correspondent, was started, to the effect that Moonlight was in league with a Chinese gardener not far from the Bean-tree Crossing, and that the pine-apple field was the hiding-place of the diamonds. The gardener was found wrapped in an opium sleep, and was sufficiently dazed to be impervious to interrogatories. There were one or two suspicious circumstances, however; the pine-apples were uprooted, the hut searched, the gardener put under arrest, and then it turned out that the trail was a false one, and the police were at sea once more.

Blake paid one or two hurried visits to the Luya, on business connected with the sale of the Selection, he said, but he did not go near Elsie; Trant was away, too – he went across the border, presumably on the same business, taking Shehan with him. The sale was now given out as a fact, and Trant had announced his probable departure for Europe. Minnie Pryde declared that Elsie was responsible for the sudden sale of the Selection, and the reason thereof was that neither of the partners would live there as neighbours to Mrs. Frank Hallett. But this of course was absurd, for there seemed no likelihood of Blake giving up his political life, and he was more likely to be brought into contact with Mrs. Frank Hallett in Leichardt's Town than on the Luya.

CHAPTER XXX

・

A Bush Picnic

But in spite of the chase of Moonlight, in spite of the great Waveryng
diamond robbery, which had furnished food for sensational leaders
and sensational telegrams, both in England and Australia – what
a fertile theme for romance-mongering penny-a-liners and society
journalists! – in spite of the tragic complications of poor Elsie's love
affairs and Frank Hallett's heart-sickness, and Ina Gage's sympathetic
dread of some terrible coming calamity, life on the Luya had to
continue its ordinary course. Its ordinary course just now meant the
carrying out of Mrs. James Hallett's scheme of a house-party at
Tunimbah, modelled on the lines of English comfort and the due
subservience of Australian roughness to aristocratic sensibilities, but
with all the dramatic fitness which local colour could impart; a house-
party which should be duly chronicled in Lady Waveryng's book of
travels, and which should pave the way for Mrs. Jem's reception into
aristocratic circles in England, when that long-talked-of trip Home
should take place; and Mrs. Jem intended that it should take place
before the Waveryng impressions had time to fade.

Mrs. Jem had for some time been silently making preparations. She
was quite as good a caterer of amusement as Lord Horace, and made
less fuss about it. The best rooms had been garnished in readiness
for the Waveryngs, the bachelors' quarters had been made ready. By
a diplomatic arrangement with the dentist, old Mrs. Hallett had been
persuaded into taking her annual trip to Sydney a little earlier than
usual, and her cottage was at the disposal of Mrs. James's guests.

She had invited a select party to meet the Waveryngs, including the
Garfits and Minnie Pryde, and such of the neighbours as were thought
either sufficiently refined for such exalted company, or sufficiently
amusing to afford 'copy' for Lady Waveryng. Dominic Trant had been

asked, and had readily accepted the invitation; and Blake had been asked also, but had left it uncertain whether he could come. It was possible, he wrote, that his official duties might prevent him from being at the picnic to which he had so looked forward. He begged his kind regards to Miss Valliant, and his assurances to Lady Waveryng that zeal on behalf of the recovery of her jewels had something to do with his uncertainty.

'Ah, Blake knows that he will have a bad time when the House meets in October,' said Jem Hallett. 'No doubt, Sir James, you and your colleagues mean to make capital out of this Moonlight business?'

Sir James Garfit smiled sardonically, and remarked drily that they had their work cut out for that summer session. He meant, for his part, to make it last as short a time as possible, and he shouldn't be surprised if there was to be a general election, and in that case no one knew what would happen.

Thus it was understood that Sir James Garfit meant to force the hand of the Government. The summer session had been a concession to public feeling. Nobody liked a summer session, and it meant an involved state of political business.

'Think, Em,' cried Lord Horace, 'the loss of your diamonds may be a turning point in colonial history – a defeat of the Ministry and an appeal to the country; and all because your vanity made you insist on dragging about these historic heirlooms.'

'It was Waveryng's vanity, not mine. He didn't like the idea of my not appearing properly, and, you see, we knew we should be in the wake of the Prince everywhere,' said Lady Waveryng apologetically.

Nature had assisted Mrs. Jem Hallett in her endeavours. Never was there a more glorious September; never had Tunimbah looked more beautiful. The pale green pods of the eucalyptus flowers were opening to let out their honied balls, the white cedars were a mass of lilac blossoms, and the chestnut trees by the creek spread their orange clusters. The young green of the quantongs showed in the scrub fringe, and here and there in the mountain gorges the flame tree shone like a burning bush. The race-course in front of the house was brilliant green, and covered with buttercups and wild violets, and the cultivation paddocks were greener still. The flat-stone peach trees were covered with bloom, and so were the orange trees, making the air almost heavy with their fragrance. And roses rioted on the fences, and the wistaria was sweet, and the purple scrub plums were beginning to ripen.

'What a pity it is that Elsie is not going to be married this month,' somebody said. 'We might all be smothered in real orange blossoms.'

But Elsie said nothing. She had grown strangely silent these days, and from her manner would scarcely have been recognised as the brilliant Miss Valliant, of Leichardt's Town renown. She rarely alluded to her marriage, nor did Frank; and Lady Garfit pronounced them an extraordinary engaged couple, and began to think there might after all be a chance for Rose. Of late, however, she had taken a fancy to Blake in the light of a possible son-in-law. She lived in hope that he might be induced to change his politics, and to join Sir James Garfit's ministry. She was very much put out that he could not be at the picnic.

For he was not to be there. A telegram had arrived, with prepaid messenger from the Bean-tree, to say that he was unavoidably prevented from joining the party. Elsie read the telegram – Mrs. Hallett handed it to her – with a curious sinking of her heart. She had been looking forward with a guilty joy to the prospect of meeting him at the picnic, and yet she had told herself all the time that she was wicked to wish for him, and that in reality she was anxious that he should not come.

The arrangements had been made with a view to the well-being and enjoyment of the elder and timorous, as well as of the rasher spirits among the young. Lady Garfit did not think camping-out was quite appropriate at her age, or that of Sir James. Besides, she had not mounted a horse for years, and her size was hardly adapted to equestrian feats. Lady Waveryng, of course, wished to see and do everything that was to be seen and done. Rose Garfit thought she would see how they got on – of course camping-out would be sweet, but she was not sure that she ought to leave her mother. Mrs. James Hallett, with her usual sense of the fitness of things, decided that it was her duty to look after her elder guests. As for Minnie Pryde, she was equal to all dangers and difficulties. So it was settled that they were to follow the buggy track as far as that would take them towards one of the Selections in the mountains, and then a very short ride on a quiet horse, into which Lady Garfit was persuaded, would lead them to the Point Row Ravine, and there they would picnic, those so disposed returning in the late afternoon, while the rest would push on past the region of human tracks into the Gorges, and camp for the night as near as might be to Baròlin Fall.

It was a goodly calvacade, the two buggies, an escort of black-boys leading spare horses, and followed by a pack of kangaroo hounds.

Sam Shehan as pioneer – Sam always dour of face, but the typical stockman, in his tight moleskins turned up at the bottom, his flannel shirt, and diagonally-folded handkerchief knotted sailor-fashion on his chest, his cabbage-tree hat on the back of his head, his stockwhip over his right shoulder, the thong trailing behind him, his waist strap with its many pouches and implements of the Bush, including a leather revolver case – for almost all the gentlemen carried revolvers, a precaution adopted on the Luya since the diamond robbery. There was always a hope of an encounter with Moonlight. The half-castes rode with Shehan, and kept somewhat apart from the other black-boys. Elsie regarded the trio with a sort of instinctive shrinking, and yet with that vague interest which in her mind associated itself with any one or any thing that was connected with Blake. Trant was there, of course, on a splendid animal, mettlesome yet docile, and, as Trant said, accustomed to the ranges. Lady Waveryng in her trim hunting get-up, and mounted on Jem Hallett's best thorough-bred lady's hack, looked like an importation from the Shires. Every incident of the little journey gave fresh material. There was a spin after a kangaroo, and then one of the stockmen killed a 'guana, a black-boy skinned it, carrying off the carcase for a camp supper, while Lady Waveryng bought the skin on the spot, and declared she would have it stuffed to take home with her. Then, as they skirted the scrub, the bell-bird rang its silvery peal, and the whip-bird gave its coachman's click. Never was September day more tender and dreamy and sweet, with always that strange exhilaration in the air which sets pulses old and young tingling.

'I *will* be happy! I *will* be happy!' Elsie kept repeating to herself. She put away dark thoughts of Blake. He was going out of her life; he must be thrust out of her life; and she would begin to-day the battle with her ghost. It was only a ghost – the ghost of a happiness that might have been. And here by her side was a happiness that was. And ahead of her, in the shape of Trant, was a means of passing excitement. She worked herself into a reckless mood. Why should she not amuse herself with Trant? He was fairly warned. 'Let us shuffle cards, Frank,' she said; 'we have been too much like Darby and Joan lately, and it isn't time for that yet. Go and flirt with Rose Garfit, and I will flirt with Mr. Trant.'

She laughed with something of her old spirit, and Frank was not displeased, but rather welcomed the sally, as a sign that Elsie was becoming herself again. He was not jealous of Trant.

So Elsie called Trant to her, on some woman's pretext, and Frank dropped back to Rose Garfit. Trant was in an odd mood, too. He did not seem disposed for pleasantry. His manner suggested to Elsie the 'villain of the piece,' and so she told him, laughing.

'Well,' he answered, a little grimly, 'perhaps. Perhaps I may turn into the hero of the piece. We are only at the beginning of the play, you know, Miss Valliant.'

'Oh no,' she said, 'we are getting to the end. The play is nearly played out, for me at least. I am to be married in a month, Mr. Trant; and we are going to Tasmania for our honeymoon.'

'Is that settled?' he asked.

'It was settled yesterday,' she replied. She looked up from her horse's mane, with which her whip had been toying. His big black eyes were fixed on her with such a fierce, devouring kind of gaze, that the girl was startled and shrank.

'I wish you wouldn't look at me like that,' she said. 'Why do you look at me so wildly?'

'Because I am wild with love of you,' he said. 'It maddens me to think of you the wife of another man. I can't stand it, and I will not stand it.' He did not speak for a moment or two, then exclaimed impetuously, 'You are right, the play is nearly played out, for me as well as for you. In a month's time, I shall have left Australia. Blake and I have agreed to dissolve partnership, and to sell Baròlin.'

'I am glad of that,' she said.

He laughed in a strange, wild way. They were at the entrance to the cleft through which wound the Point Row gulley, the scene of their picnic in the autumn. The buggies crawled along a rough cedar-cutter's track for a little way, and then at Lady Garfit's request the ladies got out, and a general shifting of baggage and dismounting and remounting took place, Lady Garfit being hoisted on the safest of the Tunimbah steeds and placed under the care of the steadiest of the Tunimbah stockmen, who led the lady and the horse along the bridle path to the lichen-covered boulders, whence it was necessary to proceed on foot. Lady Waveryng uttered cries of delight. The place was in all the beauty of spring blossom. The rock-lilies were in flower, and stuck out all over the precipice in tufts like plumes of cream-coloured feathers. Orchids, with white and purple tassels hung down from the crevices, the shrubs were nearly all in bloom, and so was the wild begonia, and the ferns were in their glory of new pale-green fronds.

They picnicked on the higher plateau. It was a very sumptuous luncheon, got up in Mrs. Jem Hallett's best fashion. She was determined that the luncheon and the expedition should be immortalised in Lady Waveryng's book. A clever young 'new-chum,' from one of the Luya stations, who had joined the party, and who had brought a Kodak, took photographs, grouping the stockmen and black-boys and guests under Lady Waveryng's direction. He insisted on including Elsie in each group; Lady Waveryng made a greater point of the black-boys. She raved about the picturesqueness of Pompo and Jack Nutty. Elsie submitted willingly to be posed. She did not want to climb higher, as Frank Hallett proposed. She had too vivid a remembrance of the ramble with Blake. And she thought of that saying of hers on which she had sadly commented. Yes; if she had only known in the autumn what the spring would bring forth!

It was a very successful day, so every one declared over the quart-pot tea. Mrs. Jem had provided cream and sugar for those who had not Mr. Micawber's sense of the fitting in regard to a colonial life. Some of the black-boys, with Sam Shehan, had been sent forward towards the Baròlin Falls early in the day, to prospect for the adventurous as to the state of the track. They brought back accounts so daunting, of the quicksands in the creek, made more dangerous by the late rains; of the density of the spinifex, through which it was almost impossible to force a way; of the close growth of the prickly bunyas in the scrub; and of the far-famed and almost fabulous 'piora' snake, said to pursue its victim, unlike its lethargic brethren, and to haunt these fastnesses of the Luya, which so frightened Miss Garfit and others of weak soul and body, that the camping-out party finally dwindled considerably below its first planned proportions, and those who turned back to the comforts of Tunimbah were more than they who faced Baròlin-wards.

It was Sam Shehan who told the tale of the spinifex and the piora. The blacks had flatly refused for fear of 'Debil-debil' to go into the bunya scrub. This to them was the forbidden region, forbidden of Pyumé, the misty one, and Yoolatanah, the Great Spirit. Only Jack Nutty and Pompo were of the emancipated from superstition's bondage, and were regarded as pariahs in consequence by their more dusky brethren.

Rose Garfit went back with her mother. So did Lord Waveryng, who complained of a twinge of sciatica. His spouse was intrepidity itself. 'Take care of them all, Frank,' plaintively adjured Mrs. Jem. Jem accompanied his wife.

'You have been drawing the long bow, Shehan,' said Frank to the stockman. 'It's my belief,' he added to Trant, 'that Shehan has a cattle-stealing plant up this way, and is afraid of my finding it out. He has been dead against this expedition, and throwing all the difficulties he could in the way.'

If, however, Shehan was dead against the expedition, certainly Trant was wild that it should be carried through. He had wakened out of his grim and apathetic mood at a suggestion on Lord Waveryng's part that the Falls should be abandoned. Ina had timidly seconded the suggestion. She did not want Elsie to go and get lost in the Bush, and perhaps bitten by a snake. Ina, herself, was one of those who turned back. She was not a coward, but she was delicate, and Lord Horace did not seem to want her company. It was quite evident that he thought Mrs. Allanby enough to take care of. Mrs. Allanby had in her way a sort of quiet recklessness. She had never looked handsomer: the slumbering fires of her eyes had darted into life, and her pale cheeks were reddened with excitement or sunburn. Trant swore that he would be responsible for Elsie's safety. He knew the country better than Frank – scrubbers from Baròlin Gorge often got lost in Baròlin scrub, he explained. Lady Horace need not be alarmed. Ina kissed her sister in a melancholy way as they parted at the lichen-covered boulders. Both afterwards remembered Ina's fears. Lord Horace grumbled – Jem Hallett laughed at her. 'I'm superstitious,' said the little woman – 'yes, I know. But I can't help it, and I shall not be happy until you all get safe back to Tunimbah.'

The party divided. Those turning their faces to the wilderness mounted and rode into the defile, with the blackness of the scrub before them and Mount Luya barring the horizon, while the others went down along the gulley, and both parties were soon swallowed up in the gloom of the gorge. Elsie seemed fated to hear the asides of Trant and his henchman. Perhaps this was because Trant kept so assiduously at her bridle rein. Lord Waveryng had solemnly committed his wife into Frank Hallett's keeping. Lady Waveryng did not like Trant – she had counted, she said, on Mr. Blake being of the party, and joined her entreaties to those of her husband. Thus Elsie found herself for the moment deserted by her legitimate protector, and it was she herself, partly out of perversity, who claimed Trant as a cavalier. The half-castes jogged ahead. Frank Hallett and Lady Waveryng followed, and then Minnie Pryde and a young bushman who showed symptoms of adoration. Mr. Craig was a well-to-do squatter, albeit rough in his ways, and Elsie thought that Minnie meant business this time, and she wondered how she should like Minnie for a neighbour on the Lower Luya, where was being built the splendid new house which she and Frank were to inhabit after their honeymoon and the English trip. Lord Horace and Mrs. Allanby were behind every one else. Sam Shehan was riding sulkily in front of Elsie and Trant.

'Sam,' called out Trant, 'you'd better push ahead and see about the camp.'

Sam took no notice. Trant looked annoyed. 'Sam is not in the best of tempers,' he said. 'This kind of ladies' picnic is not much in his way. I'll go and give him a bit of my mind.'

Trant spurred his horse, and the two were presently in a somewhat animated conference. It struck Elsie that it was Shehan who was giving his master a bit of his mind. Elsie lagged. She looked round for Lord Horace. And then she saw what gave her an odd start and opened her eyes to the state of affairs. Lord Horace was bending close to Mrs. Allanby. The faces of the two were turned to each other. Lord Horace looked very handsome: he was evidently pleading, and Mrs. Allanby was listening to him with a dreary passionate eagerness. Elsie had never seen that expression upon her still reserved face. The girl knew intuitively that the woman loved her brother-in-law. And then she saw Lord Horace bend closer still, and as the two horses touched, Lord Horace laid a kiss upon Mrs. Allanby's responsive lips. Elsie's heart swelled with anger and shame. A fierce blush came to her face, that Ina should be so insulted! – Ina who was angelic in her goodness to Horace. Did Ina know or guess? and was this the cause of Ina's pale sad face? Or was it possible that Ina knew and did not care, because she had ceased to love her husband – had perhaps never loved him? Like a lightning flash this truth seemed borne in upon Elsie. She, too, urged on her horse, and the spirited creature in a few bounds had taken her almost beside Trant and his stockman. And then Elsie heard Sam Shehan say in angry tones, 'What is the sense of bringing these swell English toffs up here – and that d – d Frank Hallett? I tell you I don't like it. The thing is too dangerous.'

'If you reflect a moment, my good Sam, you will see that it is the most diplomatic course one could possibly pursue. I was in great hopes that Macpherson would have joined our party. Now, that would have been truly dramatic. He would never have come this way again.'

'Oh, blow all that nonsense!' said Shehan. He looked round as he spoke, and became aware that Elsie was within earshot. He shut his mouth with the stockman's expressive click of his tongue and teeth, which implies reserve and caution. Elsie was quite aware of this, but she only took in dazedly the significance of Shehan's sudden silence.

She was too pre-occupied with her own discovery, and the manner in which it might affect her sister's happiness, to give much thought to the mysteries of Sam Shehan and Dominic Trant.

Trant noticed her discomposed look as he came back to her, while Shehan pushed on, as he had been bid, and joined the half castes.

'Shehan has the true native's objection to swell English people,' he said airily, though he furtively watched the effect of his words. 'I am sorry to say that he has been swearing vigorously at Lord and Lady Waveryng, and even at Mr. Frank Hallett, who he fancies is responsible for having brought them here. The fact is,' Trant added, 'Shehan wanted to have a chase after Moonlight – he has a theory that the Bushrangers are in hiding somewhere up here, and he doesn't want the game disturbed by this sort of thing. I told him that we were near having Captain Macpherson, and that we might have shown the troopers a bit of really wild country, but Sam didn't see the fun.'

Elsie did not answer. 'What is the matter?' he said. 'You look as if you had seen a ghost.'

'I have seen a ghost,' she replied. 'Never mind. Don't speak to me for a bit. I want to think.'

And just then silence became compulsory, for the track was too narrow and broken for them to ride any more together.

The sun had set when they reached the border of the scrub, where Sam Shehan and the half-castes had already lighted the camp fires.

CHAPTER XXXI

•

Camping Out

'It puts me a little in mind of a view from the Chabet Pass in Algeria,' said Lady Waveryng, 'if you could imagine a coach road here.'

'Not the least in the world,' said Trant bluntly. He did not now say 'My Lady,' having got over his first awe, being one of those persons who, too obsequious at a distance, figuratively speaking, become familiar to ill-breeding when the social barriers are at all lowered. Lady Waveryng looked at him a little haughtily, but did not reply to him, only saying, as she turned to Elsie, 'It is wild enough for anything, anyhow.'

Yes, certainly, it was wild enough for anything. The mountains rose so close that the sense of size was lost – Mount Luya and its spurs to front and right, the jagged peaks of Mount Burrum barring the horizon on the left, so that they seemed in a *cul-de-sac*, closed in by gigantic walls. Behind them were the forest wolds broken by volcanic-looking hills, sparsely covered with hoary gums, and in places with nothing but the weird, jagged, speared grass-trees, and here and there a great lichen-grown rock or cairn of gray stones peculiar to the district. The loneliness was intense. The men had set the camp on a little clear plateau, on one of the mountain spurs, with a ravine on each side, from which came the sound of a torrent rushing over stones. This torrent was one of the heads of the Luya river, forming in places a wide rocky bed bordered with dense scrub. All round, except from whence they had come, rose thick black scrub, up to where the mountains rose sheer – both Luya and Burrum being somewhat of the same conformation, their peaks girdled with ribbed precipices. But Mount Luya had this peculiarity, that the summit was flat – indeed the flatness seemed a depression, and was in truth the hollow of an extinct crater, now a lake. A lower peak, evidently also a dead volcano, stood out from the higher one like a huge flat-topped excrescence, completely surrounded, except where it joined the mountain, by a perfectly bare wall of rock, and absolutely inaccessible. The pines grew up to this wall, but there were none above it – only the desolate grandeur of the naked rock. Beyond this projecting platform, as it seemed, the precipice shelved into the heart of the mountain, with the river running below it, and another inaccessible wall of rock upon the other side narrowing into a V, so that the cleft had the appearance of a slice cut bodily from the mountain, and the hollow was black, with what appeared to be impenetrable scrub. Here was the Baròlin Fall, and some of the party fancied that they could hear in the distance the noise of the waters.

A few white gums, with peeling bark and long withes of grey moss, had a spectral appearance against the pyramidal blackness of the bunyas and the spinifex jungle. The camp fires looked cheerful in the gloom of this shut-in region, though the summits of Burrum and Luya were golden in the setting sun. Great boulders of rock strewed the little treeless place. Some rose like misshapen monoliths to a considerable height, some were piled as though by design one upon another, and smaller stones lay pell-mell, grass and ferns growing between them. On the slope of the pinch were a few twisted grass trees, and Frank Hallett, with the bushman's forethought, went to these, and directed one of the men to cut a quantity of the grassy tufts, which he spread in one corner of the tent that was being put up for the ladies to sleep in. Minnie Pryde's squatter had already cut and fixed the tent poles and was spreading the canvas.

The pack-horse was unsaddled, and from the gaping saddlebags protruded provisions and cooking implements. The tin 'billys' and pint pots and jackshays, strung together by a saddle strap, lay on the ground. The black-boys carried a dipper to the creek to be filled. As the sun sank, the stars came out all glorious in a cloudless sky, Sirius like a far-off beacon and the bright evening star and familiar constellations, with the brilliant pointers of the Southern Cross dipping below the left peak of Burrum. The men set to work to gather dead bunya cones and sticks and dry logs to make a blaze that would give all the light they needed. But Frank Hallett had brought lanterns for the ladies' tent, and it was he who, assisted by Elsie and Minnie Pryde, spread the blankets and carried in the valises and hung a red blanket for a curtain at the doorway, while Lady Waveryng and Mrs. Allanby laid the table and unpacked the provisions.

And then came the merry meal. Oh yes, it was merry, in spite of

Elsie's sad heart and Trant's melodramatic love, and the other love that was scarcely innocent between the two who to gratify it must overleap barriers. Elsie's knowledge of this secret love drowned the sense of her own pain. But was it possible that Lord Horace could feel for any woman a serious and absorbing attachment? Was his light nature capable of any tragic emotion? If not, Mrs. Allanby's nature certainly was. Elsie watched the two. Her brother-in-law was haggard and pale, and evidently consumed by a hidden anxiety. Lady Waveryng noticed that he was unlike himself, and asked him if anything were amiss, and if he was fretting for Ina. Lord Horace laughed, and became feverishly gay. A quarter of an hour afterwards he was plunged in thought. Mrs. Allanby's mood, too, was fitful. In both were the signs of repressed excitement. They appeared to avoid each other. But their eyes were continually meeting.

It was a curious and romantic scene. The lonely night and solemn mountains, the black forest in which perhaps white foot had never trodden, the fire-illumined patch and gray boulders that seemed to belong to primaeval times. And in contrast, this little group of nine-teenth-century people, all young – almost all handsome, the outside band of stockmen and the two half-castes, and this inner circle – the men in their bushmen's dress. Frank Hallett and Trant, stalwart and splendid with animal health and vigour; Lord Horace, with his Apollo face and that nameless stamp of the old-world aristocracy; Lady Waveryng, with the same stamp – high-bred, and yet simple, the natural product of centuries of civilisation; Mrs. Allanby – a perfumed exotic, not altogether wholesome; Elsie – wild, tropical flower; and Minnie Pryde – typically Australian, reminding one with a tendency for floral simile of a sprig of her own fresh native wattle.

Some one suggested songs. Trant's rich voice rose and fell on the luxurious night in those exquisitely passionate words of Shelley, 'I arise from dreams of thee,' his eyes fixed all the while on Elsie. It was to her that he was singing: it was for her that his soul was thrilling. Poor Dominic Trant! He was almost poetic when he sang.

Lord Horace's neat tenor went well with his sister's mild but culti-vated soprano, in some of the Gilbert and Sullivan airs. They both liked modern opera. One song led on to another – Gilbert and Sullivan and nigger melodies, and old English glees, till somebody – it was Lady Waveryng – cried out that it was a shame and a treachery on this Australian night, under these Southern stars, and in this lonely Australian bush, not to sing one truly Australian song.

Then Trant lifted his voice again, in that favourite bush lament for the dead stockman, Lord Horace and the others joining in the refrain:

> *For he sleeps where the wattles*
> *Their sweet fragrance shed,*
> *And tall gum trees shadow*
> *The stockman's last bed.*

And when the music ceased there came the wild sounds of the Australian night, the curlew's moan, the howl of the dingoes, the strange sad plaint of the native bear, which is like the cry of a lost child; and, through all, the clank of the horses' hobbles and the 'poomp, poom-p' of their bells. It was a long time before Elsie, on her grass-tree bed, fell asleep, and then she dreamed unquiet dreams.

And the next day, how wild and wonderful it was! They had left their horses in charge of one of the stockmen, and were threading their way through the scrub to the foot of Baròlin Fall. It was not quite so difficult as Sam Shehan's description would have made them believe, but it was still sufficiently hard going for even a stout bushman, to say nothing of delicate women. They tried to follow the bed of the river, diverging only when the waterside track became impracticable. For there were quicksands, slimy and treacherous, in which at any moment they might have got engulfed, and of which the half-castes showed a curious knowledge; and there were giant trunks of fallen trees, and there were landslips and impassable rocks and impenetrable thickets of the horrible prickly spinifex. And there was always the especial danger to beware of – the dreaded piora, of which they heard much, but which as yet they had not seen. They had, however, seen more than one deaf adder, more dangerous than the pursuing piora, for squat and sluggish and of colour and shape resembling a bit of dead wood, it may be trodden on or kicked aside with consequences, alas! too fatal.

Lady Waveryng's stout hunting habit was torn in many places, and her smart, high boots were scratched and blistered. She was the most adventurous of the party, and kept ahead with Frank Hallett, between whom and Trant there was a friendly rivalship as to which should best guide the fair being committed to his care. Perhaps more than once Frank envied Elsie's cavalier, but Elsie insisted that, for the honour of the Luya, he must in no wise desert his English charge. She herself had no reason to complain. Trant was deference itself. Whatever there may have been of underlying passion, outwardly he was quite composed, and showed nothing of the desperation of the day before. Lord Horace and Mrs. Allanby lagged somewhat. She was fragile, and he was unused to such rough climbing. But he had the spirit of race, and she would not be outdone by Lady Waveryng and Elsie.

From the spot where they had encamped it was not really any great distance to Baròlin, it was the roughness of the country that made the expedition so difficult. They had left the camp almost at daylight, and some three hours of arduous walking brought them within sight of their destination. The noise of the Waterfall had partly guided them, increasing with every step they took. They had kept on the edge of the bunya scrub. Once, when Frank Hallett had tried to push his way through the thickness of the trees, in order to avoid a stony ridge hard to scale, Trant and Sam Shehan had interposed in an uneasy manner, and had assured him that it was dangerous to venture within the mazes of the scrub, and that progress was impossible on account of the density of the prickly foliage. Frank had resented the imputation on his bushmanship, but Trant and the stockman carried their point, and they had climbed over the rocks of the river bed instead of going round.

And now, at last, they were at the base of the V. The mountain towered straight overhead. The precipice took a slight curve to the left, making another side nick in the mountain, and giving to the secondary platform the appearance of an island, or of an extremely narrow-necked peninsula. They could almost fancy that they saw the waters of a lake in the slight depression of the summit. But Trant, who had keener eyes than the others, declared that it was only the sun making a rocky surface glisten.

'By Jove!' cried Lord Horace excitedly, 'I'd give anything to get to the top of that peak,' and he went off to consult the half-castes. But both Pompo and Jack Nutty shook their heads, and declined to budge a step further. Even they had their superstitions.

'Ba'al, me go. Black no like this place. Debil-debil sit down alongside Baròlin,' sulkily replied Pompo; and Sam Shehan pointed to a smooth treacherous bed of sand, where the river course widened and wound round the precipice, and explained with a greater fulness of detail than might have been expected from his usually taciturn demeanour, that no doubt the tales of Baròlin Rock and the second Waterfall – the existence of which he flatly denied, having, he said, gone as far round the precipice as it was possible for human being to venture – and the legend of the petrified chief, waking to lure his victims to destruction, had arisen from the fact of the quicksand which made it impossible for man or beast to cross the river bed.

'Well, at any rate,' said Lady Waveryng, who was more tired than she had expected, and not altogether inclined for further exploration, 'this is well worth having gone through so much to see.'

The waterfall, fed, it was said, by a subterranean channel from the lake on the top of Mount Luya, was of no enormous height or volume, but could hardly be equalled in picturesqueness, as it stole from the black masses of the scrub, with the grand girdling precipice just above – a sharp wavy line against the sky – its colour a greenish white, the bank broken into a foamy zigzag midway in its course, and thundering in a cloud of spray into a round pool of deepest intensest blue, churned into froth where the waters met. The jagged pines gave a certain weirdness to the scene, and the utter absence of any sign of humanity added to its extreme wildness and desolation. A few giant gums hung with moss grew a little back from the river bed. Here and there was a funereal cedar, and the ti-trees on the lower banks were twisted and bent with the force of floods, which had left their mark on the precipice and had swept into the watercourse huge boulders of stone, great tree-trunks, and wrack of every kind. In places the river bed glistened with crystals as bright almost as diamonds. Close on each side the mountains rose, and always till the naked rock began, that dense black wilderness of scrub.

Pouches were unstrapped, and the half-castes, who had been the beasts of burden, undid their rolls of provisions, while flasks were dipped in the ice-cold water of the pool. There was an hour to spare when the light repast was over. The Kodak came into requisition again. Minnie Pryde and Mr. Craig wandered off to collect crystals. Lady Waveryng, anxious to secure a root of a curious fern which she saw growing on a rock beside the waterfall, claimed Frank Hallett's services, and Trant returned to Elsie.

'Will you do me a favour,' he said with repressed emotion, 'it's the last favour I shall ever ask you?'

'What is it?' she asked, snatching at a straw of excitement. A dull dead depression seemed to have settled upon her, a nausea of everything. The watching of Frank Hallett's square well-knit figure as he piloted Lady Waveryng had got on her nerves. She was grateful to Lady Waveryng for keeping him. To have talked to him would have driven her mad with irritation. All the time she was in imagination seeing Blake. Oh, why was he not here?

'You know that I love you,' Trant spoke with a deadly quietude; 'I quite see that my love is hopeless. You are going to marry Frank Hallett in a month's time. For myself, I am leaving Australia; you are driving me away, you have to a certain extent spoiled my life, you owe me something, even if it's only indulgence of a sentimental whim.'

'Well, tell me; if I can I will grant you the favour.'

'You mightn't think me a man of sentiment. But I assure you that I have fancies that are not unpoetic. Do you remember speaking about the legend of the Baròlin rock, and that you were determined at any cost to reach it? You are at the Fall, but your keenness to see the petrified chief seems to have left you.'

'Sam Shehan says there's no such rock,' she answered.

'There is. I have seen it, it's exactly as you told me Yoolaman Tommy described it, a rock like a man's head with a beard and long hair of grey moss.'

'How did you find that out?' she asked interested.

'Because I came here. I was determined that I, and no other, should stand with you before that rock. I meant to tell you there of my love; you see, however, that I couldn't wait for that. Now I want you to let me bid you there my last good-bye. No other white woman will ever have stood there, Elsie,' he went on. 'There's a secret track through the mountain known only to one or two of the blacks. Pompo showed it to me. At one time the blacks had their mysterious Bora grounds here, and then something happened – I think from Pompo's description that it must have been an earthquake shock – and since then they have had a superstitious terror of the place, and will never speak of it. They look upon it as the abode of the Great Yoolatanah, and it's sacrilege to give any information about it. But as I have told you, Pompo would do anything for me.'

'Oh! go on. This is quite interesting. Is it far?'

'Not half a mile. We could go and come back before it is time to start for the camp. Elsie, will you come?'

She looked doubtful. The man's eagerness frightened her a little. And yet she loved danger. 'Why do you so want me to go? May Minnie Pryde come?'

'Minnie Pryde!' He gave a gesture of disgust.

'Then Lady Waveryng. Think of her book.'

'No. To rob the whole thing of its poetry, its one especial charm to me! I have thought of this and nothing else since we planned the picnic. I am thankful Blake is not with us,' he went on, 'for now I can have you to myself – no one to interpose. Oh, I know you love Blake; you need not deny it. He has been here too. And you, he, and

I will for ever be associated with this wild poetic spot. Elsie, you are the one poetic element of my Australian life – you are the goddess of these wilds. I want you to be enshrined in them as it were – enshrined in my heart – in my memory. It is a fitting scene for an everlasting farewell.' He laughed in a grim way, yet his face twitched with emotion.

'Well?' he said. 'Are you afraid of me?'

'No. I have often told you that I am not afraid of you.'

'Prove it then.'

'Besides,' she added laughing, 'look here. Frank gave me this, and I have been practising. It is a precaution against Moonlight.'

She showed him a tiny pocket pistol, which she took from under the jacket of her habit.

He laughed again, too. 'You won't need it. And I don't believe you could hit a haystack if you tried. I promise that I won't even ask you to kiss me. I'll take your hand in mine, and I'll look into your eyes, and I'll say "Good-bye, Elsie Valliant –'

'No, not; not that,' she cried – 'not good-bye, Elsie Valliant. Only good-bye.'

'As you like. Will you come? They are all going off except Mrs. Allanby.'

It was so. Frank Hallett turned as he followed Lady Waveryng. 'Won't you come with us, Elsie?'

'No,' she said, and laughed. 'Two is company, you know, and three is trumpery: and I don't fancy climbing the waterfall.'

'I dare say you are right,' he said, a little wistfully; 'you must not tire yourself, and you mustn't lose yourself if you wander about. Don't let us miss each other, we ought not to be too long.'

'Oh, Mr. Trant has promised to take care of me,' she said lightly.

'And, as I have been here before,' said Trant, 'and know the country, Miss Valliant would be quite safe even if we did miss each other. I could take her back to the camp.'

Frank looked a little uneasy. 'You had better stay quietly here,' he said, 'like Mrs. Allanby, who is too tired to stir another step.'

Mrs. Allanby was reclining in a graceful attitude against a rock, and Lord Horace, not far from her, was in an absent manner prodding the crevices of a natural rockery, out of which grew ferns and strange spiky plants.

'For goodness' sake, look out for snakes,' said Trant to him. 'The place swarms with them.'

CHAPTER XXXII

The Rock of the Human Head

Elsie turned away from the married and forbidden lovers with a little shiver of disgust, and she and Trant, unnoticed by the other two, strolled presently out of the gorge. The turn of a rocky screen put them out of sight. They stood presently in front of the precipice, and apparently further progress seemed barred. 'Well?' she said.

Trant pointed with a staff he had cut from a stout gum-sapling to a hole just above her head, half covered with hoya creepers. It looked, only that it was too large, like the hole of a wallaby or native bear. He swung himself up to it. 'I could take you another way,' he said, 'but this will save time.' In a moment he had disappeared within the hole, which she now saw was even larger than it had seemed, and must have a drop within. The upper part of his body showed, and his arm and the staff, which he stretched down.

'Do you think you could put your foot in that little cleft?' he said. 'You will find it much easier than it looks; then take my hand, and I will lift you here.'

She did as he bade her. The girl liked mystery, and her face was flushed with interest. In a few moments she found herself walking on a higher level within the rampart of the rock in a kind of corridor, with the sky far overhead. 'Oh, how extraordinary! she cried.

He repeated his caution against snakes, and made her lift her habit and show him her boots and gaiters, which he declared stout enough almost to defy a serpent's fangs. The corridor dipped down every now and then, and was sufficiently rough walking for her frequently to require his helping hand. Once when it was withdrawn for him to cut away a prickly creeper, that the late heavy rains had evidently detached from the outer rock, she stumbled and fell, and in doing so hit her knee against a hard object, when she picked up. To her astonishment it was a horse's shoe.

'How could this possibly have got here?' she cried. 'It is not conceivable that a horse could have climbed that wall and come in by the hole.'

'The hole is big enough,' said Trant, with his queer laugh, 'and trained horses have been known to do more extraordinary feats even than that. The wall isn't really so steep as it looks. But,' he added hastily, 'it is far more likely that there has been a stockman here at some time – Sam Shehan, perhaps – who threw the shoe against the rock and struck our hole with it, probably, for I am quite of Mr. Frank Hallett's opinion,' added Trant with candour, 'that in the days before his reformation, Sam Shehan did a little cattle-duffing business, and made use of this place, which is out of the way, and yet close at hand, as a plant.'

'Mr. Trant,' exclaimed Elsie, 'does it not strike you that this is just the kind of place Moonlight might choose to hide in?'

'If it were,' said Trant grimly, 'I should have been a richer man by the 5,000*l*. reward which a liberal Leichardt's Land Government offer for his capture, to say nothing of Lord Waveryng's 1,000*l*. And if I had not chosen to avail myself of the opportunity, Sam Shehan would certainly have done so. We explored this spot thoroughly when Captain Macpherson was at the Gorge. Very likely the shoe was pitched over the wall then.'

They emerged from the passage, which gave out upon an open ledge, and which, as they saw, skirted the quicksand. Descending sheer from the ledge was a precipice lapped by a long, deep, black lagoon, into which the sands shelved. The ledge, though fairly wide, would have been hardly perceivable from the opposite side of the watercourse. While in the passage they had been steadily mounting upward, and now, Elsie saw, were about half the height of the lower crater peak. And then, as they turned a rounded corner, she came, still mounting, suddenly in sight of the legendary Baròin rock.

Yes, it was exactly as King Tommy of Yoolaman had described it – a great, black, bluff boulder, fashioned by Nature into the rude semblance of a human head, the back part of which, being somewhat corrugated and affording a deposit ground for drift and wind-blown particles, had become overgrown with grey hanging lichen that in the distance gave the appearance of an old man's hair. Strangely solemn and impressive did this rough-hewn image seem, set in this desolate grandeur of mountain and scrub. They were within a few yards of the rock. Here the ledge widened out into a sort of plateau, where grew some dark green shrubs with a strong-scented yellow flower which she did not know, and a quantity of the sage green aromatic plant that abounded at Point Row. Out of the precipice behind waved a profusion of feathery rock-lilies, and there were many other flowers and plants, making the spot a mass of colour and bloom. She noticed now for the first time – perhaps because it cut the vegetation – that there was a distinct track leading right up to the rock. Trant remarked the direction of her eyes. 'That must have been made by the blacks on their way to the sacred ceremony. Would you like to see a Bora ground, Miss Valliant? There's a sort of cave behind that rock.'

Elsie followed him, excited by the adventure. The rock of the human head stood out from the mountain behind it. Between it and the precipice was a shadowy space, and here the wall scooped inward. Trant put out his hand and took Elsie's. 'Take care! it is dark, and you may stumble.'

She suffered herself to be guided along what seemed a narrow gallery. Presently she knew that they were in a cave, and as they moved gropingly on, she felt by the rush of air, and a certain sense of space and dryness, that the cave was a large one. And then a sudden feeling of terror overcame her. Anything might happen to her here. How had she been so mad as to trust herself in this lonely place with Dominic Trant?

'I don't like it,' she exclaimed nervously. 'Mr. Trant, I feel frightened. I should like to get back to the others. Take me out of this.'

'In a few moments. It is the darkness that frightens you. There is light when we come to the Bora ground; and it is really worth your while to see it.'

'I don't care to see the Bora ground,' she answered. 'I hate this darkness. Please take me back to the others.'

'If you will wait a moment I will light a match,' he said, 'and then you will see where we are, and will not be frightened any longer.'

He released her hand, and she fancied that she heard him fumbling. It was so dim that she could only just see his form. Then he seemed to move behind her.

'What are you doing?' she said sharply.

'There is a draught. I want to get into the shelter of the rock,' he replied.

Elsie waited for the light. It never came. Suddenly she became aware of an odd sickly odour, and at the same instant something was thrown over her face – something wet and suffocating. She struggled,

CHAPTER XXXIII

———————•———————

Entrapped

When she came to herself, she thought for a few moments that she must be in a dream, so strange was the scene upon which her eyes opened. She was no longer in darkness. The sun shone high in the heavens, and its rays fell upon what seemed to be a grassy meadow, green with a greenness rivalled only by the cultivation paddock at Tunimbah. She was not sure that this was not a cultivation paddock. There were young oats certainly springing close to her. She seemed to be lying on the grass, and her head was resting on a roll of soft blankets. And there was a patch of Indian corn, and here was a stack of hay built against a wall. Her eyes went upward. What a high wall it was! It seemed to reach to the sky. And there were green things growing out of it, and it had a wavy outline against the blue, sharp and jagged here and there, like rocky teeth. Then her gaze came down and moved onward. There was another wall opposite, with the field between – a wall of rock all round. She was in some gigantic room without a roof, and with a floor that was like a cultivation paddock, and in the very centre of the paddock she saw a waterhole clear and darkly blue. She also saw that there were several horses grazing in the paddock – and one or two penned in a small stockyard at the further end of this natural enclosure.

Where could she be? She tried to think back. And she became conscious of a deadly nausea which made her feel like fainting, but which passed presently. She became aware also of that horrid sickly odour which clung to her. And this recalled to her the scene of the cave, and the expedition with Trant.

She staggered to her feet, and turned to find Trant leaning against the wall close beside her, and watching her anxiously. He was very pale, and his face was set and determined. Elsie understood everything now. This was the meaning of his melodramatic words. This was his plot for carrying her off. To this end had he used his knowledge of this natural hiding-place, with the secret of which only the blacks were acquainted. With what devilish cleverness and apparent innocence he had carried out his purpose! She was helpless as a trapped animal. She looked wildly round. The mountain was her prison. How was she to escape? and even if she succeeded in making her escape from this prison, how find her way through the wider prison of the bunya scrub and down the trackless gorges to human habitation? Elsie's heart sank with deadly fear. But she had a brave spirit, and she determined that she would never yield. She remembered her pistol, and felt for it at her waist. It was gone. Fool that she had been to show Trant her weapon!

'I have taken it from you,' he said quietly. 'I don't think I was in much danger of being shot by you; but I didn't want to run the risk.'

'If I had failed to shoot you,' she said, 'I should have shot myself. I understand everything now. This is what all your wild bravado about carrying me off meant; a base cowardly plot to decoy a helpless girl. Mr. Trant, I am ashamed for you; you, whom I trusted, thinking you were a man of honour.'

'Don't taunt me,' he said, with an almost sad quietude. 'I deserve everything that you could say; every reproach you could hurl at me. I have acted like a coward and a villain. But my excuse is this: I love you, Elsie; and there was no other way.'

'You love me,' she repeated, 'and you fancy that you can make me care for you by this means? Don't you know that you are making me hate you?'

'No,' he said, 'you won't hate me, because you will see that though I can do a desperate thing to win a woman's love, I can also restrain myself to act like a gentleman. I shall treat you with the respect that I should pay to a queen – to my own sister. I can't say more.'

Elsie flushed deeply, and was silent for a moment. 'I thank you for that, at least,' she said. 'Will you prove your words by taking me back to – to my future husband?'

'No,' he cried passionately. 'Do you want to madden me? I will not take you back to your future husband. You are with your future husband. I don't intend to let you leave this place till you go with me to be married.'

'Mr. Trant, this is madness – this is sheer absurdity. Do you imagine that you can keep me shut up here – do you suppose that the whole district won't rise to search for me? Do you suppose that they will not find me?'

'Let them try,' said he calmly. 'I have no doubt that the district, headed by Mr. Frank Hallett, will come out in search of you; but I don't think they are at all likely to find their way here. No one knows the secret of this place, but those whom I can trust not to betray it.'

'You said that Captain Macpherson had been here.'

'No, I did not say so. Captain Macpherson would as soon think of searching for you – or for Moonlight – on the topmost peak of Burrum.'

'Then it is only Sam Shehan and the half-castes who know it?'

'Yes.'

'And Mr. Blake?' she asked eagerly. 'Tell me, does Mr. Blake know it?'

'I cannot tell you.' A change came over Trant's face. 'No,' he added, deliberately lying, 'Blake does not know it.'

Elsie believed him. How should Blake know it? How should he lend himself to such a scheme of iniquity?

'Mr. Trant,' she said, 'you know that you cannot keep me here. The idea is nonsense. You are only trying to frighten me into making you some promise, or perhaps you are only playing some practical joke on me. Tell me, is that it?'

'Oh, no,' he answered. 'I assure you I am playing no practical joke. I'm in deadly earnest.'

'You will never frighten me into making you any promise,' she said firmly. 'You may think I'm only a weak girl, but I've got plenty of pluck; I'm not going to give in.'

'I know you have got plenty of pluck,' he said, looking at her admiringly. 'That's one reason why I love you.'

'You think that I should be afraid of getting lost in the Bush. But I tell you that I am not. I shall get out, and I shall find my way to Tunimbah.'

'Try,' he said, 'I give you full leave. I shan't handcuff you. I shan't chain you. Roam about as you please, and try to find your way out of your prison.'

She moved from him a few steps and walked on, examining the rocky wall. Then she realised how faint and weak she was. She attributed this to the chloroform. Her indignation rose.

'You have made me sick with that horrible stuff – and you call yourself a gentleman! Oh! Mr. Trant, how dared you – how could you do so mean a thing?'

'Yes, it was a mean thing. I own it, and I am ashamed of it. But I wish to tell you this. I did not take one little advantage of your helplessness beyond carrying you here in my arms. I might have kissed you, and I was tempted to do it, but I didn't. I kept my promise.'

She made no answer. 'Elsie,' he said, 'I was afraid I should never bring you to. You were so long insensible that I was afraid. I tried to make you swallow some brandy. Take some now.'

He held out the cup of his flask to her. She felt need of the restorative, but stopped as she stretched out her hand.

'How do I know that you have not drugged it?'

'I swear to you that I have not. And if it comes to that, are you going to starve yourself, and die of thirst? Everything I give you might be drugged.'

'That is true,' she said, 'and I shall need my strength.' She drank the brandy. 'What time is it?' she asked suddenly.

He looked at his watch. 'It is exactly midday.'

'And they were to start back at eleven. But they won't leave the Fall. They'll miss me, and they will hunt for me. They'll coo-ee, and they'll hear me answering back.' She began to send out long ineffectual coo-ees.

'You may save your breath,' he said. 'It would be simply impossible to hear you through the thickness of the mountain. And they will naturally suppose that we have gone on towards the camp.'

Elsie gave a faint groan. 'Oh! Frank,' she cried helplessly; 'Oh! Ina – Horace!'

CHAPTER XXXIV

———— • ————

The Tragedy of the Waterfall

But when Elsie, in her helpless despair, called aloud on Lord Horace and Ina, she did not know the tragedy which had befallen Horace, and both Ina and another woman. Frank and Lady Waveryng had gone some way in search of specimens of ferns. Minnie Pryde and her lover – for such he now was – had disappeared. The young man with the Kodak was posing the half-castes at a little distance from the Fall, and Sam Shehan was jogging sulkily back towards the camp. All these several persons, with the exception of the stockman, were recalled by piercing shrieks rising above the roar of the waterfall.

Lady Waveryng turned very pale.

'Good heavens! what is that?' she cried.

'I am afraid something has happened,' said Frank Hallett. He only thought of Elsie, and strode on over stones and fallen trees, and through patches of spinifex, like one possessed with fear. Lady Waveryng struggled to keep pace with him. Others had heard the shrieks. The young man with the Kodak was leaping the brushwood from an opposite direction, and so were Minnie Pryde and Mr. Craig.

'What is the matter?' they all cried. 'Has anything happened to Elsie?' They, too, thought of Elsie.

But there was no sound nor sign of Elsie. It was Mrs. Allanby who came tragically forward. Her face was like death. She could scarcely speak, and only pointed with nerveless hand to where Lord Horace, looking strangely dazed and heavy, was leaning against a flat-topped rock.

'He put his hand on it,' gasped Mrs. Allanby. 'It bit him.' And then she uttered a heartrending shriek. 'Oh, my God! it is my punishment. What shall I do? what shall I do? He is all I had in the world.'

Lady Waveryng gave a sudden start, and looked at her straight with her proud eyes from under her level brow. She went direct to Mrs. Allanby, never losing her presence of mind, though she seemed to see at a glance what had happened. She took Mrs. Allanby's hand.

'Hush,' she said imperiously, but very low. 'You mustn't say such things; for his sake and for your own, and for the sake of his wife.'

'It has bitten him,' cried Mrs. Allanby, 'and I fainted when I saw it, and there's been time lost. Can't you do anything? Oh, can't you do anything? But I know you can't. It's deadly –'

And then she was seized with a fit of shuddering.

Lady Waveryng shook her off, as though she too had been a reptile, and rushed to her brother's side.

'Take care, Em,' he said. 'I'm done for, dear, and the beast is there yet.'

And on the flat top of the rock, sluggish, stunted of shape, and with the cruel broad head of the deadly reptile, was the death adder which had bitten him.

Mr. Craig killed it. Frank Hallett had his knife out in a twinkling. 'Where?' he said.

Lord Horace held out his hand. Frank made one or two transverse cuts, and then unhesitatingly put his mouth to the wound and sucked the blood, while Minnie Pryde's squatter tied a ligature tightly round the arm.

'Too late, old chap,' said Lord Horace faintly. 'It's all up with me. All I can do is to die game, and whatever we Gages were, bad or good, we all of us could do that – couldn't we, Em?'

Lady Waveryng's eyes gave the answer. She was very pale, almost stunned by the blow, but she never lost her self-possession, a contrast to the weeping, panic-stricken woman whom Lord Horace loved.

'Can nothing be done?' she said, turning to Frank, and sweeping Mrs. Allanby with her gaze. 'Brandy, ammonia – is there no ammonia?'

They had already begun pouring brandy down Lord Horace's throat. No one had ammonia, an omission for which Frank cursed himself; he usually carried his injecting apparatus with him on the run, in the snake season; upon this occasion he had forgotten it. But in the face of that murderous blunt-headed reptile they all knew that neither brandy nor ammonia could be of any avail.

Lord Horace's face had become waxen in hue, and already he had the dull dazed look of a drunken man. It was only his healthy vitality which had kept the poison from working more speedily. He staggered as they walked him to and fro, and before many minutes the collapse came. Frank and Lady Waveryng did all they could to rouse him, and with an effort he collected his dying faculties.

The others had drawn aside. Only Mrs. Allanby clung to him, and Lady Waveryng, stern and stately, and yet pitiful, stood shielding them both.

'Horace,' she said, 'is there anything you would like me to tell Ina?'

Lord Horace's glazed eyes fastened themselves on his sister beseechingly, and wandered from her to Mrs. Allanby. 'Don't let Ina know,' he said, 'and take care of her. I wasn't good enough for Ina.'

And those were the last words he spoke.

As if obeying his last behest, Lady Waveryng, when all was over, took Mrs. Allanby very gently by the hand and placed her on a ledge, in an angle of the rocks, where the poor woman sank moaning hysterically.

'It is my punishment,' she cried. 'God has sent His vengeance upon me. Do you know what he was doing when that thing fastened on him? He had his arm round me: he kissed me, he had put his hand down on the rock. His kiss – oh, my God! his last kiss.'

'Hush,' said Lady Waveryng shuddering. 'He is dead. Think of his wife.'

'She never loved him,' Mrs. Allanby broke out. 'She loved Frank Hallett, who is going to marry her sister. She married him so that she might not be in her sister's way. I know it. No one told me. It came to me. I saw it in her look. It was in her voice when she spoke to Frank. I told him. She is very good, too good for him, I suppose. I was better suited for him. . . . What does it matter to her? The poor woman wandered on. 'She will be glad after a little while that he is dead. They never could have been happy. If she had been a different woman he wouldn't have wanted me. He did want me. I don't know what would have come of it. I suppose we should have gone off together; he asked me to go – it was almost settled – yesterday, as we rode out. And now he is dead. And what is to become of me? I worshipped him – I would have died for him. You should be sorry for me.'

'I am sorry for you,' said Lady Waveryng. 'I will take care of you. I will shield you. Only for your own sake – for his sake – don't betray him now that he is dead; and remember that he was my favourite brother, and that if you mourn him as having lost your all, I, too, have lost almost the dearest thing in the world to me.'

Mrs. Allanby grew more composed. Gradually she sank into a silent, tearless condition, keeping close to Lady Waveryng, while arrangements were being made for taking the dead man to the camp. It was Frank Hallett who organised these. A rough litter was prepared, on which the body was laid, and they carried it in turns through the gorges and along the scrub, to the point where the horses were waiting.

Trant stood motionless against the wall of the old crater. Elsie, strengthened by the brandy she had drunk, left him and walked on, determined to take the bearings of her prison. She walked steadily, examining every inch of the wall for an opening. She even looked for some little zigzag path, some crumbling of the stone, some wallaby hole, but there was none. For the most part the wall was of naked rock, with here and there patches of hanging creepers, and as the sun lowered, so long was the shadow it cast that she supposed the wall to be two or three hundred feet in height. She had walked almost round the enclosure when she at last saw an opening, leading, she imagined, into the cave through which she had passed from the outer world into this strange retreat. She went in and found herself in a lofty rock chamber, from which led several smaller grottos, one of which was evidently used as a kind of stable, for there was fodder in it and the trace of a horse's occupation. Saddles, bridles, and stout leather saddle-bags lay stacked on the ground near the entrance to the stable cell. She wondered vaguely how they had come there, and by whom the place was used, but she was too dazed and her mind too preoccupied with her own danger for the real truth to take any hold upon her faculties. There was no outlet to the stable cell. Of that she assured herself, and proceeded to examine the rest of the chamber, going systematically round its wall. There were two other grottos, both without an outlet, and both used apparently as sleeping quarters, for in each was a rude wooden bunk and roll of blankets, and some saddle-bags that seemed to be filled with blankets or clothes. In each also was a tin basin and soap, and some toilet implements. Elsie pursued her investigations in the larger cave. Here also was a bunk, and piled in the corner were some more rolls of blankets. Near the mouth of the cave were the remains of a fire, and there were several blackened billys and pint pots lying about. She saw also a rude settle and a sort of table made of slabs laid upon four firm stones. In a recess was a supply of provisions; bags, large and small, some sticky with sugar and white and caked with flour, and others which she supposed contained tea; several small kegs and some cakes of store tobacco. She saw also tins of preserved meat or grocery. Then the truth flashed upon Elsie. She was in Moonlight's lair!

She forgot everything in the excitement of her discovery. She rushed out into the open. Trant was standing passively against the wall. 'I know you,' the girl cried. 'How could you dare to bring me here? Are you not afraid? This is Moonlight's hiding-place. You have been lying to me; lying, lying all through. I understand everything now. I understand why Sam Shehan didn't want us to come here. You are Moonlight – you – you –'

She burst into a fit of hysterical laughter.

'No,' he answered, 'I am not Moonlight, and I am not lying to you now. It is true this is Moonlight's lair. And are you surprised that the police haven't found him? But I am not Moonlight.'

'Then who is Moonlight?' she said.

'Ah,' he answered, 'it would surprise you to know that. Perhaps you may find out later.'

'Are you not afraid that I shall betray you?' she said.

'No. I have told you that I don't intend to let you leave this place till you go with me to the nearest township to be married. You are not likely to betray your husband. Besides, I don't mean to give you the chance. I have made all my arrangements, and when I leave this it will be for good. The Moonlight drama is played out. As soon as you are Mrs. Dominic Trant, we sail for Europe.'

'Where are Lady Waveryng's diamonds?' she asked suddenly.

'Do you think I am likely to tell you that?' he said. 'Let us drop unpleasant subjects, Elsie. You know the worst that is to be known. We have never killed anybody, and we have gone in for things on a generous scale. You can't call us petty ruffians. In fact, I have heard you express admiration for Moonlight.'

Again the girl was seized with hysterical laughter. Her mind went back to various episodes, seizing the threads brokenly. 'Oh! oh!' she gasped. 'And you pretended to condole with Lord Waveryng – and when you went away from the corroboree all that story about the butcher waiting! – Oh! and at the Races – and I remember how you joked at Moonlight and Captain Macpherson being fellow guests, and you have been pretending to help Captain Macpherson. And then at Goondi – the gold-escort – at the election. Oh!' The girl's eyes dilated, and she suddenly stopped. She remembered the tall cloaked figure, the gleaming hilt of the revolver, the wild words, the flaming eyes. And then all came clear to her.

'Oh, God!' she cried, and fainted.

Never in all her life before to-day had Elsie fainted. Trant told her that she had been unconscious for a long time. When she came to herself he was chafing her hands with the tenderness of a woman. She asked him to leave her alone, and he went away. For a long time she lay on the grass and thought. She lay there till the sun had sunk behind the rampart of the old crater.

By-and-by Trant came to her, and in a humble subdued manner asked her if she would like to see the place he had arranged for her to sleep in. Always to Trant's credit it was to be remembered that he acted towards her with a certain chivalric consideration. She did not feel afraid of him now. Her very soul seemed numbed. He asked her if she would take his arm as ceremoniously as if they had been in a ball-room, and she accepted it again with that tendency to hysterical laughter.

He took her into one of the smaller caves, and she was almost touched to see how carefully he had arranged it. He had put some hay on a bunk to serve as a mattress, and had spread the blankets smoothly upon it. He had spread another blanket on the floor so that her feet should not touch the bare earth of the cave, and he had scoured the tin basin and filled a dipper with water, and laid some soap and even a raw edged cloth – torn from something – for a towel. He had dragged in some stones and a slab, and had extemporised a dressing-table, on which he had put a tiny handglass and a comb, and – loverlike touch! – in a small pint pot were a few sprays of rock lily. He must have gone out and gathered them.

'I'm afraid it is very rough,' he said, 'but it's the best I can do. Nothing will hurt you. You'll be as safe here as if you were in Lady Horace's room at the Dell. I shall be a good way off, but you can call me if anything frightens you. I'm going to camp outside, and now I shall get you some supper.'

He went out. Presently, however, he came back and called her, 'Elsie!'

She went to him.

'Did you find the way out?'

'No,' she said, surprised, and fancying he was going to release her.

'Well, I'd better show you – just that it is no use hoping to get away – in case you tried to-night. Come with me.'

He had a tiny lantern in his hand, and she followed him. At one end the larger cave hollowed inward – she had not reached so far when the horror of her discovery had burst upon her. He led her here, and along a high narrow passage into which only the faintest glimmer of light came from what was evidently the larger cave, into which they had first come yesterday. She knew now that it must have been in this narrow passage he had chloroformed her. He came to a stop and flashed his lantern against a black excrescence, which she saw was a large projecting rock. She saw also beside it an iron tipped staff, which looked as if it had been a cart pole. 'Look at me,' he said; 'I am a very large and powerful man.'

'Yes,' she answered bewildered.

'Well. Do you mind holding the lantern?' She took it from him, and he seized the pole and fixed it in a groove of the rock, using it as a lever and exerting all his strength to turn the mass outward. He was a long time at it. The sweat poured down his forehead. 'It takes two of us,' he said. 'Do you think you could do that?'

By inches he moved the block, and she now saw that it was a stone that must have been dragged sideways from the outside, no doubt by a horse, which when placed across in a perpendicular position completely barred the passage.

'That's the door of your prison,' he said. 'There's only this entrance to the cave. You have my full leave to hunt for any other. You are not likely to escape.'

'No,' she answered, submissive in her bewilderment. He led her back again, lighted the fire, and proceeded with his preparations for supper. She tried to eat a little of the salt beef he had boiled, and even told him his johnny-cakes were excellent. It was all so grim, so extraordinary. In his manner now there was nothing theatrical. He might have been doing the honours of Baròlin. When their meal was over she sat patient, supine, with no heart even to be angry. She knew that his eyes were on her all the time, but she would not look at him. At last she could bear the oppression of his presence in that confined place no longer, and got up and went outside. She longed to fling herself on the ground and sob, but pride kept her from this weakness. She would not let him think she was frightened. Presently he came out to her. 'Would you like me to sing?' he said gently.

She signified assent, and he began, his beautiful voice echoing strangely in this mountain heart. He sang on for an hour, all kinds of things, mostly sad, one or two spirited war songs, and among them 'The Marseillaise.'

Was ever stranger concert! At last Elsie got up, and said she would go to bed, and he went with her like an attentive host, lighted a fat lamp and conducted her to the door of her chamber. Then he bowed low and left her.

CHAPTER XXXV

The 'Crater' Prison

Three days went by of this curious life – days that seemed like an eternity. Elsie sometimes wondered whether she had ever passed any other existence than this one within the crater prison, with Dominic Trant for her sole companion. She wondered what was going on in the outer world – whether the Luya was all out in search of her, whether Frank Hallett thought she was dead, whether Ina was mourning her as lost. Alas! she did not know that Ina was a widow, mourning her husband – that Lord Horace was laid in his grave that very day.

Elsie had found a copy of Shakespeare. She guessed to whom the book belonged, and she stayed as much as she could in her sleeping-cave, and tried to read. She avoided Trant as far as was possible, only seeing him at meals and when she took her daily walk in the crater-field. It was in one of these walks that she noticed among the other horses a splendid black thoroughbred, which somehow seemed familiar. Doubtless this was the famous Abatos.

For the first day Trant was respectful, and almost timid. On the second day he alarmed her a little by his vehement declarations of love. On the third day he sought her persistently; she was afraid that he would come to her own compartment in the cave, and she longed for the pistol he had taken from her, and which she had since tried to wheedle from him, but to no purpose. On the night of the third day she thought she heard voices, but when she looked into the larger cave there was no sign of any one. Still she felt almost sure that Trant had had a visitor, and that the visitor had been Pompo, the half-caste.

Her suspicion became certainty on the following morning. It was her habit to remain in her cell, taking no breakfast, and only coming out at mid-day. She had kept her watch – one which Frank had given her – wound up, and knew the hours. Otherwise there was little except the rising and drooping of the sun behind the walls of her prison to mark how the time sped. To-day Trant came to her cell and pushed aside the blanket which she had propped up with sticks against the entrance. 'Elsie,' he said, 'come out. I have something to say to you.'

She obeyed him. His face had a grim determined look. She felt sure that some crisis had arrived. His eyes were flaming, and his whole manner showed that he had reached his limit of patience.

'Elsie,' he said, 'I can bear this no longer. I have been your humble slave for three days. Now I will be your master. Sit here,' he said, and pointed to the settle in the larger cave.

'No,' she exclaimed, 'I will hear what you have to say outside.'

'I had a visitor last night,' he said, when they were outside the cave.

'I know. It was one of the half-castes.'

'It was the one who would go to perdition for me if I bade him – Pompo. If Pompo had been a woman he – or she – would have died for love of me. Why can't I make you love me? Why can't I magnetise you with my eyes, with my voice? Look at me, Elsie.'

She did look at him. His eyes frightened her, and she averted her own. They had certainly a magnetic quality.

'I believe I could magnetise you if you would only look at me. Love me, Elsie; what is the use of holding out? I tell you that, by fair means or foul, by gentleness or force, I mean to have you for my own.'

'You will not,' she said, 'for I will kill myself first.'

'No, you will think better of it. And besides, you have nothing to kill yourself with now that I have taken your pistol from you. And I am so strong – so strong. I could crush you; I could seize and break you in two. How are you going to withstand me?'

He put his arms round her as he spoke, and held her facing him as in a vice, not attempting to kiss her, but simply looking at her with a smile that terrified her. Then for the first time her courage failed her. She besought him; she pleaded with him; she appealed to his honour, to his manliness, to his love for her, to let her go free. She would take any oath he chose to impose upon her; she would never betray him; she would thank him from the bottom of her heart; she would pray for him; she would always be his friend. Only would he have mercy on her and let her go back to Ina and Horace.

'Lord Horace is dead,' he said, with brutal suddenness.

She thought he was jesting. He told her the story circumstantially, as he had heard it from Pompo. The funeral had taken place the day before. Lady Horace, between the loss of her husband and that of her sister, was distracted. Mrs. Allanby was distracted also, and had made a scandal; Trant seemed to gloat over the details. As for Elsie, the general impression was that she and Trant had wandered into the quicksands and got engulfed therein, or had been lost in the bunya scrub. At first, in the confusion following Lord Horace's death, it had been taken for granted that the two were making their way to the camp. When it was discovered that they were missing, Frank Hallett had gone back to the Falls with two of the stockmen and the half-castes, and had searched in vain. Trant described with fiendish malice how Pompo had led him off the trail, and contrived that no suspicion of her real hiding-place could be aroused. Search-parties had been sent out from Tunimbah. They were exploring the scrub. But the quicksand theory would certainly be accepted, and Trant told how he had bidden Pompo find on the borders of the lagoon where the sands shelved from the bank, a handkerchief of Elsie's that he, Trant, had stolen, and the hat he himself had worn. That would settle the question, and it would be believed, for a time at any rate, that the fate of Elsie Valliant was the same as that of Scott's Ravenswood.

'Now it's time this should end,' Trant went on. 'I am going to take you away with me to-night.'

Elsie laughed hysterically. 'You can't do that,' she said. 'I am not a baby that you can carry me. I think you would find me a very troublesome burden, and I tell you that I will throw myself down the precipice rather than go with you.'

'We shall see,' he said grimly. 'I think I can find a means of making you obedient.'

She understood. He meant to drug her as he had done on her entrance. She realised her helplessness – realised also the uselessness of appeal or defiance.

'Tell me,' she said quietly, 'what do you mean to do?'

'Pompo will be here with the horses about sundown. We shall ride all night – camp out if necessary. To-morrow we will take the steamer from Myall Heads for Sydney, and once there I shall marry you, and sail immediately for Europe.'

'Very well,' said Elsie, 'I will go with you peaceably if you will give me your word of honour that you will not drug me.'

'I shall not drug you unless you defy me. You think you will escape,' he added, 'but I warn you that you won't find that easy.'

She went back to her cave. The day wore on. Curiously enough, her spirits rose at the thought of the wild night ride before her. Anything was better than imprisonment here. She heard Trant moving about in the larger cave, and supposed that he was making preparations for departure. She wondered what the robbers had done with their booty – wondered where they had put Lady Waveryng's diamonds – wondered. Oh, did *he* know that she was held captive in his secret lair? She could not bear the thought. She had tried to keep it away – had tried to blunt her senses to the horror. Now it overcame her. She writhed in shame for him – in agony for herself.

It was four o'clock. Trant came to the opening of her cell. 'Come out,' he said, 'I have made some tea. It is not good for you to stay in there.'

She obeyed. He was standing in the larger cave, and had laid the table with biscuits and tea. The light from the crater streamed into the cave. She saw that there were valises lying ready packed, and that the cave had been put in order, also that Trant was dressed for a journey. He drew forward the settle, laid a blanket upon it, and placed a rough footstool. There was a certain tenderness in his way of doing this, as well as in the manner in which he looked at her. 'You have been crying,' he exclaimed; 'and I would give the world to make you happy.'

'Let me go then,' she said; 'take me back to Ina.'

'You ask me the one thing I cannot do for you. I could die *with* you. Give you up I cannot.'

She sank into silence. He pressed her to drink the tea, but she refused. He proceeded to fill his flask, and to put up some bread and salt beef, and tea and sugar in ration bags, which were laid by the valise. Then suddenly came a sound which made Trant start for a moment, and caused Elsie's heart to leap.

'Pompo is a little earlier than I expected,' said Trant quietly, and went on with his preparations.

The rock door had been moved by an outside lever. This was the sound Elsie heard, and which Trant had taken for granted was made by the half-castes. But it was not the black-boy's step that came towards the cave. This was a firmer, an altogether different tread. Trant knew it. He darted forward with a muffled oath. Elsie rose too. She recognised the advancing figure. It was Morres Blake. He was followed by Sam Shehan.

Blake came right into the centre of the cave. He had a revolver in his hand, and Elsie saw a look on his face which reminded her of the night at Goondi; a wild, desperate, and yet exalted look.

He came straight towards Elsie, just pausing as he entered to say to Shehan, 'Get Abatos.'

Shehan went out by the crater entrance. Ignoring Trant's presence, Blake said to Elsie, 'Miss Valliant, I have come to take you home.'

And then all Elsie's fortitude gave way, and she burst into a fit of sobbing. Blake put his arms round her. 'Don't cry,' he said, 'you are safe, now.' The sight seemed to madden Trant. He sprang towards them, his revolver upraised. In a moment Blake had covered him with the muzzle of his own pistol. There was a shot. Elsie never rightly knew what had happened. When the smoke cleared she saw that the two men were grappling, and that the revolvers lay upon the ground.

'You villain!' she heard Blake say, 'couldn't you play square?'

It was as though a demon possessed Blake. Of the two he was of the slighter build, but he seemed to have the strength of a giant as he flung his adversary from him.

Trant reeled backwards and fell, his head striking heavily against one of the stone props of the slab table. Blake looked at him coolly, raised him and quickly examined the spot of blood on his temple, then laid him back and turned to Elsie.

'You have killed him,' she cried.

'No,' he answered, 'he is stunned. It is nothing. Shehan will look after him. Come with me out of this accursed place,' he said.

He took her hand, and she let him lead her as though she had been a child.

They went through the dark passage of the cave, and then once again she stood on the plateau beside the Baròlin rock. Blake had not spoken a word, but he had watched each step with the utmost solicitude, and each time she had looked towards him she had seen, when the dimness allowed, that his eyes were upon her. He took her to a ledge of rock, and asked her if she would rest there for a few minutes.

'Do you feel able to walk as far as the Fall?' he said. 'It would perhaps be safer to let Shehan lead Abatos. After that you can mount, and I know a fairly good track through the scrub.'

'Yes,' she said, 'I am quite strong, and I shall be glad to walk.'

'Then I will go back to the cave and see that all is right, and in what state Trant is. Do you mind waiting here? You will be quite safe.'

'I know that. I will wait.'

He left her. All that she could feel then was joy that she had seen him, that he was near, that he had promised to take care of her. She waited for some time, and it did not seem long. She knew that it was some time because of the lengthening shadows. At last he came, but Shehan was not with him, and he himself led Abatos.

'I was obliged to leave Shehan,' he explained. 'Perhaps it is as well. Trant had only just become conscious. He is not really hurt, but I did not like him to be alone. I have Jack Nutty here.'

Blake gave again that peculiar 'coo-ee' which Elsie remembered. In a few moments the half caste appeared. He showed his white teeth as he made an impish salute to Elsie, and took Abatos' rein from his master, leading him round the ledge, by a path which might have frightened any animal not accustomed to it. Elsie and Blake were alone.

He came close, and stood looking at her with a curious solemn gaze in which there was an infinite regret. It stirred the girl to her heart's core. Involuntarily she put out her hands to him. He took them.

'What,' he said, 'you don't turn away from me? You don't hate me?'

'No,' she said. And then her voice broke in a sob. 'Oh, tell me what it means,' she cried; 'I can bear anything – if only you will make me understand.'

'Yes, I will make you understand,' he answered. 'I said that I would on the day before you were married. I shall not wait for that. Sit here.'

He led her to a ledge of rock out of sight of the entrance to the cave, and then placed himself with his back against the precipice and began.

'I have ruined my life,' he said. 'I began to ruin it when I was a very young man in the army, and got mixed up with a Fenian Society – I need not tell you now in what way. You may have heard from Lord Waveryng, who has recognised me, that the Blakes of Coola are a wild set, Catholics, and, with the exception of the present Lord Coola, who has reversed all the family traditions, ardent Nationalists; the very stuff of which a Fenian is made. You may have heard, too, of Boyle O'Reilly, who was tried and sentenced for inciting his regiment to revolt, and finally sent to Western Australia, from which he got away to America. My offence was the same, but I was not tried. I had information of my projected arrest, and acting under orders I escaped. The whole thing was very cleverly arranged. I was seen to fall over a cliff. The man with me went for help. When he came back my body was not to be found, and I was supposed to have been washed out to sea. I am a good swimmer, and a boat was in waiting which took me to a hiding-place on the coast; and after a bit Trant joined me. Did I tell you that he was a private in my regiment, and a member of the same secret society, sworn to obey orders, as I was? We spent some wild wandering years. We both, as you know, speak

French, and we enlisted in an Algerian corps. That didn't last long. The taste for brigandage started in the desert. The adventurous life suited me. There are times when a mad thirst for excitement seizes me, works me to frenzy. At these times I am mad. It's a taint in the Blake blood. I must have an outlet, or I should be in a lunatic asylum. You may take that as one excuse for me. The other is that I am a patriot to the depth of my heart, and that I am sworn to work for my country's freedom. I have robbed – not for greed of gain, but for Ireland.'

'Ah!' Elsie drew a panting breath of relief.

'What did I care for mere existence?' he went on. 'I tell you that I know no more intense joy than the thrilling sense of carrying one's life in one's hand. If I were taken I should kill myself. I couldn't live the tame round of the ordinary English soldier in time of peace. I was about twenty when I became subject to these recurring fits of excitement – madness if you like to call them so. I know when they are coming on, and I find vent for them in some desperate adventure – a wild ride, a bushranging escapade – Abatos and I understand each other. We've thrilled together on the moonlight nights as we have galloped along, with the gum trees flying past and the black bunyas closing us within walls of gloom, only the moonbeams shining through the rifts on the track, when we have ridden for our lives through gorges and scrub to the shelter of this cave. You shudder. Yes, it is horrible, I suppose, for a woman to think of the man she loves as a common thief.'

'You are not that,' she exclaimed. 'But it is horrible; oh! it is horrible.'

'Well,' he said, 'now you understand why, much as I loved you, I could not ask you to link your lot with such a lot as mine.'

'You loved me!' she repeated as if the assurance brought her comfort.

'You knew it,' he cried. 'Did I not tell you so the night of the corroboree? I told you that I loved you when you were bound to another man – I waited for that, so that there might be no faintest glimmer of hope for me; no possibility of temptation.'

'For either of us,' she added deliberately.

'Elsie,' he exclaimed, 'it is not possible that you can love me now that you know everything?'

She was silent for a few moments. When she spoke it was in a changed tone.

'Tell me how it was that you became Moonlight.'

'By an accident; the discovery of this place. Some good people say that there is no such thing as fate. Do you believe them? One would find it hard to think that a beneficent Providence led me here. It was one of those strange chances which seemed almost an impossibility. Why should I, of all people in the world, have stumbled upon this inaccessible spot?'

'How was it?'

'We were travelling overland to Leichardt's Town. I had heard of this wild bit of country, and of the reports of gold, and Trant had fallen in with Pompo, who agreed to pilot us. I must tell you that Trant had an extraordinary influence over Pompo. He can hypnotise a little, and used to be fond of trying it with the Kabyles. He tried it on Pompo, who firmly believes that Trant is Debil-debil incarnate. Perhaps that has shaken his belief in the Blacks' Debil-debil, and reconciled him to our invasion of the sacred Bora grounds.'

Blake laughed. Elsie laughed too; but so drearily. Neither spoke for a few moments. He was watching her intently. 'You have had a bad time,' he said abruptly. 'You are much thinner, and you are terribly pale; and your face is so sad, so unlike the face of that bright, beautiful, unconscious Elsie whom I met at the creek-side not so many months ago. You have suffered.'

'Yes, I have suffered,' she said, in a low voice; 'horribly.'

'And it is I who have done this. I who have ruined your happiness and brought into your life tragedy and crime. My curse is upon you as it has been on all women who have ever cared for me.'

'There have been women then who have cared for you, and who have suffered as I have suffered?'

'Perhaps more,' he answered gloomily. 'You, at least, have the satisfaction of knowing – if it is a satisfaction – that what you suffer I suffer ten thousand fold, that I love you as I have never loved any other woman.'

'Ah!' she interrupted, with a little cry of pain. 'The other women. There was surely one, there must have been, whom you loved.'

'There was one,' he answered gravely, 'who risked much for my sake, and to whom I was bound by every tie of honour. It was in the East. Some day, if ever we are together – and that is not likely – I will tell you the whole story; I cannot now, I am ashamed to think of what she sacrificed for me, and how little I deserved it – how little real love I gave in return. She is dead. It humiliates me to remember the light way in which I played with love, in other episodes – never mind them. If you were to be my wife you should have the whole record; and it is not a stainless one; but there is no woman nor the memory of one who should stand between you and me.'

She put out her hand to him and he kissed it very tenderly, but his manner was curiously self-contained. She could see that he was holding himself under restraint.

'Come, Elsie,' he said. 'I have made my fate, and regret will not undo it. All that I can do for you is to remove myself from your life, and that I will do. Now I am going to take you back to your sister. We have a long rough ride, and we must manage it as best we can.'

He led her along the cliff edge. She walked as in a dream. Down below lay the still dark lagoon, and opposite the shelving quicksands. Blake did not take her by quite the same road as that by which she had come with Trant. She saw when they had got into the rocky gallery which she and Trant had entered by the hole in the precipice, that in several places there were deep clefts and chasms going as it were into the heart of the mountain, and scarcely noticeable in the dimness. It was into one of these fissures that Blake led her, and she now perceived that this was an opening into the outer world, almost more closely hidden than the one by which she had entered – a narrow winding passage twisting round abutting boulders, but practicable for a well-trained horse, and no doubt the entrance which the bushrangers had used. It opened into a little clear space, partly girt with rocks, and partly hemmed in by the bunya scrub, where Elsie saw a rough track had been cut.

The half-caste was waiting here holding the bridles of two horses, while a third was tethered to a sapling close by. One of those he held she recognised as Abatos: the other was the animal she had ridden at the picnic.

'I brought The Outlaw, as you see,' said Blake; 'but I couldn't manage a side-saddle. I know, however, that you are a good horse-woman, and I think we might arrange something in the shape of a pommel.'

He undid a sort of valise, strapped on to the dees of the saddle in fashion to serve as a safeguard in the case of a buckjumper, and doubling and re-strapping it, made a tolerable imitation of a single pommel. He liftet Elsie, and gave her the reins, then mounted himself, and they followed Jack Nutty, who on the third horse disappeared into the bunya scrub.

The track would have been absolutely undiscoverable to one who did not know it. No trees had been felled; only the spreading branches had been cut so as to allow the passage of horsemen in single file. The black bunyas rose dense on either side, forbidding prickly pyramids so close together as to lose the effect of sombre grandeur they might otherwise have had. At the distance of a yard or two there would be no sign of the track, if it had been possible even to penetrate a yard or two. No wonder, Elsie thought, the bushrangers' hiding-place had not been discovered by the police.

Blake held back the branches for her, keeping close and riding with his head turned so as to watch how she got on. It was hard riding. Here and there the track crossed a gulley, and there were rocks strewn among the trees. In some places, where the forest was less dense, the horses trod on slippery stone, made more slippery still by the creepers with which it was partially overgrown. Blake exhorted her to keep The Outlaw up, and mourned the omission of a leading rein. It was now dark, but Jack Nutty's white shirt was like a guiding flag ahead. There was something weird and unnatural in that black forest, with its funereal foliage and straight stems and grotesque pendant bunya cones. The stillness was oppressive – only the tramping of their horses' feet and stirring of the dead husks of fallen nuts, no sound of bird or beast except occasionally the distant howl of a dingo, or the near thud of an opossum, or stealthy movement of a wallaby. Elsie felt faint, dazed, and weary, and yet she longed passionately that the journey might never end. She longed for open country, where she might ride by Blake's side and where talk would be possible. She had so much to ask, so much to know. Perhaps this was the last time on which she should ever see him in this world. There seemed to her something tragic, strange and repressed in his air. When night came he dismounted, and brought a little lantern which he had lighted, and fastened it to the side of her saddle, so that it shed a faint weird light on the bunya trunks and the broken ground.

'We shall soon be out of the scrub,' he said. 'Are you very tired, Elsie?'

'Yes,' she answered, and there was a sob in her voice. 'But I don't mind anything if only you are safe and we are together.'

He bent passionately down and kissed her foot. 'Oh, my love,' he cried, and left her abruptly and remounted.

Tears rained from Elsie's eyes. A sense of utter desolation over-powered her. She let the reins fall loosely. And just then The Outlaw slipped, one of his forefeet became entangled, and before Elsie had time to collect herself, the horse and she were on the ground.

Blake had sprung to her in an instant. She was unhurt. But the

CHAPTER XXXVI

·

'Who Knows that the World May End To-Night?'

The black-boy's horse was restive, and had never carried a lady. There was nothing for it but that Elsie should be placed on Abatos in front of Blake.

The girl's heart throbbed with a secret and guilty joy as he lifted her up and held her close to him, keeping her firm on the saddle. Abatos seemed almost to relish the burden, so springily did he step forth. They had nearly reached the border of the scrub when the accident happened. Before long there was a breath of wind, the trees widened, and presently they were in the open again, at a point somewhat below that of the camp from which they had started for the Falls. The great mountains rose in their solemn grandeur, and the outline of ridge and gully became distinct.

What a night it was, so still but for that faint breeze which made a mysterious murmur in the gum-trees; the stars glittering and the moon showing a pale milky radiance. There were more sounds here: the dingoes were nearer and more distinct in the river-bed, and by the lagoons there was the noise of wild duck swishing the reeds, and of the sweet plaintive cry of the curlew echoed from the swamps. No need now for Jack Nutty's pilotage. Blake touched Abatos with the spur, leaving the black-boy with Elsie's lame horse far behind. They had reached a flat, one of those level tracts by the creek bank, and Abatos flew over it as lightly as a bird. Blake held Elsie closer; her head was against his shoulder, her heart beating with his, she could hear his breath come and go quickly.

'Who knows that the world may end to-night?' he whispered. 'Let us be happy, Elsie, for once; for the last and only time.'

And holding her so, as they sped along he made many strange confidences. He told her of his wild moods of excitement, during which he was scarcely conscious of anything except the overmastering need of some engrossing action; told her of how he had embarked on his reckless career; of the discovery and planning of their hiding-place; of the extraordinary success which had attended the first of the Moonlight escapades; of the manner in which he had procured his armour, and of how he had first worn it in the desert; of the woman who had followed him in the East; of his curious alliance with Trant, unbroken in harmony till Elsie had come between them; of their joint devotion to the cause of Ireland; of the fund to which their unholy gains were mostly devoted; and the secret society to which they owed their allegiance. 'Trant has feathered his nest, and so has Sam Shehan, probably,' Blake said; 'but I have laid by nothing, Elsie, and so far my hands are free from the spending of ill-gotten gold.'

It seemed to Elsie like some wonderful tale of romance. He described the fascination of the double life, the piquancy of dramatic contrast between the outlaw and the lawmaker – Blake, the Colonial Secretary, and Blake the bushranger. He told her of his gallops through the gorges and the labryinth of scrub in which he had worked off the fever of his blood; of the mad feats of courage; the fights with the gold escort; the dashes back to their mountain hiding-place and return to decorous existence again. 'And oddly enough, Elsie,' he said, 'I don't regret what I did except for you and for one other thing, which may perhaps seem to you an absurd distinction in morals – that is, the robbery of Lady Waveryng's diamonds. I suppose that, ethically speaking, there is not much difference between robbing a gold escort, or a bank, or even Peter Duncan, the miser millionaire, and stealing the diamonds of a person who can well afford to lose them, and whose family have for generations been the oppressors of Ireland; but it is the truth that I yielded very reluctantly in that business, and that I would give my right hand to be able to return Lady Waveryng her diamonds.'

'Cannot that be done?' Elsie asked.

'I am afraid not. Trant took them to Sydney, and put them, or such part as he thought fit, in the hands of our agent there, who would take means to transmit them to their destination. I have no doubt, as I said, that Trant feathered his own nest well. I was too sick and disgusted with the whole affair to care once the thing was done. That's the one act in Moonlight's career which seems somehow a blot on my honour. The gold was earth's bounty, and it is only fair that some of it should go to redress Ireland's wrongs: and Peter Duncan had been notoriously a screw to the Irish settler, and was an avowed hater of the Irish. He deserved to be bled. Slaney deserved it too; but Slaney was true to his word. He had me in his grip, and forebore. Oh, Elsie, do you know that I never enjoyed anything more in my life than that walking into the bank with the almost certainty of being arrested. It was a throw of the dice, liberty the stake.'

And then he told her of how his love for her had grown and grown; how at first he had begun his flirtation, believing her to be heartless and deserving of no quarter; and how he had gradually become caught in her toils, and had struggled against her influence, at first from mere pride, and later out of love and consideration for her. 'Till I knew that you were securely pledged to Frank Hallett; and that night I let myself go,' he said. 'I had let myself go once before, but I wanted you to believe that that was only to show my mastery.'

'And how is it to end?' she said suddenly.

'To end!' he repeated. 'Moonlight's race is run. There will never be another Moonlight robbery in Leichardt's Land. Years and years hence the cave will be discovered, and people will wonder who used it. Everything is settled. Trant goes to Europe next mail.'

'He wanted to take me with him,' said Elsie.

Blake kissed her in a passionate impulse. 'Oh! thank Heaven that you were saved from that – though I don't think he would have carried his purpose, my dear; you have too much pluck. You would have got away from him somehow.'

'Yes,' said Elsie, 'I should have got away. I had made up my mind. I resolved that I would appear to yield, and that if the worst came to the worst I would kill myself on my wedding-day. Are you not afraid of him?' she asked suddenly. 'Don't think me conceited, but he must have cared for me in a wild desperate way to have planned and managed all that scheme of carrying me off. I think he would stop at nothing. He is dangerous and revengeful. He is capable of betraying you, for having foiled his purpose.'

'You forget,' said Blake, 'that in betraying me he would be betraying himself – not only to the authorities here, but what is far more terrible, to the society, who would avenge me. No, my darling, don't think any more of that. Trant will go as he had settled. Sam Shehan wants to try ranching in America; and as for the half-castes, they don't count.'

'And you?' asked Elsie.

'I have not decided anything yet,' he said, 'except that my career is ended in Leichardt's Land. I cannot stay here and risk exposure as Moonlight. My purpose is accomplished. I have done my country some service. I shall go now and fight for it, in another way and another place. And do you think,' he added vehemently, 'that after this night I could meet you as Frank Hallett's wife?'

She was silent. She knew that she should never be Frank Hallett's wife, but she would not tell him this now.

The first faint greyness of early morning was paling the stars. They were riding along comparatively easy country, skirting the Luya on the road from Baròlin Gorge to the Dell. In a little time they would have reached the crossing. Elsie asked about her sister. Her heart smote her for having forgotten her.

'She is at the Dell,' he said. 'They buried Lord Horace in the graveyard at Tunimbah, and Lady Horace and the Waveryngs went back to the Dell after the funeral. Poor Lady Horace bore her loss with a curious composure. She seemed far more distressed and broken by her uncertainty about you. But she said that she was convinced you were not dead. She had an extraordinary intuition that Trant had you somewhere in hiding, and she had a belief that I should find you. She will not be surprised when she sees us this morning. Tell her the truth, Elsie, if you please. I mean the truth about your abduction, but keep the secret of Moonlight's lair. But if you take my advice you will let the rest of the world believe that you and Trant got lost in the mountains, and that it was only by chance I discovered you.'

'I will let all the world, including Ina, think so,' Elsie answered. 'My poor Ina! She will have no heart for such things. Tell me,' she went on hesitatingly, 'was there any trouble about Mrs. Allanby?'

'Ah! I see that you know of poor Horace's infatuation; it was very patent to other people. I believe there was some sort of scene, but that it was kept from your sister. Lady Waveryng has behaved like an angel and a woman of the world in one. It was extraordinary the way she watched over both Mrs. Allanby and Lady Horace, keeping them apart, and arranging for Mrs. Allanby to be taken to Leichardt's Town without any suspicion. She was like a sister to that unfortunate woman, from whom it might be supposed that she would naturally shrink as if she were poison. But *noblesse oblige*,' he added with a laugh. 'Race tells, after all. Lady Waveryng never seemed to think of her own grief, and it is certain that she was devoted to Lord Horace.'

'Yes, Lady Waveryng is good,' said Elsie. 'I am glad that Ina has got her now.'

It was strange, now that the novelty of the situation had worn off a little, how quietly and composedly they talked. Blake gave no hope, no hint of union. They might have been parting with a scaffold before one of them, for all the hoping or planning there was in their talk about the future. But notwithstanding the gloom and tragedy which surrounded their lives – the terrible discovery that had come upon her, the utter hopelessness of any happiness before them, this early morning on which she rode clasped in his arms seemed the opening of a new life for Elsie. Her whole being was filled with a curious calm certainty. She knew the worst. She knew his crime, she knew the bar between them. But she knew also that he loved her supremely, she knew that in life or in death she must belong to this man and no other. Her mind was made up, her course was clear.

The east was aglow when they reached the crossing, and the birds had begun to twitter, and the cockatoos to chatter. It was a strange wonderful world bathed in dew and suffused with the radiance of sunrise. Blake dismounted. He had reluctantly unfolded his arms from Elsie's form. Their kiss had a great solemnity, as was fitting after this most sad yet sweetest night in the lives of either. Blake settled Elsie on the saddle and walked beside her, holding the rein. Abatos was very quiet, and as if in sympathy rubbed his sleek beautiful head against his master's shoulder. Elsie stooped and kissed the creature's shining mane. 'Dear Abatos,' she said. 'Do you remember,' she added, turning to Blake, 'how I once wished that Moonlight might carry me off on Abatos? I have had my wish.'

'Not quite,' he answered. 'I am bringing you home. You don't know the mad longing that seized me last night as we rode together – the longing that it might be to some far-off place, where we should be together to our lives' end.'

'Why did you not take me?' she murmured.

'Because I love you, Elsie, too well to sacrifice your life to mine.'

'And if I asked you to take me?' she said.

'If you asked me I should say No – I should say, Go and marry the man who is more worthy of you than I.'

'And if I told you that I could never marry that man – never, never; that I should feel it a crime to marry him when my heart and soul belonged to you?'

'Then I would say, Go back, Elsie, and wait a year, two years, till you are sure of yourself – till I have made a new life and a new home away from the shadow of old sin, and sorrow, and disgrace. I should say, Give yourself the chance of repenting –'

'And if I gave myself the chance, and if I did not repent, but longed more ardently than now that I might make your happiness as you would make mine, what then?'

'Then I would take you in my arms, and bid you never leave them more.'

They crossed the river silently, and he led her to the house. No one was stirring. He lifted her down at the log steps of the verandah. A kangaroo hound barked, and presently a sleepy Islander came slouching out of the back premises. Blake took Elsie's hand.

'I will leave you now and ride back to Baròlin. I am to be there for a week, making final arrangements. If you wish to communicate with me, that address would find me at once. But we part, Elsie, for ever.

'Do we part?' she cried, with a wild, half tearful laugh. 'I will write to you. We shall see.'

'Good-bye, he said, afraid of her weakness, tearing himself away lest his presence should influence her against what was best for her future; 'Good-bye, my dear love. God bless and keep you.'

He mounted Abatos and rode away.

Elsie went straight to Ina's room. Ina was wide-awake. It had not occurred to Elsie that her unexpected appearance might give her sister a shock which might be hurtful. Ina gazed at her at first as though she were a ghost. Poor Ina had the look of one who had become used lately to seeing ghosts. She said not one word, did not utter a cry.

'Ina,' said Elsie, going to the bed, and taking the young widow in her arms. 'Oh! my poor Ina, my darling Ina, I have come back again. I am quite safe. I have come back to be with you in your trouble.'

'I knew that you were not dead,' Ina said, in an odd dulled voice. 'I knew that God would not be so cruel as to take you from me. I knew that you would have come to me if you had been dead. Horace has come to me often. We have talked together. He has told me – we have forgiven each other everything.'

'Oh! my dearest Ina, he had nothing to forgive you.'

'You don't know. Oh! wasn'it it sad about poor Horace?' Ina went on quite calmly. 'Mr. Blake has told you, I suppose, Elsie, all that has happened.'

'Yes, I know all that happened. My heart ached for you, Ina.'

'But it was much best that God should have taken him,' Ina went on. 'Horace feels that now. It was such a bright joyous life, Elsie – that's what makes it seem so hard, and he cared so for the things of life – poor Horace! But God will remember all that, and we don't know what the other life is like, dear. I think it must be like this one, only without the sin. Horace was taken away just in time to save him from sin. I told *her* that. I told her I was glad; and I think she understood. Poor woman, I was sorry for her. It was harder for her than for me.'

Elsie listened in silent wonder. It seemed a relief to Ina to go on.

'Yes, it was much best so. It wasn't her fault, and it wasn't his. If I had loved him he might have cared for me. That was the wrong, from the beginning. He had a loving nature, poor Horace. People cannot help caring for one person more than for another, Elsie. They ought not to be judged hardly. The sin is in marrying one person when you love another. You may think you will get over it, but you never do, you never do. It is always a canker in the heart.'

And now Elsie knew what Ina had done for her. She had vaguely suspected it as a possibility, but she had not allowed herself to think of it as a fact.

'Elsie,' Ina said suddenly, 'I have learned a good deal while I have been sitting quiet here since Horace died. I have been wrong, wrong from the beginning. There is no use ever in trying to go against nature and one's heart. I was wrong in helping to persuade you to marry Frank. You don't love him, you love Mr. Blake. And Mr. Blake loves you. I saw that very well when he talked to me after you were lost. I knew that he would find you. Love always finds the way to the one that is dearest. Elsie, don't marry Frank if you love Mr. Blake. Only harm will come of it. And God may not be merciful and take him away as He took Horace. But I ought not to tell you now. You won't understand.' And the poor thing burst for the first time into hysterical sobbing.

'Yes, I do understand,' Elsie said, taking Ina in her arms, and soothing her like a child. 'I understand everything, Ina. I made up my mind last night, dear, last night, when we rode together, and it was all so sad and solemn; don't ask me about it. I can never speak of it as it really was to anybody in the world. But I knew that he loved me, and I knew that I would rather die than be any other man's wife. I have been a vain thoughtless girl all my life, and I never knew what love meant, the sacredness and the wonder and mystery of it, and how it is the one thing in the world that comes next to God and heaven. But I know now, and I know what you feel – that it is a crime – when we know – to marry without love. I don't love Frank, he is no more than a brother to me. And I do love Morres Blake with all my soul. We shall never marry, perhaps. I don't know – not for a long time, if ever; but if I do not marry him, I will die without having been the wife of any other man. I am going to tell Frank that, Ina, as soon as I can see him.'

'He is here,' said Ina. 'He came very late last night. He was worn out. He had been searching for you through the scrub and the gorges. I told him that Mr. Blake had gone to look for you, and it seemed to relieve him. He had a feeling like me that Mr. Blake would find you. But oh! Elsie, I never noticed before how pale you are – how different. My dear, have you been wandering all this time – did you have food to eat? How did you lose yourself? Where is Mr Trant?'

'He – he had an accident,' Elsie said. 'Shehan is with him. Don't ask me about him, Ina; try and keep them from asking too many questions. Some day I will tell you all about it, but not now. You're not fit for it, nor am I. The very thought of it makes me shudder.'

'Did he lose you on purpose then?' said Ina. 'I hated that man. He wanted to marry you, Elsie. He loved you in a wrong way. Where were you all this time?'

'We were in a cave in the mountains. I was quite safe. We lost ourselves. Mr. Trant did not behave badly on the whole, Ina. It wasn't his fault, perhaps. Oh! is nothing anybody's fault?' she cried, and became hysterical with fatigue and excitement.

Lady Waveryng came in just at the right time, and forebore, at Ina's request, to worry Elsie with questions, but like the tender practical lady she was, took Elsie to her room, and a bath and hot coffee, and Miss Briggs' ministrations, and then when she had seen that Elsie was all right, and had said a few reassuring words about Ina, and spoken with tears of Horace and her own love and regret for him, and intention that Ina should henceforth take his place in her heart, Lady Waveryng went to tell her lord the good news of Elsie's return, and to see that Frank Hallett was likewise informed.

Lady Waveryng was the stay of everybody in those days: shrewd, practical, dignified, and full of womanly sympathy, which she continued to manifest in the course of that miserable episode of Mrs. Allanby. Later on, when the way was smoothed for her return to social life, Mrs. Allanby had cause to bless 'Em' Waveryng.

———————•———————

CHAPTER XXXVII

Broken Off

Frank Hallett and Elsie met later in the morning. Lady Waveryng had prepared him for the meeting, and had told him the story which Ina had related to her of the misadventure of Elsie and Trant. This was how Lady Waveryng had put the affair. She affected to treat it as the most natural thing in the world, that the two should have lost them-selves in the mountains. The only marvel was, she declared, that they had ever been found again. Trant had fallen against a rock, and had hurt himself. No doubt he had been making heroic efforts to carry Elsie back again. This accounted for their having been found quite near the Falls. They had taken refuge in a sort of cave. Elsie was very well, only terribly shaken in nerves, which could not be wondered at. Nor was it surprising that she shuddered at the thought of the whole affair, and could not bear to be asked about it, and Lady Waveryng concluded by begging Frank not to worry her at present with questions.

Lady Waveryng knew perfectly well that there was something behind, and Frank knew that she knew, and attributed her reserve to the fact of some disclosure of Elsie's feelings in regard to Blake. When he heard that Blake had found her, and that the two had ridden together through the night, he could well imagine that the pent-up emotion of both had found vent. He did not suspect Trant of having played a treacherous part. Lady Waveryng did, though it is fair to say that her suspicion was not based upon any revelations of either Elsie or of Ina, who indeed did not know, but upon her own notion of probabilities. Lady Waveryng had a faint regret that she did not know the exact details of what might have furnished a sensational episode for a chapter on Australian mountain scenery; and then she shuddered at the mere thought of describing in cold blood, for the delectation of a curious public, any scene that was connected with the tragedy of her brother's death. She broke down, and had a fit of unrestrained weeping, which did her good, and enabled her to throw herself more sympathetically into poor Elsie's difficulties.

'My dear,' she said, 'I see that there is a good deal you don't want to talk about, and it must be horrid for you to think of having been three days out in the Bush with that odious man. But there's one mercy about the Bush; it seems to me that there nothing matters and nobody minds anything; and you see, if you had been cast on a desert island with a man, it wouldn't have been your fault, and this is much the same thing; now don't trouble to make any explanations. I've told Waveryng not to bother you, and I shall tell Mr. Hallett the same thing. Ina told me that Mr. Trant had an accident, and of course, poor man, if he sprained his ankle, he could not be expected to cleave a way for you through the precipices.'

'It was not his ankle – it was his forehead,' said Elsie, blushing deeply, but accepting the pious fraud.

'Well, that is worse,' said Lady Waveryng. 'I dare say he was unconscious.'

'No – he – it was not serious; but he was unconscious,' Elsie said incoherently. 'Oh! Lady Waveryng, if you would explain a little to Frank. He is so good; he will understand how I hate talking about Mr. Trant.'

'Don't fret,' said Lady Waveryng kindly. 'I understand. I will make things as easy as they can be for you. Elsie,' she added, kissing the girl in a motherly fashion, 'take my advice. If you are going to marry Frank Hallett, tell him everything, *everything*. But ask him for breathing space. And if you are not going to marry him, don't be in a hurry about marrying anybody else. Give yourself and other people a chance to prove themselves. And I want to say something to you. Ina is going home with us for a year, or for always, just as she pleases. She is my sister, you know, as well as yours. If you want breathing time, my dear, come with us, too, and be another sister. You will be very welcome at Waveryng, and I will take care of you.'

Elsie sobbed her thanks, and became a little hysterical again, and Lady Waveryng made her lie down and drink some coffee, and went away to talk to Frank.

Lady Waveryng managed it all with the most kindly tact. She took Elsie into the little room which had been poor Lord Horace's office and sent Frank to her. There they were undisturbed.

If Frank found Elsie changed into something sadder, sweeter, and paler than she had been, she on her side was shocked at the ravages anxiety had made in him. He looked oppressed, worn out, with the reddened eyelids of one who has not slept for several nights.

'I was anxious, you know, and I suppose it has told upon me a little,' he said clumsily, in answer to her remorseful exclamation. 'It has been a horrible week one way and another. And then we have been out a good deal, the black-boys and I. I don't know how it is that we did not find you, and that Blake did. We scoured the country about the Falls, and the scrub too, as well as we could; but I knew that Trant was too good a bushman to take you there. But never mind,' he added, seeing the look of trouble and perplexity on her face. 'I know the whole thing must be painful to you. Lady Waveryng told me so, and I am not going to bother you now about the details. It doesn't matter; nothing matters except that you are here safe and well.'

'Oh, yes, Frank, everything matters. There is something I must tell you – the sooner the better – which matters very much to you and to me. I've been a wicked girl, Frank. I have acted cruelly to you. I can never forgive myself, never, never.'

She leaned over to him as he sat in the office chair by Lord Horace's writing-table, his chin resting on his hand, his other hand clenched on the table, the starting veins showing an agitation which his set features concealed. Elsie timidly touched this hand.

'Oh! Frank,' she said brokenly, 'there is no use in going on. It breaks my heart, but I *must* tell you.'

He opened his hand and took hers in it. 'Elsie,' he said hoarsely, 'I think I can guess. I haven't forgotten the time of the corroboree. If it's anything that happened last night, anything to do with Blake, and that you think you ought to make a clean breast of, don't let it weigh upon you as far as I am concerned. I trust you wholly, dear; and I forgive you wholly if there's anything to forgive. I don't want to know. Keep it till – till after we are married – if you still wish to marry me.'

'Frank, that is just it. There's no one so noble as you. You deserve to have a good wife; you deserve to be loved with a woman's whole heart, and I can't love you like that, I never have. It was wicked of me to let you engage yourself to me. It was wicked of me to accept your love.'

'We settled all that, Elsie, remember. It was my doing. I took the risk. I am content with what you give me. I am content to wait till you have got over this infatuation, for that's what it is. It's not your fault.'

'No, it is not infatuation. It is much more, Frank. When I said I would marry you, I didn't quite know myself. I did know that night after the corroboree. I ought to have stopped it all then. I can't marry you, Frank. I should be the vilest woman on earth if I married you now.'

'Why, Elsie?'

'Because I love another man so that I would die for him; yes, I would die for him, if need were. I love him so that I would follow him to the world's end if he wanted me.'

'*Does* he want you, Elsie?' Frank's voice was very grim.

'No; I cannot tell. I know nothing, except that he loves me.'

'And you are sure of that, now?'

'As sure as that I live.'

'Then,' he said quietly, releasing her hand, 'there is nothing more to be said. I don't blame you, Elsie; I took the risk, and I abide by it.'

He turned his head away, and then he got up abruptly. She felt that it was to hide the sob that for a moment convulsed his frame. She got up too, and stood helpless, agonised, her eyes following him with a dumb yearning. He turned to her at last.

'I don't blame you,' he repeated. 'I shall never think one bitter thought of you; you will always be to me the sweetest, truest, finest of women. But for him,' he added fiercely; 'why did he not know his own mind sooner? Why did he keep you on a string, and wait to declare himself till your wedding day was fixed? I think he has behaved *damnably*.'

'Frank, Frank, don't say that.' She came to him and again touched him pleadingly. 'You don't know all he has suffered, you don't know —'

'I know that he has treated you ill. And why? When are you to be married?' he added coldly.

'We shall not be married. Oh! Frank, I don't know, I can't tell you. He is not to blame. It was out of love for me that he held back. It is his secret, his and mine.'

'If you are not going to marry him, I will wait. Ten years hence you will find me the same.'

'It would be of no use. My mind is clear. Last night, in my heart, I gave myself to him for ever and ever; in death or in life, in honour or in dishonour, whether he lives or dies, or marries me or leaves me, I am his; and I can never be any other man's. I never had much religion, Frank, but it seems to me that I have learned at least the religion of love. That's why I hated anybody to come near me in that way. Yes, even you, Frank, truly as I cared for you. I was meant for him, and for him only.'

There was a look of exaltation on Elsie's face which Frank had never seen there before. It convinced him more than her words that she meant what she said.

'Frank,' she went on, 'if you will forgive me – and I know you will – be my brother, and let me be your sister. Let us always love each other, in that way. Some day, perhaps, you may be –' she stopped herself. It seemed desecration to hint at the secret of the new-made widow, but at that moment an intuition came to her that Frank would marry Ina, and that he would love Ina more truly than even he had loved herself. 'Frank,' she said, 'is it to be so?'

'Yes, if you wish it, Elsie,' he answered, in a choked voice.

She took his hand, and kissed it. He gave up his dream silently, struggling to hide from her what it cost him. Presently he knew that her tears were falling upon his hand.

'Don't cry, Elsie,' he said huskily. 'I shall get over it. If I take it badly just at first, remember that I have loved you very much, and that I have wanted you for long. I am not going to make it harder for you. I shall ride back to Tunimbah now, and when you see me again we shall be as you say, brother and sister. Good-bye, my dear; and Heaven bless your choice.'

He left her without another word. Elsie flung herself upon the chair where he had sat, and wept long and bitterly. She was not the only one who wept over Frank's disappointment. Ina Gage was crying, too, in the solitude of her widowed chamber; and not for the dead Horace. She knew what was Lady Waveryng's errand, when Em came to her door, and asked to speak to her.

Em's eyes, she fancied, were red, too. 'He wants to see you, to say good-bye. He is going away; he tells me that his engagement is broken off.'

'Broken off!' Ina repeated in a dazed sort of way. 'And I tried so hard to bring it about. But oh! Em, it's best like this.'

'I suppose it is,' said Lady Waveryng, a little drily. 'But it's hard not to feel for Frank Hallett. She would be safer with him than with Morres Blake.'

Ina went into the parlour, where Frank, booted and spurred, was waiting.

'Ina, you know how it is,' he said, without any preamble. 'She will marry Blake, I suppose, and I can't be surprised since she loves him;

but keep her from doing it too soon, for her own sake; not for mine,' he added hastily. 'That's all over now.'

'Oh, Frank, it has spoiled your life.'

'No,' he answered – 'only wrong-doing can do that. There has been no wrong-doing here, either on her side or mine. I shall always love her, but I see now that she could never have loved me, and that I couldn't have made her happy. I have felt it lately in a way that has been intensifying every day. I've had the sort of feeling that it couldn't be. It took a great deal to make Elsie love; but now that she does love, it will be for ever.'

'Yes,' said Ina. 'When one loves like that, it must be for ever.'

'Ina,' he said, suddenly startled by something spiritualised in her face, 'you are suffering, too; and I have been so selfishly absorbed in my own anxiety that I have thought little of your grief.'

'Yes, I am suffering,' she said quietly, 'but not quite in the way you think. I am glad that Horace died before he had done what all his life would have weighted him with sorrow and remorse. The wrong was that I did not love him as I ought.' She stopped, and a burning blush overspread her face.

He saw it, and a strange look came into his own face. She went on hurriedly.

'Elsie is right. There is no worse crime, when one knows, than to marry one man loving another. And Elsie knows now. I wanted her to marry you, but I am glad now that she will not.'

'Ina,' Frank said again, 'you won't let this make any difference between us. We have always been like brother and sister, haven't we? and we'll be brother and sister still.'

'Yes,' said Ina; 'brother and sister.' She gave him her hand, and he pressed it in his and went away.

That night Elsie wrote to Blake a long letter, of which only a few lines may be given here.

'My love, you won't misjudge me, and I have no shame in what I say to you. Love knows no shame, and after last night there can be only truth between us. I am yours and yours only, to take or to leave as you shall please. It is for you to decide what the future shall be, but whatever it may be – even if it were to be disgrace – I am ready to share it with you. I am ready to come to you when and where you wish, or never to see you again, if that seems better to you. I am ready to wait, as you said – a year, or many years, and then to come to you and be taken – as you said too – in your arms and bidden never to leave you more.'

His answer came by special black-boy two days later. It was Jack Nutty who brought it, and Elsie herself, being at the crossing, took the letter, and asked him the Baròlin news.

Jack Nutty grinned. 'You no tell, me no tell about that fellow cave,' he said. 'Me understand all right. Massa Blake been tell me. Ba'al me see Mr. Trant. Mine think it that fellow go off like it Sydney and ba'al come back.'

Elsie drew a breath of relief. 'Then he has not been at the Gorge?'

'Ba'al mine see him. Mr. Blake he manage all about muster by himself. In one week Baròlin Gorge belong to other fellow – no more Blake and Trant – no more Moonlight.'

'Are you sorry, Jack?' asked Elsie.

'Me sorry; cobbon sorry,' said the black, 'but mine think it police very soon find out Moonlight, best stop in time. No hanging now, suppose that fellow find out; but suppose policeman shot, then hang ba'al mine like that. . . . You been see Pompo?' he asked suddenly.

'No,' answered Elsie.

'Mine frightened about Pompo. That fellow do everything Trant tell him. Suppose Trant tell him, "You go show policeman where Moonlight sit down." Pompo no care; he go. Trant out of the country, all safe. Policeman catch all the rest.'

'Oh, no Jack,' said Elsie. 'What for Mr. Trant do that? No fear!'

'Ba'al mine know,' said the black, shaking his head. 'Trant he got plenty money; he go big steamer to America; he quite safe, and Trant he no like Mr. Blake: he want to be revenged.'

Elsie, remembering Blake's assurance, again told him that there was no fear.

But she herself had a qualm of terror. Fate was always like that – fate would step in and spoil everything, now that they were going to be happy. She had read Blake's letter. She was happy. It was a very long letter, to be read and re-read; it told her of his plans for a new life, and the burden of it was this: 'Be it as you will, love. I am yours and you are mine.'

She wrote a few lines on a leaf torn from her pocket-book, and bade Jack Nutty ride back with it to his master. It was a wild entreaty to him to hasten and wind up everything, to sell Baròlin, resign his appointment, and go and make a home where she could join him as soon as might be. She told him that she would write further by post, that he must come and see her, and that then they would settle everything.

When she got back to the Humpey she found Lord and Lady

Waveryng surrounded with letters and newspapers. Braile the postman had arrived, and it was English mail-day.

Lord Waveryng looked excited. 'They've got a clue to the diamonds,' he said; 'a fellow in Sydney has been disposing of the cross. What fools they were to risk that piece, which could be identified anywhere. However, I hope it means that we shall get the lot, or part anyhow, back again.'

Elsie's heart stopped beating. 'Is anything known,' she asked, 'of the person who first sold the cross.'

'It seems not,' said Lord Waveryng; 'there the thread breaks. But it's something to have got the clue as far as it goes. One can only hope that the New South Wales police department may prove itself a little more effectual than that which is presided over by our friend the Colonial Secretary here. I understand that Blake is at Baròlin, and I think that I shall ride over and see him about this. I have something else to tell him,' Lord Waveryng added solemnly; 'a piece of news the mail brought, which he ought to know without delay.'

'What is that?' asked Elsie.

'I don't know whether I ought to tell you,' said Lord Waveryng hesitatingly. 'It is Blake's own business.'

'I think you may tell her,' put in Lady Waveryng. 'I fancy that Mr. Blake's business is Elsie's business too.'

'I am going to marry Mr. Blake sometime or other,' said Elsie calmly, with a curious pride.

'So I imagined.'

'Well, it's this,' said Lord Waveryng. 'Lord Coola is dead, and Morres Blake is now Baron Coola.'

Oh, the Fates! Why should the threads be so knotted as to make it easier work for her of the shears! This was Elsie's first thought. A superstitious terror seized her. She could not speak; she could only listen tremblingly while they discussed the old blight that had fallen on his youth. Ina came in, and a horse was ordered for Lord Waveryng, and one of the black-boys to accompany him to Baròlin Gorge.

She waited anxiously for Lord Waveryng's return. He came back late, and reported of Blake as being deeply engaged in the transfer of Baròlin Gorge to its new purchaser. Blake's manner appeared to have impressed Lord Waveryng curiously. 'He was quite unemotional,' Lord Waveryng said; 'seemed taken aback, shocked, and sorry at the news of his brother's death, but wasn't in the least excited as to its bearing upon his own fortunes. He wouldn't tell me what he thought of doing; said he should probably leave Australia, but said he had as yet given no hint of his intention to his colleagues. I can't make him out. Somehow he gave me the idea of a man who is contemplating some great change in his life, and is quite indifferent to all other concerns. Or perhaps he is so tremendously in love that he has no thought for anything else.'

CHAPTER XXXVIII

●

The Last Baron Coola

Nearly a week later Elsie was sitting on her cairn by the crossing. She had got into the way latterly of taking up this position in the afternoon, perhaps because the place had tender associations for her; perhaps because she was always expecting Blake. He was still at Baròlin, and had written to her again, but he had not yet ridden over to the Dell, as in the letter he had promised to do. It was getting towards sundown when she heard the tramp of a horse's feet, a hurried tramp, as though the rider were in fear or distress. The sound did not come from the Baròlin road, but from that which led to Tunimbah.

Elsie got up and walked to the edge of the creek to see Frank Hallett pressing eagerly down the opposite bank.

He urged his horse across and then up to where she stood; then dismounted, his face full of trouble.

'Elsie,' he exclaimed, not waiting for her to speak. 'I am thankful to have found you here. You have heard nothing?'

'Nothing,' she repeated. 'What is there to hear?'

'Bad news for you, my poor Elsie. I thought it might have been telegraphed from the Bean-tree. That villain Trant, I suppose, has caused Blake to be denounced as Moonlight, and Macpherson with the police arrived at Tunimbah just before I left, on their way to the cave at the Falls.'

Elsie staggered, and would have fallen but for Frank's protecting arm.

'Be brave,' he said. 'I have come to you that we may save him. We will give him warning at Baròlin if he is there. If not tell me where he may be found.'

'He is at Baròlin,' she said, recovering herself. 'Come, I will go with you.'

'You!' he exclaimed.

'Yes. I will be with him whatever happens. But we will save him. Oh! Frank, we must save him.'

She was walking rapidly towards the Humpey, Frank leading his horse by her side. As they walked he told her breathlessly all he knew.

It was Pompo who had given the information, and offered to lead the police to the cave. Mr. Torbolton would not believe that Blake was implicated, but Trant had been clever enough to furnish the half-caste with conclusive proof, which had made it clear to Captain Macpherson, at any rate, that the outlaw and the lawmaker were one. Trant had either left the colony, or was in secure hiding. No trace of him was discoverable.

Pompo had not betrayed him – had indeed strenuously asserted Trant's innocence. But no one believed him. Captain Macpherson, in a state of wild excitement, had arrived with his troopers at Tunimbah on his way to the cave. There had been some little delay about the warrant, which he had counted on one of the Halletts signing. Jem was away, and Frank had refused to sign, and they had been obliged to seek any other magistrate. In the meantime, Frank had mounted and ridden furiously to the Humpey to take counsel with Elsie.

The girl stopped him at a cross-cut. One path led round by the stockyard, the other to the house. She pointed to him to take the first.

'Look here,' she said, keen and collected, with all her woman's wits about her, in the face of danger to the man she loved, 'you must go to the stockyard, where I know Ina's horse and one for Lord Waveryng are saddled. He and Em were to go for a canter at sunset. Take the horses to the crossing, and wait for me. I will slip into the house and leave a note, so that Ina may not be frightened at my being away, and I shall join you before many minutes.'

He did as she bade him. It seemed providential that the horses should be in readiness. He had not waited long before he saw her light figure flying down the narrow path half hidden by gum trees, which led from the house. No one had seen either of them, and Elsie had left a note on her dressing-table which would reassure Ina as to her safety.

She had put on her riding skirt, and had a lady's spur in her hand. It was a sudden inspiration which had made her snatch it from its peg in the passage. She was panting and breathless, but she would not let him wait a moment. He lifted her on her horse, and presently they were cantering fast along the track to the Gorge.

It was not more than eight miles, and the country was fairly level. The sun had only just set as they reached the Baròlin slip rails, and as good luck had it Jack Nutty, the half-caste, mounted on a spirited young horse, was riding down towards them. On the way Elsie had told Frank all she knew and might tell of Blake's career, and the young man's heart was less vindictive towards his rival, and more sympathetic with the woman he loved, and who, in turn, loved so unwisely. The whole story now was clear to him, the secret of the double life and of the bush-rangers' hiding-place.

They stopped Jack Nutty and asked for news of his master. At first the half-caste would give only evasive replies. Blake was not in the house; he was out on the run; then when Elsie told him wildly of his master's peril, Jack Nutty, all alert, turned his horse's head toward Mount Luya. 'Massa sit down along a cave,' he cried, and galloped thither-ward, leaving Elsie and Hallett to follow.

They knew now that the danger was imminent. It was a race between the troopers and themselves. Blake's liberty, perhaps his life, depended on which should reach the Falls first.

Oh, for Abatos, trained, sure-footed, and swift. Fortunately Ina Gage's horse and that which Lord Horace had used to ride, and which had been saddled for Lord Waveryng, were both half-thorough-breds, and creatures of pace and mettle. Hallett was, of course, a magnificent Bush rider, and Elsie a fearless horsewoman. They dashed on, never slacking, though the country grew wilder, following close on Jack Nutty, who, uttering every now and then exciting cries in the native language, rode as though possessed.

On among thickening gum-trees, over fallen logs, through dense prickly scrub, up and down gorges, and now to where the bunyas showed their black serrated wall against the spurs of Mount Luya. The moon had come out – that same moon which had faintly lighted the Falls expedition, and the ride that had been Paradise to Elsie as she had lain in her lover's arms. This ride seemed a nightmare – the flying trees, evil demons, the night noises, impish jibes, and Mount Luya and the Burrum Peaks towering ahead, till they reached the scrub, like gigantic fiends of menace. Once they thought they heard the sound of voices; it was only the cry of the native bear; and the tramp they fancied to be pursuing horses was that of startled beasts on a cattle camp by the border of the scrub. Jack Nutty got down, and carefully examined the ground for a trail, and put his ear to the earth, rising with a grim smile of satisfaction. 'Ba'al, that fellow come yet,' he said; and again they darted on into the labyrinthine depths of the scrub. Elsie's skirts were torn, her face was bleeding where the bunya spikes had scratched her, every limb of her body was tense with the strain; she was scarcely conscious of herself, her whole being seemed devoured with the frenzied eagerness to arrive in time. She remembered The Outlaw's downfall, and kept up her horse's head. The animal's side was streaming beneath her habit, where she had struck it with the spur. They were a long time in the scrub, and every moment was an agony, lest, in the darkness and difficulty of the way, one of the horses should slip or start back frightened, so that precious time would be lost.

But at last, at last! The beams of moonlight that struck down through the roofing branches became broader, and showed ahead a clear, luminous, open space. It was the clear patch behind the precipice to which Blake had led her through the fissure, the place where Jack Nutty had been in waiting with Abatos.

And Abatos was there now, testifying to his master's vicinity. Blake had evidently left him tethered, while he had made his way on foot to the cave. The animal was tied securely to a gum-tree, and whinnied at sight of Jack Nutty. The half-caste threw himself from his horse, and seized the bridles of Elsie's and Hallett's horses. Frank lifted Elsie down, and the girl fell almost fainting in his arms. But she rallied herself quickly, and drank eagerly from the flask of diluted brandy which he held to her lips. The draught gave her new strength.

'Quick!' she cried. 'I know the way. What are we to do with the horses? They must not stop here.'

'Mine plant that fellow,' said Jack Nutty – 'little way – behind that fellow rock – in the scrub.' He pointed to an abutting spur up to which the bunyas grew close, and as he did so, began to undo Abatos' bridle. 'Ba'al me go along a you,' he went on. 'Mine stop here – keep very quiet – look after horses. Suppose policeman come me ready.'

Elsie scarcely waited to hear him. She could trust herself to find the way. Once through the fissure, it was easy. She led Hallett after her, and in a moment they were lost in the bowels, as it seemed, of the mountain. Gropingly they felt their way along the gallery, and by-and-by emerged again into the moonlight, and stood on the ledge leading round to the Baròlin rock.

They walked on skirting the precipice. Hallett could hardly repress an exclamation of astonishment at the lonely grandeur of the scene, and the almost entire inaccessibility of the spot. 'No wonder Macpherson couldn't track them,' he said to himself.

The great rock of the human head looked strangely weird in the moonlight, with its withes of grey moss hanging like hair, and its majestic rugged outline of feature. Again Elsie drew him on. They had gone into the mountain once more, and here was the gallery where she had been chloroformed. She made Frank light a match, and they felt for the stone doorway. The stone lay back. A few steps, and they were in the bushrangers' cave. A fat lamp shed a dim illumination on the rough interior, the rock walls, the slab table on its stone supports, the settle, the ration bags heaped in a corner. Except for the lamp there was no sign of human presence.

Elsie took up the lamp, and with a knowledge of the cave which surprised Frank, who had not fully grasped the circumstances of her recent incarceration, flashed it into each of the other chambers, and returned to the central cave having found no one. She gave a small 'coo-ee,' but there was no answer.

'He must be outside in the crater,' she cried. 'We must look for him there. Oh! to think of this time lost!'

They went out into the great green space enclosed by its mountain walls, into which the moon shone with a clear and wondrous brilliancy. Frank gazed about him with wonder and admiration. He saw the blue waterhole of unfathomable depth, the growing corn, the animals stabled securely in their volcanic paddock. It was marvellous to him that this place should have existed all his lifetime – countless ages before him – under his very eyes as it were, and he had never known of it. He made some remark of this kind to Elsie, but she paid no heed.

'Help me to find him,' she cried, in agony. 'Go that way and I will go this – and coo-ee softly – no, it does not matter. No one could hear unless they were in the cave itself.'

But her first 'coo-ee' echoing back was answered by a voice on the other side of the crater, and presently she could see the fire-tip of a cigar thrown to the earth. Blake advanced, not at first certain who his visitors were and prepared for resistance, his revolver in his hand.

'It is I – Elsie,' she cried, 'Elsie and Frank Hallett. We have come to warn you. The troopers are on your track. They may be here now.'

'Who has betrayed me?' he asked calmly, as he approached them.

'Trant,' said Frank; 'Pompo was his instrument. You know best what motive he had for revenge.'

'It is I who am the cause of it all,' moaned Elsie. 'It is I who have ruined you, and made him mad for revenge.'

'My poor Elsie,' answered Blake with intense tenderness. 'Say rather that it is I who have ruined you.'

She caught his hand and passionately kissed it. 'Come,' she said, dragging him forward, 'we are going to save you, Frank and I; we have come for that. The horses are hidden in the scrub. Only let us get out of the mountain before the police come, and all will be well. You have Abatos, and you will ride for your life over the border, and get off into some ship or boat from Myall Heads. I have thought it all out as we rode here. You must bribe the cedar-cutters. And that's the thing – have you money? I had forgotten –'

'Yes, I have some money hidden here,' he said, 'plenty. That is what I came for to-night.'

They walked back to the cave, and he went into the inner chamber where she had slept, and which she now was certain had been his sleeping place also. She heard a sound of falling stone and a scraping of iron, and went in to him.

'Oh, quick, quick! can I not help you?'

'I have it,' he answered; and she saw him pull out a box which had been hidden in a crevice of the rock, and take from it a bundle of notes and some gold, which he stowed into his breast pocket.

'I am ready,' he said. 'But first, Elsie, my darling, tell me whatever happens that you forgive me for the blight I have brought upon you.'

'Forgive you! I love you. I would die for you. I will live for you and with you. I love you,' she repeated. 'Is not that enough? But here again I make the vow I have made in my heart. I will never belong to another man. If they put you in prison I will wait for you to my life's end. If you die I will be faithful to you for eternity.'

He caught her in his arms and pressed one hurried passionate kiss upon her lips. She tore herself from him, and led him on. Frank was before them. He had heard her words; he had seen that kiss. Her vow was the knell of his last hope.

Thy hurried through the gallery, and the further entrance cave, and across the plateau where the rock-lilies waved and scented the night air with their fragrance. Then suddenly there rang through the night the shot of a pistol, and then another. Elsie shrieked in despair. She gazed round in the helpless frenzy of an animal trapped with her young, and ready to defend them with her blood. On one side the unscaleable precipice, on the other the slimy depths of the waterhole and the treacherous quicksands. And before them nearly a quarter of a mile of that ledge path with no hope of escape to right or left.

'They are upon us,' Blake said quietly. 'We can do nothing now.'

Elsie made a frantic movement backwards.

'Go into the cave again; let us put up the stone and defy them.'

'For what use? It would mean bloodshed first and certain capture later. No, I haven't taken any man's life so far. I won't do it now.'

'You are right,' said Hallett. 'Face the inevitable. It is better to give yourself up quietly, Blake,' he exclaimed with emotion. 'I'm sorry for you. I'd have sacrificed all I'm worth to save you.'

'Yes, I know you would,' Blake answered. 'You would have done it for her sake, Hallett,' he added with deep emotion. 'I deserve nothing from you, but curses. I have also robbed you of your dearest hope, as I have robbed her of her happiness –'

'No, no!' cried Elsie passionately. 'You have taught me what happiness is.'

He turned on her with a look of infinite love and remorse.

'It is true,' he said. 'I have ruined the lives of all those I loved, of all those who have loved me; I am the scapegoat of my generation, the mad, bad Blake. Well, it ends with me. I am the last of my name, the last Blake of Coola.'

There was a rush of feet. 'Stand back, Elsie, against the rock,' said Blake hoarsely. 'Good-bye, my one love,' he whispered, 'pray for me and forgive me. Keep beside her, Hallett. Take care of her.'

He stepped boldly forward to the edge of the precipice. At that moment Captain Macpherson's voice sounded in ringing tones, as with his gun pointed he appeared round the curve of the gallery, followed by a black line of troopers, the mountings of their carbines glittering in the moonlight. 'Stir, and I fire. Morres Blake, *alias* Moonlight, in the Queen's name I arrest you.'

Blake made no answer. With one swift sudden movement he threw himself backward and disappeared. They heard the thud of his fallen body, a hundred feet below, and then a splash as it was swallowed up for ever in the depths of the Baròlin waterhole.

And this was the end of Morres Blake, last Baron Coola.

These things happened a good many years ago. This strange tragic episode was felt to be a blot on the history of Leichardt's Land, and the leaders on both sides did their utmost to shroud in mystery the facts of their late Colonial Secretary's double life. By his death Blake had done all he could to spare his friends and his adopted country disgrace. The Moonlight tragedy was never wholly cleared up. Trant disappeared and was not heard of again. Sam Shehan disappeared also. Pompo was pardoned, and Jack Nutty had been killed by one of the first shots fired that night. Lady Waveryng got some of her diamonds, but the rest were gone from her descendants for ever.

Elsie was very ill after the events of that terrible night. She had an attack of brain fever, and for weeks all was dark. She never knew of the blare of notoriety which surrounded her name, and no one ever spoke to her of Moonlight. She thought of Blake only as the embodiment of an ideal love, and as such, in her heart, she worshipped his memory, clinging fanatically to the vow she had made to be faithful to him to her life's end. It was a very different Elsie who looked on the world when she rose from her sick bed. Life was never to her the same again.

Ina nursed her through her illness, and the Waveryngs stayed till danger was over. Then they went back to England, and Ina, who followed with her mother and Elsie, joined them later. Elsie and her mother lived mostly at Rome, and Elsie developed a latent taste for art, which served her in good stead in later days. Ina spent a great part of the time she was in Europe with the Waveryngs. Elsie never went back to Australia, but it has been Ina's lot to return to her old haunts on the Luya. Two years after her departure, Frank Hallett, a prominent Australian politician, took a trip to Europe, and at the Waveryngs met again Ina Gage. There he asked her to marry him, and she returned with him as his wife.